MEN WITH A MISSION

Ezra Early: With Falling Leaf, his Ute woman, he winters in the high Rocky Mountains, riding south in the spring with his two partners for a spree in the Mexican town of Taos. A man with a painful past, Early has his reasons for taking on the easterner who had been left to die along the barren Cimarron Cutoff . . . reasons for showing him how to survive the perils of the Southwest.

Abe Rawlins: With his two *amigos*, he came west with General Ashley's brigade, and went on to carve himself a wide swath through the hard and unforgiving Stony Mountains. Rawlins prefers his own company, or that of his two longtime friends, but if Early thinks young Hobart Adams is worth teaching, he'll lend a skilled and brawny hand.

Lucien Chardonnais: Flamboyant and unpredictable, his moods change like lightning. It takes the French Canadian a while to warm up to New York reporter Hobart Adams, but once he does, he willingly offers his heart, soul, and strength to Adams's quest for vengeance against those who left him to die.

SOUTHWEST THUNDER

JOHN LEGG

HarperPaperbacks
A Division of HarperCollinsPublishers

This is a work of fiction. The characters, incidents, and dialogues are products of the author's imagination and are not to be construed as real. Any resemblance to actual events or persons, living or dead, is entirely coincidental.

HarperPaperbacks   *A Division of* HarperCollins*Publishers*
10 East 53rd Street, New York, N.Y. 10022

Cover illustration by Bill Dodge

First printing: July 1993

Printed in the United States of America

HarperPaperbacks and colophon are trademarks of HarperCollins*Publishers*

❖ 10 9 8 7 6 5 4 3 2 1

For my niece and nephew
Linda and Jake Legg.
I hope you both make some thunder of
your own as you ride through life.

1

EZRA EARLY KNELT NEXT to the thing—it was the only way he could describe it, since it was no longer a human being—lying on the desolate stretch of Cimarron desert.

The signs around the thing showed that white men had committed this loathsome deed. There had been at least a half-dozen of them that he could count. He rose to his full height and stood, leaning lightly on his Dickert rifle. Vultures and turkey buzzards circled overhead, angry at having been disturbed while feeding on the succulent carrion on the hot ground below.

Early spit a thin line of tobacco juice into the dust, making sure it was away from the thing. He still could not call it a body. She had been young, and he expected, somewhat attractive, if one thought short, dumpy Comanches were attractive. He could not

1

prove it, of course, but he just knew that she had been repeatedly raped before someone had painstakingly begun to skin her. Either boredom or a sudden dose of fear had stilled the knife-wielding hand before its grisly work was completed, but he had peeled a considerable amount of skin before he stopped. He—or they—had also mutilated the body in other ways. The scavenger birds had pretty well completed the damage.

Early padded around. He found three more bodies, all males. Two Comanche warriors had been shot, scalped, and crudely emasculated. A little distance off, Early found the remains of an infant boy, his brains dashed out on the ground. There was little left of the three, especially the baby, after the scavengers had been at the corpses.

Early shrugged. There was nothing he could do for any of them now. He could not afford the time to bury them. He wasn't even sure it would be right for them. All Indian peoples had their own ways and were touchy about them, and rightfully so. Besides, it might mean other Comanches were lurking about, and he had no desire to be caught by them out here, alone.

As Early pulled himself up onto his big Appaloosa, he knew he was bound to have more trouble before he reached Taos. The only question was when and where he would find it.

A day and a half later, he pulled the Appaloosa up and stopped to listen. The constant breeze brought to him the faint sound of rough, angry laughter. Early scratched the horse's big, broad head and said to him, "Well, boy, sounds like there's mayhap four of 'em. And they sound like they're havin' theyselves a high ol' time."

Early kicked the horse slowly into motion, the big

Dickert rifle cradled on his left arm, ready. Behind him was the single, dark gray mule, laden with the necessities of life on the trail.

He moved ahead cautiously, but unafraid. Early had been a mountain man ten years, and a free trapper for much of that time. He had not survived skirmishes with a dozen different tribes by being afraid. He had not survived by being foolish either.

In traveling alone, he knew he was vulnerable to attack, especially riding the large, strong Appaloosa. The horse would be a welcome target for any Indian— as would a lone trapper. But he had not had much of a choice. He had figured on leaving Independence, back in Missouri, with one of the caravans traveling the Santa Fe Trail. But by the time he had arrived there, all the caravans were gone.

He hadn't been too disappointed in that. He preferred his own company, except for those few people he could call friends. Most of the men who worked on the long trains of freight wagons were not the sort he liked anyway. Besides, traveling alone, though dangerous, was much faster than marching along with the plodding mule- or ox-drawn wagons that screeched and lurched and kicked up suffocating clouds of dust. No, he preferred the freedom of solitude, though it did have its dangers. Like Comanches, who he figured were up ahead.

The land stretched out before him as he reached a slight rise in the wide, falsely flat ground. About half a mile ahead, he could see the small group of warriors shimmering in the heat. He counted four of them, and they were mainly crouching around something on the ground.

"Looks like they got theyselves a captive there, boy,"

Early said to the horse. He usually talked to the animal when he was alone. He saw nothing wrong in that. The Appaloosa had no name, but it and its rider made an impressive team, whether on the hunt or in war. "Come on, boy," he said, patting the side of the horse's neck. "I reckon we ought to see if'n we can help that poor, misfortunate bastard."

He made sure his felt, wide-brimmed hat was on tight, and then urged the Appaloosa into a run. As he neared the Comanches, he dropped the pack mule's rope, figuring the animal would follow him. If not, it wouldn't go far. He shoved his rifle into the buckskin scabbard on his saddle.

Intent on the painful pleasures they were about to inflict on their victim, the Comanches were unaware of Early until he roared in on them, scattering them like chickens in a barnyard.

Early yanked both big horse pistols from the pouches on the front of his saddle. He fired one, ripping a large hole in the side of a fleeing warrior. The Indian spun, fell, and tried to rise, but failed.

The other Comanches jumped on their horses, not quite sure what kind of demon had descended on them. Nor did they want to find out. All they knew was that their medicine had suddenly and completely turned bad, and there was no need to stay here to ponder its meaning.

The three made one attempt at rescuing the dead warrior, but Early shot another Comanche. The warrior did not fall, but he was clearly wounded. He and his two companions raced away, kicking their horses for all they were worth. The dead man's pony followed.

Early pulled the Appaloosa to a stop and shoved the pistols away as he watched the Indians racing off. He suddenly laughed. "Run, ye chickshit daughters of Beelzebub," he yelled after them. Still chuckling harshly, he slid off his horse and looked down at the man the Comanches had captured.

His handsome face was contorted with fear and pain, and covered by a few days' growth of whiskers. His hair was clipped fairly short, and his clothing was fancy, completely out of place in such a desolate, foreboding place.

The man, whom Early figured was at least several years younger than his own twenty-eight, pushed himself up until he was sitting. Fearfully, as if he thought a piece of him would fall off if he moved too quickly, the man got to his feet. He was moderately tall and needed some filling out. Absentmindedly he began brushing the dust from his clothes. His knee-length coat, once beige, was dirty and tattered. Blood spots were visible on the shoulders. His tight, high-waisted, blue trousers were ripped at both knees; his shirt had once been white; and his shiny vest and red ascot were disheveled. He was probably the height of fashion in New York or Boston, Early thought, but he was as out of place here as a buffalo at a barn dance.

As he cleaned his clothing as best he could, Hobart Adams looked at his savior. What he saw frightened him almost as much as the Comanches had. The two men were of about equal height—maybe an inch on either side of six-foot—but there the similarity ended with jarring suddenness.

Ezra Early gave the impression of being much larger than he was, probably because of the breadth of his chest and shoulders and the slimness of his waist. A wad of tobacco bulged in Early's right cheek. His thick, curly dark-brown hair cascaded out from under the felt hat and down onto the broad shoulders. Except for a little stubble, he was clean shaven. Pale, faded gray eyes gazed steadily at Adams, who gulped as he looked into those piercing orbs. Adams thought Early might have been handsome at one time. But his nose was mashed flat, and his left cheekbone was distorted. Adams shivered at the thought of how the bone had gotten that way.

Early wore a faded shirt of plain osnaburg. His pants were fringed buckskin—dark, smoky, greasy, bloody, filthy, well-worn buckskin. There was a tall feather in the high-crowned hat; heavy moccasins covered Early's feet. Two big flintlock pistols were stuck in the wide leather belt, each held in place by a thin piece of iron that formed a clip. A powder horn and shooting bag hung over his right shoulder and rested against his left hip. Another buckskin pouch dangled at the other side. Adams could not see it, but a tomahawk was jammed into his belt at the small of Early's back. A large knife in a beaded sheath hung from the belt at his left hip. A rawhide thong around his neck held a heart-shaped piece of leather, through which was stuffed a small clay pipe.

To Adams, the man was a frightening apparition, all in all. He gulped.

"Well now, boy," Early said slowly. "Just what're ye doin' out here all to your lonesome? 'Sides entertainin' a Comanche war party?"

Adams ignored the question. He was still scared down to his socks but was regaining his senses rapidly. With an authority bred of good living, he looked at Early in distaste. "And just who might you be?" he countered.

Early's eyes narrowed as he felt the beginnings of anger rise in him. "Name's Ezra Early, boy," he growled. "I'm the full-growed son of a buffler bull and a wild panther. And I'm the meanest goddamn critter ye'll ever meet." He spit a stream of brown juice. It landed near Adams's foot. "Now, I asked ye a question, boy, which ye nary answered."

Adams looked down at the brown ooze near his foot and then back up at Early. "That wasn't very nice, good fellow," he said haughtily, determined after his rough treatment to take no more guff from any ruffian.

Early's eyes were now thin slits, and his face was hard as stone. "There's some folks don't take kindly to bein' talked to in such a way, boy," he snarled. "'Specially after they just up and saved your miserable ass from a bunch of shit-eatin' Comanches that was nigh onto peelin' your hide and cuttin' your nuts off for ye." Early shrugged. "But if ye ain't of a mind to be friendly to this ol' hoss, I'll just be on my way."

Early pulled himself into the saddle and looked around. "I don't reckon the Comanches'll be back here for a spell." He squinted at Adams. "But it's still a far piece to Taos or Santa Fe. Still, ye keep a good pace, they might not catch up to ye at all." He tugged the Appaloosa's head around and started heading toward his mule, which had stopped fifty yards off and was looking balefully at him.

But Adams's voice stopped him: "Wait, there. I need your help."

Early turned back to face him. "I expect ye do." He spit. "But what makes ye think I'll be givin' it?"

"You can't just leave me out here in this godforsaken desert for the Comanches or the wolves," Adams said indignantly. "Not without food or water or a horse."

"Like hell I can't," Early said flatly.

They stared at each other, Early's eyes hard and glittering, Adams's scared but determined.

The easterner broke first. "I'm on my way to Santa Fe," he said, resignation touching his words. "I'd be in your debt if you were to help me get there. If it won't take you out of your way."

"I can get ye to Taos. That's where I'm headin'. From there ye can make arrangements to get to Santa Fe, which ain't but a couple days' ride south of there."

"I'm afraid I couldn't pay you," Adams said, abashed at having nothing but the clothes on his back.

Early shrugged and spit. "Wouldn't expect that of ye. Now, ye just plunk your ass down there and rest a bit whilst I go fetch up my mule." Early was back within minutes. "I don't suppose ye got yourself a horse, do ye, boy?" he asked, dismounting.

"No," Adams said, shaking his head sadly. "I was left without one. Without anything, for that matter."

"Didn't expect so." He started walking toward the dead Comanche. "What's your name, boy?" he asked.

"Adams. Hobart Adams. Most folks call me Bart."

Early nodded, pulling his knife. From behind him he heard Adams ask, "What're you planning to do there?"

"Raise this buck's hair, boy." It was done quickly. Early wrapped the bloody trophy in on itself and stuffed it into a sack on his saddle.

Adams stared at him in horror. Early ignored him as he mounted the Appaloosa. "I hope ye got some good shoes for walkin', Bart."

Still shocked and disgusted, Adams stuttered, "But I thought I would ride." He pointed at the mule.

"Need him to tote my plunder, boy," Early said nonchalantly. "'Sides, he's the goddamnedest, orneriest, most fractious four-legged critter this chil' ary met. He'd as like to throw you and stomp you into the dirt as he would to take a drink."

"But I'll never make it on foot. I'll . . ."

"If that's where your stick floats, boy," Early said with a shrug.

"Huh?"

"If that's the way ye want it. I aim to be headin' out. Ye can walk along, or not. I ain't aimin' to set here all day jawin' with ye."

Adams's shoulders sagged in defeat. "Guess I have no choice. The wolves or the bears or those savages'll get me if I stay out here alone. I'll go along with you."

2

EARLY SET OUT, PACK mule in tow, setting a slow pace. Adams walked nearby. The men were silent mostly; Early was not much given to talking to people he didn't really know. Adams concentrated on keeping up.

The day was waning fast, though, and finally Early said, "We'll be makin' camp in about an hour or so."

His face beaded in sweat, Adams merely nodded. His side hurt, his head throbbed, and his feet were swollen. He was more certain than ever that he would not make it to Santa Fe, or even Taos.

Early finally stopped, seemingly in the middle of nowhere. There were no landmarks that Adams could pick out. No trees and no water, either, anywhere he could see, when he limped up somewhat after Early. By the time Adams got there, Early had unloaded the pack mule, unsaddled the Appaloosa, and hobbled both animals. The two beasts wandered off a few feet, feeding on the sparse brown grass and clumps of brush.

Adams surveyed the area with horror and disdain. "You're planning to camp here?" he sputtered, a note of incredulity in his voice.

"There somethin' wrong with that?"

"But there's no wood. No water. No . . . nothing."

"There's more here than meets the eye, boy." He knelt, seemingly at random and began scooping at the sandy dirt. A few moments later he rocked back on his heels and waved his hand at the hole with a bit of a flourish. "Water," he announced.

Adams walked over and looked down. Sure enough, there was water. Not much, and it was dirty, but the seepage had filled the hole. He watched as Early flattened himself on the dirt and stuck his face into the hole, slurping up water with greedy, noisy abandon. Finally Early rolled onto his back and then sat up. "It'll be a bit afore it fills again, but then ye can have at it."

Early moved off as Adams squatted with anticipation. By the time Adams emptied the hole of water, nearly getting his fill, Early was kneeling nearby doing something, though Adams could not tell what. He strolled over there, a feeling of hope rising in him, and then watched.

"What're you doing?" Adams asked.

"Buildin' a fire. What'n hell ye think I'm doin'?"

"With what?" he asked, surprised and filled with wonder.

"*Bois de vache.*" Early snapped a piece of steel against some flint, sending a small shower of sparks onto the fluffy tinder he had placed on the ground. The sparks finally caught, and Early bent over, puffing lightly on the tinder, nursing it.

"What's that—whatever you called it?"

"Bois de vache." He paused in his puffing on the tinder as a small lick of flame flicked out. "Dried buffler shit." The tinder was burning now, and Early leaned back, feeding large, flat chips to the flames. "Don't burn too long, but it burns hot. Gives the food a tinge of spice, too, I'd be sayin'."

Adams nodded, accepting and digesting the information. He had seen it used before, but no one had bothered to explain what it was.

"Ye hungry?"

Adams nodded again and sat, happy to be off his feet. He issued a sigh of relief as he began undoing his bootlaces and then pulled the footwear off. As he worked, he added, "I've not had anything to eat since the day before yesterday."

"Well, it's a damn shame I got no fresh hump meat or fleece to fill your meatbag with. Bacon and beans'll have to do." He hated the thought. He had left real buffalo country only a week ago, but he was already sick of bacon and beans. There was nothing he could do about it, though, except to press on. He would be back in buffalo country eventually.

"After no eats for two days, bacon and beans sounds just fine to me," Adams said fervently. He paused. "You mentioned hump meat. I know what that is. But what's that other—the fleece, I think you said?"

"Yep. Prime eatin'. It's the long strip of fat along a buffler's backbone. Sizzled up, it shines with this chil'."

"Shines?"

"Jesus, ye are one shit-dumb critter, ain't ye," Early commented with a shake of his head. He set a frying pan on the fire and chunked up bacon into it, followed by some beans.

Adams was stung by the words, but he realized that for this time and place, he was incredibly unknowledgeable. He sighed. Without being told, he stood and prepared some simple corn cakes. By the time he had them cooking in another old pan, Early had pounded up coffee beans and poured them into a pot of water that was sitting in the flames.

Before long, they were slurping coffee and spooning down greasy bacon and beans. They were silent as they ate. When he had finished his food, Early tossed his tin plate aside. He refilled his coffee cup, and then tamped his pipe full of tobacco.

As he lit the pipe, he asked, "So how come ye to be out here in such a place all by your lonesome, boy?"

Adams grimaced, and said, "It's none of your affair, Mister Early."

Early's eyes grew hard again. He was plumb tired of Hobart Adams already and was beginning to regret having helped the man.

Adams saw the sudden hardness in his companion and said hastily, "I don't mean to be rude, Mister Early. It's just that . . . well, dammit all, I'm simply mortified at what happened to me. I feel the complete fool."

"We all been made a fool of at times," Early said, relenting slightly. "Even this ol' chil'," he added solemnly.

Adams smiled regretfully. He patted his coat absentmindedly. With a look of sudden surprise, he reached inside his coat and extracted a cigar. It was battered but seemed smokable. He lit it and puffed a few moments, savoring the smoke as it bit inside him, settling him, relaxing him. "I guess you've earned the right to know," he finally said.

Early nodded. "I expect I have," he said flatly.

Hobart Adams stood uncomfortably in the office of the *New York Register* under the harsh glare of editor Humphrey McWalters.

"Our readers want to know the details of the growing trade with the Mexican people in Santa Fe," McWalters said in that fierce, cigar-formed growl of his. "What's being shipped out there; what we're getting in return; the trail itself; the Indians along it. Everything."

Adams didn't like where this was going, but he kept silent.

"There've been rumors that the Mexican government is heavily taxing American traders. So much so that there is danger of Americans being excluded from trading there. That's an affront to all Americans."

Adams nodded dumbly, not knowing what to say.

"The road to Santa Fe—maybe it's called the Santa Fe Trail—has been in existence for nine or maybe ten years. But from dispatches we have received from the West, it has only been in the past couple of years or so that substantial amounts of money have become involved. That makes it of far more importance to everyone. So much so that the government ordered a large force to accompany the trading caravan the year before last as far as the Mexican border, to protect them from Indians. And, I suspect, the Mexicans themselves," McWalters said haughtily. "Apparently the Americans are faring well, though there is considerable concern about the duties being charged. I want you to find out all the particulars."

"Why me?" Adams finally managed to blurt. "There are others who're far more versed in writing than I."

"You're a talented enough writer, I suppose. Certainly not the best, but adequate enough for the task."

"But—"

"Don't interrupt." McWalters cleared his throat. "In addition to your barely better than mediocre writing ability, you are well versed in sketching. When you forward your stories on this burgeoning trade, I expect them to be accompanied by accurate sketches of the land, buildings, Mexicans, wagons, whatever you can find to draw out there in that barren wasteland."

Adams left McWalters's office an hour later, sweating heavily despite the coolness of the early March day. He wanted no part of this ridiculous adventure, but he knew there was no way of getting out of it either. As he walked toward his small room at a boardinghouse, he wondered how he had gotten into such a position.

He was the second-born son of a small-time baker, and he had lived his whole life amid New York's teeming throngs. He was used to the hustle and bustle of the city, with its slums, foul docks, social whirl, culture, and interesting marketplaces. The city had everything, as far as he was concerned; the West had nothing to offer except danger and wild Indians.

Adams early on had shown an affinity for sketching

and soon after for writing also. However, he had absolutely no talent whatsoever for baking. His father had finally acknowledged that his son would never take his place in the growing family business. Once he had drawn that conclusion, Silas Adams made sure that Hobart got an education. With a lot of hard work and a liberal dash of luck Adams had managed to land a reporting job on the *New York Register* two years ago.

He had grown comfortable in the job, had managed to put aside a few dollars, and as such had begun courting Elizabeth Luyuendyke. He hoped that within another year or two he would have enough money saved to be able to ask her to marry him. But this noxious venture would certainly put an end to *that* dream. Elizabeth would never stand for it, and she was far too pretty and vivacious for him to expect her to wait for him.

The more he thought about it, the angrier he became. He was comfortable here; his life was falling into place. Yet now he was being sent to a foreign country, one chock-full of heathens and people whose language he did not speak. There were wild animals and even wilder men, if even some of the tales he had heard were true.

With determination that afternoon he made some inquiries about a position on some of the other newspapers in the city. But none was in the offing. Defeated, he ate a tasteless meal and headed back to his room. He sat there that night, knowing he had no choice. To refuse this assignment would mean losing his hard-earned job. Until he could find another, he might be forced back into the bakery with his brothers. No, he must go.

Explaining it to Elizabeth was not easy, neither was

it particularly fulfilling. She as much as told him not to bother calling on her again when he returned to New York City . . . *if* he returned to New York City.

In the morning, he began making his preparations. A week later he was on his way. The trip west seemed interminable. First there was a steam ferry ride across the river to New Jersey, followed by a jolting stage ride across that small state, and then another ferry to Philadelphia. He caught another stage there, heading westward across the rolling hills and through the forests to Harrisburg. A hand-operated ferry got him across the Susquehanna River. On the far side he caught a wagon that jarred its way across the increasingly harsh countryside.

At Pittsburgh, he paid his fare for a barge ride down the Ohio. The wet, uncomfortable journey down the miles of river did little to improve his attitude or the favor upon which he viewed this job. Another rough barge brought him up the Mississippi to St. Louis.

With increasing irritation and trepidation, he caught still another crude boat for the last leg of his preliminary journey, up the Missouri River to Independence, Missouri. *Good God, I've not even begun the real trek yet.* He thought he might be ill.

He became more convinced of that when he first saw Independence. The town was a rancid collection of shacks and festering saloons. Men, mules, and oxen swarmed all over the town, each more obnoxious than the last. For the few moments it took the boat to dock, Adams considered turning around and leaving. He could, he figured, just stop at one of the cities along the Ohio River and seek a job at a newspaper there. With his experience, it shouldn't be hard.

Despite his surface meekness, though, Adams had a streak of stubbornness in him. He would not back down now.

He reconsidered that determination when he finally met the men who would take him West along the already famous Santa Fe Trail. Led by a foul creature named Ebenezer Parfrey, they were a filthy, usually drunk, lot. Their gruffness and profanity revolted Adams.

With more than a little regret, Adams gingerly climbed into one of the three huge ox-drawn wagons loaded with goods of all sorts. He settled in as best he could, choked on the clouds of dust, and endured the epithets the freighters threw his way.

3

IF ADAMS HAD THOUGHT the journey to Missouri interminable, then there was no way to describe the trek in that creaking wagon. The dust rolled up from under the wheels in thick clouds; the crack of whips was unceasing; the men's oaths omnipresent. Adams felt after the first mile that his head would be jolted off at any time, and his spine began to hurt.

In disgust, he hopped out of the wagon at the first opportunity and walked, as did a few of the other men. The bullwhackers rode horses or mules alongside the plodding oxen. Adams realized quickly that his shoes were not designed for walking great distances. There was nothing he could do about it now, though. Nor could he do anything about his clothes, which were inappropriate for the place and activity.

The next day, Adams asked Parfrey for a horse.

"Ain't got no goddamn extra horse, sonny," the leader of the caravan said in his phlegmy, hoarse clot of a voice.

"A mule then?" Adams was attempting to keep his composure. He always tried his best not to anger others unnecessarily.

"That I got for ya." Parfrey chuckled. At least Adams thought it was a chuckle. Parfrey shoved an oversize index finger up his right nostril and prospected awhile. He wiped the results on his shirt, where it disappeared into the rest of the foulness.

Parfrey spun and bellowed a string of profane orders. In minutes, one of his men brought up a saddled mule. Adams took the reins and looked the beast over skeptically. It was a handsome mule, as far as such beasts went, and not as big as some Adams had seen. With a shrug, Adams stuck a boot in a stirrup and pulled. Settled in the saddle, he felt a little better, though he was still nervous. He had heard stories about the unpredictability of these animals, plus he had ridden in a saddle only once or twice.

The mule proved to be rather sedate, Adams found out, though he had an ungainly gait that rubbed Adams's buttocks the wrong way. Still, the fancy-dressed easterner figured it was better than walking, or even riding in one of the large, seatless Conestogas.

The land here was rolling grassland and at this time of year was covered by a profusion of flowers of every color. Adams sketched as frequently as he could, sometimes stopping the mule for a few minutes to make some hasty lines on his pad before moving off again. At night, around the fire, he would fill in the sketches, using his memory. At first he asked the teamsters about the landmarks, the identity of the flowers, and more. But the men proved so surly and taciturn that after two days he had given up. He hoped one day to find someone more talkative who might be able to identify things from the sketches.

Three days out, they came to the Wakarusa and Ottawa creeks, which had a narrow strip of land between them. It had been raining since the night before, and the neck of land seemed to be disappearing even as the men watched.

Parfrey bellowed orders and roared curses. Whips snapped and cracked, oxen grumbled, and mules brayed wildly as the men worked the noisy wagons hurriedly toward, then across, the narrows. They stopped on the far side of the second creek to rest for a few minutes. Looking back, the neck had all but disappeared.

"Well, Jesus goddamn H. Christ," Parfrey growled, laughing roughly. "Beat the bastard this time. Jesus."

The others joined in the laughter.

Ten days after leaving Independence, the small wagon train pulled into a long grove of oak, hickory, and walnut trees along the Neosho River. Wagons and men were scattered in thick profusion throughout the trees. It seemed there was even more bustle here than in Independence.

"What is this place?" Adams asked Ivor Jenkins, whom Adams had found to be about the least offensive of Parfrey's men, though that was not saying much in the man's favor.

"Council Grove," Jenkins answered in his constantly breathless voice.

"What happens here?" Adams was truly interested,

not only for his stories, but out of pure inquisitiveness.

"Usually a bunch of small companies rendezvous here. Take a few days to rest the animals. Usually form a big caravan, with all the wagons. Elect a cap'n and other leaders. Cut some extry axles out of these fine hard trees. Then hit the trail again in a big group."

He was about to say more when Parfrey roared Jenkins's name. "Gotta go," Jenkins gasped as he hurried off.

Parfrey's little caravan quickly settled in and his men gathered around a fire. Soon after, another group of men tromped up. As they were taking seats by the fire, holding cups out for coffee, one stopped and looked at Adams. "What the hell's this ya got here?" he asked in a lightly slurred voice.

"Goddamn idjit newspaper feller from back in the sonna bitchin' States," Parfrey responded. "Figures to get hisself into Santa Fe."

"Looks like his fancy ass is some out of place out here."

"Sure as hell," Parfrey snapped. "He's a useless peckerwood is what he is. Can't do shit for hisself." He shook his head and hawked up a clot of phlegm and spit it into the fire. "Don't know why I brung him along."

Adams sat a moment, stunned. But he quickly regained his senses. "For the money, Mister Parfrey," he said quietly. "That's why you agreed to bring me along. Soon's I opened my mouth, you opened your hand for my gold." He paused. "Of course," he continued, "if you continue to speak so poorly of me, I just might be unable to pay you what I owe you."

"You egg-suckin' sonna bitch," Parfrey snarled, shoving up and reaching for his knife.

"Sit down," the new man growled. He was a big burly fellow, with a fight-scarred face, beefy shoulders, and hard slabs for hands.

Parfrey hesitated but then saw that several of the other fellow's men had their hands on their pistols.

When Parfrey reluctantly sat the man said, "There ain't no call for you to take offense, Parfrey. He ain't done nothin' to you." He looked at Adams. "Name's Woodrow Eakins. I lead another of these caravans."

Adams nodded at him. "Hobart Adams."

"I expect to be elected captain of the main caravan. You figure you ain't easy traveling with Parfrey here, you're welcome to travel with me."

He nodded again. "I appreciate the offer. I figure I'll stick with Mister Parfrey, though, at least for a while. After all, I've paid him a substantial sum already to get me to Santa Fe." He was determined not to show the fear and worry he felt.

"Suit yourself, boy."

The talk drifted off to the peculiarities of their trade. Much of the talk centered on the annoyance of doing business with the Mexican officials. Adams listened quietly, jotting notes now and again.

After an hour, Eakins said to one of his men, "Hey, Charley, take Mister Adams there and fetch us up a few bottles of whiskey to cut our dry." It didn't matter to any of them that it was barely past noon.

"Sure, boss," Charley Poole said, standing. "Come on, Mister Adams."

Poole and Adams wove through the trees, around wagons or clusters of animals, past knots of sweating, working men. They reached a group of wagons, each neatly parked next to or behind the other. All were loaded with huge stores of goods. Smaller piles of supplies were on the ground, covered by oiled, waterproof canvas. The wagons, merchandise, and supplies were being guarded by several armed men, who returned Poole's greeting.

"Hungry?" Poole asked as he flipped the tarp off a pile of supplies.

"Could do with a bite, I expect." Adams felt as if he had not been full since he had left New York.

Poole turned and tossed something at Adams, who, startled, managed to catch it without dropping it. He looked at the can, nodding. He managed to get the can open and happily ate the syrupy peaches. He finished quickly. He turned to toss the can away, not wanting to hit anyone with it, and stopped, mouth agape. There, not two feet away, was an Indian.

"Get outta here, ya goddamn savage," Poole snapped, stepping up alongside Adams. The Indian glared balefully at the two white men a moment. Then, pulling his blanket around him, he spun and disappeared.

Poole glanced up at Adams, amused at the look of amazement on the easterner's face. "Ain't ya ary seed an Injun up close afore, boy?" he asked.

Adams shook his head, not quite sure any of this was real. Half of him worked it over in his mind, trying to convince himself that it was. The other half was burning the image of that Indian into his mind. He suddenly wanted desperately to get his pad and sketch that picture before it dimmed in his mind.

"He's a Wichita. Damned dirty, lazy savages." Poole almost shuddered. "Sons a bitches come around our camps alla time. Thievin' bastards."

"Thieving?" Adams asked dumbly. "What do they take?"

"Any goddamn thing ain't nailed down or held tight in your hand." He paused. "Well, come on, we'd best be gettin' back to the others." He headed back toward the heap of supplies. He grabbed two bottles of whiskey and handed them to Adams. He pulled out two more and set them down before carefully covering over the supplies with the canvas again.

"Where the hell you boys been?" Eakins asked, stomping up.

Poole finished his job, picked up the bottles, and turned. "You get lonely for me, Woody?" Poole asked. His tone was bantering, though.

"Shit," Eakins chuckled. He had a deep, clear voice. "Them other boys're gettin' mighty thirsty."

The three strode off. Just before they reached Parfrey's fire again, a burst of yells and then a gunshot broke the lazy afternoon warmth.

"Damn," Eakins snapped. He broke into a run. Poole and a somewhat hesitant Adams rushed after him.

As they ran, they heard, "Ya missed him, ya goddamn blind, dumb son of a bitch."

Eakins, Adams, and Poole burst into the opening. All the other men were standing. Some were laughing; the others looked angry. Parfrey had reloaded his rifle and brought it up to his shoulder, aiming at an Indian who was running toward the river.

"Let him be," Eakins shouted.

Parfrey fired anyway, but the Indian was behind a screen of hardwood trees and brush.

"Goddammit, Parfrey," Eakins roared as he ran up

and jerked Parfrey around to face him. "I told ya to leave him be, goddammit."

"I don't give a shit what ya said," Parfrey rasped. "You don't hold no sway over me, damn ya. That sonna bitch tried to steal my favorite butcherin' knife. Christ, the goddamn thing was stuck in that log right there next to me. Bastard just up and went for it. Shit."

"Shouldn't have left it settin' around," Eakins said simply.

"Buffler shit," Parfrey snarled, anger contorting his already twisted face. "It's a poor thing when a man can't even leave his tools 'round without some goddamn savage walkin' off with 'em."

"You been 'round Injuns enough to know how they operate. You're a goddamn fool for leavin' it out in the open." He glared at Parfrey, who held the stare for a few moments before dropping his eyes. "Well, boys, I expect we all got work to do." Thoughts of an afternoon sitting around sipping whiskey were all but forgotten. As he turned away, he added, "Come see me in the mornin', Parfrey. I'll replace your knife."

"No need," Parfrey said quietly. "He nary did get it."

Eakins whirled back to face Parfrey. "What the goddamn hell do you mean he didn't get it?" Eakins was enraged.

"Kept him from it, dammit."

"Then what in hell was all the fuss about?"

"Shit, the sonna bitch knocked me down," Parfrey said without apology.

"How'd ya stop him in the first place?" Eakins asked, trying to keep down his soaring temper.

"Knocked him on his ass with the butt end of my

whip." He waved a hand at the whip lying on the ground nearby.

"It ain't surprisin' then that he knocked ya down. I'd of done the same myself." He paused to spit. "But I'm tellin' ya, Parfrey, don't go agin no more Injuns whilst we're all here."

"Buffler shit," Parfrey said. The words were accompanied by a blast of nasal mucus. "I ain't about to let no redskin sonna bitch put his hands on me and get away with it. They gotta be taught a lesson when they pull shit like that. You know that well's I do."

"And you goddamn full well know that we got us enough problems on this trail without lookin' for more by killin' some Injun over a goddamn knife." Eakins stared down Parfrey again. Eakins turned and walked away, his own men following. Poole took the two bottles of whiskey from Adams, shrugged in a sort of apology, and hurried after his companions.

Adams stood there, not quite knowing what to do. The thought of moving to Eakins's camp and riding with him did cross his mind, though.

4

"CATCH UP! CATCH UP!"

The shouts rebounded through the long string of camps along the Neosho River. Activity was not far behind. Dozens of men herded scores of oxen and mules into a makeshift corral, where the men harnessed the animals. Then the beasts were brought to the wagons and hitched up.

Soon the cries of "All set!" rang out throughout the camp as the wagons were made ready to roll.

"What's going on?" Adams asked as the first yells went through Council Grove. He sat up in his blankets.

"Sons a bitch bastards're leavin' already," Ivor Jenkins snarled as he moved about Parfrey's small camp in irritation, his work boots sending up small puffs of dirt.

"Who? What?" Adams asked, casting off the blankets and standing. He rubbed the sleep from his eyes.

"Eakins, that mule-humpin' peckerwood, is pullin' out."

"But what does that mean?" Adams had no idea what was going on, but he figured it wasn't good.

"It means, goddammit," the nervous, fidgety little man said raggedly, "that we'll be on our goddamn own. Across Comanche and Kiowa country. Shit. It goddamn means that Eakins is movin' the caravan out already."

"But I thought it wouldn't be leaving for several days." Adams was confused. Yesterday Eakins had been elected captain of the caravan. He had told the outfits he wanted the wagons ready to move in four or five days.

"That's what that lyin' buffler pizzle said. Shit-eater musta changed his goddamn mind for some reason. Damn."

A hungover Parfrey was roaring for Jenkins, and the man rushed off.

Adams sat heavily and pulled on his boots. He was numb. He had not really considered leaving Parfrey's wagons to go with Eakins, but it had remained an option in the back of his head. He considered for a moment grabbing his things and running after the long string of wagons that was just beginning to pull out.

He recoiled, though, at any hint of quitting or of running away from a problem. He had lost too much in getting this far. He could not see running away, as it seemed to him, just because the going got rough. After all, there was no guarantee that going with Eakins would be any more pleasant than sticking with Parfrey,

though Eakins and his men certainly seemed somewhat more amiable and more intelligent than Parfrey's
small group.

Adams stood, tucking his shirt into his pants. He
watched as the wagons continued pulling out. Besides,
there was the matter of money. He could not expect
Eakins to take him along for free. And Adams had
already paid Parfrey half the price for the full trip to
Santa Fe. His editor would be furious if Adams left
now and forfeited his down payment.

Adams decided that he would stick it out with
Parfrey no matter how bad it got. He went to the fire,
squatted, and poured a mug of coffee. He sipped at it,
trying to ignore the turmoil around him.

Parfrey did not show up until past noon. The main
caravan was long gone, and Parfrey's three wagons
and seven men were alone.

"What now, Mister Parfrey?" Adams asked after
Parfrey had downed two cups of coffee, some salt beef,
and biscuits.

"We do what the hell we would've been doin' even
if that horseshit Eakins hadn't run off on us. We'll
leave when we was supposed to leave."

"Will that be dangerous?"

"Shit," Parfrey snorted. "Ain't gonna be no more
dangerous than any other time."

To Adams, it sounded like a boast, but he wondered. He had heard tales of fierce Indians west of
here. Ones with names like Comanches and Kiowas
and Cheyennes. Even if only some of the stories were
true, it was enough to make his gut knot in fear. "You
sure?" he asked tentatively.

" 'Course I'm sure." Parfrey flicked a louse off his

forearm and into the fire. "You might have to help us out some, though, 'stead of just sittin' 'round with that damned drawin' book alla time." He sneered.

"I don't mind helping out a little." Adams paused. "But I don't plan to become one of your wagoneers. I've paid you to take me to Santa Fe. I didn't pay you to work me to death on the way." He tried to sound harsh but was not at all sure he had accomplished it. Seeing the look in Parfrey's eyes made him know he had not succeeded at all.

The work he was drafted to do was not all that difficult or time consuming. Parfrey had at first tried to get him to do more, but Adams's incompetence outweighed most of Parfrey's desire to humiliate Adams.

They pulled out five days later. No one else had shown up at Council Grove in that time, and things had been mighty quiet. They crossed the Neosho River early in the morning and were on their way at long last. Adams rode his mule with a combination of fear and excitement.

The wagons crawled along, giving Adams plenty of opportunity to make notes and preliminary sketches. He was rather in awe. Having spent all his life in crowded New York, he was amazed by the limitless horizon, the gently rolling land that gradually changed to flat, short-grass prairie. There were no trees, except occasional cottonwoods along the rare watercourses. He saw no landmarks, nothing in the land to break the monotony. Adams wondered how the first men to travel this path had found their way. Now at least there were some tracks of the many wagons that had passed by.

Despite the starkness of the land, animals abounded.

There were huge herds of buffalo, sometimes stretching as far as the eye could see. At those times, the land itself seemed to be alive, shifting and moving like a brown carpet being pulled this way and that.

Six days after leaving Council Grove, they reached the Little Arkansas. Seeing it, Adams was unimpressed, since it was only fifteen or twenty feet wide. Crossing it did impress him, though, since the banks of the river were very steep and quite slick. The river bottom was like a quagmire, rather than firm. However, the men from the main caravan had made bridges of grass and earth a week earlier. They were in poor shape after so many wagons had crossed, but they enabled Parfrey's group to get across with a minimum of fuss.

They moved through sand hills and pushed on. Adams quickly grew bored again with the monotony. Making matters worse, Parfrey and his seven companions had become more sullen and withdrawn. They weren't more antagonistic toward Adams; they just kept to themselves, as if the constant wind had abraded all the sociableness out of them. Adams, a generally gregarious young man, was bothered by it.

After four more days of traveling, Adams felt a touch of excitement. There, out in front of him, bold as could be, was an actual landmark. It wasn't much; just a small hump of brown sandstone, but standing amid the flatness of the endless plains, it seemed like a mountain.

After they arrived at the rock, Adams helped set up camp, then climbed to the top of the hump. Names were carved into the sandstone face of the rock. Adams smiled, pulled out his penknife, and added his. He sat up there until it was too dark to see.

The traveling grew more arduous in the next few

days when the landscape changed again as they left the lush-grass prairie behind them. It was replaced by sparse, curly, short grass, dotted with small cactus. It was a dull, bleak land, and once more boredom settled over the men.

Three weeks after leaving Council Grove, they came to the Arkansas River. Parfrey and his men surveyed the river for a few minutes.

"It doesn't look too bad," Adams ventured.

"Shit," Parfrey snorted, expectorating a wad of phlegm and tobacco.

"Well, it doesn't," Adams insisted. "It's wide, yes, and the current seems strong. But from here it doesn't look too deep."

"Ain't too deep," Jenkins said. "But the goddamn current's treacherous. Worse is the goddamn bottom. Son of a bitch's full of quicksand, holes, and Christ knows what else. Jesus. You don't get your ass across there in a hurry, your goddamn wagon'll be sunk up to its goddamn axles afore you know it." He shook his head.

They had little problem crossing the river, except for once. One of the wagons started to topple after its right front wheel hit a hole. Parfrey and George Court grabbed the oxen harnesses on one side, and Jenkins and Tom Hartstone did so on the other. They lent their strength and that of their horses and mules, cracking their whips. The wagon lurched out of the hole and moved ahead.

Before long, they were resting on the bleak, barren sand hills on the south side of the river. The men stripped down almost to nothing, spreading their clothes across the dunes to dry.

"Hope you got yourself as much balls as ya think ya do, city boy," Parfrey said smugly as they prepared to move on. "You think the goddamn trip's been tough so far, wait till ya see the *Jornada del Muerto*."

"Journey of death?" Adams asked, surprised.

"Goddamn right. Sixty miles of not a goddamn thing. Ain't shit to see but miles and miles of goddamn nothing. Ain't no goddamn water, no goddamn animals, no goddamn trees. Just goddamn heat and horizon."

"Everyone go that way?" Adams asked.

"'Cept those that take the mountain way. But not many do. Haven't since the first couple years. It's got a shitload more water than this way, but it's a hundred miles or so longer'n this route. And them mountains are a bitch to get through."

The trip was every bit as bad as Parfrey had warned, and then some. Adams thought more than once that they were wandering aimlessly across an empty plain toward the flat edge of the earth. He was sure they would all fall off at any moment.

Parfrey kept them moving through the night, then allowed his men to sleep during the heat of the day. They moved out again late in the afternoon. Adams, refreshed by some sleep and a meal, still saw mirages dancing in the heat ahead. He was frightened, thinking they were getting nowhere. But he was afraid to say anything, so he kept his mouth shut.

At one point, Parfrey swore and growled. Somehow he had realized that he had taken them off the trail. Going two days without water wasn't too bad for the animals; three, they might still make it. But if he had gotten them off the track too far and it took four days to reach Lower Springs, the animals would be dead. He sweated, worried, but finally caught a faint trace of the wagons that had passed a couple of weeks before.

They staggered into the grassy marsh that identified Lower Spring. The grateful men and suffering animals gulped down water as fast as they could, thankful for this oasis in the midst of nowhere. They rested a day before pushing on again, following the Cimarron River's dry, twisting bed.

This new stretch was nowhere near as bad as the *jornada,* since there were springs—small but usually with water—approximately a day's journey apart. Eventually the barrenness of the dry prairie gave way to a rugged land slashed with small, sharp canyons.

A week after leaving Lower Spring, they camped at Cold Spring, then they cut away from the Cimarron River, heading southwest. The next morning, the group spotted figures moving slowly toward them.

"Who are they?" Adams asked, not really trusting his eyes.

"Comanches," Parfrey spit.

5

THERE WERE THREE OF them—two men and a woman. An icy feeling gripped Adams's bowels, until he remembered that there were only two warriors, and seven wagoneers. Still, the fear-chill lingered, as he worried that more warriors might be lurking nearby. Then he realized that was ridiculous. There was no place for anyone to hide around here.

The three Comanches stopped and talked for a few minutes. They were still almost half a mile off. Then the woman rode off, cutting southward, walking her pony. The two warriors did some things that Adams could not see fully, and would not have understood even if he had.

Then the two Comanches charged at the three wagons.

Parfrey had been well aware of the Comanches for a while, and had waited to see what they would do. He

rode quietly with a devilish gleam in his eye, his anticipation almost sexual in its intensity.

"George, Alf," Parfrey suddenly shouted, eagerness
in his voice as the Comanches charged. "Drop them
two goddamn bucks."

George Court and Alf McHugh pulled to a stop and
slid off their horses. They rested their rifles across
their saddles. McHugh fired first. Less than a second
later, Court followed suit. Both Comanches tumbled
from their saddles.

McHugh and Court whooped, then congratulated
each other, as the other men yelled in agreement at
their good deed.

"Ivor, you and Tom go fetch that bitch back here,"
Parfrey ordered. "Move your asses."

Ivor Jenkins and Tom Hartstone galloped off. The
woman had heard the shots and seen her companions
fall. She looked back and then slapped her pony into a
run when she spotted the two white men racing
toward her.

Still, Jenkins and Hartstone had no difficulty catching her. Whooping, the two men pulled up to the
woman, one on each side. Jenkins grabbed the pony's
rope and tugged, stopping the Comanche horse.

"Well, lookee here," Hartstone said with a rasping
chuckle. He pointed to an infant in a cradle hanging
from the saddle's high horn. He reached for the baby,
and the woman raked his cheek with her fingernails.
She snapped something in her language.

Hartstone slid a greasy hand along his cheek and
then looked at his finger. It was spotted with blood.
"Goddamn whore bitch," he snarled. He smacked her
with a backhand.

The woman gasped, but it was the only sound she made. She would have fallen off her horse, had it not been for Jenkins on the other side of her. She bounced off him and managed to right herself in the saddle again.

They began heading toward the others, trying to ignore the squalling baby. Near to the others, Hartstone had had enough. He pulled the infant from the cradleboard. "Goddamn noisy little critter, ain't he?" the wagoneer said with no humor. Suddenly he flung the baby to the ground. "Let's get this bitch back over there," Hartstone said with growing excitement.

Jenkins nodded. The Comanche woman was young and nearly pleasing looking. She was dark of face, and plump, with full, milk-heavy breasts, and broad, fleshy buttocks. Ravishing her would be fun, he figured. Still, it irritated Jenkins a little that he, like always, would be third or fourth in line, after Parfrey, Court, and McHugh. Next in line after them usually alternated between himself and Hartstone. The relative newcomers, Dickie Thayer and Bob Maines, were last. Neither minded. Indeed, they often vied for the "honor" of last dibs.

Jenkins and Hartstone rode slowly toward the others, one on each side of the woman. Jenkins still held the rope rein to the Comanche pony.

Parfrey had stopped his wagons not far from the two warriors' bodies. Thayer was building a small fire, while Maines was getting a mess of beans and bacon ready for cooking.

"Stake her down, boys," Parfrey said with glee in his clogged voice. Hartstone and Jenkins dismounted and dragged the woman off her pony. Thayer took his companions' horses and the Comanche pony and led them off to where the others were staked and munching the scrub grass.

The Comanche started to resist, until Hartstone punched her on the side of the head. That took the fight out of her, and she was much more pliant as the two men pounded picket rings into the ground and then tied the woman—spread-eagled—to them.

Hartstone pulled his knife and slid it under the hem of the woman's dress. Grasping a fold of buckskin in his other hand, he started cutting.

"Hold on there, Tom," Parfrey said, voice neutral. "You're too goddamn anxious. Let's leave that till we've ate."

"Shit, lookin' at a nekkid squaw makes the eatin' more goddamn fun."

"You'll shoot your juices in your pants doin' that, ya dumb bastard," Parfrey said with a crude chuckle.

"Shit," Hartstone grumbled. But he stood and sheathed his knife. Then he grinned. "Well, goddammit, let's have that grub."

"Jesus, you are an antsy bastard, ain't ya?"

It wasn't long before they were slobbering down greasy bacon and beans. The wagoneers shoveled their food in, eager to get to the woman.

Adams ate slowly. He was uneasy; had been since they had spotted the Comanches. Fear of Indian attack had been present at first, but that had given way to a dread of what he was certain these men were about to do. He remained seated when the other men rose almost as one and headed the few feet to where the young woman was tied. Then he reluctantly got up and followed slowly, a sinking, sick feeling in the pit of his stomach.

Adams got his first good look at her, and thought he

would vomit. She couldn't be more than sixteen, he thought. She looked like a trapped coyote, in a way, as she tried to hide her fear.

The wagoneers began hooting and cheering as Parfrey pulled his knife and knelt. Starting where Hartstone had left off, he slowly started to cut off the dark, well-used buckskin dress. Then the garment was fully parted, lying on either side of the woman. Parfrey stood inside the V of the girl's legs and slid the knife away.

"Lordy, she's a fine lookin' thing for a dumpy Comanche, ain't she?" Thayer said with a hoarse chuckle.

The girl struggled, which enflamed the men more. She realized that, and settled down, firming her mind to face what was about to happen. *I am a Nermernuh*, she told herself furiously.

The men's hoots, jeers, and profane epithets sickened Adams all the more, but he didn't know what to do. In unwanted fascination, he watched as Parfrey unbuttoned his pants and let them flop down at his ankles. He was turgid, bringing forth a new burst of hooting encouragement.

Then Parfrey knelt and with leering, brutal efficiency, entered the girl. The young woman kept her face blank. The blandness seemed to anger Parfrey, and he pounded on her ruthlessly. Then he stopped. Still inside her, he balanced himself on one hand. With the other, he smacked her face, one way and then the other several times. He grabbed her breasts and viciously squeezed them, sending out spurts of milk, which had the men roaring in sick humor.

Blood seeped from the corners of the woman's mouth, and on her breasts, which had been cut by Parfrey's long, ragged fingernails. Still, she would not acknowledge the pain or the horror of her situation.

"Comanche bitch," Parfrey snarled as he began pumping again. Suddenly he stiffened and grunted a few times. He slumped onto the woman, almost smothering her with his greater size. Parfrey stood and pulled up his pants. He was refastening them when Adams's revulsion got the better of his reason. "You bastard," he screamed, and he charged at Parfrey.

Adams hit Parfrey around the middle, tackling him. They rolled in the dust, swearing. Parfrey easily flung Adams off and stood, feeling the back of his head. His hand came away bloody, from where his head had grazed one of the iron picket pins when Adams tackled him. "You goddamn no-good, Injun-lovin' son of a whore," Parfrey growled. Once more he pulled his knife.

Parfrey advanced, eyes filled with rage. Adams backed up slowly, fear digging its fangs into his stomach. Suddenly he dipped, scooped up a handful of sandy dirt, and flung it at Parfrey's face.

Parfrey dropped the knife and wiped furiously at his eyes, trying to clear them. Adams saw his chance and took it. He charged. But from out of nowhere came a blow to the back of his head. He fell flat on his face, then groggily pushed up onto his hands and knees. He saw George Court putting his pistol back into his belt.

Adams fell again, landing and only semiconsciously rolling. He came to a stop on his back. Leering, rough faces swirled over him and he heard rough, derisive laughter. The world started turning dark, and he barely heard Court say, "Now we can kill that goddamn, fancy-ass sumbitch."

Adams fought to stay awake, but it was impossible. He finally gave in to the unconsciousness just after hearing Parfrey say, "We don't need to kill him." Parfrey's gargling laughter was the last thing Adams heard before the world went away from him.

Adams awoke alone and afraid. His head pounded and hunger gnawed at his belly. He had no idea how long he had been out. It had been early afternoon when the fracas started. The sun was shining brightly, so it could be just a few hours later that same afternoon; or it could be a week later.

He stood gingerly, the ache in his head threatening to topple him. He bent, placing his hands on his knees. He sucked in great draughts of hot, dusty air, trying to settle the sickness in his stomach spawned by the hammering in his head. Finally he managed to straighten up again.

Gingerly he began to turn, looking over the area with pain-clouded eyes. He stopped when he saw what was left of the young woman. At least he assumed it was the Comanche; there was not really enough left of her to tell, but the remains were still lying the way she had been, though the picket rings were gone.

It took a moment for the full horror of what he was looking at to get through to him. He bent over retching, though there was nothing in his stomach to come out except bile. He sank down to his knees, still with the dry heaves. And he cried, tears falling from his face into the dust.

Finally, though, the tears and retching stopped. He was empty inside, drained of fluids, hope, and feeling. He rose, stomach aching from both the heaving and hunger. Avoiding looking at the remains again, he searched the countryside. There was nothing here that he could use. No water, no food, no animal to transport him. He did see a faint line of tracks in the dust, heading toward what he assumed was the southwest.

Adams rubbed a hand across his face. Judging by the amount of stubble on his face, he had been out almost a full day. He shook his head, worried and angry and disgusted.

He stood, unsure of what to do. He could not stay here. It might be weeks before succor came along, but it might be only minutes before Comanches arrived. He had two choices—press on or turn back. In his notes, he had marked down estimates of the distances they had covered. Exactness was impossible, since Parfrey and his men would not give him any definite information. Before leaving Independence, he had learned that the entire journey to Santa Fe was about eight hundred miles, maybe nine hundred. He figured they had come more than five hundred miles, and probably close to six hundred.

There was only one answer: pushing on. It was a long shot, but he had no choice. It would not be easy, though. He had no food, no water, no weapons with which to hunt. He had to hope he could stumble onto a waterhole or spring. That was the most important thing. Pressed to it, he thought he might be able to eat grubs or worms or ants, or something. But without water, he would not last another day.

He cursed, silently at first, then loudly and with verve. He had unconsciously acquired much from the wagoneers, mostly their penchant for foul language. It came in handy now.

Then he set off.

6

WITHIN A QUARTER OF a mile, Adams's feet began to ache unmercifully in the fashionable, exceedingly uncomfortable shoes. Combined with his hunger, his throbbing head, the wobbliness from hunger, and the recent bout of sickness, it was slow, painful going. But he pressed on, mile after slow mile, under a broiling sun. He tried not to think of his aches and pains. He tried to ignore the thirst that thickened his tongue and the hunger that sent pains through his belly.

He tried to concentrate on the possibility of rescue. With some luck—a commodity that for him had been in mighty short supply of late, he had to admit—he might catch on with a wagon train heading back toward Missouri. Of course, one coming *from* Missouri might catch up to him, too. But he would prefer one heading east. That way he could take it back to Missouri and return to New York as quickly as possible. As soon as he got there, he would—in the most colorful terms possible, and he knew some good ones now—tell editor Humphrey McWalters to go straight to the devil. He had suffered more than enough in this vile outback of desolation.

He continued to march unsteadily through the night. Just before dawn, he stumbled on a well-used spring. Adams figured it was the spring a day's march from the previous one. It must have been the one Parfrey and his men stayed at the night after—

Adams almost had the dry heaves again as the picture of the Comanche girl's remains flickered through his mind. For the thousandth time, he wondered how men—any men, but particularly white men—could do such a thing to another human being. Even an Indian. It horrified him that anyone could be so cruel, so vicious, as to do those things to a woman. No, girl, he told himself. It was unthinkable to him.

He sighed and knelt beside a small hole, which he was delighted to see was filled with water. He plunged his face in and gulped eagerly. Bloated, he lay on his back, staring up into the hot sun. He threw his left arm over his eyes and fell asleep.

The sharp gnawing of hunger woke him. He stood up and looked around in the dying sunlight. There was little here. A stunted piece of tree and some scrubby-looking brush, beyond which the horizon spread out to the edge of forever. Adams knelt beside the hole and drained it once again.

When he came up for air, he saw a rabbit a few feet away staring warily at him. Adams wished more than ever that he had a gun. He had never really used one, but he was certain that he could hit the rabbit, close as it was.

He didn't, though, and the thought of food being so near yet so inaccessible filled him with despair. With a shrug, he stood, and lurched on. The darkness that soon arrived was cool and even somewhat refreshing, which made the traveling a bit less onerous.

Adams hoped that he could make it to the next spring by daylight. At his slow, tottering pace, though, it was almost noon when he reached it. By then, he was hallucinating a little, having seen several mirages before realizing the little oasis was the real thing. He slurped water, which revived him minutely but not enough.

He lay on his back, one arm across his eyes, the other stretched out away from him. The heat beat down on him with an unyielding ferocity he had never experienced. He was close to just giving up and dying right here. It would be so easy, he thought. Something made his hand twitch, annoying him. He shook his hand and went back to his self-pitying thoughts. It happened again, and then a third time.

"Dammit all to hell and back again!" he shouted, sitting up. He looked at his hand. It was crawling with ants. He was filled with disgust, and was all set to fling the ants loose. Then he stopped. With great reluctance, he moved the hand slowly toward his mouth. He stopped again. Then, steeling himself to what he was doing, began licking the ants off his hand, mashing them flat between tongue and the roof of his mouth. He swallowed quickly, trying not to think of what he was doing.

Suddenly Adams spun to the side and regurgitated.

It left him shaken and weak. It also gave him a renewed determination. "Dammit, if some of those other bastards can do it, I can do it, too," he muttered. He set his hand out again, hoping he could attract more ants.

He did, and he ate them with iron resolve. The meal, such as it was, stayed put. Adams cast aside thoughts of dying for the moment and drank some more water. Then he covered his face with his coat and fell asleep.

Adams awoke in the darkness. He drank water and then started picking ants off his clothes and hand. The thought of eating them still revolted him, but he kept himself from thinking about it.

He delayed leaving as long as he could, trying to eat as many ants as possible. But he knew he had to keep moving. If he didn't move, he would die here. The ants, as small a meal as they had been, helped him a little as he shuffled off.

He walked through the night and into the day, finally managing to make it to another small spring. At that spot of pleasantness in the harsh countryside, he found more ants and some rotting scraps of an unidentifiable meat. He managed to choke the bits of meat down, surprised when it did not come right back up on him. He also swallowed more ants.

He stood and looked around. With a gasp of excitement, he spotted some berries. He had no idea what they were and more than half suspected they might be poisonous. But he had to try them. He collected all he could find, maybe two handfuls, and shoved them greedily into his mouth. He did not get sick, neither did he die.

After more water, he slept again, sweltering under

the coat covering his face to keep the brutal sun out. He awoke several times, sweating and feeling like he was choking. Then he would fall back to sleep.

Once again he awoke after darkness had spread its coolness over the land. He felt like all the wagons that had ever passed on the Santa Fe Trail had ridden over him. He ached all over and he was as weak as a baby. But he drank water, found another small handful of berries, and then moved on.

By first light, his faltering steps had slowed until he was not doing much more than shuffling. He had little strength left, and less resolve.

Then they appeared. He heard horses, and Adams's dull mind slowly roused from its almost stupor to search for the source. Off to his left, riding hard, were four Indians.

"Good Lord almighty," Adams whispered. With a reserve of strength he did not know he had in him, he began to run.

It did no good. The mounted horses swooped around him. One raced close and smashed Adams across the back with his bow. Adams fell headfirst into the dirt, bouncing painfully on his nose.

Another warrior leapt off his pony and yanked Adams's head up by the hair. Adams was more frightened than he had ever been. All his pains and weaknesses and worries fled in the face of this frightening apparition. Adams just lay there wide-eyed, fear immobilizing him.

The Comanches crouched around their prey and jabbered among themselves for a while. Adams figured they were arguing over how to kill him, since there was no question that they would.

The four warriors were still arguing about it when an avenging angel charged into their midst. One of his pistols roared, and a Comanche fell dead. The others scattered, leaping on their ponies and racing off.

"So, you see, Mister Early," Adams said, "my trek hasn't been easy. It has, I'm afraid, made my tongue more harsh than it usually is."

"Well, I can see that mayhap such a thing's true, boy," Early said easily. He had had journeys every bit as rugged as this and had lived through them. So had many of his friends. Others were not so fortunate. But no one he knew made a big deal of them. Still, he could understand it coming from a greenhorn like Adams. And he could even empathize a little. "So don't ye go frettin' over it no more, *amigo*. I'll not go holdin' it agin ye."

Adams nodded gratefully. He did not know how to thank Ezra Early, though he knew that someday he would have to try. "How far are we from Santa Fe, Mister Early? Or Taos?"

"Slow's we was movin' today, I'd expect mayhap three more weeks, give or take a day or so. There's a heap of travelin' to be done yet, boy, afore we get anywhere near them places, and don't ye doubt it." He shrugged, letting go another large cloud of pipe smoke. "'Sides, ye've been through a pile of trouble and ain't as spry as ye might be elsewise. That'll slow us even more. It could be a month afore we get into Taos."

"What if I had a horse?"

"Prob'ly do it in a week, week and a half, mayhap." He pointed the stem of his pipe at Adams. "But ye ain't got a horse, so there's no call for ye to go wishin' ye had." He grinned, surprising Adams a little. "Ye in some kind of a rush to get there?"

"No, can't say as I am. Still, being in Taos would be more comfortable and appealing than being out here at the mercy of the elements and the savages. But the more walking I must do, the slower I'll get. I can't keep up now. Another couple of weeks, and I'll be so far behind I'll never catch up."

"Well, some good food'll help. Ye've had that, and there'll be more. That'll help build up your strength."

"I suppose," Adams said doubtfully. "More importantly, though, I'm keeping you from your business. I can't expect you to slow down to my pace." He shrugged. "If you could spare a little of your food, you could be on your way. I'll follow along as best I can."

"Shit, ye're just lookin' to get your goddamn hair raised, ain't ye?" Early snorted. "Then your death'd be on my conscience. Such doin's don't shine with this chil' none so ever. Nope, goddammit."

Adams didn't really think his death would weigh very heavily on Early's conscience. But he did seem willing to help. Adams was not about to turn the aid down. "Well, I just didn't want to hold you up, Mister Early."

"When I get tired of bein' held up by ye, boy, I'll ride on. And not a goddamn minute afore that." He paused, then added bluntly, "It might help your cause, too, was ye to lose them goddamn fancy shoes ye're wearin'. Goddamn things're more useless. They ain't doin' ye a lick of good, and I expect they're doin' ye more than a little hurt."

"I'd be worse off barefoot. I'm not used to that." He

shrugged apologetically. "City born and bred, I'm afraid. All this is rather overwhelming to me."

"I reckon I could find enough shit in my pack to be able to make ye a pair of mocs ye could use. They ain't gonna be too purty to look at, but they'd let ye walk without pinchin' your toes all up into a knot."

"I'm not sure that'd work," Early said quietly. "Again, I'm not used to them and I'm afraid the cactus thorns and such would go right through them. At least my shoes protect me from that."

"Suit yourself, boy. Ain't my feets that're hurtin'."

"I'll think it over."

7

ADAMS WAS SILENT FOR a few minutes, then he asked, "Why're you going to Taos, Mister Early?"

"That's where I make my home durin' the summers."

"Winters?"

"I'm a mountaineer, boy. A beaver trapper."

"Are there many companies that hire trappers in Taos?" Adams asked, interested.

"Shit," Early snapped. "I'm a free trapper." There was unmistakable pride—no, arrogance—in his voice. "I don't work for nobody but myself. Me and my two *amigos*—Abe Rawlins and Lucien Chardonnais—trap the southern Rockies, mostly. We generally winter up somewhere in the Uncompahgre country, sometimes over toward Bear Lake. Spring we trap our way down, and then trade in our plews at Taos."

"I've heard there's something called a rendezvous in the mountains. A sort of trapper's market, where they trade in their furs, buy supplies, and have themselves something of a good time?"

"Yep." Early grinned. "Can be right pleasurable doin's, too."

"Then why not go there instead of all the way to Taos?"

"Ye ask a heap of damn questions, boy," Early said, not too harshly.

Adams laughed a little. It startled him, since it was the first time he could remember laughing at all since he had been given this assignment. "I am, after all, a correspondent, Mister Early," he said.

"I expect ye are," Early acknowledged. He knocked the ashes out of his pipe. "I been to rendezvous, boy, includin' the first 'un, back in '25. They're some shinin' doin's for goddamn certain. Christ, mountaineers from all over, Injins of all kinds. A heap of shinin' doin's, too—shootin', ax throwin', horse racin', wrasslin', gamblin', and yarnin'. But mostly drinkin' and fornicatin'." He laughed. "A goddamn heap of both, I'm tellin' ye."

He paused, thinking. "Main trouble is them suppliers at rendezvous're goddamn thieves. Christ, I swear those bastards'd sell their mothers if they thought they could do so at a thousand percent profit. I don't spend a whole goddamn winter freezin' my balls off in beaver streams just to give all my money to some goddamn thief from Saint Louis." He laughed again. " 'Course, sellin' plews in Taos ain't the easiest thing in the world, neither."

"Why not?" Adams asked, surprised.

"Goddamn greaser officials."

"I thought they favored American trade."

"The people do." Early sighed. "The Mexican peo-ple're nice folks for the most part. It's the goddamn officials. Money-grubbin' sons of bitches always have their goddamn hands out lookin' for someone to give 'em some cash to look the other way to do whatever business you got to mind."

"I overheard the wagoneers saying much the same thing about their goods. They spoke of bribes and such things."

Early nodded. "Those boys got to pay out the ass to do business in Mexico." He grinned. "The officials come up with all kinds of schemes to keep us foreign-ers out of the fur trade in their land. Won't give us licenses, for one thing."

"Then how . . . ?"

"We just hire some Mexican feller to get a license, then buy it from him. More times than not, we either take him with us—as a cook or camp helper, not as a trapper. Them Mexicans may be nice folks, but when it comes to some hard work, which trappin' is, they're lazy critters."

Early shrugged and grinned again. "The American boys down in them parts've come up with a heap of ways to get around some of the shit the officials try'n pull. Mainly smugglin' our plews in. 'Course, it don't always work. I know more'n one ol' hoss lost all his plews—a whole goddamn winter's work—when they was confiscated by the goddamn customs folk and the *soldados*. Shit." Then he laughed. "Me and my *amigos* been lucky though. They ain't ary took even so much as one plew from this chil'."

He sighed. "It'd be a heap easier on us was one of us partners to become a Mexican citizen like some others we know of has done. But such doin's goes against the grain of this chil'. The others, too."

Adams nodded. "How'd you get out here in the first place?" he asked, curiosity gleaming in his eyes.

Early glared at him a moment. Like most mountaineers, he was not fond of questions, especially ones about his past. Too many men had fled the settlements to avoid the law, a shotgun wedding, or other trouble, and it had become a code not to pry. Still, Early saw that Adams was not asking to cause trouble. He was just a naturally curious type and meant no harm.

Early took the time to refill his pipe. He found a small piece of brush, hardly longer than his pinkie and about as thick as a piece of string. The fire had gone out, but there were a few embers left. Early put the twig on the ember and blew, until the twig flared. He used it to light his pipe.

When it was going to his satisfaction, he settled his rump a little more comfortably. "Well, me'n Lucien come out here back in '22 with Ashley's brigade. A heap of us boys from that trip has made good since. Ol' Gabe Bridger, Frenchie Sublette, Jed Smith, more. Abe come up the next season. We worked for Ashley's company another two years. Right after the first rendezvous, me, Lucien, and Abe bought our way out of his employ with no hard feelin's on either side. We been free trappers since."

There had been a sight of adventures since then. The next year, the three had gone down to Taos with Etienne Provost. The portly Provost had worked for Ashley that year but wanted to get back to Taos. His tales about the town and the friendliness of its inhabitants, especially the women, convinced Early, Chardonnais, and Rawlins to go see what it was like.

Provost had also alerted them to the possibility of losing their plews to the authorities if things weren't handled right. Following his advice, they cached their bales of beaver fur before riding into Taos and looking around. Within a short time, and with Provost's help, they found several men who were more than willing to bend the rules to help American trappers unload their furs. It was a pattern they still generally followed.

"Do you have a woman there? In Taos, I mean." Adams smiled to remove the possible intemperance of the question. He felt relaxed for the first time in longer than he could remember.

"I got me a heap of women in Taos. Them women're just fallin' all over theyselves to get near me." He winked. "But the closest thing I got to a wife is a Ute. Me'n Fallin' Leaf've been together six year or so now."

"You live with an Indian woman?" Adams asked a little incredulously.

Early's eyes narrowed a bit. "Ye got somethin' agin such doin's, boy?" he asked, voice harsh.

Adams saw the look and was frightened by it. "Well, no, not exactly," he answered nervously. "It's just that . . . Well, hell, it just don't seem right somehow." He shrugged, knowing he was not explaining himself very well.

"Felt the same way myself once," Early admitted quietly. "But that were a passel of years ago. But I come to find that Injin women—most Injin women—are about the best ye can find."

Adams didn't know what to think of that, so he settled for asking, "Is she waiting for you in Taos?"

"It don't shine with this chil' to bring my woman to such a place. Hell, us three critters have us one hell of a spree every summer down there. It ain't fittin' to bring no squaw to such doin's." He laughed. "The greasers ain't real fond of it neither. They got they-selves enough trouble with Taoseños and Apaches and such to be happy about a bunch of Americans bringing their squaws and young 'uns into town."

"Then where is she?"

"Me, Abe, and Lucien drop our women off at their village every year afore headin' on into Taos."

"How'd you ever get a Ute squaw?"

Early shrugged, letting his mind drift through the clouds of pipe smoke back a few years. "We was up in the Uncompahgre country—that's Ute land—back in '25, just after we'd left General Ashley's employ. We come on a couple of Ute warriors being chased by a shitload of Crows. Not likin' the odds we saw—and since we figured to be trappin' in Ute country for some spell—we pulled them Utes aside, gave 'em some weapons, and helped 'em send those scum-suckin' Crows packin'.

"Them two critters was some grateful, I'm tellin' ye. They took us back to their village and tol' everybody there what great heroes we was in savin' their miserable hides."

Adams was beginning to wonder about the veracity of Early's story. Then he saw the twinkle in the mountain man's eyes, and he knew Early was exaggerating, which was all right with Adams.

"Them boys met us up with some squaws. Me'n Fallin' Leaf been together ary since."

"Is that her name? Falling Leaf?"

"It's what I call her. I can't rightly pronounce her Ute name, which means She-Who-Came-During-the-Time-of-the-Leaf-Falling."

"That's a pretty name, Mister Early."

"Why, thankee, boy. I think the same. Trouble is, it's one hell of a mouthful, so I shortened it some." He knocked the ashes from his pipe again. "Well, boy, I'd like to set here the whole night jabberin' with ye, but it's robe time for this ol' chil'."

He moved a few feet away from the fire and spread his thick buffalo robe on the ground. He lay on it and pulled its lushness around him, but he had trouble getting to sleep. The talk about Falling Leaf had turned his mind toward her. He realized that he missed her. It was not a usual thing for him, but then again, he generally was not out here alone much.

He pondered what he felt for her. He didn't think it was love, though it might be close. Over the six years, he and Falling Leaf had come to respect and care for each other. He treated her as well as he could, and he figured she did the same.

It was an odd thing, he thought, that he rode into Taos every year and had himself some dalliances with the *señoritas*. He never mentioned it to Falling Leaf, but he was fairly certain she knew, figuring that men were like that. Perhaps she was spending her summers with a man from her Ute band. If she were, he did not want to know about it, since he didn't know how he might react.

He had thought about that more than once in the six years they had been together. She was not the most beautiful woman he had ever seen, but she was plenty attractive. He liked her smooth, dusky skin, firm buttocks, and full breasts, heavier now since the birth of their daughter almost three years ago. Her hair gleamed in an ebony cascade, and her dark eyes often glittered with joy. He figured that if Falling Leaf was so attractive to him, she would be so to other men, too. Plus she was a good cook, a hard worker, and a willing bed partner.

Because of the possibility of her taking up with a warrior, Early had considered not riding into Taos, and instead going to rendezvous, where he could bring Falling Leaf. But the pull of Taos was strong on him, as was the thought of the *cigarrillo*-smoking *señoritas* there.

He never dwelled on such things overly long. He was a simple man with simple needs, one who did not worry about what he could not control. If Falling Leaf wanted another man, Early would not stand in her way. Of course, there was a good chance that he would pound the living daylights out of whatever man Falling Leaf might take up with before he rode out and found himself another wife.

Early began to relax. It would not be long before he was in Taos, where he would have himself a goddamn good spree. And in a couple of months, he and his two partners would be riding out, heading for the Uncompahgre country . . . and Falling Leaf.

While they worked breaking camp in the morning, Adams said, "I know I've asked many questions already, Mister Early. But one more?"

"Reckon that won't hurt none," Early offered. "But first I'll give ye a wee bit of advice. There's many a mountaineer don't shine with bein' asked questions, 'specially so many personal ones."

"If I've offended you, Mister Early," Adams said stiffly, "I'll . . ."

"Didn't say no such thing, boy. Just tellin' ye for times to come when ye meet some others. Now, ask your question."

Adams nodded. "You said you spend each summer in Taos, that you come down out of the mountains. Yet you came from the northeast, along the Santa Fe Trail. Why?" He was quite perplexed.

A look of sadness briefly crossed Early's face. "I were back in the settlements on family business, boy," he said gruffly. He jerked on a rope that held the canvas covering the supplies.

8

EARLY AND ADAMS PULLED out soon afterward, following the upper reaches of the Canadian River. Early had decided he better share the Appaloosa with Adams or they would never get anywhere. So he walked this day, allowing Adams to ride the big spotted horse. Adams had been impressed at the mountain man's generosity, and said so.

To which Early growled, "Don't set your sights on ridin' that horse every goddamn day." Then he stomped off, his .54-caliber Dickert rifle resting in the crook of his left arm.

Early hated walking, at least out in the open like this. Walking was fine around camp or Taos, or even rendezvous, but out here it was a hateful task. One reason he hated it was that he lost a great deal of sight advantage being on foot. Up on the horse, he had a good view of the land, and so could spot danger before it arrived. Down on foot, though, he lost that small advantage. But he said nothing as he walked briskly along, several feet from the horse.

It was an uneventful day, one broken only by the boredom of their slow movements and the tedium of traveling in the dry, blistering heat. Because of the monotony, Adams near midday asked, "Would you have any paper among your supplies, Mister Early?"

The mountain man stopped and looked at Adams. The few feet separating them suddenly seemed like an abyss. "Now what in hell would I be doin' out here totin' paper?"

Adams shrugged. "Just thought I'd ask, Mister Early."

"Call me Ezra. And what'n hell do ye want with some paper, anyway?"

"I thought I'd sketch some of the land. All my belongings are still with the wagons. I have a few pieces of paper in my pocket, but not enough, certainly, to do justice to this wide land."

Early shrugged and started walking again, but he moved a little closer. "Ye'll just have to make do with what ye got, if'n ye aim to make yourself any pictures," he said unapologetically. He stopped again and looked at Adams. "Them drawin's ye made afore important to ye, I suppose?"

"Lord, yes," Adams said fervently. He grew agitated at the thought of what might be happening to his papers in the hands of those animals.

"Ye'd like to get 'em back then, would ye?"

"Yes, dammit."

Early grinned. "Then ye best get ready to fight for

'em. I don't know any of them boys you was with, but I know others like 'em. They ain't likely to just up and give 'em back to ye, ye know." He started walking again, but moved still closer. "That's if they even got 'em."

"What do you mean?" Adams asked, his irritation increasing.

"Boys like them're the kind to up and start tossin' such things to the four winds."

"That'd be a sin, Ezra. An affront to all that's right and good."

"Ye think some fractious shit balls like the ones did that to that girl back there are gonna be worried over tossin' away some goddamn papers and shit just 'cause it'd cause ye some misery?" Early asked scornfully.

"I suppose not," Adams grated. He tightened with impotent rage, conjuring up an image of that . . . thing. He vowed that he would not only get all his effects back, but he would exact some revenge for that unfortunate Indian girl.

Early shook his head, wondering about the mind of the odd fellow he had helped. Adams was an odd one, that was for sure, but Early was beginning to see a bit of spirit in his companion. He might be able to pull through after all, and maybe even take a run at Ebenezer Parfrey and his companions. He wondered, though, why he was taking such an interest in Adams, but the thought of one possible reason was uncomfortable for him, so he kept from thinking it.

" 'Sides," Early said, "what'n hell're you gonna make pictures of out here?"

"That." Adams pointed to a double-peaked mountain off to the southwest. "What is it?"

Early almost smiled. "Called the Rabbit Ears. One of the main landmarks on the trail." Early shrugged, not understanding why someone would want to sketch the ragged mountain. To him it was a landmark, something to guide him on the trail, allowing him to find good campsites and such. No more, no less.

They traveled in silence for another hour or so, before crossing a small, shallow, muck-bottomed creek.

"What's this place?" Adams asked. He had stopped, pulled out one of his few pieces of paper and was making some lines on it. His forehead was corrugated with concentration.

"McNees Crossing." Early stopped, too, kneeling to scoop water into his mouth with a cupped hand.

"Odd name."

"I expect." Early stood and looked around. "Two fellers headin' east on the trail was ahead of their *compañeros* by some distance. They was attacked here a couple years ago by some Injins. Goddamn Comanches, I expect. Their companions found 'em here. One of the fellers was named McNees. They buried him right over there, from what I heard." He pointed to a spot ten feet away. It looked no different from the rest of the surrounding area. "The men took the other feller with them, but from what I hear, he died up on the Cimarron and was buried there."

Adams scribbled notes as fast as he could, muttering, "Interesting. Damn interesting."

Early walked on, allowing Adams to sit there a few more minutes and savor whatever it was he found so fascinating at the bleak river crossing. The easterner caught up in a few minutes.

"Where're we heading now, Ezra?" Adams asked.

"Turkey Creek."

Early was tired when they finally pulled to a stop at Turkey Creek Camp, a well-used site. He was irritated at the slow pace and at the miles his feet had put behind them. As such, he was in no mood for an evening of idle chatter. He allowed Adams to cook up a mess of bacon and beans, while he cared for the horse and mule. When Early was finished, he went back to the fire and sat down after pouring a mug of coffee. He leaned back against his saddle, eyes closed.

Adams tried a few times to draw him into a conversation, but without success. Annoyed now himself, he finally kept his silence. The two men ate without speaking, after which Early puffed his pipe. For no good reason that he could think of, Early said quietly, "Me and my *amigos* were trappin' our way down toward Taos, like we always do. It was early spring, but snow was still fallin'."

In the firelight, Adams could see the light of longing in Early's eyes. It was clear that Early liked the place he was thinking of, or the time of year, or maybe both.

"We was up in the Sawatch Mountains, along the Roaring Fork. We was to meet Falling Leaf's people there, so we could leave off the women and then mosey on down to Taos. The Utes was there, along with a couple traders we knew up from Taos."

Early's pipe went out. He considered refilling and lighting it, but decided against it. He knocked the ashes out of it and slid it into the heart-shaped piece of buckskin around his neck. He pulled a twist of tobacco out of his possible sack, cut off a chunk, and stuffed it into his cheek.

* * *

As soon as the three men rode into the village, a trader named Jacques Ducharme, who worked out of Taos and was well known by the three, gave Early a letter.

"Zis come to Charlie Bent's new store for you near a mont' ago, Ezra," Ducharme said.

While Chardonnais and Rawlins argued with Ducharme over the state of business, Early read the letter. It was a laborious process, since he was not the best reader in the world, but he could make do. It just took time. As soon as he was through with it, he interjected himself into the semifriendly argument.

"Can ye spot me some powder, ball, and other such plunder to get me back to the settlements, Jacques?"

"Trouble, Ezra?" Ducharme asked, pointing to the letter.

"My pa's ailin', accordin' to my sister Irma. She says here she don't think Pa'll make it. I pull out now, I can be back there in a month or so. Mayhap I'll find him still alive."

Ducharme nodded. "All my plunder is over zere." He pointed. "You take whatever you need, and let me know what you took. You can square wit' me when you get back, eh?"

"Thankee."

When Early had picked out all he thought he would need, Rawlins and Chardonnais helped him load his supplies on one of their pack mules.

"Anyt'ing we can do for you, *mon ami?*" Chardonnais asked.

"Nope." Early pulled himself onto his Appaloosa. "I aim to be back in Taos afore ye boys head out again," he said. "If I ain't, ye get me my supplies, along with yours. Head on back here and pick up the women. I'll either cut your trail somewhere or meet ye up in the Sawatch."

"*Oui.* Dat will be good."

"Get your ass movin', boy," Rawlins growled. He swatted Early's horse on the rump, and the horse trotted off, heading down the trail that wound eastward through the San Juan Mountains.

Early stopped as little as possible and made it back to his family's farm in Indiana, down near the Ohio River, in twenty-eight days. Ignoring the looks of disgust and shame on the faces of his relatives, he went in to look at his father. It seemed to the family that Early's father had held on until he saw his firstborn son, which irked them even more. Ezra Early, Senior, died the day after his namesake arrived.

Early spent two weeks helping with the funeral and making sure his mother would be taken care of. His brothers and sisters, who lived nearby and were married, agreed to see to things. Irma, the next oldest after Ezra, however, was the only one who would talk to him. Indeed, his two brothers, Lucas and Daniel, blamed Ezra for the death of the second oldest brother, Ethan, and were not about to let him forget it.

The day before Ezra was set to leave, he called his two brothers outside, back behind the barn. Full of curiosity at what their savage-looking brother wanted, the two strolled behind him.

Ezra stopped and turned. "Ye two buffler peckers've been riding my ass since I rode in. Now it's time for ye to back up your hard words."

Lucas, who was almost seven years younger than Ezra and nearly as big, grinned. "I been waitin' for a chance to knock you on your ass, big brother," he said almost eagerly. "I was beginnin' to think you was a coward."

"Have at it," Ezra said coldly.

Lucas spit on his palms and rubbed them together. Then he charged. Ezra braced himself and Lucas ran into him. Ezra was shoved back only a step, and Luke fell. He sat there a minute, looking up, thinking he had just run into a boulder.

"That the best you can do, you peckerless little bastard?" Ezra said with a sneer.

Daniel, the youngest of the Early children, launched himself wildly at his oldest brother. Ezra ducked a punch and then pounded Dan in the chest with a big right fist. Dan slammed into the barn wall and slid down it, thinking he would die here if he couldn't catch in a breath.

Lucas had gotten up and was looking warily at Ezra.

"You want some more?" Ezra asked Luke. The younger brother shook his head. He had had more than enough of this buckskin-clad savage.

"You?" he asked Dan, who was still sitting, back against the barn.

He shook his head, wondering if he would ever be able to get up.

"Next time ye boys want to ride my ass, I'll make wolf bait out of ye."

"Like you did with Ethan?" Luke accused.

Ezra's eyes glazed over with pain and anger. It took him some moments to regain control of himself. Then in icy, harsh tones, he said, "Don't ye nary accuse me of such again, ol' hoss. I've lived four year now with that and mayhap'll have to live with it the rest of my days. But this ol' chil' ain't about to be taken to task about it by the likes of ye. Ain't neither of ye got half the balls Ethan had." He paused, trying to settle the anger down in him some more. "Now, Ma's gonna need your help considerable, so you best see to it."

"What about Pa's things?" Luke asked, his voice still accusatory. "Hell, he left you damn near everything."

Ezra shrugged. "Ain't a thing out of all of it that I need, or want, except for two."

"What's that?" Dan asked. He had managed to slide up the wall, using it for support, until he was standing. He decided he had better see if his voice worked.

"Pa's flintlocks—the rifle and pistol he used in the war."

"That's all?" Luke asked, incredulous.

"Yep." He paused. "I'll be pullin' out come mornin'. I been here too long already. Until then, I don't want to see either of ye mewlin' pukes." He strode off, heading for the house.

The next day, just after dawn, Early pulled himself up onto the Appaloosa and turned the horse's nose west. Irma was the only one to see him off.

Early hoped to make it to Independence to catch on with one of the caravans heading down the Santa Fe Trail. It would be safer that way, though considerably slower. All had been long gone, though, by the time he got to Independence, so he pressed on by himself. He figured he would catch up to the slow wagons somewhere between the Cimarron and the Canadian.

Early finally grew silent. Then with a sigh, wishing he hadn't opened up as much as he had, he spit out the tobacco. "Robe time for this chil'," he said quietly.

As Early spread his buffalo robe out a little away from the fire, Adams watched a moment. Then he asked tentatively, "Do you have another of those buffalo skins, Ezra? I'm afraid my coat isn't sufficient against these cool desert nights." He could not believe the nights were so cool when the days were so blasted hot.

"Can't say as I do, boy," Early said tersely, angry at his weakness, as he saw it. He lay on the hide and pulled it around him.

As Adams lay close to the fire, which was almost out, and covered himself with his coat, he wondered what was wrong with Early. But tiredness swept over him with the warmth the coat provided, and he soon fell into a fitful sleep.

9

THE NEXT DAY, EARLY rode, putting him in good spirits. It also was a short day, which surprised Adams. "Stopping so early?"

"Yep."

"This place have a name?"

"Rabbit Ears Creek."

Adams nodded and scribbled it down. "Why stop here? We haven't traveled that far today. What, maybe fifteen miles?"

"More like ten." Early started unpacking the mule. "It's a good campsite," he offered, not really feeling a need to explain further.

"There's got to be more to it than that."

"Next good camp's a fair piece. Forty mile or so. I figure to rest up here the rest of today, mayhap tomorrow, too. Ye still ain't too goddamn steady, ye

71

know. Then we can get an early start and push hard."

Adams nodded and began gathering fuel for a fire.

A few minutes later, Early mounted the Appaloosa again. "Ye get a fire goin', boy," he said. "I'll be back directly."

"Where're you going?" A sudden knot of fear tightened Adams's belly.

Early did not answer him. He returned in about an hour, though, with a piece of bloody buffalo hide wrapped around some chunks of fresh meat.

"Now ye'll have some goddamn good eatin'," Early said happily.

"I've had fresh buffalo meat before, Mister Early," Adams said stiffly.

"Shit," Early drawled, unfazed. He would cook it no differently than the wagoneers had, but that didn't matter to him. He tossed the bloody package at Adams. "Still, if'n ye aim to eat, ye'd best get to cookin'." Early unsaddled his horse, while Adams gingerly unwrapped the hide.

Before long, the men were downing chunks of half-raw meat, as well as pieces of fried fleece. Adams was surprised at the tastiness of the latter, though he could not say the same for the boudins Early offered him.

Adams was finished quickly, and as he sat sipping coffee, he watched in amazement as Early kept bolting down hunks of meat. Eventually he stopped and leaned back, tamping tobacco into the bowl of his clay pipe.

"You always eat like that?" Adams asked, still incredulous.

Early belched and smiled, proud of it. "Ever' chance I get," he admitted. He laughed at the look on Adams's face. "All us mountaineers do so. Injins, too. Reckon it's 'cause we see starvin' times more often than we'd like to admit. So we kind of fill up whenever we get the chance."

"The wagoneers did that, too, but not to such a great extent."

"Man works hard, he needs to have a full meatbag." Unembarrassed, Early reached for the last piece of meat. He belched again, happily.

Early was still in a good frame of mind and spent the evening regaling Adams with tales of his life in the mountains. He told of the thin air and frigid temperatures, of plush beaver plews pulled from freezing streams, of starving times as well as feasting times when fat buffalo were plentiful, of warfare against Indians, of the good times at rendezvous.

Adams had trouble falling asleep since his mind was filled with Early's tales. He wished more than anything for his notepads. He wanted to write it all down, editor be damned. The story of the mountain men—this one in particular—was far more fascinating than the tedious journey on the Santa Fe Trail. He was sure his readers would feel the same.

The day after next, they set out just after dawn with Early riding his Appaloosa again. Adams strode along, eyes flickering over everything. "What's that?" he asked early on. He pointed to the northwest horizon.

"Called Point of Rocks. It's near where the Mountain branch and the Cimarron branch of the trail meet back up. Most folks head southwest from there, headin' toward the southern edge of the Sangre de Cristos, which they go around, and then back up to Santa Fe."

"And us?"

"I'm fixin' to head north, toward the trail to Taos. Ye can do whatever the hell ye want to."

They traveled in silence after that, with Early half dozing in the saddle. He came awake—and instantly alert—at a startled shout. His head snapped up and he scanned the countryside, looking for the danger.

He saw nothing except a horrified-looking Adams off to his right about thirty yards, kneeling by a sagebrush, staring at the dull bush.

"What'n hell's wrong with ye, boy?" Early called, trotting toward Adams. "Ye snakebit?"

Adams seemed frozen, as if afraid that moving would do himself some damage.

Early pulled up ten feet away, nose wrinkling in offense. "Goddamn, boy," he snapped, "ain't ye got enough goddamn sense not to go messin' around with no goddamn skunks? Jesus."

Adams finally moved, simply shaking his head. "I'm from the city, Ezra. Never been away from it till now."

"Shit," Early said, spitting tobacco juice at another bush. "Well, get away from the goddamn critter afore he doses ye again, and, Christ, maybe me, too."

Adams rose and moved slowly backward, away from the angry skunk. Early rode on. "Ye just make goddamn certain ye keep your stinkin' hide far downwind from me, boy," he warned over his shoulder. "I got no hankerin' to smell like no goddamn skunk. And ye'll likely scare the horse and mule ye get too goddamn close. Damn." He moved on, muttering, "Damn fool."

It was another long day, covering more than thirty miles, and Adams was exhausted and footsore by the time they finally stopped. Ezra had ridden a little ahead and had a small camp made near a pool in Spring Canyon, tucked into the rocky point. A fire was going and meat roasting.

Early held his nose when Adams arrived. "Ye ain't gonna set in my goddamn camp whilst ye're smellin' that high, boy," he snapped, but there was humor in his voice.

"But what am I supposed to do, Ezra?" Adams was tired, angry, disgusted with the smell that clung to him like his own skin. But he did manage to keep the whining tone, if not the exasperation, out of his voice.

"Well, now, I expect the fust thing ye'll do is shuck them goddamn clothes ye're wearin'. Then ye bury 'em. Deep."

"But I have no other clothing."

"I reckon I can find an ol' set of 'skins of mine ye can wear. They'll set on ye funny, but I expect they'll do."

"But—"

"Don't ye sass me, boy," Early said, the humor melting away. "Ye either do like I tell ye, or go make your camp elsewhere. That high smell don't shine with this chil' the least littlest bit. Nosirree."

"Guess I have no choice, do I?" Adams said sourly. Then he grinned, shaking his head at his latest predicament. "What about my shoes?"

"That little bastard dose 'em?"

"Don't think so. Mostly got my lower stomach and my pants."

Early nodded. "I expect that'll be all right."

"Thanks," Adams said dryly. "Can I keep this, too?" he suddenly asked, tugging gently at his red ascot.

"Toss it over here, boy." Adams did so, and Early

caught the fluttering piece of cloth and tentatively sniffed at it. "I expect it's all right, *amigo.* But ye best get rid of them other things ye're wearin'. And god-damn soon."

Adams nodded. He kicked off his shoes and moved off a ways to dig a small, deep hole, using his hands and a pocketknife Early had given him. When it was done, he emptied his pockets, being careful with his papers. Reluctantly he began to strip. A puff of wind swept down off the dull brown rocks and over him, bringing a fresh blast of skunk stench to his nostrils. It encouraged him to finish shucking his clothes quickly, and then he hurriedly buried the garments.

Inactive all of a sudden, he shivered as the breeze touched his sweating skin. With a shrug, he ran to the nearby pond and jumped in. He scrubbed himself vigorously to try to rid his flesh of the odor. He was not entirely successful, but it helped.

Embarrassed and shivering in the stronger wind, he tried to cover himself with his hands as he hurried toward the fire. Early had dumped a pair of greasy buckskin pants and a worn calico, puff-sleeved shirt near Adams's shoes.

With a look of distaste, Adams donned the outfit and his shoes.

Early thought it highly amusing, and he sat grinning through all of Adams's shame and annoyance. When Adams was done, Early said joyfully, "Ye are the sorri-est lookin' critter this chil's ary seen." He started laughing.

Adams glared at Early, a little anger starting to heat up his face. Then he looked down at himself. He could not help it; he, too, started laughing. The shirt was long enough, but hung loosely on his thin frame; the pants were tight in the waist and loose at the seat, the fringes hanging limply down the sides. Adams wrinkled his own nose. "Lord, Ezra, this smells nearly as bad as those things I buried."

"Mayhap, lad," Early said, still laughing, "but them're good smells ye're wearin' now."

"Good?" Adams tried to hide his disbelief.

"Why, sure. Goddamn, boy, there ain't nothin' wrong with the lingerin' 'roma of dried buffler blood, hump grease, woodsmoke, and mayhap a touch of Blackfoot blood."

"I sometimes think you're mad, Ezra," Adams said, still chuckling.

"Ye ain't the first ary suggested such, boy," Early said with a laugh. "And I'd wager a season's catch ye ain't gonna be the last neither."

The laughter died out, and Adams poured a mug of coffee and then sat. Finally he said seriously, albeit nervously, "I would think that most men who said that to you wouldn't live long enough to ever say it again."

"That's a fact, boy," Early said without arrogance or apology.

"But you let me get away with saying it."

"Knew ye didn't mean it." Early shrugged and tossed a pair of moccasins to Adams. "I made ye mocs, boy, if'n ye choose to wear 'em. I used your boots for sizin'." He scratched his nose. "I didn't have much time, ye understand, so I just used what was here and threw 'em together."

"Well, thanks, Ezra. That was mighty nice. But . . ." he hesitated, then pushed on, "I've still got my boots."

"Ye looked at them goddamn boots?" When Adams

shook his head, Early added, "They're full of holes, and the bottoms ain't much thicker'n one of them goddamn pieces of paper ye've been cartin' 'round."

Adams inspected his footwear, nodding sadly. "I suppose you're right, Ezra." He pulled off his boots slowly and tossed them aside. Before he pulled on the moccasins, he touched the red ascot. It was all he had left of his old life. Everything else was gone. Still melancholy, he tugged on the moccasins and tied them. Then he stood, wiggling his toes in the supple but substantial footwear. "They're a little big," he said tentatively.

"I figured. Here." He threw two strips of blanket material to Adams. "Wrap 'em 'round your feet."

Adams sat and did as instructed. He stood once more and again wriggled his toes. "I'll be damned," he muttered. "These are almost comfortable." He flopped back down again, stretching out his legs, still marveling a little at the hastily made moccasins.

Early said nothing. He simply hacked off a hunk of buffalo meat and handed it to Adams.

The easterner took it and began eating. Between bites, he asked, "What's it like in Taos?"

"Low, flat houses made of 'dobe. Nice'n thick. Helps keep 'em cool in the summer and warm in the winter. Town centers on the plaza. Nice place, with somethin' goin' on nearly all the time."

"What're the Mexicans like?"

"Nice folks, mostly. Warm, friendly. Leastways, this chil's always thought so. 'Cept for the *soldados* and them goddamn officials sent up from Mexico City to run things. Goddamn buffler peckers, each and ary one of 'em, far's I've seen. Seem to change all the time, too. A few of 'em ain't too bad, but some is the sneakiest, schemin'est bastards ye're likely to meet."

"The women?" Adams asked slyly.

"Some of the purtiest ye ary seen. And fond of sharin' their favors with a man they like." He grinned. "Ye got to watch their fathers, though. At least the rich ones, of which there's a heap. Them *ricos* don't like nobody—'specially Americans—messin' with their daughters. Get downright mean about it, they catch you at it. But," Early added with an even larger grin, "there's ways of gettin' around that."

"Sounds like a nice place."

"Heap better'n Saint Louis. Or ary other goddamn city I've been in."

"Why don't you stick closer to there, then, instead of trapping all over the mountains, as you said you did?"

"Shit, all them mountains near Taos are all trapped out already. Have been for years. Too easy to get to."

"Too easy to get to?" Adams asked incredulously. "Seems to me we're near the end of the world."

"Hell, boy, trappers've been crawlin' over the Sangre de Cristos for years. Spanish, Injin, Mexican, French, Americans. I figure there ain't a beaver left in the Sangre de Cristos."

He paused, looking through the darkness, eyes a little sad. "'Sides, a man needs his freedom, boy. It don't set right with this ol' hoss to be all cooped up inside some city for too long. Stunts ye, it does, by Christ."

His eyes were wistful as he peered across the fire at Adams. "Ye ain't ary rode the high mountains, boy. Nor run buffler like the Injins. Nor set your face in a stream so cold it numbs ye to wake ye up of a mornin'."

"Never had the chance," Adams interjected. "Nor the desire."

"Don't turn against such doin's, boy, less'n ye try some of 'em. Them mountains give ye a feelin' I can't rightly explain. No matter how good ye're feelin' down there in Taos or Santa Fe, them mountains're callin' ye, whisperin' your name, just pullin' at ye."

Adams laughed. "You almost have me convinced to try it, Ezra." He waved a hand at himself. "At least you have me lookin' the part."

10

WHEN THEY PULLED OUT in the morning, Early was walking and Adams was riding high and happy. Early grumbled some about having to walk again, but it was more because of the slow pace than because he was on foot. It bothered him, since at this rate Abe Rawlins and Lucien Chardonnais would almost be ready to leave Taos by the time Early got there. It meant Early would get no spree, and that soured his disposition a little. About midday, he growled at himself in annoyance and shrugged. He could do nothing about the pace, so he would have to make do.

A few hours later, Adams broke into his thoughts, saying, "I see somebody coming. Off to the right."

"I saw 'em," Early said with a nod.

"You know who they are, Ezra?"

"Can't tell just yet. Could be whites. Or Injins."

"Doesn't it worry you?"

"Nope."

Adams could not understand it.

"They seem to be gettin' closer, boy," Early said. "So get your ass down from that horse, and let me up there so's I can get a look-see." Adams slid off the horse without question. Early immediately swung into the saddle. He stood in the stirrups and shaded his eyes with a hand.

"Well?" Adams asked impatiently, worried. He was sure the blazing heat could not account for all the sweat streaking down his face and along his ribs.

"Injins," Early said flatly.

"Comanches?" Real fear began to edge up into Adams's throat.

"Can't be sure. Still too far off. But they ride like Apaches," Early said sourly. "Comanches ride like they was born on a horse. Apaches can ride well enough, but they look like shit doin' it."

"Are they warlike?"

Early looked down at Adams in amazement. "Goddamn, ye are a know-nothin'. Christ, the goddamn Apaches're about the meanest, toughest critters south of the Blackfoot."

"Who are the best fighters among the Indians, Ezra?" Adams asked, trying to keep his mind off what he assumed was an impending attack.

"Well now, I expect that'd be the Utes," Early said, a smile tugging the corners of his mouth. " 'Course, I might be some favorably disposed toward them boys. Come on." He moved forward, Adams walking right beside the horse, hand on the buffalo robe rolled up and tied behind Early's saddle.

"Actually, who're the best fighters depends on what

ye're lookin' for. Comanches, Blackfoot, Cheyennes, Sioux, are about the best at fightin' from the back of a horse. The Utes, though, are poor horse riders and so a sight better from behind cover. Excellent shots, and brave as they come. Still, was I goin' into battle in the mountains or in the desert, I'd want Apaches on my side. Waugh! Them're some hard critters, those boys."

Adams licked his lips worriedly. "Are you friends with the Apaches?"

"Ain't nobody but other Apaches friends with Apaches. I think even one band of Apaches don't get along with any of the others."

"How many bands are there?"

Early shrugged. "White Mountain, Jicarilla, Mescalero, Coyotero, Chiricahua. There's others, but I don't know much about 'em."

"Which ones are these?"

"Can't say till I see 'em up close. But 'round here, I'd say Jicarillas."

They plodded along for a few more minutes, Adams growing more and more fearful. Finally he asked, "Can you trust any Indians, Ezra?"

"I can trust the Utes. Some of 'em, anyhow. But ye'd best not put your trust in any of 'em. Leastways, not till ye get to know 'em real well." He paused. "Then again, it don't pay for ye to put your trust in any people till ye get to know 'em pretty well." He looked down at Adams. "Some folks get theyselves in a heap of trouble by puttin' their trust in the wrong folk."

Thoughts of Ebenezer Parfrey and the other men on the freight wagon passed through Adams's mind, conjuring up visions of that poor Comanche girl. "You're right," Adams said sadly. "I was a fool, and—"

"Shut your trap now, boy. Them Injins is comin' over for a look-see."

"Are they going to attack?"

"I misdoubt it. Just stand here and stop your frettin'. Keep your trap shut and your hands in sight. If'n I tell ye to do somethin', do it sprightly, without askin' a pile of questions."

"All right." Adams gulped and said softly, "I'm scared, Ezra."

"Ain't the fust time somebody was ever scared. Ye'll get over it, I expect. Just don't let them see it. They'll take it as a sign of weakness."

The Apaches trotted up, mostly quiet, but menacing with their broad chests and dark, hard faces.

Early knew nothing of the Apache language, but most of the Jicarillas knew at least some Spanish, which Early could muddle along with. Early also was well versed in sign language. Between the various languages, the white man and the warriors managed to converse.

Using signs and Spanish, the Apache leader asked for tobacco.

Early replied in the same fashion that he would give tobacco and a knife to each man, but only in exchange for a horse. That would wipe out anything of value he had to trade. "You have many horses, and could spare one for my friend, who's on foot," Early said. Since the Apaches had several stolen horses, Early hoped they would be willing to part with one without too much argument.

"No," the Apache leader signed roughly, "we can't spare even one." He had only asked for some tobacco, he signed, because he had none and thought it would be friendly for the visitor to give him some.

"But," he added, "if you were to give me your fire stick"—he pointed to Early's rifle—"then maybe I could spare one horse."

"Shit," Early muttered. He spit off the left side of his horse, a sign of contempt. When he straightened, he thumbed back the hammer of his Dickert rifle, and moved the barrel skyward. He rested the rifle's butt on his right thigh. His left hand looped the Appaloosa's reins around the saddlehorn, and then rested on one of the big pistols in the saddle holster.

Not willing to use his hands for sign talk, Early said in the best Spanish he could muster, "You'll get some tobacco, and maybe some other gifts, too. But only if we get a horse."

The Apache also replied in Spanish. "We can't spare any."

"Buffler shit," Early spit out. He was tired of it all now. In his own version of English, he said, "We get a horse, ye get presents. We don't get a horse, the only present ye'll get is a lead pill from my rifle here." He didn't know if the Jicarilla would understand him. Nor did he much care. If the Apaches didn't understand the words, they most likely would get the intent.

The Jicarilla leader's eyes narrowed. He understood well enough. He grinned. In Spanish, he asked, "You have things to trade for a horse?"

"I already said I did. But before ye get anything, pull your men back."

The leader nodded, and his warriors moved back some.

"Take the possible sack down from the saddlehorn here," Early said to Adams. "And go easy. These bastards're itchier'n a wolf with fleas."

Adams pulled the sack off, set it down, and opened it.

"Pull out a knife for each of 'em, and some of that buckskin-wrapped tobacco." He paused a moment, while Adams rummaged around in the bag. Then he added, "Best get out that part-used bar of Galena and that half-empty tin of DuPont." He sighed. "And the jug of awardenty."

"Huh?" Adams looked up at Early in surprise.

"Whiskey, ye dumb son of a bitch. I hate like hell to give it up, since that's all I got, but it'll probably make those bastards look on this trade a heap more favorable."

When Adams had retrieved all the items, Early said, "Put 'em all out there on the grass 'tween us'n them."

Adams moved cautiously but quickly. When everything was sitting on the grass, he moved back to stand beside the Appaloosa again after putting the bag back on the saddlehorn.

"For you," Early said in Spanish. He jerked his chin toward the gifts.

The Apaches eyed the goods, coveting mostly the lead, powder, and whiskey. The Jicarilla leader nodded and signed, "It is good." He called to one of his warriors, who brought up one of the stolen horses.

Early glanced at the animal. He nodded and signed, "It is good." The warrior brought the horse close. "Take it, boy," Early said to Adams. "And get your ass on it."

The Apaches laughed at Adams's awkwardness in getting on the horse. Adams's face reddened.

The young Apache who had brought the horse picked up the gifts and handed them around. The whiskey, powder, and lead went to the leader.

"Ye can ride bareback, can't ye, boy?" Early asked.

"If I have to," Adams vowed.

Still wary, Early moved his hand from the saddle pistol and unlooped the reins from the saddlehorn. "Let's go."

They pushed through the Jicarillas, Adams's face ashen with fear. Then they were past. "Just keep a slow pace, boy," Early said calmly. "Leastways till we put some distance 'tween us and them critters."

When they had ridden for maybe fifteen minutes, Early finally looked back. The Apaches apparently were passing around the jug of whiskey.

"Let's move, boy," Early said. He kicked the Appaloosa into a trot. If the Apaches got drunk, they might get mean and come looking for the two white men. They rode until after dark, though after the first hour away from the Apaches, their pace had slackened considerably. Still, Early had kept a lookout for them.

"What're you looking for?" Adams had asked at one point. "Those Apaches're miles behind us."

"Apaches've been known to ride a couple hundred miles in hardly any time at all, boy. Those goddamn critters get it into their minds to come for us, they'd be on us afore we knew they was there."

But there was no pursuit, and after dark had fallen, Early finally pulled to a stop for the night next to a snaking dribble of a stream.

Adams slid off the horse, rubbing his seat and smiling ruefully. "Guess I'm not all that good at riding bareback. Or even riding with a saddle, for that matter."

"How'n hell did ye get around back in New York?" Early asked, as he began unsaddling the Appaloosa.

"Carriages, mostly. But have no fear—"

"Do some work whilst ye're yappin', boy. We'll need a fire, which means we'll need firewood. That's a good start."

"Right." He began searching under the low silver shimmer of the quarter moon and the many stars. "As I was saying, now that I have a horse, I won't slow us down anymore. If I get a sore rump in the doing, then so be it. At least we can make better time."

"That we can, boy." Early smiled into the darkness, thinking of how good it would be to rejoin Rawlins and Chardonnais. He began rubbing down the big Appaloosa, thinking that he now was assured of getting to Taos with plenty of time for a spree. "Now, quit your yammerin'. We got us work to do," he said.

11

"YOU SEEM MIGHTY EAGER to get to Taos, Ezra," Adams said around chunks of buffalo and sips of coffee. "But I thought you liked being out in the wilds, away from the city and all its closeness."

"Well now, I sure as hell do that," Early said with a laugh. "I most purely do. But after all them winter months up in them mountains, ye just get a hankerin' in your bones for lettin' loose a little."

"But winter is long past."

"Goddamn, don't I know that." He popped another piece of meat in his mouth. "But, I nary did get my chance for lettin' loose, seein's how I had to head East. I aim to have that spree, I get back soon enough."

"Will we?" He stood and stretched his legs, wanting to get off his sore rump for a while.

"Yep. We hadn't gotten that horse, though, we'd of nary made it."

Talk of getting the horse brought Adam's mind back onto the Apaches. His fear returned. He looked out over the way they had come, seeing nothing in the darkness, especially since he was so close to the fire. "You think those Apaches're going to come after us?"

"There's always that chance. But I reckon not. For a couple reasons. For one, if they finished off that awardenty, they'll most likely be lookin' for a place to sleep it off. Even not, there ain't enough profit in it for them to come after us. They don't know me, but they know the kind of man I am. They know they come after us, and at least a couple of them are gonna go under. For what? A couple horses? Shit, it ain't worth the bother. Not when they can go raid some ranches down toward San Miguel or somewhere."

"They were some scary-looking fellows," Adams said, retaking his seat. For some reason he felt more at ease by the fire.

"I expect they were."

"But they weren't what I expected," Adams said, almost musing. "They weren't like the Comanches at all."

"All Injins is different. Different languages, different dress, customs, dances, and such. Some are mostly peaceable toward whites; others're walkin' shit heaps." He shrugged.

"We've heard of Apaches back East. Some of the others, too, like the Blackfoot. It is said they are quite mean."

"Aside from the Apaches, the Blackfoot're about the meanest bastards ye can meet. Don't get along with whites at all, 'cept maybe for a few of the Britishers from the Hudson's Bay Company."

"You ever fight them, Ezra?"

"Ye ask a heap of goddamn questions, boy," Early snapped, his anger only halfhearted.

Across the fire Adams could see the light dim in Early's eyes. "I'm sorry, Ezra," he said quietly. "I meant nothing personal by it."

"Aw, hell, boy, it ain't your fault." He sliced off a piece of meat. Nibbling at it, he said softly, "I fought them bastards more'n once, for goddamn certain. Fust Injin I ary killed was one of Bug's Boys."

"Bug's Boys?"

"Blackfeet. Sons of the goddamn devil his own self."

Adams nodded and ate silently. He figured that if Early was going to say more, he'd do so in his way, at his pace. The silence dragged until Adams couldn't stand it anymore. "Maybe it's none of my business, Ezra, but it sounds like you hate the Blackfeet above all others. Why?"

Early sighed, anger revived by the memories. "Shit," he mumbled.

"You needn't say anything if you don't want."

"Hell, it don't make no difference now." He filled and lit his pipe. When he spoke again his voice was softly insistent, lending import to his words.

Early, Rawlins, and Chardonnais had pulled into Taos late in the spring of 1827. There, Early found his brother Ethan waiting for him. Early, still angry over the death of a woman companion the year before, gave up his thoughts of revenge in the joy of seeing his brother.

"What the hell're ye doin' here, little brother?" Ezra asked after whooping it up for a few moments. Ethan was the only sibling Ezra had ever really gotten along with.

"Come to see you, and"—he looked abashed—"go into the mountains with you."

"No," Ezra said firmly. "No goddamn way."

"And why not?" Ethan asked, pulling himself up straight.

"You're too goddamn young," Ezra growled.

"I am, huh?" Ethan said with a touch of anger. "I'm the same damn age you was when you left to go with Ashley. Hell, I ain't done nothin' more'n you did. You left home early and wandered before endin' up in Saint Louis and hiring on with Ashley. Well, I wandered a little, too, and then ended up in Saint Louis, thinkin' maybe I'd find you there."

Ethan shrugged. "When I didn't see you, I went to Independence. Some feller named Charlie Bent said that if I wanted to find you, I'd best go on to Taos. I hired on with him and, by Christ, here I am."

Ezra looked his brother over. Ethan was almost as big as Ezra, though he did not have the big shoulders and hardness that came with half a decade of working in the mountains. He still remembered Ethan as a boy. They hadn't seen each other in almost six years, since Ezra had been home only once after leaving at the age of eighteen. Ethan was eighteen now, and Ezra could see no real reason for not taking his brother along. He nodded, but then said, "I got to see if my partners don't mind none."

"Partners?" Ethan asked, surprised. "You own a company now?"

Ezra laughed. "Naw, I ain't no booshway. I meant my trappin' partners. We been together almost since the beginnin'."

"You think they'll mind?" Ethan asked, suddenly a little worried. He had just assumed that his brother was trapping with some big company and that it would be no trouble for him to get hired on, too.

"I don't expect so," Ezra said with a laugh. "Come on, boy, let's go find them two squamptious critters."

Chardonnais and Rawlins were in one of their partner's favorite *cantinas*. The Early brothers came up and slopped into chairs. Ezra reached for the jug of whiskey and drank from it, rather than wasting time to put it into a cup, then held the jug out to his brother. Ethan took it and sipped tentatively. It wasn't as bad as he had feared, though it did make his eyes water and seemed to leave a trail of flames behind on the way down his gullet.

"An' who is dis?" Chardonnais asked, pointing to Ethan.

"Boys, meet my brother Ethan. Ethan, meet Lucien Chardonnais, the foulest, ugliest frog this side of Saint Louis. The big, dumb-lookin' critter there is Abe Rawlins." He grinned.

Ethan smiled tentatively and shook hands with the two, not quite sure what to think.

"Ethan here says he come out to find me and become a mountaineer. He wants to join us."

"Mais non!" Chardonnais said emphatically. "We don't need no udders wit' us."

Ethan looked crestfallen, as well as angry.

Chardonnais suddenly laughed. "I make de joke, no?" he said.

Rawlins swatted Chardonnais with his hat, sending up a puff of dust. "Goddamn frog fart. Jesus, ain't got no goddamn manners." He looked at Ethan. "Glad to have ye along, boy. But mind, there's a heap of work involved."

Ethan nodded. "I'm aware of that."

"Den welcome, *mon ami,*" Chardonnais said with a huge, warm grin. He stuck out his small, hard hand to shake. "I am sorry I make dat joke wit' you, my frain."

Ethan chuckled. "It's all right, Mister Chardonnais."

Chardonnais clutched at his chest. "Oh, I am wounded. *Mister* Chardonnais, 'e calls me now. And I do not'ing to him." He was laughing the whole time.

"He don't like when someone calls him 'mister,'" Rawlins chuckled. "He prefers to be called buffler pecker most times."

"These fellers always like this?" Ethan asked his brother.

"Usually worse," Ezra smiled. "Of course, they're usually worse because I'm usually helpin' 'em out."

The four pulled out when they normally did, along about the middle of August. During the summer, Ethan Early had sampled the many delights of Taos, including the *señoritas.* At Falling Leaf's village, they arranged for Ethan to have a young woman from the tribe, and then they rode off in fine fettle and boisterous spirits.

A month later, the two Earlys were on their way to check their trap lines one morning when a dozen Blackfoot jumped them. Chardonnais and Rawlins came running and drove the Blackfoot off, but it was too late for Ethan.

* * *

"Killed?" Adams asked, gulping.

Early nodded. "Some son of a bitch damn near took his head off with a tomahawk. Bastards nary got to raise his hair, though. I made goddamn certain of that."

Adams was shocked at the vehemence in Early's voice. "You were all right then?"

Early shrugged. "Took two arrows that time," he said nonchalantly. This was no case of exaggeration. He was simply stating a fact, not making a hero of himself. He grinned savagely. "And there's two of Bug's Boys're roamin' around lookin' to get into the spirit world, but they ain't gonna make it. Ever."

"Why?"

"I raised their hair, boy," Early said viciously.

"You've used that term before, Ezra. What does it mean?" He was fairly certain he knew, but he wanted to make sure.

"Scalped 'em," Early said flatly.

Adams looked a little sick. The thought of a white man taking a scalp, even an Indian scalp, was still foreign to him. He didn't know what to say, and the sad look on Early's face kept Adams's mouth closed. He suddenly figured it was a good time to sleep. He curled up near the fire, missing his coat that he had buried along with his shirt and pants.

Suddenly he felt more than heard Early looming over him. In fright, thinking Early was going to kill him for being such a busybody, he looked up with fright-widened eyes. But all Early did was lay a blanket over him. He started to offer thanks, but Early put a finger to his lips, and Adams nodded.

Early kicked him awake in the gray of the predawn.

It was chilly, though he knew that in only a couple of hours it would be sizzling again. Still, right now he was reluctant to leave the warmth of the blanket.

"Best get your ass a-movin', boy," Early said, all trace of last night's melancholy gone. "Afore I douse ye with cold water from yonder spring."

"Damn, Ezra," Adams grumbled, shoving aside the blanket. He shivered a moment after standing up. The fire warmed him a little, and a cup of coffee soon afterward helped even more. He gobbled bacon and beans and then hurried to clean up. By the time he finished, Early had the Apache horse saddled and his bedroll tied behind. Adams hastened to get the rest of his work done.

"You shouldn't have done that, Ezra," Adams said, pointing to Early's saddle on the Apache horse. "I would've made do."

"I expect ye would've. But I'm a heap better at ridin' bareback. Ye ride a couple more days without a saddle and your ass'll be so sore ye won't be able to move."

Adams nodded and pulled himself onto the small-boned chestnut. "I think you're right, Ezra. I'm thankful."

Early leapt on the Appaloosa. "Don't get too thankful till ye've really ridden with me a few days. Now that ye've got a horse, I intend to move fast. The itch to have me a *fandango* is gettin' stronger all the time."

They rode out, with Early setting a bone-jarring, stomach-shaking, backside-busting pace for someone who had met a saddle only once or twice in his life before this. But Adams kept to it gamely, uncomplaining. Still, he grimaced almost constantly as blisters grew, and his thighs felt as if they had been thrashed with large sticks.

They rode almost nineteen hours that day. When they pulled to a stop that night, Adams was exhausted. He managed to accomplish his chores, but then he fell asleep with a half-eaten piece of fresh deer meat in his hand. Early smiled when he saw it and threw a blanket over the journalist.

Sometime the next day, a pain-filled Adams noticed that Early had turned them westward, and several hours later, northward. He could feel the ground steepen as they moved into mountains, and he noticed more jagged peaks. The ground was rougher, too, with more stones in the way. It meant that at times they had to slow the horses to a mere walk.

Adams felt bruised over his whole body, but he was determined not to show it. More than once he drew blood from his own lips as he bit them to keep from crying out with a new jolt. During the ride, he simply followed the wide back of the mountain man; at night, he would fall asleep almost as soon as he was out of the saddle. He cursed at himself for his weaknesses of body and of spirit. He would not allow himself to complain, though, and he pushed himself as hard as he could, trying to complete whatever chores he could manage before he collapsed.

They traveled north another day and started that way the next morning. Then Early turned them west on a small track that seemed to go nowhere but up.

"What is this?" Adams asked as they stopped for a few minutes to let the horses rest.

"Mule track. Heads across the Sangre de Cristos, right into Taos."

"How long?"

"Three, four days. Think ye can hold up?"

"I'll make it," Adams vowed. He didn't know how, but he would either make it or die trying.

Three days later, Adams was surprised to find the trapper pulling into a campsite rather early. Adams slid out of the saddle and stood on shaky legs. He had to hold the saddle to keep himself upright. "Why're you stopping so early?" he asked in accusatory tones. "It's because of me, isn't it?"

"Well, now, I wouldn't go and say that, exactly." He grinned. "We'll be in Taos afore noon tomorrow. I figured ye'd need a little rest. 'Sides, this chil' don't think it's right to go ridin' on into Taos this way." He indicated his shabby clothing. "I got to get myself all fancied up to make a proper entrance into Taos."

"You always do that?"

"Most always. Leave the same goddamn way, too." He laughed a little. "Such doin's shine. 'Sides," he added conspiratorially, "it annoys hell out of the *alcalde* and the other goddamn officials."

Adams laughed in spite of himself and all his aches. Then he groaned.

"Feel like shit, do ye, boy?" Early asked with a grin.

"Worse. If that's possible." He smiled weakly.

12

EARLY LET OUT A screech that might have carried all the way to Mexico City, and kicked the Appaloosa into a run. As he thundered into the bustling town of San Fernando de Taos, he fired the Dickert and then jammed it into the scabbard on his saddle, which he had taken back for this occasion.

Halfway down the main street toward the plaza, he bellowed, "Here I am, boys, to show ye how to *fandango!*" Then he fired both saddle pistols just before releasing a war cry. Women, children, dogs, soldiers, civilians, horses, burros, chickens, everyone and everything scattered out of the path of this raving wild man.

Early pulled the Appaloosa up in the center of the plaza. The horse reared once. When it landed, Early laughed long and hard, a deep-seated belly laugh that freed his feelings of joy.

A half mile back, he could see Adams riding sedately into town. People had begun moving into the plaza. A few *señoritas* waved, holding out lascivious promises with their dark eyes. Early hurriedly reloaded both pistols, just in case one of the *soldados* wanted to take exception to his expressing his joy so freely. None did.

Then he heard, "Well, it's about goddamn time ye showed your mangy ass back here, ye flea-bitten son of a bitch." The voice came from the crowd, drifting through the cloud of dust that lingered in the air.

"That ye, Abe?" Early shouted. He scanned the crowd, looking for the familiar face.

"Now who the hell else would it be, ye damn fool? Ain't no one else gonna give a wanderin' hoot about some raggedy ol' chil' like ye."

Early grinned and shouted, "Well, then, drag yourself out here where I can see ye, 'stead of hidin' behind the dust and *señoritas*."

The dust was settling, though it had never really been thick enough to prevent him from seeing. It just limited his vision some and with all the noise and the bustle of the people, it was hard to pick out where Abe was.

Suddenly a strong hand grabbed Early by the back of the shirt and yanked him off the horse into the dirt. He landed with a thud, but he rolled with it and was on his feet almost instantly.

"That weren't nice, *amigo*," Early said with a grin. "I just might have to get ye back for that one day."

"Shit, ye talk too much." He gave Early a great bear hug, which Early returned enthusiastically. "How's things back in Indiana?" Rawlins asked.

"Pa went under."

"Sorry to hear that, hoss." He wasn't sure how to

take it since Early had never been all that close with
his folks back in the East.

"He lived a long enough life, I expect," Early said
with a shrug. He thought to say more, but there was
nothing more to say.

Abe nodded.

"Where'n hell's Lucien?"

"Around and about." Rawlins suddenly laughed.
"Last I saw him, he was tryin' to get some leetle
señorita into the robes."

Early joined the laughter.

Adams rode up and stopped. He dismounted gingerly, still feeling bruised and abused. He was weak in
the knees.

Rawlins glared at Adams. "Ye know this here chil',
Ezra?" he asked, pointing to Adams.

"Abe Rawlins, meet Hobart Adams. Bart, meet Abe."

The two men shook hands, then Rawlins said, "He
looks to be about the greenest coon this chil's ary
seen."

Early laughed. "He is that for goddamn sure. About
as useful on the trail as tits on a buffler bull. Found
him wanderin' loose, all on his own. Figured I just
couldn't let him stay out there by his own self, at the
mercy of all sorts of wild animals, and worse men."
His chuckle expanded. "Hell, when I met up with him,
he was entertainin' some Comanche bucks."

"He don't look none the worse for it."

"I come on 'em afore they could do him much damage." He was about to say something else when
another voice intruded.

"Don' you even said *bonjour* to your ol' *ami*, eh?
You get citified manners out dere back East?"

Early spun. "Lucien!" he said joyfully. "How the hell are ye, boy?"

"*Très bon*," Lucien Chardonnais said as the two men embraced.

"Abe says ye was off tryin' to romance some *señorita*."

"*Oui.*"

"Well, goddammit, how'd ye do?" Early asked in mock exasperation.

"How you t'ink, eh?" He laughed.

"Christ, ye'd hump a goat was there no woman around."

Chardonnais shrugged, unashamed. "You are just jealous, eh, because you are less *homme* den me." He thrust out his chest proudly and grinned, showing two missing teeth on the left side.

"Shit, I'll match up with ye inch for goddamn inch anywhere, ye stinkin' little frog fart, ye." He pulled off his hat and began swatting Chardonnais with it.

"Stop dat," Chardonnais said, not really angry. "Dat *chapeau* probably 'as lice all over it, goddammit. An' I don' wan' no lice on me. At least not until de wintair."

Early grinned and stuck the hat back on his head. "Hell, ain't no self-respectin' lice gonna want to live on your fat ol' hide no ways, ye buzzard-humpin' sack of frog shit."

"Bah," Chardonnais shot back.

Despite all his aches and pains, Adams had stood there and watched the exchange with mounting interest, taking it all in. He wanted to remember it all for later, when he had a chance to get some paper and render drawings of the scene.

Early he had down pat, as far as looks and movements went. But Chardonnais and Rawlins were new to him and warranted investigation. Rawlins was much like Early: a big, rangy American with broad shoulders, slim waist, no behind to speak of, and long, powerful legs. He had a long, dour face that bore some resemblance to a sad hound dog. Under his wide *sombrero* fell a thick mane of wheat-colored hair that reached down to his shoulders. He wore a fat mustache that dropped around his slim lips and hung off the points of his square chin. Otherwise, he was clean shaven, though it looked freshly done; still kind of raw.

Adams was surprised to see that Rawlins did not wear moccasins. Instead, he had on a pair of boots, with spurs that had huge rowels. His pants were tight-fitting, with fringes and conchas alternating down the outside seam of each leg. *Botas* covered the bottoms, from knees to ankles. His shirt was simple cloth, and not much of it was seen under the short, Taos-style buckskin jacket. A knife in a plain, hard-leather case hung from the left side of his wide leather belt, just in front of a pistol clipped to the belt. A matching pistol was on the other side. Behind him, at the small of his back, he carried a tomahawk in his belt, as Early did. At the moment, he was leaning his gnarled hands on the muzzle of a long flintlock rifle, the butt of which was in the dirt.

Chardonnais was not nearly as tall as the other two, and was, to Adams's surprise, bowlegged. Thick, black hair covered his swarthy face from eyebrows to past his chin. The tangle continued down to the limited amount of chest seen beneath the bright red calico shirt. The hair on his head was long, too, and slightly curled upward just below the level of the shoulders.

His eyes were dark glittering coals that Adams figured would be expressive in joy or in menace. Chardonnais had a short, squat nose that evidently had been broken more than once.

Where Rawlins and Early seemed rather somber as far as clothing went, Chardonnais was a blaze of hues. Below the red shirt, he wore buckskin pants that had been beaded, bangled, and decorated in a splashy pattern. His moccasins were fixed in a bold pattern of blue, green, and white beads. A wide red sash circled his waist. Two big pistols were stuck through the sash, as was a colorful sheath encasing a large knife. A small patch knife dangled by a thong around his neck, as did a large heart-shaped ornament of silver. He casually carried a large-bore flintlock rifle. On his head was a vivid green knitted wool cap, the top of which flopped to the side.

Both Chardonnais and Rawlins had the customary possibles bag hanging at their side, while on the other were powder horn, priming horn, and shooting bag.

Rawlins dropped his mental sketching when Early introduced him to Chardonnais. The man had a steely handshake, and his eyes were piercing.

Accustomed to reading men quickly, it had taken Rawlins and Chardonnais only moments to size up Adams. As soon as Chardonnais got his hand back, he asked, "Where is dis chil' from, eh?"

"New York, of all goddamn places," Early said gleefully. "And more recent of the Santa Fe Trail."

Rawlins suddenly started laughing. "Where'n hell'd ye get them rags ye're wearin', boy?" he asked between growing gales. "Ye ary see anything looked quite like that, Lucien?"

"Mais non!" Chardonnais had tried not to laugh, but he could not help himself. "I don' believe I see anyt'ing like dat. Even de Diggers dress better."

Adams's face flushed with anger, and his eyes dropped. When they did, he saw his outfit. He had been so full of pain on the trail that he had forgotten just what he looked like in the outlandish getup. He grinned, just a little at first, but it quickly built strength. He lifted his head and looked from one to the other of the three men facing him. "It does seem I need a new tailor, doesn't it?" he said evenly.

Rawlins and Chardonnais were nearly rolling in the dirt, laughing all the harder. "How long dead was the feller ye took 'em from?" Rawlins managed to gasp.

Adams looked slyly at Early, who shook his head vigorously, not wanting Adams to say anything. But the easterner's grin enlarged some more and he said, "Well, actually, it was Ezra here who gave them to me."

Rawlins snapped his back straight and managed with some difficulty to put a look of indignation on his face. "Ye mean to tell me, Ezra Early," he said in a high, whining voice, "that ye're standin' here in the broad light of the day all fancied up in your finest outfit, all ready to *fandango,* whilst this here poor bastard's been ridin' in them rags? Ye got yourself some explainin' to do here, boy." He could not keep a straight face, though, and within moments lost himself to the laughter again, tears of joy leaking from under his eyelids.

"Shit," Early said stiffly. "I expect they ain't the finest clothes this chil's ary seen, but they're better'n runnin' 'round bare-ass naked, or stinkin' of skunk like he was." He shrugged. "I expect I could've let him ride on into town here wearin' nothin' but that little red fancy of his." He pointed to the bright, out-of-place ascot.

Rawlins and Chardonnais laughed all the more, but finally Chardonnais managed to say, "Some of dese *mademoiselles* just might've taken a fancy to dat. Hell, yes, dey would."

Early and then Adams joined in the laughter, which finally wound down. The four men wiped their eyes, still ignoring the crowd that was warily watching the antics of these *loco* Americans.

"Well now," Early said at last, "seein's how ye two boys've had your fun, it's time for me and Bart here to tend to business."

"What ye got in mind, ol' hoss?" Rawlins asked.

"Well, fust off, I expect ye and Lucien should buy me and Bart a jug or two. Seein's how ye two have had so much fun at our expense."

"It looks like dis fellow 'ere," he pointed to Adams, "can use a few drinks, eh. But you . . . ?" He gave an exaggerated shrug.

"Aw, hell, Lucien," Rawlins offered, "I suppose we can even buy ol' Ezra a sip or two, don't ye think, *amigo?*"

"Dat would be all right wit' me, *mon ami.*"

"Good. But let's move. This dust's got me drier'n a spent well."

Rawlins and Chardonnais accompanied the two newcomers to a livery, where they dropped off their horses. Then they strolled to their favorite *cantina*. While the three Americans cleared some drunks from a table, the French Canadian went and bought two jugs of Taos Lightning.

13

CHARDONNAIS PUT THE JUGS down and sat. Early grabbed one, Rawlins the other. They pulled the corks and drank deeply. Especially Early. It had been awhile since he'd had more than a swallow of whiskey, and he aimed to make up for lost opportunity. He finally slapped the jug down and wiped a hand across his mouth and beard. "Damn, that shines with this chil'." He pushed the jug in Adams's direction. "Here, boy, have yourself a taste."

Adams pulled the jug toward him. He had never been much of a drinker, so he was wary. Still, Early had swallowed a healthy dose without so much as a by-your-leave. He figured he could do the same.

"Just pour some down into your guts, boy," Rawlins snapped. "It ain't gonna get there through the sides of the jug. Damn fool."

Adams looked at the grinning faces around him and knew he was about to be had. He shrugged. It was all in good fun, he figured, and Early had done nothing to hurt him. He lifted the jug and tilted it. He drank cautiously, letting it seep rather than roar down his throat. It still sent a harsh jolt through his system. His eyes began watering and he pulled the jug away. Carefully he set it down on the scarred wood table. He sat very still, staring into nothingness, looking like he was having trouble catching his breath. When he thought he could speak, he gargled carefully, "Good."

The three other men laughed, and Early pounded Adams heartily on the back. Adams winced as old pains returned with renewed fury.

"Ye made 'em come now, boy. Ye sure did," Early said. "But ye can breathe, boy. It should've stopped burnin' by now."

Adams sucked in a deep breath and winced, but within seconds he was back to normal. He watched as the three mountain men tippled steadily from the jugs. "That's some stuff," he said quietly. "What's it made out of?"

"A little of this, a little of that," Early said. "Mainly just homemade whiskey with a few extras added for some flavor."

"What kind of extras?" Adams asked suspiciously.

"Maybe a little tobacco. Maybe a little DuPont powder. Most often down this way, they just throw in some chili peppers."

"What's a chili pepper?"

"Little peppers. Some of 'em's green. Some's red. All of 'em hotter'n the fires of hell. Folks here use 'em for all kinds of cookin'. Ye wait till ye get your first taste of Mexican cookin'. Your belly'll nary forgive ye for it."

Adams laughed, feeling more at ease. "Sounds like between the whiskey and the food, I'll not live out the week."

"Don' you listen to dat ol' fart, *mon ami*," Chardonnais said. "'E is a chickenshit, afraid of everyt'ing. You will like de food. It is *très bon*."

"Eat shit, ye dumb bastard," Early growled goodnaturedly.

After another round of sips, Early asked, "Ye boys have any trouble with the plews?"

"Hell, what makes ye think we'd have trouble with the plews?" Rawlins growled.

"Nothin'," Early said with a shrug. "Just askin' ye is all."

"Ezra said there was sometimes trouble in selling your furs here because of the officials."

"Dey are a pain in my ass," Chardonnais snapped.

"How do you do it so you don't lose your furs?" He pulled out one of the last scraps of unused paper, wetted the tip of a pencil and waited.

"We always stop somewhere north of the Pueblo," Early said. "We take a day or two to cache our plews."

"Cache?"

"Hide 'em. We dig a hole, put the plews in, and cover it up so's even a goddamn Injin can't find it." He paused for a sip. "Then we ride on into town. Then we poke around tryin' to find out who'll give us the best price. Once that's done, we make arrangements to bring 'em into town." He looked at his two partners. "Who'd ye go with this year?"

"Charlie Bent and Ceran Saint Vrain went into business together the end of last year," Rawlins said. "They got a store here in town. Way I understand it, Charlie's gonna ride the trail, Ceran's mostly gonna stick with the store here in town."

Early nodded. "Good. Charlie's a fair man, and ye can't get no better'n Ceran, even if he is a goddamn frog."

"Bah," Chardonnais said. "For dat, I will 'ave anudder drink." He made good on his promise.

Rawlins grinned. "Couple nights later, I took some of Charlie's boys to the cache. We hauled them plews back on the mules the next night."

They drank in silence for a while, with Adams even venturing a few more tentative sips. He did not think he would ever come to like this foul brew, but he did not want to be left out. Besides, it was wet and that counted for a lot. He did feel, though, that he was being accepted by these men, and that pleased him.

Suddenly Early said, "Goddamn, I got me a hankerin' to fill my meatbag. What about ye others?"

"Hell, that'd suit this chil' just fine," Rawlins offered easily.

"*Oui*. Me, too."

"How about ye, Bart?" Early asked.

"I haven't felt like I've had a full belly since I left New York." He flushed momentarily at the mention of his home. He did not want these men to make light of him for it again. They did not.

Each man took one more healthy slug of the whiskey, then strolled out into the warm, early afternoon sun. Since it was not yet *siesta* time, the plaza was bustling. The four men strolled up the dusty street.

After hearing Early speak about the place, Adams had expected some great, wondrous city. He was disappointed to see the dismal little place with its brown dirt and brown adobe houses and shops, the squalid alleys with clucking, squawking chickens. Goats and sheep wandered aimlessly, unfettered. Mounds of horse manure and garbage were piled here and there. Everything— except the people—looked drab and poor.

Adams's eyes drank it all in: Indians going about their mysterious business; shopkeepers and customers arguing over prices; peddlers selling everything from *tortillas* to woven rugs from their *carretas;* pretty, dark-haired *señoritas* walking along, *cigarrillos* dangling from full, pouty lips; young men, cocksure and proud, leaning against walls while ogling the women; old men strolling, leading burros laden with God knew what; old women covered by *mantillas,* heading for the church off the plaza; arrogant soldiers. To Adams it was a whirl of colors, images, and sounds.

The four entered the cool, dim interior of a small adobe restaurant and sat at a large round table. In their best Spanish, they ordered huge amounts of food—flat corn *tortillas;* spicy hot bean dishes; chicken covered in savory, fiery sauce; *chile huevos;* fried bread, like that made by the nearby Indians; soup made of acorns and corn; cornhusk-wrapped *tamales;* fresh goat's milk.

They ate without talking, breaking the quiet only to grunt with satisfaction at the tasty dishes. Even Adams was hushed, although his face turned red and he whistled more than once when he bit into a burning pepper that decorated his food. He would not back down from the fiery dishes, though, especially after he learned that the fresh, cold goat's milk could ease the sting some in his mouth, throat, and stomach.

But finally even these voracious eaters had enough,

and they leaned back, patting full bellies.

"Damn, such vittles shine with this ol' chil' for goddamn sure," Early said with a sigh of pleasure.

"It purely does," Rawlins agreed. Then he called out to the young waitress, the daughter of the owner, "*Señorita*, some coffee, *por favor.*"

The waitress brought a big pot of hot coffee and set it in the middle of the table. Then she brought four cups, a bowl of sugar, and one of honey. Rawlins passed around cigars, made down in Santa Fe of tobacco brought all the way up the Camino Real from Mexico City.

"Now," Rawlins said, as the men relaxed and sipped coffee and puffed on cigars, "tell us how ye met ol' Bart hyar. Ye nary did say."

"Well, goddamn, there's a tale there, for goddamn certain," Early said. He explained it all, embellishing here and there.

When Early was finished, Rawlins looked at Adams and said, "Ye done all right for yourself, boy. 'Specially with Ezra findin' ye. Many's the other chil' would've left ye to the Comanches' tender mercies."

"I'm aware of that, Mister Rawlins," Adams said seriously. "And it's an episode of my life I'd not care to repeat."

"I'd think not," Rawlins said, grinning. Then he asked solemnly, "Ye are aimin' to get the critters what done this to ye, ain't ye?"

"Hadn't really had time to think of it," Adams said. "I was too worried about getting to safety." The idea of revenge was, in some ways, pleasant. Then reality hit him. He stood no chance against Ebenezer Parfrey. "But I think I'll leave it to the authorities," he said pensively.

"Shit," Rawlins snorted. "Them goddamn greaser officials ain't gonna help ye none, boy. They ain't about to send no *soldados* to end a feud 'tween two Americans."

"We'll just see about that," Adams said firmly. His mind was suddenly made up, and he was flooded with determination.

Rawlins shrugged. "Suit yourself, boy." He looked at Early and then Chardonnais. "I reckon it's about time this ol' hoss got down to some serious drinkin'. Ye boys aim to join me?"

Early grinned hugely. "This chil' thought ye'd nary ask. But since ye did, I can tell ye, this ol' beaver's more'n half froze for a good drunk."

"*Oui,*" Chardonnais added hastily.

They strolled outside and leisurely headed back to the *cantina.* The plaza was fairly quiet, as the *siesta* had started. When they entered the saloon, the four men ignored the monte game in progress in one corner. They took a small table near the back. The others in the *cantina*—mostly peasants who worked in nearby fields, or less-fortunate shopkeepers—ignored the Americans. These were hard men, and best left to themselves.

They sipped steadily and quietly, until Early suddenly said, "Ye boys remember that time we was caught up in that spinnin' wind?" He winked at his two old friends.

"*Mais oui!*" Chardonnais said eagerly. "Dat was somet'ing, I tell you."

"Why don't ye just tell ol' Bart here about it," Rawlins said. "I reckon that since he's a newspaper feller, and all of them folk is nosier'n a rootin' hog, he'll be wantin' to hear about such doin's."

"Would ye like that, boy?" Early asked.

Adams had perked up attentively. "I sure would. It will make an interesting tale for the readers back home."

"Well, then, boy, ye just let me fire up my ol' pipe and then I'll set to tellin' ye." He lit the pipe, then sat back. As he talked, he clutched the pipe in his fist or between his teeth. A jug was never far from his hand.

"We had been up in the upper San Juans, stayin' with the Utes. We decided we'd head on out to the flats with 'em to make meat."

"Make meat?" Adams had found a few scraps of unused paper and was scribbling notes. He looked at Early expectantly when he asked.

"Huntin', with the purpose of puttin' up some dried meat to last a spell." When Adams nodded, Early went back to his story.

"We was ridin' along, nice as ye please, enjoyin' the sunshine and such. When all to a sudden, the sky turned dark as night. Goddamn, boy, that was somethin' now. Clouds come up hard and fast. All of it like to scare the shit out of them Utes."

He paused for a sip of whiskey. "Then, by Christ, all of a sudden up comes this howlin' son of a bitch of a wind, twistin' and turnin', whooshin' and spinnin' like ol' Beelzebub was standin' there encouragin' it. It was flingin' bufflers and horses and everything else this way and that . . .

"Well, ol' Abe there, he sees this goddamn wind a blowin', weavin' all over the goddamn countryside, and he says, 'This here's damp powder, and ain't no good in denyin' it. We best run for our lives.' With that, he was off and runnin', with me and Lucien followin' right on his heels, and the Utes right behind us. But all that goddamn runnin' didn't do us no good though."

Early paused again for a few well-timed puffs of his pipe and a few swallows of whiskey. Adams sat wide-eyed and attentive, waiting in anticipation.

"Because there ain't a goddamn tree out there on the peraira. So there we was, out on them goddamn flats, racin' our horses like all the Blackfeet in the goddamn world was nippin' at our asses, when that windy goddamn piece of the devil's work caught us, like we wasn't movin' at all. It just sucked us up into its spinnin' belly and then spit us out again. Flung us all to hell and gone, I'm tellin' ye.

"I was flung all the way north to Absaroka, by Christ. Abe there was tossed down into Comanche land." He paused. "But Lucien there, well that French son of a bitch always had the luck with him, like he was carryin' it in his possible bag. Jesus. He was thrown about, too, but goddamn if that ol' wind didn't set him down right where we was plannin' to do our trappin' that year. Plunked him down on the very goddamn spot. Nice as ye please. He just made himself a camp and started takin' plews."

Smoke billowed up from his pipe. "Took me'n Abe near half the goddamn winter to get back together and find that French-Canadian rascal. Hell, by the time we rode into Lucien's camp—in the midst of a goddamn howlin' blizzard, no less—that ol' son of a bitch had himself near two thousand plews already. Had 'em stacked up higher'n a lodgepole pine."

Adams looked from one man to the other, a grin playing across his lips. With a straight face, he said, "I'm glad to see you fellows came through it all right. I don't know as if any others would've been able to do so."

Early burst out laughing. The others joined him. "Ye mean to say I didn't fool ye even the least littlest bit?" Early asked, chuckling.

"You had me going, until you had people being flung all over the West. I did look at some maps before I left New York, you know."

Laughing, Rawlins said, "Hell, Ezra, mayhap he ain't so bad after all."

Two young Mexicans entered the *cantina*. One carried a guitar, the other a fiddle. Standing near the small bar, they began to play. There were few women in the shabby side-street bar, but those who were there were willingly taken up and spun around the floor by the men.

Early leapt up and grabbed a toothless old harridan and whirled her around the floor. Both made up for their lack of grace with enthusiasm. They crashed around the floor, spinning wildly, bumping into others and knocking over chairs and tables in their abandon.

As they did, Rawlins and Chardonnais howled in laughter, holding their sides, at their friend's antics. Adams watched with disbelief as the carnage mounted.

The song finally ended, and Early bowed gracefully to the woman. When the next song started, Early spotted a fat-bottomed half-Navajo, half-Mexican prostitute. He began twirling her unresisting but unhelping body around the floor. His enthusiasm soon got through to her, and she began to respond, laughing with—and at—this crazy Anglo.

The night passed in frivolity, as the four drank and danced. They sang—badly—and bought drinks for all more than once. They clapped and shouted and whooped, full of mischief, fun, and alcohol.

14

EARLY AWOKE WITH A head that pounded with each movement. He felt as if his skull was a blacksmith's anvil that was being used regularly and hard. He groaned as the light coming through the shutters over the small window seared his bloodshot eyes. For more than an hour he lay there, trying to dampen the intense pain and quiet his stomach, which was writhing like a nest of rattlesnakes. All the while knowing that only time would ease it.

Finally he could lay there no longer. With slow, careful movements, he inched himself up the wall until he was sitting. Then he eased himself to the edge of the sagging bed and placed his feet on the floor. With an effort, he rose, swaying as the hangover kicked the bejeebers out of his innards.

He fought the nausea but lost. He did manage to

make it to the window before he vomited, splashing the outside wall. He hung there, half out the window, retching and heaving, until his stomach was empty. Still the violent contractions in his gut continued, ebbing until they shuddered to a halt. He groaned. "Jesus goddamn Christ."

Sucking in great gobs of air, he at last pushed to his feet. He was unsteady but vertical. He lurched toward the small table and poured water from the pitcher into the basin. Then plunged his head into the water and held it there as long as he could.

He finally came up for air, whipping his head from side to side, water flying. "Damn," he mumbled at himself, "ye are one sorry son of a bitch. Jesus." He was glad Adams was not there to see him in such a state.

Early shoved his long, wet hair back, combing it through his fingers. Then he drank the water left in the pitcher, gulping it greedily. The liquid sloshed over his beard and shirt.

The door opened, and Adams entered quietly. He was scowling but his greeting was polite.

"What's eatin' at ye, boy?" Early asked, leaning back against the wall. He needed the support.

Adams shrugged.

"Where ye been off to?"

"Around town. Here and there."

"Ye went to see the *alcalde*, to tell him your tale of woe, didn't ye?" Early said more than asked. His voice was touched with condescension. When Adams nodded, Early asked, "Well, what did ye find out, boy?"

"I was told that since both the freighters and I were *Americanos*, and because what happened was on the trail, it was outside their jurisdiction. There's nothing they could do. They were apologetic, and suggested I take it up with the governor, but . . . " He shrugged.

"We told ye, boy. Ye should've listened."

Adams grinned lopsidedly. "It was the proper thing to do."

"Mayhap in New York it is. But not here. These boys play by different rules. They ain't gonna go out of their way to help the likes of us. Not the officials, anyway." He paused. "Ye offer 'em money?"

"A bribe?" Adams was not surprised. "That wouldn't be right."

"It's the way things be here, boy. Ain't a one of them goddamn wagons travel the trail come into Santa Fe that don't bribe officials—on top of the goddamn taxes they got to pay."

Adams shrugged. "I have no money anyway," he said with regret.

"They know that?"

"I don't think so."

"Good. Keep it quiet. They know ye ain't got no specie, they'll likely toss your sorry ass into the *calabozo*—jail."

"Why?" Actually, he was not all that surprised. They still had debtor's prisons back in New York. He figured that all he could learn about the Mexican people and their customs, the better.

"Ye ain't no Mexican citizen, boy. Ye got no license from 'em to trap or trade. They'll just figure either ye're on the run or ye're a spy. They don't take highly to *Americanos* with empty pockets."

Adams looked even more dejected. "Having empty pockets will present other problems as well. I have no money for food, or even to get paper and ink so that I might earn a living."

"Don't ye go worryin' about money, boy. Me, Abe, and Lucien got enough. Ye'll not starve."

"I can't take any money—any *more* money—from you, Ezra. You've gone out of your way far too much on my account already."

"Christ, boy, don't argue with me when my head hurts so damn bad. Ye'll get enough specie from me'n the others to keep ye goin' till ye get back on your feet again. Ye can pay us back, if'n ye're of a mind to, when ye can."

"I don't know how to thank you, Ezra. You've been very kind. No, far more than very kind. You are a lifesaver, a—"

"Christ, ye're gonna make me blush, boy," Early said sarcastically. "But if'n ye're truly thankful, ye can start thankin' me by lowerin' your voice. That *fandango* last night was a little more than this chil' could take, I expect. You ate yet?"

"No."

"Well, then, let's go fill our meatbags." He grimaced. "I just hope the food stays in mine."

"I'd think some food would help." Adams was slightly hungover. He had drunk more than he was used to last night, but he had worked off most of it in his walks around town.

Early only grunted. He grabbed his hat and led the way out of the room. As they hit the bright, sunny street, Early winced. "Jesus, who the hell brought this goddamn sun?" he muttered. He blinked furiously a few times before his eyes started working more or less properly again. "Ye seen Abe or Lucien this mornin', boy?"

"Morning?" Adams said with a short laugh. "It's near noon. You've slept away most of the day already."

"Don't ye go start naggin' me, goddammit," Early snapped. "And answer my question."

"I've not seen either."

They entered a restaurant. It was a finer one than the one in which they had eaten the night before. It was cool, quiet, and dim, all of which suited Early quite well. Early ate sparingly, since each mouthful threatened to erupt right back out again as soon as he swallowed it.

Adams, on the other hand, ate heartily. It was obvious that he had taken to Mexican food like Indians had taken to horses.

When they were finished and sipping coffee, Adams coughed in embarrassment. When he had Early's attention, he said tentatively, "I feel like an ungrateful lout mentioning this, Ezra, but I could use a little of the money you said you would lend me."

"Well, sure, boy," Early said, unconcerned. "Soon's we finish here, I'll see to it. What're ye gonna do with it?"

"Get some writing and sketching materials. I fear I've already waited too long before starting to chronicle the tales I've heard and the many wondrous things I've seen so far."

Early nodded, then regretted it. When the pounding settled to a dull throb, he rose. "Come on," he said, heading out. They walked slowly through the sleepy, dusty streets to the new Bent–Saint Vrain store. Charles Bent had told Chardonnais and Rawlins that he, or Ceran Saint Vrain, would be happy to act as a bank for the independent trappers who used Taos as their base.

Early got some money from Bent's clerk and then handed Adams a few gold coins. He slid the others into a small buckskin pouch and dropped it into his possible sack.

Outside, Adams said, "I'll find you later."

"Why didn't ye just get 'em in there?" Early asked, chucking a thumb over his shoulder toward the store they had just left.

"He didn't have what I need. I found another store down the street there this morning when I was walking around. Their materials are of much better quality. Cheaper, too."

"Well, then, boy, go on about your business. I ain't about to stand between a man and his duty. I aim to go take me a goddamn *siesta*."

Early felt considerably better when he awoke late in the afternoon. He strolled down the hall to the room Rawlins and Chardonnais shared. They talked of plans for the evening before Early went back to his own room.

Soon after, Adams hurried in, full of excitement. He handed Early a large pad. Early scanned the sketches, surprised at how good they were. He nodded in satisfaction as he studied the pencil drawings of adobe buildings, Mexicans, mountain men, including himself, Indians, animals, peddlers' carts, dancing couples, the musicians from last night, mountains, Santa Fe Trail landmarks, and more. It was an impressive display.

"Well now, boy," he finally said, "ye sure can make 'em come with them pictures. That ye can." He paused, thinking, then said, "Ye know, boy, I expect ye could make yourself some decent specie of your own by doin' this. I expect there'd be a heap of folks willin' to pay out good *pesos* for some of these here pictures."

"But I must send them back to New York, Ezra," Adams protested, though not very strongly. "My editor will be expecting them." He almost shuddered thinking of an angry Humphrey McWalters bellowing at him.

"Waugh!" Early grunted. "When's the last time ye sent drawin's back there?"

"Just after leaving Independence. I met some fellows on the road and paid them to post the sketches and some articles from Independence."

"Shit, that was, what, two months ago? 'Sides, ye can't be certain them critters didn't just take your cash and toss your precious papers into the nearest mudhole."

"If that's true," Adams said thoughtfully, "it's even more urgent that I get these drawings, and what little writings I've done, back to New York."

"Now, lookee here, boy," Early chided gently, "them folks most likely figure ye been rubbed out already, so they ain't gonna miss nothin'."

Adams sat, looking uncomfortable, as Early continued, "Most of the folks gonna be takin' the trail back to Missouri will be leavin' in about a month, give or take a few days. I expect ye can find somebody here to get your drawin's and such down to Santa Fe and have one of the wagoneers take 'em. Or we can ride down there with ye. But what I'd suggest ye do is spend more time sketchin'. Sell half and save the other half for sendin' back to your newspaper. They ain't gonna find a use for all them drawin's anyhow. Hell, ye done all those in one damn afternoon. Think how many ye can do in a month. Shit, ye'll be a rich man, ye sell even half of 'em."

Adams pondered that briefly. Then a grin spread across his face. "By God, I think you're right, Ezra. I could at least earn my own keep. Plus enough to pay for sending the rest to New York, *and* to pay you back."

"I ain't worried about that, boy," Early said gruffly.

Adams nodded. "I'll do it!" he said suddenly, joyfully. He stood and paced the room. "I've done enough already to sell for money to buy additional materials." The thoughts were coming to him hard and fast now. "Yes, I can go to the plaza. Now. There's still some daylight left."

"Hold your horses, boy," Early said with a laugh. "Ye got time. Ye can start tomorrow. Ye got to eat, boy. Ye ain't had nothin' since we ate this mornin', have ye?"

"No," Adams admitted. "But that was noon. Or later."

"Shit." Early snorted. "A man's got to fill his meat-bag regular he wants to do a decent day's work. By then it'll be dark." He grinned widely. "'Sides, a man's got to have time to *fandango*."

Adams chuckled. "You going out to get drunk again tonight?"

"Naw, expect not. I'm about half froze for some monte."

"What's that?"

"Christ, ain't ye ary done nothin' in your life, boy? Monte's a card game. Ye wager on whether ye can match what the dealer's got."

"I might have to give that a try."

15

ADAMS SUDDENLY STOPPED WALKING and stood rooted in the street.

Early was some steps beyond before he realized he was alone. He stopped and looked back. "Well, what'n hell's wrong with ye now, boy?" he asked, annoyed.

"I just realized," Adams said in embarrassment, "that I spent almost all the money you lent me on writing and sketching materials."

"So?" Early shrugged.

"Well, I have no money now for gambling."

"I'll lend ye a few pesos."

"That's not all. You said this place we're going . . ."

"Doña Montoya's."

"Yes, that's it. You said it was a nice place."

"Doña Montoya's ain't no flea-ridden place like we

was in last night, boy. All the *ricos*—rich folk—go there. A woman named Doña Tule opened a gamblin' place down in Santa Fe. The governor's sweet on her, if the tales told are true. Anyway, the *alcalde* here decided that if such a thing's good enough for the governor down there, then it's good enough for him here, especially since the *alcalde* has took a fancy to Doña Montoya."

"But therein lies the problem, Ezra," Adams said. "I can't go into such a place like this." With a short, choppy arm motion, he indicated his worn, smelly clothes, the ones Early had given him more than a week ago.

"That's a goddamn fact, boy," Early said with a nod. "Well, then, we'll just have to find ye a fancified outfit. After we've eaten. Come on, boy, this chil's facin' starvin' times, and ain't happy about it."

They ate a leisurely, filling meal of acorn stew, thick buffalo steaks, corn, spiced beans, roasted piñon nuts, dishes made with red chili peppers and others made with green chilies. Fresh milk from cows and goats washed the food down. Afterward they polished off pie and *sopapillas*. Coffee sweetened with honey or sugar topped it off as Adams enjoyed a cigar, and Early puffed on his pipe.

Sated, the two men headed back out into the dusty streets. The day was fading fast, but some stores and shops were still open.

Early took Adams to Bent's, where the young journalist picked out a pair of flared-bottom pants of bright blue wool and a matching short, Taos-style jacket. Both were decorated with red and gold embroidery and silver buttons. Under the jacket he would wear a white shirt of pure silk, with billowy sleeves.

For around his waist he bought a sash of the same hue as the ascot he still wore. A wide-brimmed blue *sombrero* embossed with gold embroidery went on his head. Heavy black boots with large-roweled spurs of fine silver completed the outfit.

"Waugh! Ye sure are gonna cut a shine in this here town tonight, boy," Early said as he and Adams walked back to their room. "Them *señoritas* are gonna set on ye like an Injin dog on a piece of meat."

Adams beamed with pride.

Back in their room, Early ordered a tub and plenty of hot water. The trapper went first, scrubbing up quickly, then Adams took his turn, using the same water. While the easterner bathed, Early had a barber remove his new beard.

Then Early started dressing with care, pulling on his tight, soft buckskin shirt. His Ute wife, Falling Leaf, had painstakingly decorated the front with tiny bits of silver, beads, and porcupine quills. The sleeves were fringed with long buckskin whangs. His buckskin pants also were fringed along the outside seams, and the bottoms flared ever so slightly. Shirt and pants were so finely tanned as to be almost white.

Early tied a blue sash around his waist, then buckled his wide leather belt over it so that he could carry his usual assortment of weapons and accoutrements. He slid his feet into soft moccasins, which also were painstakingly decorated with quills, metal, and beads. A tiny bell on each tinkled with each step. From out of a box he pulled a beaver top hat. He wore it only occasionally.

Adams finished his bath, rubbed himself dry with rough cloth, and dressed in his new finery. "We are some sight, ain't we?" He grinned.

"Goddamn right." Early howled and whooped. "Waugh! Them *señoritas* best run for cover tonight, if they want to save their virtue, for this ol' chil' figures to count coup on at least one of 'em."

Adams did not need to have that new term explained to him. In context, it was crystal clear.

They pounded on the door of their friends' room. The two mountain men came out, looking as resplendent in their finery as Early and Adams did in theirs. They wandered outside. The darkness was broken by the many candle lamps that lined the streets or shined from windows and doorways.

With anticipation, they entered the gambling hall run by Doña Luisa Montoya. Adams was amazed at the elegance inside this building that on the outside looked like every other flat brown adobe in town. The place was small and very crowded. Monte, faro, and *chuzo* tables were crowded under the pall of tobacco smoke. The noise was loud but somehow refreshing to men used to the solitude in the high reaches of the Rocky Mountains. The four stood just inside the door, allowing Adams to take everything in. The easterner stood transfixed.

Early glanced at Adams and grinned. With a straight face he asked, "What'n hell are ye starin' at, boy?"

"All the women." There were many women gathered around the gambling tables, loudly making their bets and crowing or groaning as loudly as any man at their victories or losses.

"Ain't ye nary seen a woman afore?"

"Not gambling," Adams said. He was still too amazed to register indignation at the insinuation.

Early laughed. "Shit, 'round here they're prob'ly

bigger gamblers than the men." Early took another look around the room, then said, "Well, boy, ye're on your own. This chil's got business to tend to." He bulled his way through the crowd where necessary, strutting when he had the chance, heading for one of the tables.

Rawlins and Chardonnais followed in Early's wake for a moment, before veering off, each in a different direction. Adams was left standing, a little uncomfortable now that he was alone. He began to relax a little when he realized he was holding his tablet of paper, and his pencils. Moving casually through the crowd, he found a spot of relative solitude and took a seat near the wall. He watched for a while, taking in the sights and sounds of the swirling mass of humanity. Then he began to sketch.

It was nearly an hour before anyone noticed what he was doing. It was a pretty, young *señorita,* made even prettier in Adams's eyes by the colorful, long, shoulderless dress she wore. He was a little taken aback by the *cigarrillo* she adroitly wielded, but the warmth of her smile overcame the feeling.

In Spanish, she asked him something. He had trouble understanding her, but finally puzzled it out. Haltingly, in English and with the very few Spanish words he knew, he tried to explain.

It did no good, though. Finally, in exasperation, he bent his head over the paper. Working quickly, he soon made a sketch of the young woman. He tore the paper free and held it out to her.

She hesitated, then took the paper and stared at it in pleasant surprise. She smiled at him and said something in Spanish, the words pouring rapidly from her full lips.

He smiled back but shrugged to show that he did not understand. She stopped speaking, then placed a hand against his chest a moment, indicating that he should stay there. She spun and hurried off.

When she returned moments later, she had in tow four other giggling young women. One had been taught English at her father's large *rancho*. She acted as interpreter. "My name, *señor*," she said, "is Dolores Ortega y Delgado."

"What's her name?" Adams asked, pointing to the one he first met.

"Isabel Salazar."

"Is she married?"

"No," Dolores giggled. "But she has many suitors."

"I'll bet she does." Adams smiled and bent over his pad.

Across the room, Rawlins sidled up to Early. "Seems like your new *amigo* is doin' all right for himself." He pointed.

Early looked up from his cards. Through a temporary gap in the crowd, he spotted Adams and grinned. "I expect he is."

"Her ol' man gets wind of it, he'll find himself in a passel of trouble."

Early shrugged and went back to his game. "He's a big boy. He ought to be able to take care of himself. This chil' ain't gonna worry about him. I got my own eye on that purty *señorita* over there." With a jerk of his chin, he indicated a young woman gambling at the next table to his left.

"Ye best tread lightly with that 'un, *amigo*. Ye know who her pa is, don't ye?" Rawlins laughed.

" 'Course I do. But when did such doin's ever scare me off?"

"Nary did, far's I know."

"Ye remember that time a few years back, when I was humpin' that little *señorita* Margarita?"

"Certain I do," Rawlins said with a laugh. "Wasn't her pa the biggest *hacendado* in these parts?"

"Yep." Early made his play. "He were some put out when he learned of it, too, wasn't he?"

"Jesus, we had half of Taos chasin' our asses that time, didn't we?" Rawlins laughed some more, remembering when he, Early, and Chardonnais had frantically tried to get out of Taos before Ricardo Escalante de Valenzuela could round up enough of his *peóns* and *vaqueros* to capture the three mountain men.

"Waugh!" Early started laughing. The wealthy patrons of Doña Montoya's tossed looks of distaste at the two Americans for their crudity. "Ran their asses all over hell and creation before we let 'em catch us."

The two laughed all the more at the memory of Escalante's men running for their lives as the three trappers stood them off from behind a pile of boulders. The Mexicans had had no heart for the fight to begin with and had gone along under the command of Escalante's son only because their *patrón* had ordered it.

They had ridden far, suffering from heat and thirst and hunger. Escalante had not provisioned them well, thinking it would take only a day or two to capture the offensive *Americanos.* So the Mexicans were in poor shape by the time they ran the mountain men to ground.

Withering fire from the mountaineers cut down two Mexicans, four horses, and a pack burro in the first few minutes. After the first volley, the Mexicans scrambled for whatever cover they could find, but they were of no mind to continue facing the deadly accuracy of the mountain men. So they fled, unceremoniously but relieved.

The three had ridden a little apprehensively back into Taos the next summer. Ricardo Escalante de Valenzuela had the largest *rancho* in the area, and with such wealth commanded much respect and inspired much fear. He could cause serious trouble for the mountain men should he choose to hold a grudge. The old *hacendado* had, however, died over the winter. His son was not disposed to continue the feud, so it was forgotten.

"We ain't had us a doin's like that one in a coon's age, have we, Abe?" Early said, laughter winding down.

"Nope. And, to tell true, I'm gettin' too goddamn old for another one. That's why I hope you—or that young hoss over yonder—don't bring some girl's papa down on us."

"Christ, ye are gettin' old, ain't ye, boy?" Early said with a grin. "Gone limp in your doterage, have ye?"

"Shit. I'll out hump ye any goddamn time."

"I misdoubt that. Hell, ye ain't even looked at a *señorita* since we been in here. Christ, I've picked out half a dozen, just in case that one over there goes skittish."

"Damn," Rawlins said with a chuckle, "ye're gettin' to be as bad as that goddamn Frenchie." He strolled off, shaking his head and laughing.

Early went back to his game.

16

ADAMS LOOKED UP FROM his sketching and past the tight circle of admiring young ladies. He was a little startled to find that Early had disappeared. It worried Adams a little. He knew nothing of the town or its inhabitants, and he suddenly felt very alone and somewhat vulnerable.

Then he looked at the smiling faces of Dolores and Isabel. Things would be all right, he decided. He handed out more of his drawings to the young women, realizing that he had quickly sketched the likeness of nearly every woman in Doña Montoya's.

"I think I've done enough drawing for one night," he said with a smile. Dolores translated.

The girls began drifting back to the gaming tables, which were still in full swing, until only Dolores and Isabel were sitting near him.

He talked with them, growing more comfortable as time passed. To his surprise, he began to find himself more drawn to the darker, full-bosomed Dolores. It was easier to talk with her, he told himself, because she could speak English, while the fairer Isabel could not.

The latter evidently sensed the same, for eventually, she left. She was cheerful about it, standing, then chatting a moment in Spanish with Dolores. The two young women giggled before Isabel drifted off.

Adams opened up completely. He chatted in animation, talking about his life in New York, and questioning Dolores about her life on the *rancho* just outside Taos and at her father's house in town. Finally gathering up his courage, he managed to ask, "Would you like to walk outside? It's very smoky in here, and much too loud."

Dolores smiled knowingly and said conspiratorially, "*Sí*. But we must not be seen leaving together. It'd be trouble." Her voice was soft, velvety rich. Though her speech was heavily accented, she was easily understood.

"Where shall we meet?" Adams's heart was pounding in anticipation.

"The home of a friend." Dolores gazed levelly at Adams. "It's not far, and no one will be there now."

As she gave directions, Adams listened with a mixture of eagerness and worry. It was hard to believe she was proposing that they meet in an unattended house in the dark. But that seemed to be what she was doing.

Dolores finished and asked if he understood. After he nodded dumbly, Dolores left. Adams waited a little, walking nervously around the establishment, watching the gambling. Then he made his way to the door and slipped outside. He walked swiftly to the appointed place, having no trouble finding it. He slipped through the gate into the courtyard and across it. He rapped quietly on the door, which Dolores opened expectantly.

He decided to test what he thought was happening. Throwing caution to the wind, he stepped inside and then boldly kissed her passionately.

She squiggled away—after a few moments. "Not here," she whispered hotly. "Come with me." She took him by the hand and led him through the almost dark house to a room near the back. A candle burning in one corner provided the only light.

The room was simple, though somehow elegant. A small bed covered with a fine blanket was against the rear wall, about in the center. On each side was a small table. The candle sat on another small table, next to which was a tall, many-drawered dresser. Across the room was another table, slightly larger, on which was a pottery basin and pitcher. A crucifix and painting of Jesus adorned two walls.

"You sure no one will come home?" Adams asked, his nervousness returning with a vengeance.

"*Sí.* It is safe here." She turned to him, all willingness and desire now.

Adams tossed his sketchbook aside, embraced Dolores, and kissed her. She returned it with vigor, straining against him. His fears fled in the heat of his rising passion, and they tumbled onto the bed. They pawed at each other, urgent in their needs and desires.

Adams's mind was awhirl. He was not innocent of women, though he was not all that experienced either.

Women—the wealthy ones, at least—in New York simply did not do such things. And it was evident that this was a woman bred in high station.

Those worrisome thoughts also fled as he shoved her long cotton skirts up and managed to get his pants opened and shoved down some. Then he was inside her, groaning with the pleasurable feelings that flooded through him.

He gasped and shouted once, loudly, as he peaked. He kept pumping, though, until Dolores was squirming with the release of her own passion.

Sometime afterward, they began exploring each other again, this time more slowly. Clothes were removed with eager expectation. Adams was stunned at the magnificence of Dolores's body. In the flickering dim light of the candle, her smooth brown flesh excited him. Her breasts were large, dark and soft to his touch; her legs long and perfectly formed; her stomach slightly rounded. Dolores's raven hair spread in soft waves over the pillow.

It was an evening of exploration and discovery for both of them. Dolores's earthiness surprised and delighted him. She squealed and moaned with the pleasures his body gave her, making Adams worry a little that she might be heard and the two of them discovered. But he pushed the worries aside and gave himself over to the ecstasy.

Dolores suffered her own bout of confusion. Though she was but eighteen, Dolores had had lovers. None, though, had been granted her favors quite so quickly as had Hobart Adams. She wasn't sure why she had done so. She only knew that after an hour or so of talking with Adams, she was tense with desire. She had never felt that way so suddenly and so completely. She also knew within moments of that overwhelming feeling that she would give in to it, and the consequences be damned. Finally, though, she whispered, "You must go now." There was regret in her voice.

Adams was reluctant, but Dolores was gently insistent. "My friends will return soon. We don't want to be caught together like this."

"No," he admitted. "No, we wouldn't." He rose and pulled on his clothes. He did so slowly, wanting to prolong every moment with Dolores. Also, he was watching Dolores, who was getting dressed on the other side of the bed.

Finally they were done, and there was no more reason to linger. He slipped out through the side door through which he had entered.

Adams happily strolled through the quiet streets to his room. He was not surprised that Early was not there. He grinned, figuring that Early most likely was doing the same thing that he himself had been doing not long ago. He dropped his sketchbook and pencils on a table. He undressed quickly, folding his clothes neatly over a chair. Then he flopped into bed. He fell asleep quickly, thoughts of Dolores lingering in his mind.

Adams was still asleep when Early returned well past noon. The mountain man looked at the blissfully sleeping Adams a moment. Then he smiled and bellowed, "Hyar now, boy! Waugh! Get your ass up and movin'."

Adams's eyes popped open and his heart pounded. Thoughts of Dolores's angry father flooded his mind. Then he saw Early.

"Ye gonna lay there all the goddamn day, boy?" Early asked with a large, friendly grin.

"I suppose not," Adams grumbled. He sat up, rubbing the remainder of sleep from his eyes. "Where've you been all this time?"

With a grin, Early said, "Ye see, there was this purty leetle *señorita* who just couldn't resist this ol' hoss." He winked and began pulling off his fancy buckskins.

Adams grinned. "You been with her the whole time?"

"Well now, I expect I was. It don't set with this chil' to leave too soon durin' such doin's. Ye seemed to be doin' all right with the ladies yourself last night. Ye had a heap of 'em stickin' to ye like burrs to an apishamore."

Adams grinned again and looked at Early slyly. "That's true. It was delightful. Especially when me and—" He stopped, his face coloring pink.

"Why ye son of Satan," Early said, laughing. "Waugh! Stealin' away with one of them girls ye set your trap for with your fancy outfit and your sketchin' book. Ye ought to be ashamed of yourself, boy. Takin' advantage of them poor *señoritas* like that. No better'n a bull elk in the rut."

Adams's face was bright red now, but his smile beamed throughout the room. "You would've done the same yourself, were you in my position." He shrugged in humor. "I had no choice."

Early roared with laughter. "Mayhap I ought not to let ye out of my sight no more. Ye'll likely get your ass in big trouble with such doin's, boy."

"I'll take my chances," Adams laughed.

Early roared all the more. "Waugh! Ye sure made

'em come now. Goddamn if'n ye didn't." He paused. "Well now, seein's how ye had yourself such shinin' times, best get yourself dressed. I expect your meatbag's plumb empty. Ye'll be needin' to fill it, so's to build your strength back up." He winked again. "C'mon, boy, get movin'." He threw on his old, worn buckskins.

Adams hurriedly dressed in his finery—the only clothes he had—and the two men headed to the restaurant. Rawlins and Chardonnais were there, seated and waiting.

Early stalked up to the table and plopped into a chair. "Mornin', boys," he said cheerily. "Ye have a pleasurable evenin'?"

"Well now," Rawlins said in that slow, quiet way of his, "I sure as hell did. Don't know about ol' Lucien here, though."

"You should know not to doubt such a t'ing, eh," Chardonnais said, laughing. "I love de ladies. *Mais oui!* And dey love me!" He laughed.

"How about ye two?" Rawlins asked, chuckling.

"Well now," Early offered, "I done all right. But Bart here, well he was really shinin'. Waugh! Ye boys remember all them little *señoritas* was hangin' all over him over to Doña Montoya's?"

When the other two men nodded, Early continued, ignoring the angry look Adams shot at him, "Seems like one of 'em was fool enough to be caught in ol' Bart's trap."

"*Mais non!*" Chardonnais said in mock horror.

"He done that to some poor, brain-addled, upstandin' young lady? Actual took advantage of her?" Rawlins offered.

Early nodded in fake solemnness. "Damn, he purely did, boys. It's a sorry thing. I am plumb ashamed to have his acquaintance, I'm tellin' ye. I took him under my care, snatched him out from under the very noses of them murderous Comanches, and this is the way he pays me back. It ain't right, I'm sayin'. Goddamn no, it ain't."

The three mountain men broke into gales of laughter. Adams looked embarrassed for a few moments, ashamed of himself, then he realized they were only kidding him. He laughed, too, feeling a warm rush of camaraderie with these three tough men.

They ordered food and sat back to wait. In the silence, Early turned to Adams and asked, "What're ye fixin' to do to pass the day, boy?"

"I thought I'd make some more sketches," Adams said seriously. "Your idea of selling them was a good one, but all I've done is to give them away." The other three grinned, but he pressed doggedly on. "I don't have any clothes other than these fancy ones I'm wearing. I need new. Besides, if I can make some money, I can pay you back, then start paying my own way."

Early nodded. "Sounds like a right good idea to me, boy."

Their food came, and they ate quickly and quietly, more interested in the meal than in conversation. Adams found the hot beverage of milk and chocolate to be another in a long line of gustatory surprises since arriving in Taos. The Mexicans considered it a delicacy, and with one taste, Adams had to agree. As soon as he had finished his meal, he hurried out.

Watching him, Early said, "I expect he'll do all right." With a faraway look, he added, "There was times I wondered, though." He chuckled.

"Ye seem to be takin' a shine to that ol' hoss," Rawlins said flatly.

"I notice dat too, *mon ami*," Chardonnais said. "Why is dat?"

Early shrugged. "I don't rightly know," he said quietly. "Mayhap 'cause the damn fool's so goddamn useless."

"Shit, ye've seen a heap of others who was—"

"Leave him be, Abe," Chardonnais said. He had seen something in Early's eyes. He could not figure out what; he just knew his friend did not deserve to be questioned right now. " 'E 'as 'is reasons, I say, and we 'ave no business giving him trouble over dis."

"All right, Frenchie, goddammit," Rawlins growled. "Just seems a might queersome to me." He paused and sighed. He had the remarkable capability of putting aside things that would plague other folks. "What're ye plannin' for today, Ezra?" he asked.

Early shrugged. "Thought I might do some huntin'. Town's gettin' a mite close already. Ye interested?"

"That shines with this chil'."

"*Mais oui.*"

17

EARLY AND CHARDONNAIS WALKED to the stables and saddled the animals, while Rawlins went back to the boardinghouse to get their guns and other possibles. He was waiting when his two companions rode up with his horse and a pack mule in tow. They headed slowly north up the valley past the tiered pueblo, taking in the fresh warm air. Colorful flowers offered a friendly aroma, but they could smell autumn, too, in the wisp of a breeze.

"Fall's comin'," Early said. "We'd best start thinkin' of leavin' soon."

"*Oui*," Chardonnais agreed. "But we 'ave *beaucoup* time yet. Time for more 'umpin' wit' de *mademoiselles* dere in Taos, eh!"

Early laughed. "*Oui*, Lucien. There's always time for such doin's."

Chardonnais sighed sadly. "Alas, but dere is not enough time, dere nevair will be enough time, to 'ave all dem *mademoiselles* in Taos." He brightened as suddenly as he had gotten sad. "Oh, well, dere is always de fun in de trying, eh?" He laughed and his two companions joined in.

The raucous sounds sent birds flying in chattering annoyance from nearby trees. The men wound through patches of spruce and firs interspersed with spindly aspens. Though game abounded, they did not kill anything for a long time, preferring just to ride and enjoy the high country. They liked the solitude, the quiet, the grassy meadows amid the trees in the shadows of ragged peaks. Mostly they didn't want to make meat since once they did they would have to head back to town, and they were not looking forward to that just yet.

Around midday they pulled up in a grove alongside a creek that emptied into the Rio Grande not far away. They unsaddled the horses, built a small fire, and cooked up a mess of bacon and spiced beans, as well as a pot of coffee. They ate quickly and efficiently. After smoking a pipe, they lolled indolently as the heat of the summer day, the gentle breeze, and the buzzing of insects lulled them. Finally Rawlins said lazily, "That there water looks plumb refreshin'."

" 'Spect it does," Early agreed.

"*Oui.*" With that, Chardonnais stood and began shucking his clothes.

The other two quickly followed suit. Minutes later, they were all splashing around like children in the clear, cold water. They saw it not so much as a bath, as a swim. Still naked, they stretched out to let the warm air dry them, then fell asleep. As with eating, such men took advantage of whatever opportunity loomed.

Rawlins was the first to awaken a couple of hours later. He padded down to the stream and sunk his face in the water to revive himself. Scratching and yawning, he wandered back to the others and unceremoniously shouted, "Come on, ye lazy bastards. *Levé, leché lego.*"

Early and Chardonnais came awake instantly, hands reaching instinctively for weapons, until their brains told them what had woke them. As if one, the two charged Rawlins and tackled him. The three men tumbled in the grass, cursing good-naturedly. Early and Chardonnais managed finally to get a grip on Rawlins. They pinned him down momentarily, then shifted position. They rose, carrying Rawlins toward the water.

Swinging the bellowing mountain man in an arc, Early and Chardonnais suddenly released him, sending him flying out over the water. He landed with a loud splash and came up sputtering.

"Now I'm all goddamn wet agin," he roared.

"Tough shit," Early said gleefully. "Might teach ye to be more circumspect when ye rouse folks."

"I'll get the both of ye critters for this," Rawlins said with mock severity. "Waugh! That's for goddamn sure." He laughed as he waded out of the stream and up onto the grassy bank.

All three dressed quickly, tightened their saddles, and mounted. They moved away from the river, heading east a while before turning south toward Taos. A few minutes later they jumped a small herd of deer. Rawlins and Early fired while Chardonnais waited with loaded rifle, since Jicarillas often roamed this area. The two brought down a deer each, which they quickly skinned and butchered while Chardonnais kept a lookout. They loaded the hides and meat on the pack mule and pulled out again.

Half an hour later, they jumped a good-size cow elk. Chardonnais got the shot this time, and easily brought the animal down. Rawlins and Early stood watch as Chardonnais took the hide and meat and added them to the rest on the pack mule.

They gave the meat and hides to some needy families they knew could use them. Then they walked the animals to the livery and tended to them.

Adams was in their room when Early arrived. The easterner sat quietly near the window, writing earnestly in a notebook with a pen he kept dipping into a small jar of ink.

Early tossed his hat on his bed and then walked over to peer over Adams's shoulder. A moment later he backed off. He had no interest in writing. "Well, boy, how'd your drawin' go today?"

Adams finished scratching out a sentence, then looked up. "Very well," he said. "I sold seven of them. And for much more than they're worth." He rose and reached into a pocket of his short jacket. Extracting a few coins, he held them out to Early. "Here's most of what you've advanced me, Ezra. I am most thankful for your help—monetary and otherwise."

Early looked skeptically at him. "Ye sure ye got enough to last ye, boy?" he asked.

"Yes. I've made enough for a new set of clothes and to feed myself a few more days, I think. By then I should be able to sell more sketches."

Early nodded. He took the coins and dropped them

into a small pouch that he placed back into the belt possible sack. He grinned. "Ye best get movin' if'n ye want to get that new outfit in time for the *baile* tonight."

"What's that?"

"Spanish. Means a ball. I reckon this'll be some big doin's. It'll be in the plaza, and I expect near everybody in town'll show up. There'll be dancin' and food and singin', all kinds of doin's."

Adams brightened, thoughts of Dolores Ortega y Delgado pounding in his head. He had thought of her most of the day, hoping to see her again, but she had not come by his perch in the plaza, where he had taken up residence to make his sketches, and that worried him. But surely she would be at the ball tonight.

"I'd better hurry," he said, excitement creeping into his voice. "I'll be back soon." He grabbed his *sombrero* and hurried out. Adams realized when he hit the street that he had become quite comfortable about being in Taos.

Upstairs, Early smiled and pulled his Green River knife. With careful, easy strokes, he began honing it. When he was done, he did the same for his tomahawk. Then he looked to his two belt pistols and the heavy Dickert rifle, cleaning them with care. The mundane tasks helped keep him occupied enough to forestall thought.

He was almost finished when Adams rushed back into the room, bundles in hand. Early set the Dickert aside and wiped his hands on a clean cloth. Then he began stripping off his buckskins. "Best start fancifyin' yourself up, boy, if'n ye plan to leave for the ball with me. I ain't aimin' to sit and watch ye primpin' and preenin'." He started pulling on his fancy buckskin outfit.

Adams's clothes flew off and paper went sailing about the room as he tore open packages. Hurriedly he donned his new clothes. The outfit was of the same style as the one he had purchased the day before, but more elegant. The pants and jacket were of scarlet cloth, striped with silver thread. Buttons of real silver gleamed down the outside of each leg and down the front of the jacket. A bright red sash was held about his waist with a silver clasp. A new white shirt and an extra-wide *sombrero* that matched the pants and jacket completed the outfit, along with his old red ascot.

"Well now, if'n ye don't look just like a buck peacock flexin' his tail feathers, boy," Early said with a grin. "Ye settin' another trap for them unsuspectin' women again?"

"I sure hope so," Adams said stiffly, though there was a gleam in his eye and hope in his heart.

"Waugh! That get-up ought to do it for ye, then. I expect all them women'll think it plumb shines."

Grinning hugely, Adams said, "Shall we go?"

Early pulled out a comb made of porcupine quills and began running it through his hair. "I expect so," he said.

They walked down the hall and pounded on the door of their friends' room. Rawlins and Chardonnais, both dressed in their finery, came out.

"Jesus, would ye look at that," Rawlins said, pointing to Adams. "Ol' hoss there's sportin' more colors than a week of sunsets. Damn, boy, ye're brighter'n the sun at noon."

"Well," Adams said in mock offense, "better than

being some drab old fellow like you." His heart pounded with some fear. He had come to feel mostly comfortable around these three men, but one could never be sure with such people. They had short tempers at times, and it seemed that the oddest things set them off. He was suddenly afraid his statement would be one of those things.

But all Rawlins said was "Shit," drawing the word out. Then he grinned, turned, and led the way out of the adobe rooming house. They could hear the music while they joined the streams of people flowing toward the sounds in the plaza. A fiddler and three guitar players stood on a small stage off to one side of the plaza. Along the remaining sides were tables laden with beef, mutton, chicken, buffalo, deer, rabbit, partridge, turkey; seasoned stews; spicy beans; tortillas; tamales; fresh fruits, vegetables, and nuts; soups; sauces; Indian fry bread; cakes; pies; milk and coffee. On a more surreptitious table were bottles of whiskey and wine. Men and women dressed in bright, colorful garb, spun around the dusty plaza. The billowing skirts of the women made a dazzling swirl in the torch-lit plaza.

The four men filled plates with food and found benches to sit on while watching the dancers. Early, Rawlins, and Chardonnais made several trips to the food tables; Adams only one.

Adams had never seen the likes of this in New York—happy couples dancing with abandon, the women's skirts flying up, showing their calves. It was astounding to him. But by the time he had finished eating, the initial shock had worn off and he began looking anxiously for Dolores. He finally saw her being twirled around the plaza in the arms of a dashing Mexican soldier who was dressed nearly as gaudily as he was himself. A flash of anger crossed his face, but he forced it away. He would wait until the dance was over, then approach her.

He watched until the soldier gallantly escorted Dolores to a chair. An imposing-looking man, finely dressed, his hair and short beard gray, sat there, as did a plump older woman, two girls younger than Dolores, a handsome young man, and a boy. Dolores took her seat, breathing heavily and fanning herself as the soldier moved off.

Gulping back his fear, Adams approached and boldly asked, "May I have the next dance, *señorita?*"

"*Sí.*" She nodded. "Papá?"

The gray-beard glowered at Adams but then nodded. Dolores smiled dazzlingly at Adams and stood. As Adams walked her toward the dancing area, he asked, "Where have you been all day?"

"Getting ready for the *baile.*"

"I missed you."

Dolores looked at him strangely. She had missed him, too. She had found herself longing for him and thinking about him all day. She never expected, though, that he would feel the same about her.

The music started. Adams licked his lips. "I'd like to spend more time with you."

Dolores smiled again, her warmth heating him already. "You will," she promised. She suddenly turned sad. "But you can't have all my time here. I must dance with others."

Adams didn't like it, but he had to accept it.

18

THE *BAILE* WAS IN full swing before Adams finally had another dance with Dolores. The easterner had been fidgety the whole while, watching Dolores as she danced with others. Anger started to build. Then Early and Rawlins, who had been wandering around having themselves a high old time, drifted by and began chiding him for his mooning look.

With that, Adams grinned, the anger dissipating. "What the hell," he mumbled. He found Isabel, the girl he had first met at Doña Montoya's. Using the little Spanish he had learned from Dolores, he asked her to dance. Giggling, she accepted, and they joined the swirling couples in the plaza.

It became easier after that, as he asked other young women to dance. He seemed to be something of a favorite among the young ladies. Finally, though, he was in Dolores's arms again, dancing lightly, his heart soaring. As the song neared an end, Dolores said softly, "Meet me. Thirty minutes." Then she was gone, and he stood there flatfooted, heart pounding, dumbfounded.

The music started again, and Adams realized he was still standing there alone. He shook his head to rid himself of the cobwebs of confusion. Then he lurched off, asked a young woman to dance, and let himself be swept up in the melody. His feet moved and his body followed. The young woman smiled, but he was unaware of it. His whole mind was focused on Dolores and their meeting.

As soon as that dance ended, he courteously though distractedly led the young woman back to her seat. Then he slipped quietly through the throngs until he was out of the plaza. Breathing deeply of the warm night air to settle himself, he started walking down the street. Despite his desire to get there, he forced himself to slow down. It would not do to get there too early and be seen skulking around while waiting. Better to dawdle on the street a little and arrive a few moments later.

He was certain his pounding heart would be heard for blocks as he moved quietly toward the door. It swung open before he needed to knock. Once again, Dolores was waiting for him. Taking his trembling hand in her own, she led him through the dark passageways of the house.

Just before entering the small bedroom, Adams stopped at a sound. It took him a moment to realize it was the sound of someone else making love, not in this bedroom but not far away either.

"What—?" he started, whispering, but stopped when Dolores placed her soft fingers against his lips. "It's all right," she whispered.

"But . . ." he mumbled into her fingers.

"My friend. That's all." Then her mouth replaced her fingers, and he decided this was a good time to ignore those other sounds and his worries about them. It was obvious Dolores did not care; he shouldn't either.

Though this was no longer completely new to Adams and Dolores, there was still plenty of opportunity for exploration and discovery of each other. They took full advantage then, and twice more later.

In between, Adams found it a little disconcerting at the noises coming from the nearby room. He found it more disturbing when he realized that the other couple would be listening to him and Dolores when they were being intimate. He did not like that much at all, but the heat of renewed passions served to erase those worries, at least temporarily.

He found, somewhat to his surprise, that it was more difficult leaving Dolores this time than it had been before. As he walked slowly through the dark, quiet streets of Taos, he was sad. At the same time, he was happy, and whistled one of the joyful tunes he had heard at the ball. Halfway back to his room, he stopped, standing there shaking his head in worried amazement. He had realized with a burst of insight, mingled with desperation, that he loved Señorita Dolores Ortega y Delgado.

What the hell do I do now? he wondered as he began walking again. He had no answer for himself. Nor did one present itself over the next several days.

He did, though, speak with his friend about it the next day, after a hungover Ezra Early had had some food and a few jolts of whiskey to settle his stomach.

"Goddamn fool," Early muttered. "Set your goddamn traps for some purty young thing and instead, get your own miserable ass stuck in hers. Waugh! Ye is some now, boy."

"Lord, Ezra, don't stand there jabbering at me. Help me out." He was humorously plaintive.

"Damn, I don't know, boy. I ain't ary been caught up in such doin's myself. Let me think on it a bit once my head clears." Then he cackled with friendly nastiness as he left the restaurant.

Somewhat absentmindedly, Adams gathered his pencils and pad and headed toward the plaza, where he wandered around in the bright, warm sunshine. The air and exercise settled his mind some. After browsing through the shops and peddlers' carts, he found an open space, and managed to usurp a chair. He sat, leaned back, and began sketching vendors and passersby. Soon, people were stopping to watch. Eventually someone hauled out some pesos and bought a drawing. Then another.

It became a pleasurable life over the next several days. In the warm sunshine, he would sit for most of the day, sketching and selling his works. Dolores would drop by for a while, not getting too close, but hovering around, swelling Adams with pending excitement. Adams's evenings were spent at a restaurant and *cantina* with Early, Chardonnais, and Rawlins.

The nights—or at least part of the nights—were spent with Dolores. They would stroll through town or sit on the porch of her father's Taos house. He chafed during these outings, wanting only to be with Dolores alone, but knowing it was not possible. Such frustrations made those nights when he could be alone with her—in stolen moments in that dark, out-of-the-way friend's house—all the more exciting and fulfilling.

After five days, Adams realized he was completely, if not hopelessly, in love with Dolores. Yet he still was not sure what to do about it.

Early was a little more willing to discuss Adams's dilemma, but could offer no more help than before. Perhaps even less.

"I'd like to marry her, Ezra," Adams said. His face was pale and his voice wavered.

"I don't expect her ol' man'll allow such doin's, boy," Early said flatly. He had thought Adams was just infatuated with Dolores and would get over it soon. It seemed apparent, though, that such was not the case. Now he figured he would have to extricate Adams from this mess. Or, more reasonably, help Adams get himself out of it.

"But why?" Adams's agitation at his helplessness was growing.

"Heap of reasons," Early said, some harshness evident in his voice. "For one, ye ain't a Mexican citizen. For another, ye're a *vide-poches,* a goddamn empty-pocket *Americano.* I'd wager ye ain't Catholic neither."

"No, I'm not," Adams said almost defiantly. "I don't rightly know what I am, but it ain't Catholic."

"Ye ain't got a goddamn thing goin' for ye, boy. Her pa's gonna want her to marry a good, local boy. Mexican, and a Catholic, and if he really gets his way, somebody's worth some cash money."

"But I—"

"Goddammit, boy," Early snapped, "get it through that buffler-thick skull of yours that ye ain't got nothin' to say about none of this. Ye've taken your pleasure with that *señorita,* mayhap'll even do so again. But that'll likely be as far as ye'll get with such doin's. Enjoy it whilst ye can, boy. It'll be over soon, and ye both'll go on with your lives."

"No," Adams said fiercely. "I'll find a way, damn you."

"Best thing ye can do, boy," Early said just as savagely, "is get your ass out of town for a spell. Let ye forget all about this *señorita.*"

"No, I—"

"Ceran Saint Vrain's asked me, Abe, and Lucien to take a couple wagons down to Santa Fe. He's sold a couple wagonloads of goods to a feller down there who cain't spare no one to come up here for 'em."

"No, dammit, I'm not . . . " He paused and squinted at Early. "Can you take a package?"

"Nope. This chil' ain't no goddamn delivery boy. Ye got a package to take down there, ye do it your own goddamn self."

"But . . . " Adams paused, then nodded. "When're you leaving?"

"Tomorrow mornin'."

Adams nodded. "I'll be ready." He spun and hurried out the door. It was a fine, beautiful day, and he had many things to do. He did not like the idea of leaving Taos—and especially Dolores—but he had to get some articles and sketches back to his editor. If Early wouldn't take that package, Adams figured Chardonnais and Rawlins wouldn't take it either. Besides, he told himself silently, he wasn't all that sure he could trust any of the three mountain men to do with the package what was necessary to get it back to New York. Better that he handle it himself.

He took up his position and began sketching, but his mind wasn't on it. After a while, he put aside his pad and instead tried to write some of his impressions. He had not been as faithful as he should have been in recording things. But for the first time since he had become a reporter, he found it difficult to write. *How can I explain men like Ezra Early or Abe Rawlins or Lucien Chardonnais?* he wondered, gazing off into the bright blue sky. *Or how can I explain a woman like Dolores Ortega y Delgado or any of the other earthy señoritas here in this strange, almost magical place?*

That train of thought was broken when a shadow crossed his face. Adams blinked a few times and then smiled at Dolores. She returned it. During a moment when no one was near, Adams said, "I have to talk with you. Tonight. Alone."

Dolores looked panicky. Adams saw it and said, "It's important, but you shouldn't worry." *I'm the one who has to worry,* he thought.

They met in the usual place. After making love, almost desperately, Dolores asked quietly, "What did you want to talk to me about?"

Adams paused, not knowing where to start. When he did, he sputtered, "I . . . I . . ."

Dolores touched a slim index finger against his lips. "I feel the same." She was desperately afraid that she was reading Adams wrong. She was sure he loved her; and she returned that feeling. She wanted him to say it but sensed that he couldn't. At least not yet. Still, a kernel of doubt was there.

"You do?" He was hoping beyond hope that she was thinking the same thing he was.

"*Sí.*" She held her breath, the fear growing again.

"We have to think of what to do," Adams offered softly.

"Yes." She was at a loss. She loved Hobart Adams; and now she was sure he loved her. She also knew that her father would never allow a union between her and this poor American.

"But I don't know what."

"Nor I."

He lay quietly, happy to have Dolores in his arms. Still, the subject must be broached. "I have to go away for a little," he finally whispered.

"What?" Dolores was shocked. They had just spoken of their love for each other, though the word had not been mentioned. And they had talked about having to figure out their future. Now he was going away.

"Just a couple of days," Adams said hastily. "To Santa Fe. I'm accompanying my friends, who are taking a few wagons down there for a Mister Saint Vrain. I need to send some articles and sketchings to my editor in New York. I want to make sure it gets with the right person—a trustworthy person—on one of the wagon trains heading east."

"You'll be back?" she asked skeptically, almost sick with worry and feelings of rejection.

"Just as soon as I can." His enthusiasm was infectious.

Dolores embraced him. "Hurry back," she whispered.

19

SANTA FE WAS NEARLY a carbon copy of Taos. Adams thought it might be a little larger than Taos; or maybe it was just the long portico of the misnamed Palace of the Governors that made it seem that way. That and the bustle. Otherwise it was the same—the same low, flat-roofed buildings; the same *señoritas* strolling by, *rebozos* around heads and shoulders, *cigarrillos* dangling from full lips; the same vendors and their *carretas;* the same swaggering soldiers in worn uniforms; the same sharply dressed men with practiced nonchalance; ragged laborers and teamsters in torn, soiled clothing; Indians; a smattering of *Americanos.*

Early and his two old companions seemed to know half the people and spent a considerable amount of time exchanging greetings with people who passed by on the dirt streets.

It had taken them five days to get from Taos to Santa Fe, since they were in no real hurry. The trip had been quite interesting, like everything else Adams had seen since leaving Independence. They roughly followed the course of the Rio Grande southwestward, away from the blocked, rugged humps of the Sangre de Cristos.

A day later they headed southeast, back toward the Sangre de Cristos and Santa Fe. As they had since leaving Taos, Early and Adams rode in one medium-sized overloaded wagon that had a seat added. Rawlins and Chardonnais rode in a similar wagon. Both wagons were pulled by a team of large mules and the men's saddled horses were tied behind.

They crossed large, grassy meadows spotted with willows, cottonwoods, and pines. They camped in a stand of live oaks and yellow pine. Among the trees were wild rose, chokecherry, rabbitbrush, and white sage. The mules and horses ate well on the thick, rich blue grass. Chardonnais brought down an elk, so the men ate well also.

The next day and night were much the same, the countryside changing little as they plodded along. At one point, Early stopped his wagon. Wrapping the reins around the brake handle, he hopped down and prowled about both sides of the faint trail.

"What is it?" Adams asked, interested as well as worried.

"Injin sign." He paused. "Apache."

"How many?" Rawlins asked.

"A dozen or thereabout."

" 'Ow old?" Chardonnais asked. He sounded unconcerned.

Early was already climbing back onto his wagon.

"Couple days," he called back. "They were headin' northeast."

They all pressed on, unworried, except for Adams. As they rode, Early, sensing Adams's discomfort, said, "It ain't likely they'll double back down this way, so it ain't worrisome."

Adams nodded, trying to calm himself.

There was no trouble, and just after noon the next day they rode into Santa Fe. They creaked straight to Antoine LeBeau's store, through the wood gate in the adobe fence out back, and into the yard.

LeBeau himself came out of the store as the four newcomers climbed down from the wagons. He was a short, stocky, hard-visaged man, with a thick beard. *"Bonjour, bonjour, mes amis,"* he said with a joviality that belied his harsh exterior.

Being something of a fellow Frenchman, even though one of a far inferior class, Chardonnais grinned and greeted LeBeau in French. The two men embraced briefly and whisked a kiss near each other's cheeks.

"Jesus, Abe," Early said with a chuckle, leaning on his rifle, "another minute and they'll be humpin' each other here in the dirt!"

Both Americans always felt uncomfortable in the presence of such displays. They settled for a friendly, "How's doin's, ol' hoss?" and a handshake when the two Frenchmen had completed their greeting.

"Did you 'ave any trouble, *monsieurs?*" LeBeau asked.

"Nope," Rawlins said. "Saw a little sign, but it were old."

"Bon. Who iz zis?" He pointed to Adams.

"Hobart Adams," Early said. "He come out here all

the way from New York just to write tales and draw pictures of the folks hereabouts."

LeBeau grunted a greeting and shook Adams's hand. Then he dismissed the easterner. "Let's get zese wagons unloaded," he said.

"I aim to fill my meatbag fust," Early growled. "And see that the horses're took care of."

"'Sides," Rawlins added, "we ain't gettin' paid for unloadin' no goddamn wagons for ye, Antoine. Ceran just said to haul them damned wagons down here. We done that."

LeBeau's face colored in anger. He was a feisty man and had been in the mountains as long as these three and had become a well-off, well-respected businessman. He was not used to being spoken to in such a way. "I suppose you'll want more money for ze work?" he asked harshly.

"Dat wouldn't change our minds, *mon ami,*" Chardonnais said. His face was as hard as an outcropping of the Sangre de Cristos. LeBeau might be a fellow Frenchman, but they were not brothers.

LeBeau glared. "I am not pleased with zis," he barked.

"Don't mean shit to me, Antoine," Early said evenly. "Ye don't hold no sway over this chil'. Nor my *amigos* neither, I expect. We're all free trappers, goddammit, as ye well know, not no goddamn ass-kissin' laborers. We brung these wagons down here as a favor to Ceran, not to hire on to ye."

LeBeau glowered for a few more moments, before spinning on his boot heel and stomping back into the store. He shouted a stream of smoking French and Spanish as he did.

Rawlins grinned and let a little laugh escape. "Waugh! Made that chil' come, now, didn't we?"

The others agreed. They turned and headed for their horses. Climbing aboard, they rode out of the yard as half a dozen Mexicans came out of the store and began unloading the wagons. They rode to a livery stable and turned their horses over. Then they headed to a restaurant. They ate heartily of *tamales,* goat's milk cheese, and *atole.* While doing so, they flirted with the Mexican girl who was serving them.

She flushed and blushed, but gave back as good as she got, all in all. As they paid her and rose to leave, she said coyly, "And will I see you *señors* at the *baile* tonight?"

"We'll be there, *señorita,*" Rawlins promised. "Where?"

"The plaza."

The four Anglos nodded and left. "Best find us a place for the night," Early said eagerly. "If they're havin' a doin's, this chil' plans to take part, and I ain't leavin' out in the middle of the night." He laughed. "Not when I aim to be spendin' my time with some willin' *señorita.*"

They found rooms and headed to LeBeau's store. He might be an obnoxious man at times, but he had the best goods and prices. They had brought nothing with them but the clothes they wore—their working outfits—and their weapons. Now they had to buy some fancy duds.

LeBeau looked at them coldly when they walked in, but his edges began to soften minutely when he realized they were there to make some purchases. When they had gotten all they needed and laid the things on the counter, Early said, "Waugh! Ye're a sour-face ol' fart, ain't ye, Antoine?"

The stern visage cracked.

"Looks like the ol' critter ate hisself a lemon," Rawlins agreed.

"You know wha' I t'ink?" Chardonnais said. "I t'ink he ain't 'ad a shit in a couple days. Maybe a week. Is dat it, *mon ami,* eh? Your bowels are so impacted you 'ave become dis foul-tempered old beavair, eh?"

Early, Rawlins, and Chardonnais were stifling chuckles, while Adams watched interestedly.

LeBeau finally grinned. "You try ze patience of a saint," he said.

"Shit, ye're a far sight from bein' a saint, ye ol' buffler fart," Early said with a laugh.

"Bah. You are buying zese t'ings for ze *baile?*"

"Goddamn right," Rawlins said with a firm nod. "Some purty leetle *señorita* invited us personal. We can't go disappointin' her now, can we?"

"*Mais non!*" LeBeau laughed. "It should be a grand ball, too. Zere will be fireworks and all zem doings."

"Ye gonna be there?" Early asked. He liked LeBeau mostly. The Frenchman was often crotchety, stubborn, and hard-headed, but any good man was, as far Early was concerned. He did not hold that against LeBeau.

"*Mais oui!*" For the first time since Adams had met LeBeau, animation moved the Frenchman's face.

"I expect we'll see ye there, then."

"*Oui.*"

The four men paid for their clothes, took their bundles, and walked out into the sunshine.

"What now?" Adams asked, excitement beginning to bubble in his innards. He didn't know why he was so eager for this ball. He did not expect it to be much different from the ones he had attended in Taos. But he was excited, and he tried just to accept it.

"Well, this chil' aims to get some shuteye," Early said with a lecherous grin. "I don't aim to get me too much sleep tonight. I aim to find me some willin' *señorita* and get me some robe time with her."

"Jus' don't get in my way, *mon ami*," Chardonnais said with a friendly growl. "Or you'll get trampled by dis bull."

"I ain't so worried about gettin' trampled by ye, boy," Early said, laughing. "I'm only worried that ye won't be able to trample me and in the confusion ye mayhap might mistake me for some female."

"*Mais non!*" Chardonnais said in mock offense. "I would not do dat. No, no, no."

"Shit. Ye let your pecker run ye half the time. And when ye do that, ye don't think. Ye'll hump anything gets in your path."

"You are jus' jealous of me because I am *le grand homme*," Chardonnais said with something approaching dignity. Then he burst into laughter, joining his two longtime friends.

The four men were quite a spectacle in their finery as they stepped out of their adobe rooming house and into the street. People were heading by the dozens, it seemed, toward the large plaza. Violin and guitar music drifted over them.

Adams found the excitement growing again as he and his companions joined the throngs. There seemed to be something more interesting in the air this night than there had been at the *baile* in Taos. It seemed to infect even the three hardened mountain men.

The dancing had begun by the time the four reached the plaza. Within minutes, Early, Rawlins, and Chardonnais had joined in, grabbing any available woman.

Adams was more reserved, partly because he felt out of place. There was Dolores to consider, even though she was in Taos. He was not comfortable with the possibility of any kind of intimacy with another woman, not when he had so recently proclaimed his love for Dolores. He wondered how Early and his two partners could so easily go off with a woman, or a series of women, when they had wives waiting for them, even if their wives were Indian. Adams figured that such men married such women solely for convenience rather than for love. Still, it seemed strange to him.

After a few minutes, though, he decided that dancing would hurt nothing, and Dolores would expect him to do that. He presented himself to an attractive young woman. He enjoyed the dance, and when it was over, he politely escorted the girl back to her seat. He turned, and spotted a familiar figure across the plaza.

"Parfrey!" he muttered through teeth suddenly clenched in rage.

He started off across the plaza, but was stopped by the whirling circle of dancers. He stood, fuming, as the revelers went by. Finally there was a break and Adams darted into the midst of the crowd.

20

"WHAT'N HELL'S GOT INTO ol' Bart?" Rawlins asked Early, pointing to Adams. "He was just standin' there, lookin' all angry, then took off like a bee-stung cat."

Early watched a moment. "That hoss looks like he's blackened his face agin somebody. I expect I'll just mosey on over there and see if'n I can keep him out of trouble. He pisses on this here *fandango,* and the governor'll have his balls."

Rawlins nodded. "I'll see if'n I can round up Lucien. Trouble comes, we'll need all the help we can get."

Early just stalked off, making his way nimbly through the dancing Santa Feans. He was only a few feet away when Adams grabbed a dirty-looking American by the back of the shirt and yanked him around.

"You bastard," Adams yelled at the man.

Early picked up speed for the last several feet and slammed to a stop. He grabbed Adams and pulled him away from the other man. "Whoa, there, ol' hoss," he said softly. "Ye don't need to go causin' no trouble here, boy."

Adams struggled against Early's powerful grip. "That's the son of a bitch who left me to die," Adams raged, face twisted with hate.

The other man look levelly at Adams and said evenly, "I ain't ever seen you afore, mister." He looked at Early. "I got no idear what this feller's talkin' about."

"You lying, murdering son of a bitch," Adams bellowed.

"I tol' ye to settle down, boy," Early said harshly. He was aware that others were beginning to watch what was going on. He also suspected more than saw that soldiers were heading in their direction.

"But—"

"But buffler shit," Early hissed. "Ye start trouble here and them *soldados*'re gonna kick the shit out of ye and then toss your ass into the *calabozo*. Then they'll forget you're there."

Adams reluctantly settled down.

"Now, ye sure this here's the critter what tried to put ye under?"

"Of course I'm sure. His name's Ebenezer Parfrey. He raped and then butchered that poor Indian girl, then left me out there in that wasteland to die." He paused a moment. "Stole all my things, too. Where are they?" The last was directed at Parfrey.

Parfrey looked at Early and shrugged. "I don't know

where this feller's got his thinkin' from, but he's got me mistook for someone else. My name's Rafe. Rafe Stockover." He sounded quite convincing.

"You lying—" Adams started, but Early clamped a callused hand over his mouth.

Parfrey's sallow face turned mean. He looked at Early. "Now, I've told you both I don't know this feller from the governor's sister, and I've took about all the insults from him that I aim to take. He opens his mouth agin, I'll gut him."

"Ye hear that, boy?" Early said more than asked. "I reckon he means it, too. Now shut your trap."

Adams nodded, and Early removed his hand. Early stepped forward a little, inserting himself just between Adams and Parfrey. He spit some tobacco juice in the dirt, barely missing Parfrey's foot. "My *amigo* here ain't given over to lyin'," he said flatly.

Rage crackled across Parfrey's face a few moments before he got himself under control. Then the malevolence dropped, replaced by a tight smile as Parfrey endeavored to look friendly. He was of no mind to tangle with a mountain man, especially one as big as Early. "Well, I didn't 'zactly say he was lyin', now did I? No, 'course not. I just said he was mistakin' me for some other feller. A common mistake, I reckon."

"Ye mayhap are right, ol' hoss," Early said easily, but his eyes narrowed in warning. Parfrey noted it. Early turned. "Let's go, *amigo,*" he said to Adams. "There's a *fandango* waitin'." He gave Adams a shove.

He was not sure. He had come to know Adams well in the past few weeks. It was possible Adams was mistaken, but Early didn't think so. Adams was not a man to act as he did without good reason. As they walked away, Early heard a voice behind him ask, "Who was that, Eb?"

Early also heard the reply. "That damned pencil-scratchin' greenhorn sonna bitch we left on the trail. I figured he was done for."

Early stopped and looked back. Parfrey saw him and stood there glaring defiantly. Early spit tobacco juice in his direction. Then he turned and hurried after Adams.

"It was him. I know it was him, Ezra. No matter what he said," Adams offered when Early caught up.

Early stopped Adams and pulled him around so they were face-to-face. "I know ye was right, boy. But this ain't the time nor place for raisin' hair. Ye just keep away from him tonight. We'll figure out what to do with that murderous bastard tomorrow."

"But he might leave."

"He ain't goin' nowhere, boy." Early shrugged. "Even if'n he does, we could catch him without much trouble."

Adams nodded and drew himself up in determination. "This isn't your affair, Ezra. I'm grateful for all the help you and your friends have given me, and I appreciate your offer to help now. But it's not your concern."

Early shrugged. "If'n that's where your stick floats, so be it. But ye best be careful. Ye ain't used to his kind. He'll carve ye up, or backshoot ye. And he'll do it without a second thought."

"I'm not afraid of him, Ezra. He's a coward."

"Cowards can be dangerous, boy, and don't ye doubt it. Ye seen what he's done. He's as likely to treat ye as poorly as he did that Comanche girl."

Adams grimaced at the thought of the mutilated

young woman—or what was left of her—lying in the dirt. "Maybe you're right, Ezra." He was suddenly cold with fear. Any man who could do that with no conscience would think nothing of killing him. "But I can't let him get away with this. I have to fight him."

"Ye aim to do that, ye best learn some things fust. For one thing, ye just don't go up to some son of a bitch like that and grab him. Ye're lucky ye're at a *fandango*. Ye had tried that on him somewhere else, ye'd've been put under already."

"I'll remember that," Adams said through a suddenly dry mouth.

They continued walking, Rawlins and Chardonnais falling into step beside them. They stopped at the tables laden with food. The three mountain men began loading tin plates, while Early explained briefly what was going on. They happily stuffed their faces.

Adams stood fuming. He desperately wanted to do something, but knew it was hopeless and useless against a man like Ebenezer Parfrey. Especially if Parfrey had any of his cronies with him.

Early kept an eye on Adams as he ate, wanting to make sure the easterner did nothing foolish. He wondered, too, why he was so concerned about Adams. He came to no conclusion, and so cast off the thought. Finally, though, Early had the urge to dance. He had been making easy progress with a young lady and wanted to get back to her before she offered her attentions elsewhere.

"Ye ought to go find yourself some *señorita* and set to dancin', boy," Early said. "It'll make ye feel a heap better."

"No," Adams responded flatly.

"Suit yourself. But I ain't aimin' to set here all night watchin' over ye to make sure ye don't go get yourself killed. Not when there's a passel of purty young *señoritas* settin' there just a waitin' for this ol' chil'."

He grinned, but it had no effect on Adams. He shrugged. "Just don't go causin' no trouble, boy. I aim to have me a shinin' goddamn spree. And such doin's don't include savin' your ass from your own goddamn foolishment. Ye understand me, boy?"

Adams ignored him, staring fixedly ahead.

Early shrugged again. He, Rawlins, and Chardonnais went off, happily looking to their own entertainment.

Adams stood for a few minutes, feeling the rage seethe hotly inside him. It was almost a living thing, growing and nurturing on the hate in him. He had never before experienced this depth of anger, and it surprised and worried him. He sighed. The ball no longer held interest for him, but he did not know what else to do. So he remained standing there, furious.

Gradually even that began to subside a little, and he could think more clearly. The rage was based on fear, he realized. Men like Ebenezer Parfrey frightened him. Such men found it so easy to kill someone, especially those who were not as strong or adept as they. Like the Comanche girl. Or himself, for that matter. Through deceit, malevolence, and intimidation, they bullied their way through the world. It was this that so filled him with hatred. More than the rape and butchering of the Comanche girl. More than the knock on his head or the leaving him out there in that hellish wilderness to die. More than the theft of all his papers and belongings.

His fury finally dimmed to a dull ache that sat inside his stomach like a piece of rancid meat. Still, he was in no mood for the joviality of the ball that flashed around him. He was tired, though, and decided it was a good time for him to head back to his room.

He turned and began threading his way through the people on the fringes of the dancing area. He suddenly wished he was back in Taos. Were that the case, Dolores would be around to help soothe him. Her support and loving comfort, however, might make him feel all the worse, he realized. He most likely would see himself as less than a man and would be afraid that she, too, would see him that way. He shuddered at the possibility.

So distracted by his mental ramblings was he that he bumped into someone. "Sorry," he started to mumble, focusing his eyes. He gulped.

"You should've died out there on the Cimarron, boy," Parfrey hissed. His face was a sneering mask of hatred and disgust. He felt better now that Adams was alone, and he was backed by George Court and Alf McHugh.

Adams felt like he had to make water in his pants. His mouth was dry and his hands damp with a sudden fear-sweat. He licked his lips, trying several times to say something before the words came. "You'll pay for what you did, Parfrey," he finally managed to say.

"I'm all a-tremble," Parfrey said scornfully. "How 'bout you, boys?"

Court and McHugh both allowed as how they were petrified.

"Legally, or otherwise," Adams said tightly, "you'll pay."

"Buffler shit." Parfrey had his thumbs hooked in the ratty sash that served him as a belt. He rocked back on the heels of his worn work boots. "Your sonna bitchin' mountaineer friend ain't here to help ya now, you peckerless bag of shit."

Adams wouldn't have thought it possible to feel more fear than he had moments before, but he did. It was as if his limbs were made of stone, and his stomach had congealed into a solid ball of ice. He found he could not move. He watched, almost in fascination, as Parfrey slid out a large knife and ran his thumb along the side of the blade, near the edge.

"You do remember that Comanche bitch, don't ya, boy?" Parfrey asked with a sneer. "I ain't ary done the same to a man." He laughed harshly, his voice rattling in his throat. "Might still not've even after I've done you, since it still ain't been shown you're a man."

Adams's testes tried to shrink up inside his body. It was all he could do to keep from shivering with terror.

Early's eyes lowered in anger. Though the song was not done, he led his young partner back to her seat. She protested some, but he was of no mind to explain anything to her. On the way he grabbed Rawlins, who had been whirling in wild abandon. "Find Lucien," he said urgently. *"Pronto."*

Rawlins did not argue. He simply headed for the sidelines, where he deposited his evening's potential paramour. Then he moved off, looking for the wild, lady-loving French Canadian.

Early had spotted Adams heading off. When he had made one more spin around the plaza, he had caught sight of Parfrey moving toward Adams, ready to intercept the easterner. By the time Early had left his dancing partner, Parfrey had slid out his knife. Early picked up his pace.

21

ADAMS WAS STILL STANDING there like a stone, watching in fascination as the knife moved slowly toward him. The blade glittered in the smoky yellow light of the lanterns. His legs were rooted to the ground. He thought it odd, though, that he suddenly felt no fear. It was there certainly, he just didn't really feel it.

Another oddity, he thought, was the slowness with which everything and everyone moved. Though he knew in his brain that things were proceeding at normal speed, it all seemed so slow. He could see every glint of light on the blade, almost count each and every whisker on Parfrey's sickeningly grinning face.

Sounds, too, were warped and distorted. The music droned on in some otherworldly pattern that sounded unlike anything he had ever heard. Parfrey's laughter and that of his companions came as if through yards and yards of thick cloth.

Another sound came, seemingly from far away. He sort of recognized what had made it, but Adams could not place it.

Early put on another burst of speed. He watched as Adams stood like a statue, with Parfrey's blade arcing toward him. With a bellow, Early launched himself. He slammed into Parfrey's side, knocking him sprawling.

As Early bounced atop the flattened Parfrey, he jerked an elbow forward. It cracked against Parfrey's forehead, splitting open the skin over the left eyebrow. Blood flowed.

Someone kicked Early in the side. It lifted him off Parfrey and rolled him several times. Enraged, Early scrambled up. A hard fist slammed against the side of his head. The blow was accompanied by a muttered oath in Spanish.

Early staggered back and to the side, knocking into a table and a soldier there. The soldier shoved him forward hard. He used the momentum to slam headfirst into the chest of the other soldier—the one who had hit him. That man had been coming at him again, smiling arrogantly. The smile exploded off his lips as Early plowed into him. Both men went down.

"Son of a bitch," Early muttered as he tried to rise. He made it as far as a squat when he noticed that the soldier also was making substantial progress toward getting up. Early punched him in the face, his hard

knuckles breaking the soldier's nose and bringing forth
a spurt of blood.

Early partly saw a boot flying toward his head from
the left side. He managed to twist himself a little. The
movement deflected most of the kick's power, but he
still caught a portion of it. The boot slid across his jaw,
but as it did, he half turned and lashed out with his left
elbow. It caught the kicker just above the back of the
knee, bringing a sudden shout of pain as the nerve
endings in the man's hamstring bruised and short-
circuited. That soldier went down, bouncing hard on
his buttocks. He grunted as he fell toward the side,
clutching his damaged leg.

Early got to his feet, blood lust in his eyes. The soldier he had hit was up, too, and moving warily toward
him, trying to draw his sword.

"Ye pull that pig sticker on me, ye bean-fartin' son
of a bitch and I'll shove it up your ass so far you can
use the tip for a hat rack."

The soldier growled an epithet low in his throat and
spit. With a wicked grin, the soldier continued to draw
his sword, slowly, almost enticingly. He never finished.

Early kicked the soldier in the stomach. As the
Mexican doubled over, Early rammed a forearm
against the soldier's forehead. The man's head
snapped back and Early grabbed his throat in two
strong hands. He squeezed, and within a few seconds,
he cast the soldier's lifeless body aside.

He straightened and swung to the right, eyes wild
with a desire to kill again. Two Mexican soldiers—the
one Early had fought with earlier and the one into
whom Early crashed—hit him, high and low. They
went down in a jumble of arms and legs.

They crashed to the ground, biting, kicking, gouging. Within moments, Early's fancy new buckskins and the soldiers' sharp uniforms were speckled with dust, sweat, and blood.

In a moment when everything seemed to stop for a heartbeat, the three pulled apart and stood, eyeing each other. The two Mexicans were breathing heavily, but Early's large, lean body seemed none the worse for his activity.

Early was unaware of the crowd that had gathered, and of the music that was no longer playing. He was focused on nothing but the two men facing him. He hated them with a raw intensity. It was inexplicable to him as to why on rare occasions, for what seemed like no particular reason, he felt such a flare-up of such loathing for another man; it just happened, and there was no bridling it. Like now. He didn't really hate these men. They had not done anything to him to warrant such a depth of feeling. Yet here he was, blood lust in his veins.

Without warning, Early leapt at one of the soldiers—someone had called him Luis. The Mexican swung at Early, but the mountain man blocked the punch. Early head-butted Luis, stunning the soldier.

As Early moved in for the kill, the other soldier slipped up behind him and with both hands locked together, he hammered Early on the back of the neck. Early's grunt exploded in a sharp gust, and he sank to his knees.

Luis swooped in and joined the other in raining blows on Early's head. The mountain man surged up like a wounded grizzly.

"Greasy sons of bitches!" he roared. "Waugh! This hoss'll show ye."

Early snapped an elbow back at the soldier behind him. The blow caught the soldier in the face, and he staggered back.

Ignoring that soldier, Early then grabbed Luis's tunic and then kneed him in the stomach. The soldier folded in half. As he did, Early snapped his knee up, cracking the soldier's face. Blood spurted from Luis's battered nose and mashed mouth over Early's buckskin pants. A tooth fell in the dust.

Early whirled, eyes flaming, and smashed his forehead into the other soldier's nose. It, too, burst in a shower of blood and mucus. As the soldier stood, eyes fluttering as he fought to retain consciousness, Early ripped out his Green River knife and plunged it into the soldier's breast.

"Waugh!" Early growled as the blade melted through organ flesh. "See how them doin's set ye, goddammit."

He jerked the knife free as the light died in the soldier's eyes. The body fell against him before flopping to the dirt of the plaza. Early spun, eyes but narrow slits of rage. He stalked Luis, who seemed unable to move, except for his mouth. His lips flapped open, giving him the look of a freshly hooked fish.

Before he could get more than two steps toward Luis, a violent pain exploded in the back of Early's head. As he went down, he caught a glimpse of Sergeant Pedro Chacón holding a pistol by the barrel, like a hammer.

"Take that, señor," Chacón said with an oily, humorless smile.

Early tried to push himself up but slumped down. As the blackness crept over him, he wondered where

Chardonnais and Rawlins were. He had always been able to count on them. Besides, they were not the kind of men to pass up a good fight, especially if it meant kicking the stuffing out of some Mexican soldiers. He worried that his two friends might have been hurt. Elsewise, he knew, they would have come to his assistance. His last thought, though, was of Adams. He hoped the easterner was all right.

Adams finally found himself capable of movement, but only after a maniacal Ezra Early had hit Parfrey. He didn't know for sure what he was doing. He only knew that Early's leap had snapped him out of his trance.

Adams acted without thought. One moment he was standing there, the next, Early and Parfrey were in the dust, and Adams was aware of his right foot flashing out. He kicked Court in the groin. Court doubled up, his breathing whistling quick through his gapped teeth.

Before Adams could follow up his attack, Alf McHugh knocked him ass over teakettle. Adams landed and rolled a few times. When he came to a stop, his head was ringing. He sat up woozily, shaking his head. It did little good. The world dipped and wove before his eyes.

Then he felt powerful hands dragging him up. He looked with dazed eyes into McHugh's bloodshot orbs, and he smelled the man's foul breath and body odor. There was little he could do, though, to prevent McHugh from doing whatever he wanted to him.

"What you done to George ain't nice, sonny," McHugh snarled. He was angry, but the prospect of pounding the living hell out of a fancified fellow like Hobart Adams pleased him to no end.

With his left hand, he held Adams up at arm's length. With his right, he pounded Adams three times, twice in the face, and one staggering blow to the abdomen. Adams's knees buckled; only McHugh's grip kept him up.

McHugh laughed and let Adams fall. He turned and walked back to Court and Parfrey. Court was standing bent over, sucking in breath. His face was etched with anger and pain as he looked up at McHugh.

"I'm gonna kill that sumbitch," Court said tightly.

"He's over there now jus' a waitin' for ya," McHugh said in agreement. "I softened him up just a bit for ya."

"Weren't necessary."

"I know." McHugh grinned. "I just wanted to."

Court nodded and straightened all the way. They were oblivious to Early's fight with the soldiers going on not far away. Court drew in one more breath to settle himself. His testes felt like they were on fire, and they seemed to be swelling. He wasn't sure he could walk, but he could not let Adams get away with such a thing. He took a step, gingerly, toward where Adams lay. Then another step. It wasn't as bad as he had feared. But it wasn't easy either.

"No," Parfrey said, grabbing Court's arm.

Court looked at Parfrey in surprise. "What the hell do you mean, no?" he asked in anger. "I'ma kill that bastard."

"Not here; not now," Parfrey said evenly.

"Bullshit. I—"

"The soldiers, you dumb bastard." He pointed.

Soldiers were pouring into the plaza. Two hauled Adams up by the arms and were dragging him off.

Court looked again. Early was stabbing a soldier. Another soldier lay dead in the dirt not far from the wild mountain man. Court turned his gaze to Parfrey. "I'ma get that sumbitch Adams."

"I got no problem with that. He'll have to get back East sooner or later, which means he'll be takin' the trail."

" 'Less he's ridin' with that crazy bastard over there," McHugh said, pointing to Early, who was still battling. "Him and his two goddamn friends."

"Them boys don't scare me none. Hell, you hadn't of kicked him off me before, I would've stomped his ass. But no, them goddamn soldiers had to stick their noses in where they weren't wanted. Shit, me and you and George would've took care of him, his two goddamn friends, and that fancified sonna bitch."

Court nodded at Parfrey. He allowed Parfrey to take him under one arm, and McHugh under the other. He was not fond of getting help, but there was little he could do about it right now. And, truth to tell, he was grateful he didn't have to put all his weight on his feet and legs. His groin throbbed like nothing he had ever experienced before. He vowed that someone would pay for the pain.

The three shuffled out of the plaza, hoping the soldiers would not stop them for some reason. Parfrey figured that once they were clear of the plaza, they would be safe from arrest. Parfrey did not want to get tossed in the *calabozo* and have to explain why Early had attacked him.

22

EARLY AWOKE IN A foul, dank-smelling place. At least he thought he awoke, since he was loathe to open his eyes. The pain in his head was intense; and he did not want to aggravate it any by raising his lids. He wasn't overly fond of moving, either, including such necessary actions as breathing, since that sent throbbing pulses of pain slamming through his head. He settled for lying as still as he could, breathing shallowly, trying to will the agony away.

Early realized he was on some kind of hard cot, and he wondered where it was. Then he decided that for the moment he really didn't care. Also of little importance right now was not knowing how long he had been here—wherever here was—since the fight or how long he had been awake.

One thing he did know, though he was reluctant to dwell on it, was that he could not lie here forever. The pain would go away eventually. He had been in pain before, like that time he had taken a couple of Blackfoot arrows in the chest, back when Ethan went under. That had been painful. He would have sworn he also was going to go under that time. But he had survived. He figured he would live through this, too.

He almost grinned at the sudden thought that he was not sure he liked the idea of surviving, considering the pounding that rose up from the top of his spine and splashed across his cranium.

Early sucked in a deep breath, trying to settle the pain as best he could. He opened his eyes. The dimness was a pleasant surprise, and he continued to lie there a bit longer, enjoying the soft dullness. He realized that he was in a dank cell in the *calabozo*.

At last, though, he knew he had to get up. He managed to swing his feet around and put them on the floor, while pushing himself up to a sitting position. He puffed his cheeks and blew out the chestful of air he had been holding in. It helped. He hung his head in his hands, breathing noisily.

"Waugh!" he finally groaned. "Ye sure done it this time, ol' hoss."

"You all right, Ezra?"

Early's head snapped up, sending another burst of pain through it. He stared across the dark, fetid cell at Hobart Adams. "Jesus goddamn Christ, boy," he muttered, shaking his head several times before resettling it in his hands. Again the head came up. "I expect we're in the *calabozo*?" he asked.

Adams nodded. He looked sick with worry and fear.

"We're in a heap of shit here, boy. Ye know that, don't ye?"

"I'm not a fool, Ezra," Adams said with as much dignity as he could dredge up from his disheartened soul.

"I expect ye ain't, boy," Early said flatly. He was a little angry thinking about the fight. Had Adams done his part then, the two of them might not be in this predicament now.

Adams paced slowly around the small room. "I know I haven't acquitted myself all that well by your lights, but—"

"Shut your trap, boy," Early growled. He was queasy with the pain and with hunger. "How long we been here?" he asked.

"As best as I can tell, a few hours. I think dawn is still some time off."

"Ye take notice when I first woke?"

"I'm not sure. Your breathing changed there for a while, but you didn't open your eyes."

"That'd be it."

"Half hour, if I estimate correctly."

Early nodded. He ignored the renewed thumping in his head as he stood up. He spit. "Waugh!" he muttered. "These doin's don't shine with this chil' the least goddamn bit."

"There's nothing we can do, I'm afraid," Adams allowed, still shamed by his lack of courage. He knew he was the cause of their troubles. It seemed that all he had done lately was get helpful people into trouble.

"We'll see about that, I expect."

"You think you can get us out of here?" Adams asked, his despair overwhelming his surprise.

"Sooner or later," Early vowed. He stopped pacing and spun. "Ye see anything of Abe? Or Lucien?"

"No," Adams said thoughtfully. "No. I haven't seen Lucien since shortly after we got to the plaza. I didn't see much of Abe. Nor of you, for that matter, until . . . One minute I was facing Parfrey, waiting for him to carve me up, then you were flying through the air like some deranged bat." He almost smiled. "I saw Abe clubbing some soldier down. Then I . . . I . . ."

Early's lips curled up in a half-sneer. "Then ye tried to hightail it, eh, boy?" His anger returned.

"No. I . . ." Adams shrugged. He couldn't explain to this hardened mountain man that he had finally overcome his fear enough to at least lash out, no matter how feebly.

"Ye get some licks in, boy?" Early asked, cocking an eye at Adams.

"Not many," Adams said sheepishly. "But one or two." He felt a chuckle rising up out of the wellspring of fear. "I can say, though, that George Court isn't going to be servicing any women for a while."

"Well, now, boy, that's some better." Early sat on the bed. "Now shut that flapping hole in your face." He stretched out and fell asleep.

Adams stood there for a few moments, staring at the silent figure on the hard iron cot. Then he lay on the floor and tried to sleep. It was not easy in coming, but he finally managed.

The next morning, Early awoke when he heard Chardonnais's voice outside the cell, calling, "Ezra? Ezra? Are you in dere?"

" 'Course I'm in here," Early offered. "Where'n hell

else am I gonna be?" Actually, he knew he would be taken deep into Mexico and hanged.

"Me and old Abe will come and 'elp you, my frain. We—"

There was a commotion capped by a hoarse bellow. Early thought for a moment that he knew the voice, but he could not place it. Then came the sounds of a running horse, followed by shouts. A few shots were fired.

"Lucien!" Early roared. He stood on the cot and jumped, grabbing the single iron bar in the slit of a window. He pulled himself up and looked out. He could see nothing but sky and the flat tops of nearby buildings. He dropped back down to the cot and sat.

Sergeant Pedro Chacón opened the cell door a few minutes later. Early glared in hate at the sergeant. "You," he breathed.

"*Sí,*" Chacón said with a cruel smile. "Pedro Chacón. And I am a sergeant now," he added with arrogance.

"Where's Lucien?" Early asked, biting back his anger.

Two other soldiers hurried in and set down two bowls of a thin, fetid gruel. They scurried out.

Chacón grinned maliciously. "Your friend will not be back, *señor*," he said in heavily accented English. "He was killed as he ran away like a frightened dog."

Early's eyes turned red with fury. The sorrow would come later; now was the time for rage. As Chacón smugly turned to leave, Early said softly, "I'm gonna cut your heart out, ye snake-humpin' sack of shit."

Chacón half laughed.

"Don't ye doubt it, ye greasy bastard. Ye killed my friend, and this chil's gonna raise your hair for such doin's. For that, and for that goddamn time you—" He clamped his mouth shut suddenly.

Chacón smiled malevolently and walked a few steps back into the room. "Ah, yes, the señorita. She was . . . adequate. But she died noisily. And messily." He sighed with satisfaction, then his face hardened. "You will do nothing, *Americano* pig. Within the week, you'll be taken to Chihuahua, where you will die. And I will watch, and laugh." He spit in Early's face and then walked out, as haughty as ever, and locked the door behind him.

Early was livid. There would be no way that the fat slug of a jailer would live once he opened the cell door to take Early to Mexico. But patience began to well up, calming him. He wiped the slime off his new growth of beard. He would wait. The time would come to take care of Sergeant Pedro Chacón. He was rash sometimes, but this was not a time for it. He sat on the cot. Almost calmly, he picked up his bowl of slop and ate.

Sadness crept over him, but he shoved it back. It would serve him no purpose to rehash the times he and Lucien Chardonnais had spent together, the adventures they had shared, the starvin' times and the *fandangos*.

Throughout the day and into the evening, Early sat, keeping his mind as blank as he could make it. Until the time Chacón and his two aides returned again to bring more slop, Early and Adams were left alone, except for the several rats that called the small cell home.

Weak sunlight came through the thin slit of a window high up in the adobe cell. Early found a small poke of tobacco in his belt pouch. He put some in his mouth and chewed. For an hour or so, he sort of amused himself by spitting at the rats, who made skittering, rapidly moving targets.

Then the boredom began to vie for attention with his anger and sorrow. Early was calm outwardly. Inside, he seethed, thinking only of killing Chacón. He was sure there was little chance of getting out of this jail cell, other than chained and being dragged to a *carreta* for the long ride to Chihuahua. He vowed that he would not make the journey. He also knew with absolute certainty that Chacón would not live more than two minutes after that cell door opened to take him on that trip.

Early had a heap of patience when it was necessary. He had acquired it by sitting around infinitely long and deadly dull council fires with his Ute friends, and with other tribes. He called all that training into play now.

Adams, on the other hand, had no such experience. He paced almost constantly until Early would growl at him to light awhile. The easterner would sit uncomfortably for a few minutes, perching awkwardly on the iron cot. Then he would be up and stomping nervously around again.

The next few days were much the same. Each morning and each evening, Chacón would stick his bloated face in the door, look around in smug superiority, then nod at his two assistants, who each carried in a bowl of the slop and set it down. Then they fled out the door. Early ignored them.

Two days later, when the evening meal was brought, Chacón was annoyed at the lack of attention he received. Early had taken to ignoring the fat jailer, mostly to annoy Chacón, but also because it helped him remain at peace. Rage would get him nowhere right now.

To show his disdain for the prisoners, Chacón spit tobacco, barely missing Early's bowl. *"Gozar, señors,"* the jailer said with a sneer. "Enjoy."

"Eat shit, ye fat, bean-fartin' son of a bitch," Early growled, grinning viciously.

"El muerto," Chacón snarled, hate darkening his jowly face.

Early laughed. "No, no, Señor Puerco," he said harshly. "You're the one who's dead."

An angry Chacón slammed the wood door and clomped away.

"That what he said?" Adams asked with his spoon halfway to his mouth. "That we're dead?"

"Yep." Early was a quarter of the way through his rancid soup already. He glanced over at Adams, who looked stricken. "Shit, ol' lard ass is just tryin' to scare ye, boy."

"He did a good job of it, then," Adams said stiffly. Then again, he realized, Early's chilling tone scared him even more than Chacón's words.

"Shit," Early said, drawing out the word. "Eat your slop."

Adams spooned in a mouthful and grimaced. "Lord, this is horrible," he said, trying to lighten the mood.

Early shrugged. "It's food, boy, and it'll keep ye alive." He slurped down the rest of his and put the bowl down. "Ain't nothin' more important to this chil'." He belched. "Damn, that is some poor shit, though, ain't it?" Then he shrugged. "But, hell, I've et worse. I mind the time me, Abe, and Lucien—" he paused, feeling a stab of grief, "were up in the

Absarokas. It was colder'n a witch's tit and starvin' times was on us."

Adams listened with rapt attention, his gruel forgotten.

"Damn, I hate to speak of such doin's, but me and my two *compañeros* was startin' to eye each other to decide who was the plumpest, and so best to be made meat of to keep the others from goin' under."

Early pulled out his tobacco and shoved some into his mouth. There was about enough left for two more good chaws, he figured. He dropped the rest back into his pouch.

"Hell, we et our moccasins and half the whangs on our 'skins. When they was gone, we started playin' hand to see who'd go under. Then this Crow come staggerin' into camp. He looked about half done in, but there was some meat on his bones."

"And how do you know that?" Adams asked weakly.

Early leaned over and spit at a rat, hitting the rodent on the head. "We et him," Early said nonchalantly. "That hoss's meat was some stringy and didn't have a heap of flavor, but he lasted us a couple weeks, after which we brung us down some poor ol' buffler."

Adams looked like he wanted to vomit. He was torn between the desire to be sick and the desire to laugh. He wasn't sure, but he was more than half certain that Early was making it up. Still, a kernel—a large kernel—of doubt remained. He was not foolish enough either to challenge Early on it. So he turned his attention to his bowl, choking down the foul broth.

"What in hell's in this?" he asked after a few more mouthfuls. He pointed his spoon at the liquid in the bowl.

"I don't expect ye'd want to know that, boy," Early said blandly. "Just feed your face and don't go thinkin' too much about what it is you're feedin' on."

Adams nodded and dourly went back to eating.

The day dragged, the hours seeming endless. Sometime in the afternoon, Adams stopped his pacing long enough to ask, "You come up with a way to get us out of here, Ezra?"

"Not yet." He hadn't really given it much thought. He figured there was still time. Despite the poor food, he knew he could last for some days yet, and still retain his strength. He was sure the Mexicans would leave them here at least a few more days, to try to soften them up, make them more pliable on the trip to Chihuahua. That should give him some time.

What he was counting on was the arrival of Abe Rawlins. Since he had not been seen, he must've cached as soon as he saw trouble the night of the *fandango*. He would have lingered nearby just long enough to find out that Early and Adams were still alive before trying to get help.

As Early lay down on the bare metal cot that night, he decided he would give it two more days. If no one arrived to help them by then, he would devise a way to get out. There was little he could use, but that did not bother him. The Mexicans had left him his belt pouch, but had taken his fire-making kit and folding knife, leaving only the little tobacco and a few innocuous odds and ends.

None of that mattered. He would not need anything but his own hands. The first thing he would do would be to get his big hands around Chacón's fat neck and squeeze the life out of the blubbery Mexican.

Chacón, despite his flabbiness, was a hard and dangerous man. Once the soldier was made wolf bait of, Early would take things as they came. His only worry, if it could even be called that, was for Adams. Early would not—could not—coddle the easterner. He would try to prepare Adams as best he could, but once things started happening, the easterner would have to know that he was on his own. He knew it was not a great plan, but it was the best he could do under the circumstances. He was satisfied with that. With those thoughts firmly in mind, Early drifted off to sleep.

23

A DULL ROARING OF gunfire woke Early. He was instantly alert, though he didn't move except to open his eyes. He wanted to try to place the sound, find out just what it meant, before he acted. It came from outside, that was obvious in the first couple of heartbeats.

He rolled out of bed, glanced at Adams, and indicated with a forefinger to his lips that Adams should be quiet. Despite the thickness of the adobe walls, he thought he could hear Rawlins's voice. He frowned and scowled when he thought he also heard Chardonnais's voice.

As he stood on the cot and pulled himself up to the small window, more gunfire erupted, but it seemed to move around the side of the building. Early couldn't see anything outside but a pall of powder smoke.

The shooting stopped, but a commotion suddenly

started moments later inside the jailhouse. Early dropped down onto the cot and sat. He grinned as he watched the door somewhat expectantly. The noise was coming toward the cell.

Then Rawlins was standing just inside the door, the key to the cell in one oversized paw. "Ye about ready to move your ass out of here, *amigo?*" he asked slowly, with a small grin. "Or have ye gotten too cozy here?"

"I expect it'd shine some with this chil' to see the outside again," Early said with a tight grin. He paused and chucked a thumb over his shoulder. "What'n hell's goin' on out there?"

"Ye'll see." He dropped the keys and spun, saying, "Let's go, boys."

Early walked calmly, almost jauntily, out of the cell. After a few moments' hesitation, Adams followed the two mountain men. He felt a little queasy as he stepped over two dead soldiers.

They stopped in the office part of the jail and quickly found Early's weapons. He checked his rifle first. When he was sure it was loaded, he set it on the desk. Then he saw to his pistols, made sure they, too, were loaded, and slid the iron clips over his belt so the pistols hung snugly. He grabbed his long, wood-handled knife and slipped it into the beaded, hard-leather scabbard on the back of his belt, held fast diagonally over his right buttock. Finally he jammed the tomahawk into the belt at the small of his back, the flat side of the sharp blade resting comfortably in the little hollow there. "We got business to finish, Abe, if ye're of a mind for such doin's."

"Reckon it wouldn't put me out none to teach some of these goddamn greaser soldiers that goin' agin boys like us ain't a healthful way to spend their free time," Rawlins drawled laconically.

They stepped outside and Early stopped, blinking in the bright sunshine. His eyes teared up and overflowed at the sudden onslaught of light. "Damn," he muttered.

He blinked again, this time in wonder as his eyes quickly adjusted. More than twenty free trappers from Taos, led by Ceran Saint Vrain, sat on their horses in a rough circle in front of the jail. Inside the circle were what Early thought might be all the soldiers in the city, close to fifty of them, he guessed, and all looking decidedly unhappy. A few soldiers lay dead in the street along the plaza.

"What'n hell's all this?" Early asked in amazement.

"Dese here are your own *amis,* boy. You should know dat," Chardonnais said from Early's side. There was a touch of arrogance in the Frenchman's voice.

Early jerked his head around so fast he thought for a moment it would fly off. "Lucien!" he roared.

"Mais oui," Lucien Chardonnais said nonchalantly, though a large grin split his thick, flat face.

"But where . . . ? How . . . ?" It was an uncommon thing for Ezra Early to be at a loss for words. His friends were enjoying it. "Chacón said you was gone under. Shot runnin' away from the soldiers."

"Merde," Chardonnais snorted. Then he laughed. "Dose *fils des garces* couldn't hit a buffalo if dey had their rifles stuck muzzle first up de buffalo's ass."

Early couldn't help but laugh. "So, what happened?"

"Once we knowed ye was safe," Rawlins said with a hearty laugh, "me and Lucien hauled ass back to Taos as fast as we could. We rounded up a few of the boys, as ye can goddamn well see, and made our way back here."

"Took ye long enough," Early said in mock anger.

"Well, some of us boys is gettin' a mite long in the tooth for such doin's. Ol' Lucien there ain't as spry as he used to was."

"Shit," Early said, drawing the word out. Then he grinned. "Well, ye sure made 'em come now. Such doin's plumb shine with this ol' chil'."

Early looked around. "Well, boys, what're ye plannin' to do with all them critters?" He pointed at the soldiers.

"Reckon that depends on the governor."

"He around?"

"Waitin' on us outside the palace." He headed in that direction. Early was on his right, and Chardonnais on Early's right. Adams walked slightly behind the three mountain men. Other mountaineers greeted Early warmly. He returned the greetings.

Most of the mounted mountain men were Americans, Adams saw, with a smattering of Frenchmen, and even a Mexican or two. They were a fierce, tough-looking lot, all in all, with their heavy rifles, pistols, tomahawks, knives; their greasy dark buckskins and long, thick beards. Even when they were smiling, they looked deadly, Adams thought. He almost shuddered. He would not want to tangle with this bunch.

"He don't look none too pleased with all these doin's," Early said as he and his friends approached Governor Ramón Castillo.

Rawlins shrugged. "Hoss ought to know better'n to sic his shit-eatin' soldiers on the likes of us." He stopped and rested the butt of his rifle in the dust, and leaned on the muzzle. "Well, now, *amigo*," he said, voice heavy with sarcasm, "just what should we do with all your boys there?"

"Let them go," Castillo said tightly.

"So's they can shoot us down first chance they get? Shit."

"What do you want then?" Castillo asked. His lips formed a small, thin slit. He looked mean and mad, but also helpless.

"Mostly just that the *soldados* let us be," Rawlins said simply. "Ye give us your word on that, we'll set 'em loose. Ye don't . . ." Rawlins shrugged, indicating he could not be held responsible for what would happen.

Early's eyes glassed over with a film of rage when he saw Chacón standing nearby. The jailer had a smirk on his fat face. "All of 'em but one," Early interjected, before Castillo could answer. "That bean-fartin' fat sack of shit's got to answer to me for the miseries he inflicted on me and others."

"No," Castillo said flatly. "They must all go free. I'll keep them away from you."

"Ye ain't holdin' a good enough hand to go issuin' orders, *amigo*," Early snarled. "Ye can have all them others, but Chacón is mine. I aim to make wolf bait out of his fat ass and then lift his hair."

"I cannot stand here and let you kill one of my soldiers in cold blood, *señor*," Castillo said in what he thought was a reasonable tone. He had trouble keeping the officiousness out of his voice, though.

Early lifted his head up a little and idly scratched at the fuzziness under his chin and on his neck. "Well now, I'll tell ye what," he finally said, dropping his chin and hooking his thumbs into his belt. "Ye keep your other boys outten it, and I'll give Chacón a fair shot at raisin' my hair. Just him and me, face-to-face. It's a better chance than he'd ary think of givin' me."

Castillo thought about it for some moments, then asked, "Will weapons be used, *señor?*"

"Well now, that's up to him, I expect. Were it left up to me, I'd choose knives. Less'n he wants to go agin me with rifles."

"You will use only hand weapons," Castillo said, as if he still had some authority here.

"Don't put me out none."

Castillo nodded again. He was not a faint-hearted man, and he was quite politically astute. He knew he could do nothing about this situation. Not now at least. He figured it best to let this take its course for the time being. Once his soldiers were freed and safe, he could take the time to formulate a plan to bring these American brigands to justice, if that seemed politic. Right now, though, he was helpless. He knew quite well what these mountain men were capable of. He would not admit it publicly, but to himself he acknowledged that there were no finer fighters in the world. His soldiers were no match against them.

"When will you do this?" Castillo asked. He suddenly thought that it was quite possible that Chacón might win. That would make the situation more palatable. Castillo knew he would be able to swallow his wounded pride a little more easily if his sergeant could defeat this arrogant *yanqui.*

"Right now shines with this chil'," Early answered. He was not about to let Chacón live a second longer than necessary. "That way my *amigos* here can keep your boys under their watch."

"So be it," Castillo said wearily. He suddenly wanted this all over with. The sooner this fight was done with, the sooner the Americans would be out of Santa Fe. He might even be willing to forget about this whole thing—if the mountain men kept away from Santa Fe for a while. They would all be heading back to the mountains north of Taos soon, Castillo figured. By the time they returned to Taos next spring, almost everyone in Santa Fe would have forgotten this episode. If they didn't, well, Castillo was still the governor, and he could make them see the error of pointing out Castillo's troubles. He also was fairly certain most of the mountain men probably wouldn't even come to Santa Fe. They tended to favor the looseness of Taos to the more civilized restraint of his own Santa Fe. That would certainly make his life more pleasant. He did, however, make a mental note to request that more soldiers be sent here from Mexico City.

The mounted Americans began shepherding the soldiers out of the way, while Chacón and a corporal who was hurriedly appointed the sergeant's second huddled with Castillo just out of earshot of Early, Chardonnais, Rawlins, and Adams.

"Ye sure ye want to go through with this now, Ezra?" Rawlins asked. "Ye been in that *calabozo* some time, and I figure them critters weren't none too generous with fillin' your meatbag. Ye're likely to be some weak, boy."

Early spit into the dust. Then he shrugged. "I got me too much hate for that son of a bitch to go worryin' about bein' a mite weak."

"Why do you hate that fat slob?" Adams asked.

"It was him hit me on the back of the head over at the *fandango* so's I could be drug over to the *calabozo* in the first place."

"That's not enough reason for hating him so much."

"Expect not." Early glanced over at Chacón, and the hate was rekindled. "Son of a bitch tol' us he kilt that dumb little French bastard there next to ye."

"But 'e did not kill me," Chardonnais said with a grin. "As you can see, I am 'ere in de flesh."

"I can see that, dammit," Early said gruffly. "I expect what really made me half froze to raise his hair is the way he did it. Son of a bitch took joy in baitin' me with the news. It was kind of like he stuck a knife in my guts and then stood there grinnin' whilst he twisted that knife 'round and 'round in the hole." He grinned viciously. "'Sides, me and Chacón go back a little ways, ye know that."

"*Oui.* Dat time with dat *mademoiselle,* when he—"

"We all remember that," Rawlins threw in hastily, not wanting to dredge up the episode and knowing the memory would do little to improve Early's mood.

"It's time an end was put to it," Early said. He handed Rawlins his rifle. With excitement and anticipation, he moved toward the center of the plaza. He stopped.

"What's he mean, Abe?" Adams asked, worried.

"Keep your trap shut, boy," Rawlins said icily.

Adams suddenly was frightened. He no longer seemed to be one of these men's friends.

"Come on, Chacón," Early roared. "Get your fat ass out here."

24

CHACEÓN WADDLED FORWARD, A sword clasped in his fat right hand. He was well versed in its use, and he felt comfortable with it. He was so good that his self-confidence bordered on arrogance.

Early saw it, and his rage flared underneath. It did not show on his face, but he remembered Chacón and his sword. It was five years ago now. Early was a lot younger then, and it was his first trip to Taos. Etienne Provost had shown Early, Rawlins, and Chardonnais how to get their plews sold without getting them confiscated, and introduced the three young men to the delights of Taos. Particularly the delights of the dusky, warm, affectionate *señoritas*.

At first, Early felt a little odd about dallying with the *señoritas*, since he had just spent the winter with

Falling Leaf. Still, he was not about to be celibate. He, Chardonnais, and Rawlins had gone into a *cantina* where Early soon found himself attracted to a young *señorita,* the daughter of the *cantina*'s owner. Early spent a considerable amount of time with Valencia Lopez. He was not in love with her, by any means, nor she with him. They were young and hot-blooded, and enjoyed each other's company.

A few weeks after meeting Valencia, Early was in Juan Lopez's *cantina* and swept Valencia up for a spirited dance. The young couple whirled around the floor, heedless of Early's youthful clumsiness. Finally, a soldier, bolstered by his size and the inflated ego that came with the abundance of whiskey he had consumed, had had enough of the happy dancers. With a muttered oath, he grabbed Early and yanked him to a halt.

"Su bailar malo," he hissed, breath reeking of cheap wine and garlic. "Your dancing is bad."

Early looked at the shuffling bear of a corporal for a moment. He was unimpressed by the great sloping shoulders, the tight tangle of dark beard and matching hair, the fleshy face and deep-set, piggish eyes. Early also had enough *aguardiente* in him that, combined with his usual touchiness, he was offended by the soldier's words, actions, and even looks. "Best go set your fat ass down, boy," he snapped. "Less'n ye get me angry."

"I am Corporal Pedro Chacón," the soldier said, puffing out his already bulging chest. Well, actually, it was his stomach that bulged all the more for the added air.

"I don't give a good goddamn if'n you was God almighty himself."

Chacón and his comrades were shocked at such a statement. Several crossed themselves, just in case.

Early shrugged. "So, now if you'd set your fat ass back down, me and the *señorita* can get back to dancin'."

Chacón muttered another oath in Spanish, and he suddenly swung at Early, catching him high on the left cheek. Early staggered back a few steps, stopping only when he ran into several people.

The mountain man stood for a moment, touching the blood from his split flesh. He figured the bone was broken, but he also knew there was not a damn thing he could do about it right at the moment, so he put the pain out of his mind. Without a word, he charged, slamming his right shoulder into Chacón's broad expanse of uniformed abdomen. Chacón's air popped out in a rush, and his knees buckled. He went down with Early half atop him.

Early leapt up and kicked Chacón in the face. A blood rage surged through Early's veins, and he kicked Chacón again. Without thinking about it, he reached for his knife.

Suddenly half a dozen other soldiers had him in their grasp. Early fought and kicked, bit and spit. He bucked like a wild mustang, and the soldiers had a heap of trouble keeping him in their grasp.

The fight was beginning to wear him down a little and a sharp blow to his midsection slowed him even more. It also boosted his anger. With a sudden surge of rage-bolstered strength, he flung the soldiers off him.

Rawlins and Chardonnais had waded into the thick of things, and suddenly only the fat one, Chacón, was on his feet, facing the three mountain men. Chacón had his sword in hand.

"Come on at me, ye puss-gut son of a bitch," Early

hissed. "Pig-sticker and all. I'll raise hair on ye sure as shit."

Chacón's piggish eyes glared from beneath the rumpled slabs of eyebrows. He ran a plump thumb along the side of the sword's blade, as if caressing a woman's soft thigh. Then he said slowly, "You and your *amigos* better go now, *señor*. But we will meet again one day."

"I see ye again, damn ye, and I'll—"

"*Allons,*" Chardonnais said, interrupting Early. He pulled at his friend's sleeve. "We better go, eh. More soldiers dey come."

Early swept his hat off the floor and slapped it on his head. He turned and grinned at Valencia. Then he and his friends hurried outside.

The three rode out of town that evening and lay low in the surrounding mountains for a few days before riding back into town. Fall was nigh, and they needed to get their supplies and ride out.

Except for the broken cheek, which never did heal quite right, Early thought little more about the fight in Lopez's *cantina*. Soldiers and mountain men were always having run-ins, and it usually passed over quickly enough. The two proud groups were wary of each other, and fights broke out frequently, only to be forgotten in a few days.

Because Early and his companions were pressed to leave, he did not get a chance to visit Valencia. He did, however, see her one day stealing away with a local youth. It did not bother Early, as he had thought it would, since they had no claim on each other. The night before he was planning to leave, Early went to Lopez's *cantina* to say good-bye to her.

"She is dead, *señor*," a grief-stricken Lopez said.

"How?" Early said. He found it hard to believe that such a vibrant young woman could have been snuffed out. He wasn't sure whether to be angry or hurt or worried.

Lopez shrugged, tears spilling unbidden from his eyes. "All we know, *señor,* is that she was found in a house a block from the plaza." He was sobbing. "She was killed by a sword."

"Jesus," Early whispered. He was sad and wondered who could—or would—do such a thing to a young woman. But the press of getting ready to leave the next morning pushed some of his sadness away.

Occasionally over the autumn and winter, he wondered about Valencia and who could have killed her. All the soldiers carried swords, and many men carried knives long enough to pass for a short sword. Then one day in winter camp, Early suddenly thought of the fat corporal and the way he had caressed the sword. Early was convinced that Chacón was the murderer. He vowed to kill him in the spring when he got back to Taos. Not for any great love for Valencia, but because he saw it as a challenge by Chacón.

Early went looking for Chacón as soon as he pulled into Taos. But he was told that the corporal had been posted to Chihuahua. Or was it Mexico City? Or Durango? Or Saltillo?

A few days later, Early had met his brother Ethan in town. His joy and excitement over seeing his brother pushed thoughts of Valencia Lopez out of his mind, and over the next several years, Early mostly forgot about Valencia, and Corporal Chacón.

Then Chacón, now a sergeant, had returned to Santa Fe, and had clubbed down Early before tossing him in the *calabozo* and baiting him there. It rekindled Early's rage against the fat soldier, particularly when he thought about an innocent girl dying only because of her fancy for a young, wild mountain man.

"That isn't fair!" Adams suddenly shouted, pointing to Chacón's sword. He had been quiet, afraid to speak, feeling decidedly out of place. But now he could not hold back. "That'll give him too much extra reach."

"All hand weapons were agreed upon," Castillo said smugly.

"But—"

"Shut your trap, boy," Early snapped. "That sword don't mean shit to me." He pulled the foot-and-a-half-long tomahawk from his belt. He slapped the slightly rounded back edge of it against his left palm, waiting.

Chacón was a little shorter than Early but out-weighed him by at least fifty pounds. And the sword added substantially to his reach. He advanced, sword held lightly in his hand. He swished it in front of him a bit, the darting weapon looking like a snake about to strike.

Adams felt as if he must do something, but he didn't know exactly what. Suddenly an idea sprang to the fore. "Your gun, Abe," he said hastily. He held out his hand.

"What'n hell for?" Rawlins asked, surprised.

"Even the odds a little." He pointed to the two combatants. Early also was moving forward, easily, on the balls of his feet. He seemed to glide across the dirt, hardly kicking up puffs of dust.

"Shit," Rawlins drawled. "Lard ass there thinks he's

hot shit with that sword, but ain't nobody in the mountains better with a 'hawk than Ezra Early. He'll hack that big tub of shit into wolf bait, certain, boy."

Adams gulped, knowing he would not be able to help his friend. With sick fascination, he watched.

Early and Chacón faced each other, sizing the other man up. Suddenly Chacón moved, surprisingly fast for such a lumbering, obese man, slicing open Early's buckskin shirt. A thin red line gleamed across Early's chest.

Chacón smiled cruelly. "Just a taste of what I will do to you, *señor.*"

Early didn't even look down. He simply smiled chillingly. While Chacón stood gloating with his success and superiority, Early moved. He was far faster than Chacón. He swung the tomahawk in what seemed to Adams to be wild arcs, but Early knew where every one was going.

Chacón whipped the sword back and forth as he gave way. With the glittering sword, the soldier managed to fend off the whistling tomahawk. Step by step, he moved backward across the plaza, oblivious to the shouts of the men who ringed the dusty plaza.

Finally Early whacked the sword near the hilt. The weapon went skittering across the dirt. Chacón dived for it, bouncing on his well-padded stomach, fingers scrabbling for the weapon.

Early leapt on him like a mosquito on bare skin. One quick flick of the tomahawk and the shirt and flesh opened down the length of Chacón's back. The sergeant froze, waiting for the death blow. It did not come.

Early stepped back, tomahawk dangling in his right hand. Chacón, still lying on the ground, looked back over his shoulder and up. Early shook his head. "That'd be too easy for the likes of ye," he said without mercy. "We're even now." He lightly touched his fingertips to the blood on his chest. "Ye won't get another chance."

Chacón pushed himself laboriously up, grabbing his sword as he did. As he brushed the dust off his uniform with one hand, he glared at Early. Chacón was a professional soldier, and proud of it. He had underestimated this hard-eyed mountain man. He vowed silently not to repeat the mistake.

The two moved toward each other again, feinting, testing. Neither gave way. Once or twice, Early moved like he had the last time—fast and hard—hoping to catch the Mexican off guard. Chacón was wary now, though, and each time he nimbly stepped aside, deftly fending off the insistent tomahawk.

The heat and strain were wearing on both men, and they slowed their pace a little, though their deadly intent remained the same. Early blinked quickly, as the perspiration seeped into his eyes.

It was what Chacón had been waiting for, and he swarmed in. The sword darted like the tongue of a snake. Five times it pierced the mountain man's skin. Early was moving away from Chacón, so none of the wounds were deep, but he knew they would begin to take their toll soon. He fought back his increasing rage, looking for an opening. He was tired, his arms heavy, and he realized that the week or so in the jail cell had sapped him more than he cared to admit.

He kept retreating, which annoyed him. He suddenly decided he would do it no longer. His mind set with deadly purpose, he stopped. His left hand flashed out, grabbing the sword. He ignored the searing pain of the blade biting into his hand. He grasped it with all his strength. As he tensed his arm and shoulder muscles, he jerked his head forward, smashing his forehead into Chacón's. At the same time, he yanked, tearing the sword from Chacón's hand.

The Mexican stood flatfooted and stunned as Early dropped the sword from his bloody left hand. *"Madre de Dios!"* Chacón whispered in shock. He shook his head in wonder and pain.

Chacón looked around frantically for help, but none was in the offing. In desperation, he squatted quickly and grasped a handful of dirt. As his tree-trunk legs pushed him back up, he threw the dirt at Early's face. Then he turned and ran. He slammed into a mountain man's horse and fell. He scrambled back up and whirled. Spotting a Mexican hunter, Chacón punched the man. As the hunter fell, Chacón yanked out the man's pistol.

Early stood calmly in the plaza, wiping his eyes. He could see well enough and knew what Chacón was up to. As the Mexican moved a bit for a clear shot, Early could hear several rifles being cocked behind him. He knew his friends were ready to blast Chacón into eternity.

"That chil's mine," Early roared.

As Chacón began bringing the pistol to bear, Early threw back his right arm. Then he whipped it forward, hurling the tomahawk. The blade chunked deep into Chacón's chest. As he staggered backward, Chacón fired the pistol, sending the ball harmlessly into the air.

There was a whoop and a shout from the group of

mountain men. The soldiers were silent, though a few were trying to stifle grins of satisfaction. With his bulk, nasty humor, and rank, Chacón was not well liked by his men, or his superiors, for that matter.

Breathing heavily, Early turned and walked to the governor. "Ye aim to keep your end of the bargain?" he asked roughly.

Castillo nodded silently, lips compressed. "You'll free my men?" The soldiers must be freed, he told himself, or he would be a laughingstock.

"Yep."

The soldiers scattered as Early headed toward Chacón's body to retrieve his tomahawk. Rawlins already had the weapon in hand. He handed it to Early. "Reckon ye ought to go see a doc, if we can roust one up."

"I reckon that ol' fart used to patch folks up is still around." He felt stiff and sore, and the pain began to assert itself some. He wasn't too worried about it, but he didn't like it much either.

Chardonnais and Adams joined their two friends, and the four walked off under the watchful eyes of their little "army."

25

EARLY AND ADAMS PACKED their few belongings, while in a nearby room Chardonnais and Rawlins did the same.

Outside, the small army of mountain men kept watch. No one had bothered them yet, and it began to seem unlikely that any would. That was no disparagement of the Mexican soldiers. Many of the *soldados,* like soldiers everywhere, had little desire to be soldiers. It made them less than eager to fight when their country or their families were not in danger.

"Damn!" Adams suddenly exclaimed.

Early half turned to look at him, partly amused, partly irritated. "What'n hell's ailin' ye now, boy?" he asked. The irritation arose partly from the bulky bandage on his left hand. On the way to the rooming house, he had stopped at the doctor's and had it stitched up, poulticed, and bandaged.

Adams held up a small, oil-cloth-wrapped package. "My writings and sketches. We never made arrangements to have them sent off."

Early shrugged and went back to work. It was of no concern to him.

Adams stood there, still holding the package up, suddenly feeling like a fool. Ezra Early had been his savior countless times, and now here he was looking to the mountain man for a way to save him again, in a way. He shook his head and dropped the package onto the small bed.

The thought of the package plagued him, though, and his eyes kept darting back to it. Suddenly he stopped working again and straightened. His mind was made up. "Where would I find some men—trustworthy men—with whom I can send my materials East?"

Early straightened and looked at Adams in surprise again. Maybe the easterner had more gumption than he thought, though he had seen precious little evidence of it. He rubbed his chin, thinking. "El Toro Cabeza, maybe." At Adams's blank look, he added, "The Bull's Head. A *cantina* over in an alley, a few blocks west of the plaza. Maybe at the little *cantina* run by Armando Abrego, over toward the river. Place doesn't have a name, but you can't miss it. Just follow the stink." He stood watching Adams.

The easterner nodded, oblivious to Early's attempt at humor. "Is there someone I should try to find?" Adams paused. "Or avoid?"

"Ye know at least one critter ye'd want to avoid," Early said dryly.

"Yes, I expect I do." Thoughts of Parfrey made his stomach roil with self-disgust.

"Try'n find an ol' hoss named Luther Whiteside. Another'n you can trust is Woody Eakins."

Adams's eyes widened. "I met him. Back at Council Grove. He was captain of the main Santa Fe Trail caravan."

"What happened that ye didn't travel with him?"

Adams shrugged in embarrassment. "I had hired Parfrey. They were planning to join up with the main caravan at Council Grove, like everyone else. Parfrey went and killed some Indian, though, for no good reason, and Mister Eakins refused to let Parfrey join. He offered to take me, but I wasn't sure he meant it. Besides, I had paid Parfrey a portion of the money and thought . . . well, I thought . . . " His voice petered out. He felt like an absolute idiot about it all.

"Well, if'n ye can find Woody and he agrees to see your package East, ye can be certain it'll get there."

Adams nodded with renewed determination. "I'll be as quick as I can. But if you want to hit the trail before I get back, I'll understand. I'll follow along as best I can."

Early gazed levelly at Adams, who held the stony, serious look. Then a small smile tickled the edges of Early's lips, shuffling the mustache just a little. "Shit, boy, ye'll be wolf bait before ye get to the plaza."

"That's my affair," Adams said stiffly.

"I expect so." He paused. "But finish packing your possibles first."

Feeling a little better about himself, Adams tossed his few remaining belongings into a cloth satchel—everything, that is, but the package he intended to post. As he did, a question arose in his mind that he had to ask. "Why have you helped me so much, Ezra?" He paused. "Don't get me wrong, I'm very grateful, but I couldn't help wondering."

"I got my goddamn reasons," Early said gruffly. "Ye done yet, boy?"

Adams nodded. Rawlins and Chardonnais were waiting outside with the other mountain men.

"Ready to get our 'orses, *mon ami?*" Chardonnais asked Early. He stood leaning against the adobe wall of the rooming house, picking at his long, grimy fingernails with a sharp knife.

"Expect so." Early grinned. "Then we got us one more stop to make. Bart here needs to ship his papers back East."

"I told you I could find Mister Eakins. Or that other fellow you mentioned," Adams said stiffly.

"Reckon ye could, boy," Early said agreeably. "But I figured I'd go along just to make sure ye didn't take out after any of them soldiers."

"Like hell."

"Ye gonna stand there jawin' all goddamn day, or are ye aimin' to get your horse and go find a delivery man?"

"Oh, all right, dammit," Adams snapped. Secretly, though, he was glad to have Early along, not only for the companionship, but also for the protection. He felt even better when he realized all the mountain men were coming along, too.

People cleared the way as the buckskin-clad group rode slowly toward the plaza, off onto a side street, and then into a small, dismal, foul alleyway. They stopped at a dank, dark-looking saloon. Loud talk and

Mexican music wafted out through the cracked adobe, and the smell of Mexican food overpowered even the stench of the alley.

Adams was beginning to have doubts about all this, wondering why a man like Woodrow Eakins would spend time in such a place. But he dismounted and followed Early and Rawlins inside the *cantina*. The rest of the men stayed outside.

Adams was quite surprised at the inside of El Toro Cabeza. It was warm and seemingly friendly. Two Mexicans, dressed in tight buckskin pants that flared at the bottom and short buckskin jackets typical of the area, plucked guitars, sending up pleasant melodies. The bar itself was little more than planks resting on sawhorses. A heavyset man wearing a bright calico shirt and worn wool trousers was behind the bar. He grinned at the newcomers.

The small place was loud, and a haze of tobacco smoke hung under the low ceiling. No one seemed to be shouting, though, and the buzz of conversation was somehow comforting. Several women wandered about, either trying to drum up business or serving drinks and food.

Early pointed, and Adams nodded when he spotted the barely remembered Woodrow Eakins. The three mountain men headed toward the man, who seemed to be holding court at the large, heavy wood table. Halfway there, Early stopped and shouted violently, "Eakins!"

The thick, fight-scarred face rose and the dark, mean eyes glared through the pall of smoke. Men began to scatter, figuring violence was but moments away. Then Eakins grinned. "Ezra. Ezra Early!" He shoved his burly body up and held out his hand as Early approached.

Early shook the hard slab at the end of Eakins's arm. "How've ye been, ye ol' mule-humper, ye?" Early asked.

"Couldn't be none better. And you, you fractious ol' bag of wind?"

"This chil' still shines with the best." He grinned. "And here's a hoss ye know." He jerked his head toward Adams, who was at his left side.

"I know ye, boy?" Eakins asked, glaring, hard eyes aimed at Adams.

"Yessir," Adams offered, hoping that his voice was not as quavery as it sounded to him. "We met—"

"You was with that skunk Parfrey, warn't ya?" Eakins demanded. "Had a hard time recognizing ya with that outfit."

"Yessir." Adams gulped. *Coming here was a big mistake,* he thought worriedly.

"Whatever happened to that peckerwood son of a bitch?" He waved, indicating that Early, Adams, and Rawlins should sit.

After they had done so, and drinks had materialized before them, Early gave Eakins a quick summary of the feud between Adams and Parfrey.

"You should've come with me when I offered ya the chance, boy," Eakins growled.

Adams nodded. "It's too late for that now," he offered meekly.

"Reckon so. You make that son of a bitch pay for what he done?"

Adams shook his head, too embarrassed to speak. He suddenly wanted to get Parfrey, though. To find the foul miscreant and challenge him, even though he knew Parfrey would stomp him into the ground.

"We ain't 'zactly had time for such doin's, Woody," Early said easily. "In fact, ol' Bart here set on Parfrey at the big *fandango* a week or so back."

"Oh?" Eakins asked, looking in surprise at Adams, who could not meet the big wagoneer's iron gaze.

"Sure as shit. He was half froze to raise hair on that dumb fart." He gave an exaggerated sigh. "Then a passel of soldiers took exception to such doin's, and . . . well, me'n ol' Bart was guests of his majesty the governor for more'n a week. Till a bit earlier, when Abe here, and Lucien—he's outside—showed up with a bunch of boys from Taos and set us free."

"I heard there was some doin's over at the plaza," Eakins said dryly.

"Me and Chacón had us a mite of a disagreement we had to settle."

"Chacón? He that lard ass of a sergeant?"

"*Sí.*"

"Did Señor Fat Ass survive this disagreement?"

"Nope," Early said flatly.

"Good." Eakins polished off a large drink and waved for another. When it arrived, he tasted it. Approving it, he set the glass back down. He pointed to Early's bandaged hand. "Lard ass give you a hard time?"

Early shrugged. "He was a mite reluctant to give over his sword, so I took it from him."

Eakins nodded, never doubting Early for a second. "So, why'd you boys come lookin' for me?" he asked.

Silence grew and stretched taut for some moments before Adams realized that everyone was waiting on him. He started to speak but found he could not. He took a drink of whatever harsh whiskey had been placed in front of him. Then he cleared his throat and tried again.

"I was hoping you would deliver a package for me, Mister Eakins."

"I don't do such things for free, ya know, boy."

"I wouldn't ask that of you."

Eakins nodded. "What's the package?"

Adams laid it on the table. "If you may remember, I am a reporter for the *New York Register*. The package contains articles and sketches of my journey here, plus my stay in Taos."

"I ain't goin' but to Independence, maybe Saint Louis."

"You could make arrangements there to have it sent on to New York, couldn't you?" Adams asked eagerly.

"That'll cost extra."

"Understood." Adams reached into his pouch and pulled out most of his coins. He placed them atop the package. "Is that enough?" he asked.

The great bullet head moved slowly from side to side.

Adams shrugged. He placed the rest of his cash on the table. "That's all I have, Mister Eakins," he said, not too abashed. He wasn't the first man ever to be down on his luck financially. It was nothing to be ashamed of.

Eakins nodded. A ham-sized paw moved out, half circled the coins and scooped them toward the barrel chest. Then the big hand pulled the package to him.

"Ezra tells me you're a man of your word, Mister Eakins," Adams said.

"I am," Eakins responded without arrogance. It was a fact—nothing more, nothing less.

"Then you'll see that my package gets to its destination?" Adams felt funny asking, but he felt he had to.

"Come hell or high water, boy," Eakins said, not offended. Then he smiled a little. " 'Less'n the Comanches take exception to it."

Adams nodded.

Eakins picked up his glass, tilted it partway toward Adams in a salute, and then drained it. He called for another. Then he said, "You could carry this yourself, Mister Adams."

Adams was surprised by the comment, and he took a few moments to think it over. The idea appealed to him. Getting back to New York would be nice, he figured. But something would not let him leave now. Perhaps it was knowing that Parfrey was still here; perhaps it was the thought of Dolores. He wasn't sure, but the reason didn't matter much right now.

He shook his head firmly. "Thank you, Mister Eakins, but I must decline your offer. There's business to be done here. Perhaps next year?"

"Wouldn't put me out none."

26

THEY PULLED OUT SOON afterward. The group of mountain men roared out the north end of town onto the road to Taos. No one molested them or even so much as stood in the way. Early figured that Governor Castillo and the soldiers were glad to be rid of him and his wild and woolly friends.

Once out of Santa Fe, the men rode slowly. To Adams it seemed as if the mountain men paid no attention whatsoever to the world around them. They all seemed to ride slack in the saddle, their heads bobbing with the stiff, rhythmical walking of the horses. A few seemed to be asleep.

Adams was so perplexed that he finally rode up alongside Early to ask him about it, but not until his friend looked like he might not mind being disturbed.

The rangy mountain man leaned over and sent a

spout of tobacco juice into the dust to give himself time to think of how to respond to Adams's question. Then he straightened. His eyes swept the countryside.

"Well now, boy," Early allowed slowly, "it might *appear* to ye that we're inattentive, but such ain't true by a long shot." He paused. "It's some hard to tell it to a hoss like ye who don't know the way of things, but when ye come to live in these mountains, ye develop senses that work even when it appears ye ain't payin' attention to nothin'."

"A sixth sense?" Adams said hopefully. He couldn't understand the details of what Early said, but he thought he was on to the essence of it.

"What'n hell's that, boy?" Early asked. He seemed neither surprised nor annoyed, though he was a little of both. Citified ways and any kind of book learning bothered him, though he would never own up to it. Such things were so outlandish to him, and so useless in his chosen world and profession, that he usually gave them little time or thought.

"Sixth sense," Adams repeated. He paused, chewing his lip as he thought a moment. "It's kind of the power of intuition." He looked at Early, hoping the mountain man would understand.

Early stared back evenly. He did not feel bad about not understanding, but he did not want to admit it vocally either.

Adams could see in Early's eyes that he did not grasp the idea. Adams thought some more, wondering how he could explain such a nebulous concept to a man who had so little education, so little school education, Adams corrected himself. There were, Adams acknowledged silently, probably fewer men who were

more educated in the ways of the wilderness than
Early was. Still, without a basis in theory or philoso-
phy or any of the other school-taught disciplines it
would be almost impossible to explain.

"That means," Adams said slowly, trying to shape
his explanation even as he went, "that you know something without reasoning it out. Your brain does it for
you without you having to think about it." *That should
do it,* he thought. He looked at Early expectantly.

Early thought about that some. The idea made sense,
even if the words were strange and fancy-sounding
strung together that way. As he mulled it over, he
knew that it mostly did explain how he and his col-
leagues operated. Little thought was given to most of
what they saw and did, as far as survival in and traveling through this land was concerned. They saw a flock
of birds, a branch bent or broken, foot- or hoofprints
in the snow, and their minds processed it immediately
and without any conscious thought. Even the seeing of
the things was unconsciously done more often than
not. The mind just took it all in, and barely a blink
later the man reacted or didn't, as was necessary.

Early's impression of Adams did not rise any. He
still didn't trust in book learning or other city ways.
He never had and was certain he never would. He
could not see that there would ever be a time when
having someone along to explain things in such ways
would be handy. Still, in some ways it seemed almost
to set his mind at peace, knowing that there was an
explanation for the way he did things he never thought
about. He smiled inwardly then, suddenly realizing
that the only reason his mind had not been at peace
before the explanation was because Adams had raised

the question in the first place. Had Adams not done so, Early would never have even wondered about what he was doing or why or how.

"I expect that'd explain it, boy," Early said after spitting again. "It's just that there ain't no call for us hosses to think about such doin's." He shrugged. "It just gets done is all." He had no better rationale for Adams. Things were the way they were. That was enough for Early. With growing annoyance, he jerked the Appaloosa's head and moved away from Adams. "Damn citified ol' chil'," he muttered.

Early wondered why he was so irritated at Adams. Early didn't like some things about Adams—his reliance on books and thinking things out and reasoning, and all his trying to explain everything he or anyone else saw and did. Neither did Early like Adams's penchant for avoiding confrontation, his lack of desire to face up to men who would take advantage of him. The easterner had his own ways, that was sure, but so did all men. Early knew that not everyone liked what he did or how he acted. That had never made any difference to him or his friends. Early rarely if ever doubted himself. He lived his life as best he could, doing things his way and to hell with anyone who didn't like it.

Early soon realized that what irritated him so much was that he was somewhat embarrassed at his lack of schooling. He could write his name but little else, and he could read only with great effort. It left him at a disadvantage in business sometimes. Such thoughts rarely plagued him, since his life consisted mostly of trapping beaver and dealing with Indians, but there were occasions when he knew that with some schooling, he would be in a better position to deal with businessmen in Taos and Santa Fe. He relied mostly on his instincts in such dealings. He thought he could generally tell good men from bad, and he dealt with those he figured were good and avoided those he suspected would cheat him. He had done well enough for himself that way and had no complaints about any of it.

Once he figured out what was bothering him about Adams, he dismissed it from his mind. He had acknowledged his faults—to himself only, of course—and that was where it would end. He knew in his heart, and in his head, that he was superior to Adams in all ways that mattered. The easterner wouldn't last two days in the mountains without help.

Such things were what really counted, Early knew. Being able to survive on roots or insects or grubs or one's moccasins or even long pig, if starvin' times was really bad, was important. Being able to read sign and tell a warrior's intentions at a glance; being able to fend off a war party of Blackfoot who had their faces painted black against you; being able to avoid or kill a fractious grizzly—these were the needful things in life. Being able to explain how one did them was a talent as useless as a buffalo bull with teats. With his faith in himself restored, Early rode on.

Riding behind Early, Adams watched the mountain man's broad back. He was worried. He knew he had angered Early but wasn't sure why. He thought perhaps that showing off his intelligence and education was the culprit. He sighed. He always had a tendency to try to impress people that way, often with the wrong results. *You'd think I'd learn,* he thought ruefully.

Still, he never meant to show anyone up when he

did it. He simply wanted to distinguish himself from everyone else. Like all men, he wanted to stand apart from the crowd in whatever way he could. These mountain men did it all the time—their dress was often gaudy, and they bragged incessantly about their prowess in love, in war, in the hunt. Each tried to set himself up as a little better than the others, to prove to the world that he had worth. Adams knew he was only trying to do that himself, using what talents he had been given.

It was unfortunate, he thought, that his talents were so utterly useless out here. Or so they seemed to be. His education might have helped some in impressing Dolores, but that was about as far as he could tell. All the education in the world was not about to help him find food in the wilderness; nor was it going to help him when confronted by a bloodthirsty band of Comanches. And it would not help him get even with a man like Ebenezer Parfrey, he thought in disgust.

That, he realized with a sudden stab of anger and fear, was his biggest problem. To feel himself a man again, to put himself on a level with Early and the others, he needed to confront Parfrey without terror freezing him. He needed to best Parfrey, and to do so in front of others, to humiliate the man who had done such unspeakable acts, to make Parfrey pay for all he had suffered at the wagoneer's hands.

Rage built in his chest, threatening to burn a hole in his heart. Hobart Adams had never experienced such a depth of fury, and it worried and frightened him. His hands where white-knuckled on the saddle horn as he battled the rage. He could not even think for a while.

As he rode, though, the anger subsided a little. That

allowed him to ponder it some more. He knew he had to analyze it to find out what to do. Early and his companions would simply react, most likely violently, and be done with it. But he would have to mull it over for a while before acting.

He knew that his anger and disgust were based in fear. He had never encountered someone like Parfrey before, and he felt like a craven coward.

This was a new opinion of himself. When he thought how full of righteous indignation he had been when trying to defend the Comanche girl, he wondered how that had changed to cowardice and fear.

With a sinking feeling, he knew that the sight of the Comanche girl's remains had gone far in bringing about the metamorphosis. That and the realization that his education and all his words and explanations were meaningless in the face of Parfrey's ruthlessness. Adams had thought that the ability to explain things could change people's thinking and actions. Now he knew it could not. Men like Parfrey—and even those like Early and his companions—would never be swayed by words. They were men of action, whether good or bad action depended on the man and the circumstances. It was a chilling thought.

Adams saw the men had stopped and were making camp. As he dismounted, his self-disgust rose up in tidal waves, smothering him. He couldn't breathe, and the muscles in his chest squeezed his heart. His stomach was a knot of squirming, bile-washed snakes.

Suddenly he turned and ran behind some pines. Bracing his left hand on a tree trunk, he doubled over and vomited, trying to puke out the demons eating at him.

Not far away, Early, Rawlins, and Chardonnais were unsaddling their horses. "What is wrong wit' him?" Chardonnais asked, jerking his head in Adams's direction.

Early shrugged. "I expect somethin' ain't agreein' with him," he said easily. It wasn't his concern.

27

ADAMS STAYED OFF TO himself, remaining behind the tree where he had been sick before moving toward another tree nearer his horse. He wanted to get away from the sickness he had spread. There he stood, disgusted with himself, as the mountain men set up their camp.

It went with well-oiled precision. Once each man had taken care of his own horse, he set about his task. Some gathered firewood, others built fires—one for each group of four or five men—and put fresh elk meat and coffee on to cook. Still others stacked gear and supplies.

Adams unsaddled his horse where he was. When Early and his two friends seemed to be occupied, Adams hurriedly carried his gear toward their fire and set it neatly down nearby. He waited a spell before tying his horse with the others, since he did not want to encounter anyone.

As Early, Chardonnais, and Rawlins sat cross-legged at their fire, Adams licked his lips. Despite having just been sick, he was ravenous, and the coffee and roasting meat smelled enticing. He still did not want to face anyone, though.

Early had been surreptitiously watching Adams while setting up camp. He had no idea what was plaguing the young easterner, but he could understand that Adams did not want to be around the other men just now. There were times when a man just needed to be alone with his thoughts and feelings, his hungers and fears, and wrestle with his own devils. Mountain men were a standoffish lot to begin with, and many of them, including Early, suffered periodic bouts of melancholy. They almost never talked about those times, but the mountaineers knew when to leave well enough alone. On the rare occasions when Early wanted to be left to himself, even his closest friends—Abe Rawlins and Lucien Chardonnais—would leave him be.

When the food was ready, Early found a cup and a tin plate. He carved off a slice of meat and tossed two biscuits alongside it. He filled the cup with coffee. Nonchalantly, he wandered away from the fire with the plate and cup in hand. Not far from where he knew Adams was lurking behind a tree trunk, Early set the two items down on a semiflat rock.

Without a word, Early went back to the fire and sat. Chardonnais, noticing what Early was doing, had filled Early's coffee cup. Early took a sip, then pulled his knife and carved off some meat. He gnawed at the chunk of half-seared flesh on his blade.

Behind his tree, Adams breathed a silent prayer of thanks to the Lord for having brought Ezra Early into his life. He wondered how an unlettered, uncouth, high-smelling, violent man like Early could be so astute in knowing people, and how he could be such a good Samaritan.

Adams stole out from behind the tree as dusk spread over the camp. He picked up the food and coffee and went back behind his tree, where he straddled a large log. He placed his plate on the log in front of him and the cup on the ground next to his right foot. Being sick had left his stomach empty, so he dug into the food with a vengeance.

As he wolfed down meat and biscuits and gulped coffee, he wondered again about Early. The mountain man was much like Parfrey. Both were, more often than not, dirty and unkempt. They were violent, quick to anger, almost as quick to kill. They were tall, rangy, and hard as hammered iron. Yet Parfrey was a lying, back-stabbing, vicious man, more savage than any Indian or bear, from what Adams had seen.

Early, on the other hand, while not the friendliest man God had ever put on earth, was the opposite of Parfrey in so many ways. There had been no reason for Early to expose himself to danger in the Cimarron desert to save Adams's life. Adams wondered how many of these other mountain men would have done the same. He figured not too many. Nor was there any call for Early to continue to help Adams. It was, Adams decided, a mystery he would never be able to solve. He accepted it as that, simply being thankful that it was Early who had found him and not someone else.

Such thoughts, though, saddened him in a way. Early had done so much for him in the short time they had been together, and there was no way for Adams to pay him back. It was, Adams knew, not a question of money. The cash Early had loaned him could be reimbursed readily enough. It was the intangibles that could not be paid back. Adams knew he was a disappointment to Early, though the mountain man had never really said anything about it. Adams also knew that the best way he could pay Early back would be to do what was needed against Parfrey. Adams shuddered at the thought.

By the time he had finished his food and coffee, the rage and self-loathing had dulled to a dim, constant ache in his guts. He felt a little better than he had, but he was still in no mood for company. He put the plate and cup on the rock from which he had gotten it and went back to his log. He wished he had some decent, smooth wine—a nice port perhaps, like he often drank back in New York—but he would settle for some of the cheap *aguardiente* the mountain men drank in Taos and Santa Fe. He didn't though, and wishing for some would not make any materialize.

Adams jumped when a voice came out of the night right next to him: "Your troubles ain't gonna go away with ye just settin' here lookin' at the stars, boy." Though he respected Adams's right to solitude, Early knew that he was not one of the mountaineers. He was still new from the East, and not used to the ways of things out here. While he had eaten, he began to wonder if perhaps Adams was contemplating something foolish, and decided that he should find out.

Adams thought at first that he had not heard Early

approach because he had been so wrapped up in his troubles. Then he remembered that Early always walked as silently as a ghost, even when drunk. Adams looked up at the shadowy figure, a dim glimmer in the moonlight filtering through the pine needles. He tried to work up a smile, but he couldn't. "I know," he said quietly.

"What's plaguin' ye, boy?" Early puffed on his pipe, working it back to a fine burn. It had almost gone out on him.

Adams shrugged. Realizing Early couldn't see it, he said, "I don't know."

"Buffler shit," Early said bluntly. "Was there some others to tell me that, I'd believe 'em. But ye got too much goin' on inside your head, and too many words for explain' to tell me such shit." He paused. "Ye don't want to talk about it, that I can understand. Ye tell me so, and I'll leave ye in peace, boy. I ain't one to pry into affairs that ain't my concern."

"It's Parfrey," Adams said flatly. Even mentioning the name these days made his bowels tighten.

"What about him?"

"I don't know what to do about him." He paused, chewing his lower lip. "I know what I *should* do about him . . ."

"Why don't ye then?"

Adams fought back tears of frustration. "I don't think I could do anything about him even if I could find him again."

Early stroked his chin for a few moments, while puffing his pipe. Then he pulled the clay pipe from his mouth. As he spoke, he jabbed the air with the stem of the pipe. "Lookee here, boy," he said calmly, "I know ye ain't no chickenshit. Parfrey's a shit-eatin' coward, the kind who picks on those can't fight back real well. He ain't got the balls to go agin somebody like me. He whomped the shit out of ye, boy, a while back, and so thinks he can lord it over ye. But if ye was tellin' true all along, it took him and his whole goddamn pack of coyotes to whomp your ass so bad. Hell, I might've even had a touch of trouble with that many boys comin' agin me."

Adams thought he detected a smile accompanying the last. "I know he's a bully. Still, he's big, strong, and tough. I don't think I'm a match for him." Self-disgust clutched at his insides anew. It made him want to vomit again to admit such a thing to a man like Early, but he held the bile back.

"He's that. But size and strength ain't everything. If'n ye knew how to handle yourself, boy, it'd make a heap of difference. Ye put aside your desire to want to go agin him right now, give yourself time to learn a few things, ye'd be able to make wolf bait of him. If'n that's what ye really want." The last was mostly a question.

Adams nodded unhappily. "Yes," he said through a constricted throat, "it's what I want." He looked up at Early, sadness in his eyes, though Early could not see it. "It's not easy for me to wish another man dead. It's even harder for me to admit I want to kill that man. But it must be done."

"I know that, boy, but ye need to convince yourself of that. Ye go agin Parfrey without bein' certain that ye *want* to kill that son of a bitch, ye might as well just put yourself under here and now."

"That ain't so easy, Ezra." Adams tried to keep the whine out of his voice. He wasn't sure he was successful.

"This here's a hard, unforgivin' land, boy," Early said harshly. "It don't make no compromises for nobody. The men who make their way successfully in these lands are the same goddamn way—hard and unforgivin'. Even cowardly bastards like Parfrey. Ye want to take a man like Parfrey, ye're gonna have to give up your citified ways and your highfalutin' ideals and set yourself to bein' as mean as a mountain blizzard and as hard as the Stony Mountains themselves."

Adams swung his left leg over the log so he sat facing Early. He thought about what the mountain man had just said, and it made a lot of sense. The trouble was, he was fairly certain he would be incapable of doing it. Cowardice and fear were not things that one could just wish away. They were usually part of a man, deeply ingrained and inflexible.

"What do you suggest, Ezra?"

"Learn to handle yourself. Ye ary fired a pistol? Or a rifle? Used a 'hawk?"

"I've fired a gun a few times," Adams said weakly, "but not enough to say I know how to use one. As for a tomahawk, I've never even held one, much less used one."

"You can bet your ass Parfrey's used 'em. More'n once, and with good effect. Knife, too, and I expect he knows how to handle himself in a brawl."

"He would seem the type," Adams admitted, feeling the fear come up in him again. He was not at all certain he was capable of killing a man, even one as heinous as Parfrey.

"Parfrey might be an asshole and a bully," Early said quietly. "But men like him're mean as hell. He's killed afore and won't hesitate to do so again."

"So've you."

"Difference is, I don't get any joy from killin'. Leastways not most times." He paused, then added, "Ye set to go agin him, ye'll have to be as mean as he is."

Adams tried to speak but was unable to. Thoughts crowded into his mind: the feel of men pounding on him and the sound of their harsh laughter; the sight of the Comanche girl's remains after Parfrey and his men were done with her; the slow arc of Parfrey's butcher knife as it curved toward him at the *fandango;* the sour taste of fear in his mouth as he waited for death at Parfrey's hands.

How in hell can I ever overcome this fear? he wondered. *How can I ever face a cold-blooded killer like Ebenezer Parfrey?*

"Ye don't need to make your decision now, boy," Early said quietly. "I just wanted ye to know what ye're facin'. Ye ain't up to it, ye'll have to live with that. But livin' with it ain't gonna be no easier if ye set here the rest of your days wishin' things'd been different. Ye either got to make up your mind to do what's needed to raise Parfrey's hair, or ye need to decide ye can live with him still walkin' the earth after all he's done."

Adams nodded glumly in the darkness. He looked up, not knowing what he should say to Early, but thinking he should at least say something. But Early was not there. He had left as silently as he had come.

A long while later, Adams walked as quietly as he could toward Early's fire. He rolled out his blankets. It took awhile to get to sleep.

28

SOMEWHERE IN THAT DIM, surreal time between real sleep and real wakefulness, when things are at their fuzziest yet somehow crystal clear, Adams made up his mind. It came to him not with a flash of light or a herald of trumpets. Rather, it snuck up on him, creeping along on the soft summer night's breeze until it insinuated itself firmly and deeply into his brain.

When he did awake to the sound of a rising camp, Adams was absolutely sure of what he had to do. What he didn't know, as he squatted with a tin mug of coffee in the coolness of the predawn, was how to go about accomplishing it.

He sipped his coffee quietly, trying to think of a way to announce his decision calmly and quietly to Early, Rawlins, and Chardonnais. He didn't want the other mountain men to know. Indeed, after his abysmal display of weakness the day before, he didn't even want the other men to see him, let alone be privy to a deeply personal—and worrisome—decision.

He jumped at the chance when Rawlins and Chardonnais moved off a few feet to tend to personal business, and Saint Vrain's group of mountain men were busy at their own fires.

"I've made up my mind, Ezra," Adams said hastily, an edge of nervousness tickling the words.

"That right, boy?" Early said nonchalantly. He knew what Adams had to do, but he was not certain he had it in him to do it. And Early was not about to try to force the easterner's hand.

"Yes." Adams stared across the fire at Early, who was pouring coffee, not even looking at him. "I aim to get Parfrey." It seemed such a simple thing, saying it so quickly. And it used so few words.

"And just how'n hell do ye figure on doin' such a thing?" Early asked, settling back on his haunches to sip coffee. He watched elk meat sizzling as it dangled from a stick over the fire. He was hungry and looked forward to eating.

"Not sure," Adams admitted. He felt a little better, now that things were in the open. "You said something last evening about teaching me how to handle myself; how to use guns and tomahawks and whatever. If that's true, I'd like to take you up on that offer. I'll put Parfrey from my mind for now. And I'll worry about taking him on when the proper time comes."

Early smiled into his coffee cup, not wanting Adams to see it. He was impressed by the easterner. Adams never ceased to amaze him—every time Early figured Adams was about to give up and go running back East, he found some backbone. But he would not let Adams know it. Besides, Adams's determination did not automatically mean action. Instead, he commented, "I nary said I'd teach ye such things."

"What?" Adams asked, surprised. "You said last night that—"

"I know what the hell I said, boy," Early growled only partially in mock fierceness. "And all I tol' ye was that if ye was to take on Parfrey that ye'd have to learn such things. I nary said I'd do the teachin'. Now that I set my mind to thinkin' on it, I realized that we're nigh onto fall. Me, Abe, and Lucien need to get on the trail soon. A chil' can't make no beaver come if'n ye get out there too late."

"But . . ."

" 'Sides," Early continued, paying no heed to Adams, "I got me a real hankering to see Fallin' Leaf. Them *señoritas* shine, boy. Waugh! But, goddamn, an Injin woman has a way of gettin' under a man's skin and makes him want her somethin' powerful." He suddenly laughed, the sound somehow odd in the quiet camp.

Adams shook his head, taken in again by the mountain man's *joie de vivre*. It was so natural, yet in some ways so out of place at the moment. Then the worry about his situation swept over him again. "But what about Parfrey?" he asked quietly, trying to fight back the resurgence of fear.

Early rubbed his chin for a moment, a smile touching the corners of his mouth under the curve of mustache. "Well now, I expect I can put aside a day or so to teach ye a few things to see ye don't get your fool ass killed."

Adams breathed a sigh of relief, as Chardonnais and Rawlins wandered back up.

"Meat ready?" Rawlins asked, not really caring whether it was. He simply squatted next to the fire, hauled out his knife, and then whacked off a hunk of elk.

Chardonnais chuckled. "You'd eat buffalo shit if we seared it a little," he said, following Rawlins's lead.

"I've et worse than burnt buffler shit," Rawlins said, unconcerned. "So've ye, ye fat little frog. Don't ye go puttin' on airs around your friends."

Early also reached for the half-cooked meat. He cut off a chunk and pitched it to Adams, who caught it and then tossed it from hand to hand to cool it. "Best fill your meatbag good, boy," Early said. "Ye got some work ahead of ye."

"Puking ain't enough work for dat old beavair?" Chardonnais asked as his teeth worked noisily on a mouthful of meat.

"Waugh! Goddamn fool's half froze to raise hair," Early offered.

"He painted his face black against that goddamn Parfrey asshole?" Rawlins asked.

"Yep."

"Ye're gonna have your hands full with that fractious son of a bitch," Rawlins commented, as his teeth tore off another bit of meat. He masticated quietly, gazing levelly at Adams.

"I know," Adams acknowledged, still having trouble fighting the fear.

"And just 'ow do you intend to accomplish this *grande* feat, eh?" Chardonnais said, slurping coffee.

"I know three ol' critters gonna help him some," Early said blandly.

Rawlins cranked his head around slowly to stare balefully at Early. "Ye got shit where your brains ought to be?" he asked.

"*Oui*," Chardonnais said unhappily. "Dat is foolish, eh. We 'ave to get our possibles and 'ead into de mountains soon." He looked anguished.

Early laughed. "Eat shit, Lucien. Ye just get weak-kneed at the thought of going more'n two days without a woman. Shit, ye need to learn to keep your pecker in your pants of a time."

Rawlins joined in the laughter, and even Adams had to stifle a grin. Chardonnais's strangled look only encouraged the others' amusement.

"Bah," Chardonnais spit. Then he grinned.

The laughter finally dwindled, and Early said seriously, "All the funnin' aside, boys, I aim to help ol' hoss there. Ye boys don't want to come along, ye're free to head on back to Taos."

"Hell, I was gettin' tired of all the *fandangos* anyway," Rawlins said, popping the last of the meat from his hand to his mouth.

Chardonnais sighed a great gust of disappointment. "I will come wit' you, too," he said.

Early started chuckling again. "Christ, Lucien, don't look so goddamn glum. Hell, maybe ye can find yourself a buffler cow or somethin' to hump whilst we're out here."

Chardonnais seemed to be considering the thought seriously, as the others laughed.

"Where're ye fixin' to go, *amigo?*" Rawlins asked. He didn't much care. Abe Rawlins was a man who had few cares in life. Some fine beaver plews to trade in come summer; a good drunk once in a while; a woman

to satisfy his lust now and then. And the companionship of a few good, carefully chosen friends. He was a
man who didn't need much to enjoy life.

Early shrugged. "It don't matter. We'll find a place.
What's important is gettin' hoss there to where he can
handle himself some. And we gotta do it fast. I don't
figure to miss out on prime fall plews for nursemaidin'
him."

"We best move then," Rawlins said, feeling the
desire to be on the move. He snapped the mug in his
right wrist, and the remains of his coffee splattered
hissing into the fire. He stood.

The others followed suit. Rawlins, Chardonnais, and
Adams began packing supplies on a mule. Early went
and squatted across the fire from the short, burly,
black-bearded Ceran Saint Vrain.

"*Bonjour, mon ami,*" Saint Vrain said quietly. He
looked at Early with a question in his eyes.

"First off, Ceran, I want to say I'm obliged for what
ye and the other boys here did for me and Bart. Ye
sure made 'em come now."

"Dere is more you want to say?" Though Saint
Vrain was a generally jovial man, he was also direct.

Early nodded. "Me and my *amigos* got us some business to tend to. 'Sides," he added with a slight smile,
"I reckon we ought to lay low for a spell. Even from
Taos. Ye never know, that goddamn Castillo might
send his goddamn soldiers after us."

Saint Vrain's head bobbed twice. "Will you ride wit'
us anymore?"

Early shrugged. "Mayhap we'll set out with ye, but
we'll cut off the trail afore long I expect."

"*Bon.*"

There was nothing more for him to say, so Early stood and headed back to his own fire. His companions were saddling their horses, and he hastened to do the same with the Appaloosa. They pulled out before Saint Vrain's men were ready. With a wave and a whoop, they rode off. Early set a strong, steady pace. He didn't really feel like having Saint Vrain and the others catch up to them. On the other hand, since he wasn't sure where he was going, he wasn't in all that much of a hurry.

Adams rode with eyes open wide, still enjoying the scenery. He thought he would never tire of the harsh, stark mountainsides, the thick green and heavy scent of the pines, the rustling of the leaves atop white-trunked aspens. He could not sketch while he was riding, but he vowed to remember it all, and then get it down on paper later.

By midafternoon, Early had turned off the main road to Taos. There was no real trail to follow; Early just let his Appaloosa pick its way through the grama grass and widely spaced trees. The ground rose steadily, but there were enough flat meadows that the ride was not a strain on the animals.

Well before dark, Early stopped. He rose on the balls of his feet in the stirrups and looked around a bit. "I expect this'll do," he commented.

The others could see no reason to argue. The cottonwoods, pines, and aspens would block the wind, offer shade, and provide sufficient firewood. There was abundant grass for the animals, game seemed plentiful, and the small, rushing mountain stream would provide water.

They made camp with swift, certain efficiency

before stretching out to rest. Adams pulled out his pad and began scribbling furiously, wanting to get the information written down before he forgot it. Once he did that, he could draw some scenes, the words helping him remember the pictures.

The four men took it easy for what remained of the afternoon. After a short nap, Early and Rawlins rode out to hunt.

As soon as those two left, Adams looked at Chardonnais. "You mind if I ask you something, Lucien?" he asked.

"Dat depends on what you wan' to ask," Chardonnais said bluntly.

Adams hesitated, then said, "You must know Ezra as well as anyone."

"*Oui.*" Chardonnais filled his pipe and lit it. "So?"

"I'm very grateful for all the help you and Abe have given me. But Ezra's help has been invaluable. Not that I want to slight you and Abe or anything, but—"

"Ask de goddamn question. *Mon Dieu!*"

Adams smiled nervously. "Why has Ezra given me so much help?"

"Ask him dat."

"I did. All he said was he had his reasons."

"Dere, 'e tell you."

"Hell, Lucien, that doesn't tell me a damn thing."

Chardonnais grinned. "And what makes you t'ink I would know dis? Or dat I would tell you if I did know?"

Adams shrugged, defeated.

Chardonnais puffed his pipe a few moments, then asked quietly, "Did Ezra ever tell you about his brodder Ethan?"

"Some," Adams said, surprised. "He said Ethan was killed by the Blackfoot. Ezra was hurt in the same battle."

"Dat all is true, but dere is more." Chardonnais poured himself some coffee. "Me and Abe, we t'ought Ezra would be gone under dat time," he said, eyes distant. " 'E was bad 'urt. He came around, though it took a couple of mont's. I never seen 'im like he was den. Nor since den, either."

Adams was caught up in the story.

" 'E was, how you say . . . inconsolable. 'E wanted to go after dem Blackfeets right away, but me and Abe, we stop him from such a t'ing." He shrugged. "But, before de winter was all gone away, 'e rides out by 'imself. 'E come back before de spring. 'E don' say not'ing, but 'e 'ad five Blackfoot scalps wit' 'im."

"Lord," Adams breathed.

"*Oui*," Chardonnais agreed.

Adams mulled it for a bit, then said, "That's a hell of a story, Lucien, but what's it got to do with me?"

"Ezra probably would put dis ol' chil' under if he learns dat I say anyt'ing about dis," Chardonnais warned. He sighed. " 'E took 'is brodder's deat' hard. 'E blame himself even though me and Abe, we tell him dis is not true." Chardonnais shrugged. "It took some time before 'e seemed to put dis behind him. 'E 'as not say anyt'ing, but I t'ink 'e sees you as 'is chance to make amends to Ethan. To do bettair for you dan 'e did for Ethan."

Adams was stunned. He had never thought these crude, hard, uneducated men capable of such philosophical thoughts, even if they were subconscious. It placed a heavy burden on Adams, one he was not sure he could carry too long or too far.

Chardonnais seemed to read Adams's thoughts. "You won't let Ezra down, *mon ami*," Chardonnais said softly.

Adams wasn't at all sure about that, but Early and Rawlins were riding back into the camp, and he had to compose himself.

After supper, Early and Chardonnais lit small clay pipes and puffed contentedly. Rawlins pulled out two cigars and handed one to Adams. "Best enjoy it," Rawlins rasped. "I reckon Ezra's gonna work your citified ass off." Adams started to smile, thinking that Rawlins was joking. Then he saw Early's stern face, and he realized with a jolt of horror that what Rawlins had said was true. He wondered if he had made a mistake. As he held a burning twig to the end of his cigar, his resolve firmed once again.

"I can take whatever he can dish out," Adams said with more ease than he felt. Worry about disappointing Early washed over him again.

29

As was their custom, the three mountain men were up just about dawn. Quietly they moved to the stream, sprawled on the bank, and dunked their heads in the cold, swift-flowing water to remove the dregs of sleep.

Early sat up, grinning into the grayness. He filled his hat with water and gleefully crept up on the still-sleeping Adams. Then he poured the water on Adams's head.

Adams rose up with a shout, sputtering. Fear as cold as the water raced through his veins, and his heart pounded with it.

Early, Rawlins, and Chardonnais hooted and laughed at the dismay on Adams's face. The easterner glared angrily at the three whooping mountain men. The initial shock had worn off, and with it the deep-seated fear that came with not knowing what was happening.

"Time to get your ass up, boy," Early said cheerily.

"There was no need for that," Adams said, scrambling to his feet. He stood stiffly. "No need at—" Suddenly he stopped. His face worked through a series of contortions. Then he laughed a little. "I think I've just learned my first lesson, haven't I," he said evenly.

"And ye said he was a dumb shit, Ezra," Rawlins ruminated. Still chuckling he turned and stoked up the fire.

Early put meat on to cook, while Rawlins whipped up what his two companions facetiously referred to as biscuits.

Chardonnais took a pot to the stream, filled it with water, and placed it near the rekindled flames. While the water was heating, Chardonnais pulled a brick of Chinese tea from the supplies. " 'Ow about we 'ave us some tea dis time, eh?" he asked.

Rawlins shrugged, and Early nodded.

Chardonnais whacked off a hunk of the black tea and wrapped it in a piece of cloth. Then he pulverized it with the back end of his tomahawk. He tied the cloth closed with a whang pulled from his buckskin pants and dropped the makeshift bag into the pot of boiling water.

They ate quietly. When they had finished and were puffing pipes or cigars and leisurely sipping hot, pungent tea, Adams cleared his throat and asked, "Well, boys, what's the first thing I must learn?"

"Ye answer him, Ezra," Rawlins said with a grin. "This here was all your goddamn idea."

"Eat shit," Early responded without rancor. He shrugged at Adams. "I ain't ary taught such things to anybody afore. Hell, all us boys just learned 'em by doin'. Don't even remember learnin' 'em, to tell ye true. We can show ye a few things, I expect, but the rest's up to ye."

Adams tossed his cigar stub into the fire and wiped his food-greasy hands on his fancy trousers and rose. "Then we'd better get started." He suddenly was eager to get on with this.

"Ye sure are in a hurry, ain't ye, boy?" Early said levelly. "One thing ye got to learn is some goddamn patience. Set back down and take your ease. I aim to finish my pipe here afore we start on anything else."

Adams shut up and sat. He was edgy, but he forced himself to calm down. He watched the others, eyes flicking from one to the other, and wished he could sit like them, as if they had not a care in the world.

He tried to emulate them, making a conscious effort to keep his jittery legs still, trying to refrain from picking at the grass or tossing pebbles. He was the kind of man who needed activity, always needed to be doing something no matter how innocuous. He had never learned to take his leisure when it was available, to conserve his strength and energy for the times when they were really needed.

In sitting there now, though, and listening to the mountain men, he began to appreciate the importance of such things. He knew his three companions were as strong, as resolute, as courageous as any men alive. Adams began to suspect that they were that way because they knew the value of their resources.

The mountain men talked quietly among themselves, mainly ignoring Adams. They discussed the prospects for the upcoming beaver season, the prices they had gotten for the plews in Taos that year. They pondered where they would trap this year, and they talked fondly of once again seeing their Ute wives. They pondered the signs they read, or thought they read, in the wind about how harsh the winter would be, and where they would make their camp for the cold months.

Adams sat silently and drank it all in. While he knew that what he was learning here would do him no good in a confrontation with Parfrey or anyone else, he was fascinated by what the mountain men had to say. He also had an inborn, deep-seated curiosity about people, places, and things. It was one of the things that had driven him into reporting. He might not be the best writer in the world, he had to admit, but when his interest in his subject was high, it showed through in the words he wrote.

He was so enthralled by the three men's conversation that he never saw Early's knife blade glittering for a moment in the sun as it twirled in the air. Then it stuck in the dirt, a scant inch from Adams's left leg. The wood hilt quivered for a few heartbeats.

Adams reflexively jerked his leg back and stared incredulously at Early. "What the hell—?" he started.

Early rose in a single, fluid motion, seemingly without effort. He moved two steps, bent, and pulled the knife out. He wiped it on a pant leg before sliding it back in the sheath. "I expect the first goddamn thing ye need to learn, boy, now that I've thunk on it some, is to keep yourself ready all the goddamn time. Ain't too many folks this chil' knows of'll give ye warnin' afore they kill ye."

Adams was pale with fright. He had thought for a few moments that Early had suddenly, inexplicably turned against him, and it scared him. More so, he was suddenly frightened by the thought that he might never be able to learn the skills that meant survival out in these rugged, wild mountains. Death and violence rode with these men every minute of every day. So much so, that they seemed oblivious to danger. They knew it was there, certainly, but they seemed to pay it no heed until danger reared its head. "Another lesson," he said flatly, nodding.

"Yep." Early resettled himself and drained his mug of tea. "Like I said before, boy, I can't teach ye much. Ye have to learn it on your own. I can show ye how to shoot a rifle or a pistol, but I can't teach ye to shoot plumb center every goddamn time. Ye got to learn that yourself." He paused and spit into the fire.

"Just like now. Ye wasn't payin' no attention to the world around ye. Ye was simply sittin' there listenin' to us three flappin' our gums. That's somethin' I can't teach ye neither—how to be alert all the time."

"I understand," Adams said with a nod. "But I'm beginning to doubt I'll ever be able to do such things." He felt marginally better at having voiced his fears.

"I expect ye will, boy," Early said with a confidence he really didn't feel. "Hell, me, Abe, and Lucien didn't know shit from beans when we come out here the first time. I'd done me a little huntin' and trappin' and such back in Indiana. But I didn't know shit about stayin' alive out here in the goddamn Stony Mountains."

"That's a fact, boy," Rawlins said. "Had me a heap of learnin' to do afore I knew my ass from a badger hole."

Adams nodded again. "Well, I still have my doubts, gentlemen," he said with a tight, determined grin. "But I'm not about to quit just yet. No, sir, not by a long shot."

"Didn't expect ye was, boy," Early said honestly. He rose, stretching out his long, lanky body. "Well, then, boy, I expect we ought to get to doin' somethin'."

Adams scrambled to his feet, the eagerness surging back.

"Reckon I'll try'n teach ye how to shoot first," Early said. "Go fetch that ol' fusee we gave ye." Like most mountain men, Early kept a spare rifle or two on hand. One never knew when an extra would come in handy.

Adams hurried off to get the .36-caliber fusil. The weapon could not compare with the finely crafted Dickerts and Hawkens the three mountain men carried, but it would do for Adams's purpose at the moment.

"These doin's are hopeless, *amigo*," Rawlins said as the three mountain men watched Adams.

Early shrugged. "Hell, mayhap so. I don't know what—or how—to set about teachin' that chil' what he needs to know. But, shit, the three of us learned. I expect he can, too."

"We learned, *oui*," Chardonnais offered. "But we all 'ad some knowledge in de forest and such, eh? 'E is from de big city, and 'e don' know *merde* about anyt'ing out 'ere."

"Ye boys don't want no part of these doin's, ye can leave off," Early said. "I told ye that afore."

"Shit, Ezra, don't gets your balls in an uproar," Rawlins said defensively. "We wasn't . . ."

He shut up as Adams returned carrying his rifle and matching flintlock pistol Rawlins had given him. Copying his companions, Adams had stuck the pistol in his belt. Over his shoulder hung a shooting bag and powder horn. Those had been donated by Chardonnais.

"Ye know how to load that fusee, boy?" Early asked.
"I'm not sure."

Early shook his head, wondering what he had gotten
himself in for. "Let's go on over there." He pointed to
a glade. Early grabbed his rifle and they all walked to
the glade, stopping about fifty yards from some trees.
Early stood a moment, probing the air with nose and
eyes, seeking sign. A quick smile flickered over his
face. He whipped the rifle up and fired.

"Waugh! Drilled that critter good," Rawlins said.

"What critter?" Adams asked, stunned not only by
the suddenness of the shot but also because he had
seen nothing.

"Turkey back in those trees," Rawlins noted. "Come
on, Frenchie. Let's get that goddamn bird." He and
Chardonnais hurried off.

"Now, boy," Early said calmly, "ye best watch close
how I load my piece. I ain't about to show ye but once
or twice."

He slowly, methodically loaded his Dickert rifle. It
gave him some problems to do it so slowly, displaying
each step, since he was so used to doing it by rote. His
bandaged left hand did not help much either. When he
had finished, he said, "Now, ye try it, boy."

Adams blinked a few times, trying to remember
every step of what seemed to him now to be an endless
process.

"Take your time, boy. Just make certain ye get it
right."

Adams poured a measured dose of powder down the
barrel. Stopping to think out the next step, he reached
into his shooting bag. He came out with a roll of
greased patching material and a lead ball. He placed

the patching on the muzzle and the ball atop it, then sliced off the patching material and put it back into the shooting bag.

"Ye ary get to where ye need to do this for real," Early said, "ye'll learn to either cut patches so ye have 'em ready, or ye can partially cut 'em. That'll make the goin' quicker and easier. There's other ways of cuttin' down the time it takes to reload when ye be in a hurry, but I expect ye don't need to know 'em just yet."

Adams nodded as he started the patched ball down the barrel with a short starter. He pulled out the ramrod and forced the ball all the way down. Lifting the rifle, he half cocked the hammer, snapped open the frizzen, and poured some fine-grained priming powder into the pan.

"Did I get everything right?" Adams asked somewhat nervously.

"Yep." Early pointed. "Ye see that aspen over yonder? The one with the branch danglin' down some?" When Adams nodded, Early said, "See if'n ye can hit that branch."

30

ADAMS RAISED THE RIFLE and steadied himself. He took his time, aiming carefully. He had seen Early and the others shooting while hunting, and it seemed so easy. Now, though, as he looked down the barrel, it was suddenly an imposing task.

Early, Rawlins, and Chardonnais, who held the turkey Early had shot, stood waiting. Finally Early said sarcastically, "Ye gonna stand there all goddamn day lookin' at it?"

"Shoot," Chardonnais said in exasperation. "Dat branch ain' going nowhere. It ain't gonna come no closer just because you are standing dere staring at it."

"I want to be sure I hit it," Adams said stiffly.

"Shit," Rawlins muttered. "That was Parfrey, ye'd have lost your hair, and your balls, long ago."

Adams, a little flushed with embarrassment, set

himself again. He fired almost right away this time. He peered through the cloud of powder smoke, waiting expectantly to see the branch fall.

"I don't know what'n hell ye're lookin' for," Early said dryly. "Ye was off by a mile. Not only was ye far left of plumb center, but ye was low, too."

"But I thought I aimed straight for it." Adams was annoyed at himself. He was also irritated at the others for making fun of him.

"Well now, I expect ye did," Early said soothingly. "What ye did wrong, though, was to scrunch all up just as ye fired. Threw ye plumb off. Ye got to be steady at it. Squeeze the trigger easy. Try it again."

Adams carefully loaded the rifle under the watchful eyes of the three mountain men. He took a long time at aiming again, too, and missed widely once more. "Oh, damn," he mumbled. "I'll never be able to do it."

"Ye aim to give up already, boy?" Early asked harshly.

Adams took a deep breath. "No," he said firmly.

"Then try it again. Ye were a bit closer that time, but ye're still scrunchin' all up. Ye got to relax, boy. Stand up straight and hold yourself steady. Ye do that, and your shot'll be plumb center."

Adams nodded and began reloading.

"Well, maybe ye boys got nothin' better to do than waste powder and ball," Rawlins said lightly. "But I sure as shit do." He strolled off.

"An' me." Chardonnais, carting the turkey, followed Rawlins.

"Don't ye pay them critters no mind," Early said.

Adams nodded and finished loading. As he brought

the rifle to his shoulder, Early said, "Don't take so long this time, boy. All ye'll do is tire your arms. Bring the damn thing up, sight fast, and fire."

Adams did as he was told, and missed again. Jaw set in determination, he began to reload. He fired and missed, fired and missed. Before he could reload once again, Early said, "Best wipe down your barrel, boy."

"Huh?" Adams looked at him, baffled.

"Ye got some of that tow in your pouch, don't ye?"

"Tow?"

"That stringy shit we sometimes use for startin' fires."

Recognition dawned in Adams's eyes. He nodded and pulled out a wad of coarse but thin fiber.

"Yank off a piece, rub a little grease on it, and then swab out your barrel with it."

As he did that, Adams asked, "What's this for?"

"Powder fouls your barrel fast, boy. Ye're in the middle of a fight with the goddamn Comanches or somethin', mayhap ye don't worry over it so goddamn much. But even then, ye don't do it every now and then, your rifle'll quit on ye. Mayhap even explode in your face."

Adams swabbed the tow on the ramrod up and down the barrel with increased vigor, until Early told him to quit. Adams reloaded.

They kept at it throughout the morning, Early patiently coaching Adams. Somewhere in midmorning, Rawlins and Chardonnais rode out of camp, hunting. When they rode back in, Adams was still at it, firing steadily, if not very rapidly.

"How's ol' hoss there doin'?" Rawlins asked, riding up as he and Chardonnais came back to camp from their short expedition.

Early grinned proudly. "Hit plumb center six times straight. And twelve of his last fifteen." He laughed. "And one of those he missed was when he heard a shot off yonder from ye boys. Son of a bitch was certain we was about to be set on by a passel of goddamn Apaches. He got back on track right after that, though. I ain't sayin' he's ready for keepin' us all in meat just yet, but I expect he's got the hang of it."

"Now that's makin' 'em come, boy, sure as shit," Rawlins said. Adams wasn't sure if Rawlins was being sarcastic, though he suspected it.

"We 'ave any powder and ball left after all dis shooting?" Chardonnais asked hopefully, stopping his horse next to Rawlins's.

"A mite," Early said evenly.

"Bon." Chardonnais said, but he sounded disappointed. "Well, we 'ave meat. Deer meat, eh? And de turkey you shot dis morning. It'll be ready soon." He rode off, looking glum.

Rawlins laughed, shaking his head as he watched Chardonnais. "Goddamn horny frog," he said. "He was hopin' ye'd say we was gettin' some low on powder or ball or somethin'. Then he could ride on into Taos to get some new."

Early started to laugh. "That sneaky ol' bastard," he commented.

"What's going on?" Adams asked. He was entirely confused.

Still laughing, Early said, "Not only would that horny bastard get us some supplies, he'd also hump himself a couple of them *señoritas* whilst he was there. But since we ain't run out of anything, he's gonna have to set here with his blood runnin' high, just achin' for some woman flesh."

Adams smiled, then laughed.

Rawlins rode off, while Adams went back to his practicing. Soon after, though, the two headed back to the fire. Adams stopped, watching Chardonnais, who was digging a hole near the fire. "What're you doing, Lucien?" he asked.

"Digging a 'ole."

"I can see that. Why?"

Chardonnais did not answer.

Early sat and poured himself a mug of whiskey from the jug Rawlins and Chardonnais had brought out. It was the only one they had been able to bring along from Santa Fe. "Ye just watch, boy," he said.

Adams also sat and filled a cup with whiskey.

A few minutes later, Chardonnais set aside his small shovel. He dropped the deer's head into the hole, grabbed the shovel, and started scooping hot coals over it.

Adams gulped. "Why's he doin' that?" he asked tentatively.

"That's good eatin' there, boy," Early said.

"You're going to eat that?" Adams was horrified.

"No," Rawlins snapped. "We just put it in the fire for the hell of it."

"Why would we do dat, eh?" Chardonnais asked, surprised, as he sat down.

Adams remained seated. "Well, I've watched you boys for quite a while now, and well—" he hesitated, not sure he should proceed—"well, I wouldn't put it past you to do that just to play a trick me. Make me gag at seeing it, then try to get me to try some of it while you all sit there and laughed your asses off at me."

Early laughed. "I expect we could've been doin' that, boy," he finally said. "But deer head really does shine with this chil'." He winked at Adams. "I'd warn ye, though, boy, to be on your guard against such pranks. Ye nary can tell with these two crepunctious bastards."

"I'll do so." He licked his lips nervously. "And if you don't mind, I'd as soon cook some deer haunch, or some of that turkey."

"If that suits," Early said with a shrug. He couldn't force anyone to eat something.

While they waited for the meat to cook, they chewed on blueberries Chardonnais had found. The berries were a little overripe, but a welcome change nonetheless.

Adams started eating first, enjoying the half-raw deer meat and the hunk of turkey he had roasted. Soon after, he watched with revulsion as Chardonnais dug up the deer's head and the three mountain men started eating it. There was no way they could convince him to try any.

After eating, the men dozed, their full bellies leaving them drowsy. Finally, though, Early stretched himself lazily up. He yawned, scratched, and belched. Then he kicked Adams lightly in the ankle. "Let's go, boy," he said none too kindly. "Ye ain't finished yet for the day."

"You're a cruel taskmaster, Ezra," Adams grumbled as he rose. He rinsed off his head and face in the cold stream and then joined Early. Rawlins and Chardonnais were still napping.

Throughout the afternoon, Early taught Adams the basics of using a tomahawk and knife. Adams stared at Early's unerring accuracy in throwing both weapons. It seemed uncanny the way Early threw them.

After a while, Rawlins and Chardonnais awoke and strolled over to where Adams was enduring his lessons. The two made small bets between themselves, wagering on Early's accuracy—and on whether Adams would be able even to get the tomahawk or knife to stick into the stump they were using as a target.

Adams wondered about whether he would be able to do that, too. Time after time, he threw one or the other weapon. But only rarely did he manage to get the blade into the stump. Within a half hour, he was sweating from the heat and from self-anger. By day's end, he was tired, sore, and most of all discouraged. He sat with low spirits and ate without enthusiasm.

Finally Early said, "Don't get disheartened, boy. Ye can't learn everything in one day. Hell, ye didn't learn all that newspaper shit all in one settin', did ye?" Early demanded.

"No." His voice had little life to it.

"See, there ye go, boy. Ye learned them things, ye'll learn these, too."

"But I couldn't hit anything with the tomahawk or knife. I did a little better with the rifle, but not much."

"Let me tell ye somethin', boy," Rawlins said. "There ain't nobody in all these goddamn Stony goddamn Mountains can throw a 'hawk like that chil' over there." He pointed at Early. "He pure makes 'em come now. Ary time. And he's just as good with that goddamn big Green River of his."

"*Mais oui,*" Chardonnais added.

"I'll tell ye somethin' else, *amigo,*" Rawlins continued. "If'n ye think Ezra's good with them weapons throwin' at a stump, ye ought to see him use 'em on somebody, one to one."

"I did," Adams reminded him. "Against Chacón back in Santa Fe."

"Hell, that was nothin'," Rawlins boasted for his good and longtime friend. "He was just toyin' with that fat piece of shit. He wanted to, he could've cut Chacón six ways from Sunday afore lard ass knew he'd been touched. Ain't arybody better'n ol' hoss there in such doin's. Don't ye get so goddamn gloomy just 'cause ye can't use them things as good as he can. Hell, even me'n Lucien can't match him with those weapons."

Adams brightened fractionally. "Maybe you're right, Abe. But it seems like I'll never be able to learn how to use them at all."

"Give it time, boy," Early said. He seemed for some reason, more quiet and thoughtful than usual.

Adams's resolve solidified. "I won't give up. Maybe I'll never learn any of these things. But it won't be from lack of trying." He persevered, day after day. Adams learned, not realizing at first that he was learning, but doing so just the same. Rawlins and Chardonnais began taking more part in his education, and Adams was often wide-eyed at the abilities of his teachers. What amazed him the most was their ignorance of their own prowess.

Not that it was easy. He suffered physically, especially early on, before his body got accustomed to being used. He also bore up under the sarcasm of his three teachers. It was usually given in the spirit of friendship, but it still cut him on occasions.

After two weeks, he tested himself, and his newly developed skills and strength, against his three companions. These semifriendly wrestling matches left him bruised and battered, but they served to harden him. They increased his confidence, too, even though he always came out the worse of the two combatants. He learned, too, to be constantly aware of his surroundings. Rarely now was he caught unawares by his companions.

He began to feel more comfortable carrying a weapon in his hand, too. At first he had felt funny about it, but then he convinced himself that there was nothing unusual about always having a knife or tomahawk or pistol near to hand in this territory.

Despite it all, though, he managed each day to find time to write and to do some sketches of himself in various activities. He was very self-conscious about it for some time, but eventually grew to be more comfortable about it.

After several weeks he was feeling rather good about himself. He wasn't under the delusion that taking Parfrey would be easy, but he began to think that taking Parfrey might not be impossible either.

31

AFTER A WEEK, RAWLINS and Chardonnais risked a trip into Taos, both to see if anyone was on the lookout for Early and Adams and to get supplies. They returned three days later in good spirits, and reported to Early and Adams that all seemed normal in Taos: that there were no more soldiers than usual and no one seemed to be lying in wait for any of them.

Moreover, while they had been there, they had spoken to Ceran Saint Vrain and some of the men who had gone to rescue Early and Adams in Santa Fe. They had not seen any increased activity against the Americans either, so all was considered safe.

Rawlins then grinned as he tossed a bone over his shoulder into the growing darkness. "And, by Christ, that goddamn horny frog there finally had himself a goddamn woman."

"Oui," Chardonnais said with a cheek-stretching grin. He seemed at peace. *"Trois femmes,"* he bragged. "Three women."

"It's a damn good thing, too," Rawlins growled in mock severity. He laughed, then. "Lecherous ol' fart was startin' looking at me funny whilst we was ridin' to Taos. Had to keep my goddamn Hawken primed lest he come up behind me and try humpin' me when I weren't lookin'."

Chardonnais was unashamed of his libido. He laughed uproariously and said, "It would be de bes' 'umping you ever 'ad, *mon ami.*"

"Shit," Rawlins muttered. There was nothing else he could say to such a statement.

The others laughed and hooted at Rawlins for a few minutes.

Then Adams asked shyly, "Do you and Abe also have Indian wives, Lucien?"

"'Ell, yes. Good women, dem Utes. *Mais oui.*"

"If they're that good, and if you are—" Adams flushed in embarrassment, unsure whether he should continue.

Early laughed. "Hell, boy, ye started on the journey, ye best have the balls to finish up what it is ye got to say."

"Well," Adams went on hesitantly. He was still red-faced but was determined to proceed. "Well, if you're so . . . needful of a woman all the time, why not bring your Indian wife down to Taos with you? That way . . ."

The rest of his statement was drowned out by the guffaws that erupted from Early and Rawlins.

Chardonnais did not see what was so funny. He let loose a string of French that none of the others understood. Not that they wanted to know what he was jabbering about anyway. Finally the laughter and Chardonnais's babbling wound down until it halted.

Into the new silence, Adams asked, "What's so funny about all this?" He was hurt that the others would laugh at him for asking a question on a suggestion that to him made perfect sense. "If he had brought his Indian wife with him to Taos, she'd be with us now. That way he wouldn't have to worry about finding a woman in Taos. Or maybe even paying for some woman's favors."

Rawlins smiled. "To tell true, boy," he said, "after a winter cooped up with three goddamn Ute squaws, we're in the market for a change, if'n ye know what I mean." He winked in lecherous camaraderie.

"But if you're married to them—"

"Hell, boy," Rawlins said in exasperation, his irritation never far subdued, "it ain't like we was married by a preacher."

"You weren't?" Adams was surprised, but when he thought about it for a moment, he realized he shouldn't be shocked. It would not be the way out here. For one thing, there were no preachers out in the wilds. He supposed the men could've brought the women into Taos for a marriage service, but they certainly didn't seem the kind to do such a thing. Besides, no respectable clergyman—even a Catholic, which was all there were in Taos—would perform such a service, he figured.

"Jesus goddamn Christ, boy," Rawlins muttered.

"Such doin's ain't no big deal," Early offered. "Ye find yourself a woman ye want, then go to her pa and offer him a couple horses or a sleepin' robe or some other such goddamn foofaraw he might want. If'n she agrees, and her pa thinks what ye're offerin' is fair, ye move into a lodge together. It that's simple."

"Less'n ye want to go through the smoke ceremony," Rawlins added, irritation tempered again.

"What's that?" Adams asked, interested.

"Ye and your woman go into a small lodge that's got a godawful smoky fire in it. And ye set there for a couple hours or so."

"That sanctifies the marriage?" Adams asked. He was still interested, but he was beginning to suspect he was being made a fool of. Still, he figured he would withhold judgment just yet.

"Not really," Early said. "It just tests ye and your woman in several ways. For one, it shows how much endurance ye got. If ye make it in there a while, it also shows ye're resistant to sickness."

Adams looked from one to the other of the men. All seemed serious. He could see no lurking smiles or smirks of derision. He began to believe.

"Most important, though," Rawlins continued after lighting up a corn-husk *cigarrillo,* "is that if ye and the woman can stay in there a spell without tryin' to raise hair on each other, the Utes figure your marriage'll last ye both a good long time."

Adams nodded. It made sense, once he thought about it. He also thought that Christian preachers might be wise to develop a similar test for the people they were about to marry.

"And they stick with you during the summer, while you're gone to Taos, even though there's no formal union between you?" Adams asked. That was the real surprise to him.

"Mostly," Early said. He shrugged. "There's times, of course, when a hoss'll get back to the village and find his woman's gone off and attached herself to another. Don't happen too often, though." He suddenly grinned. "Happened to Chardonnais quite a few times. Seems them women get some tired of his goddamn pawin' at 'em and wantin' to hump 'em every hour or so. That happens, ye go get yourself another."

"Bah," Chardonnais spit. He was still in a sour mood.

"What about love?" Adams asked.

The other three just shrugged. It was not of much importance to them. All of them cared for their Ute wives after a fashion. But mostly their marriages with the Utes were ones of convenience. They picked women who were strong, who traveled well, who would bear and raise children with little trouble, who would be good companions, in the robes and out, who were good cooks, and who could work plews well. The concept of romantic love was, if not alien to both parties, an awkward luxury. If love bloomed between the couple, which happened often enough, so much the better.

Adams was shocked again, as he had been by so much he had seen and heard in the past few months. He got over it more quickly this time, though, realizing that this was not a land or a life that would breed love. Come to think of it, he was shocked to discover, the life in the slums of New York was not really conducive to breeding love either. Indeed, it was probably worse. So much so that the people who lived there had to delude themselves into thinking they were in love in an effort to make their pitiful existence a touch better. These mountain men, and the Indians, too, he suspected, had no such need.

Suddenly, Adams thought about his fiancée. Former
fiancée, he corrected himself. He had not thought of
her in what seemed like months. She seemed a distant
thing, almost unreal, though he knew that she was
real. As had been their love. Or had it? he wondered.
He had loved her. He knew that for a fact, unless he
was deluding himself far more than he thought he was
capable of. Even now the pain at losing her was
sharp.

He had always thought she had loved him as deeply,
but now he was not so sure. Removed by time and distance, he could look back almost dispassionately. In
doing so, he could see the flaws and chinks in their
love. Just the little things that he had been too blinded
to see when he was in New York. She did not really
love him, he knew now. Or if she did, it was a superfi-
cial love, the kind he had reasoned deluded their pos-
sessors to lighten their lives.

No, there was little love there. For him, at least.
Though from a poor family, Elizabeth wanted to get
ahead in life. She wanted a good home, fine clothes,
the best food and drink. She wanted to socialize with
people who were not poor and downtrodden like herself. Thing was, Adams acknowledged painfully, with
her beauty she would probably succeed.

He also admitted to himself now that she had only
been using him. Even as a reporter for a well-respected
newspaper like the *New York Register,* he would not
gain entry to the social circles in which Elizabeth
wanted to circulate, but it would have been a start. He
could have gotten her one step up the social ladder.
Then she would have dropped him to find another
man to take her to the next step, until she married a

rich suitor. Adams could see that clearly now. It made him sick to think that she had so ill-used him. "Damn woman," he breathed, barely audibly. But the irritation lessened when he thought of Dolores.

"Ye all right, boy?" Early asked, looking at him strangely.

"Yes," Adams said dumbly, as he painfully and slowly climbed out of the morass of self-pity into which he had worked himself.

"Ye sure? Ye looked like ye've just et somethin' don't agree with ye."

"I'm all right," Adams insisted, though without much conviction. He sucked in a deep breath and then blew it out. He smiled with rue. "Just some unpleasant thoughts of the past came back to me."

"Ye can't do shit about what's gone afore, good or bad," Rawlins commented. "Best to think of this day and the ones to come." Rawlins was a man who did that, and he could not understand people who lived in the past.

"You're right, of course," Adams said after some moments to mull the statement over. "I take it, then," he said, remembering now what they had been talking about, "that getting shed of an Indian woman—or she you—is as easy as getting married?"

"Yep," Early acknowledged. He leaned forward and carved off another piece of mountain lion meat. He took a bite and chewed slowly. "All ye got to do is take your possibles out of the lodge. Either of ye. Then it's over."

Adams nodded. "What'd you mean, Abe, when you said you all needed a change after a winter?"

Rawlins thought about that for a bit, while he finished off another mouthful of meat and then spit out a piece of gristle. "Now don't get me wrong, boy," he said slowly. "Utes're good Injins. Clean, dependable, good company. But after a winter closed up in a lodge with a squaw—any squaw—ye get a hankerin' for a woman don't smell like buckskin and grease."

"*Oui,*" Chardonnais said emphatically. His mood had swung completely around. He was like that, one minute down in the dumps, the next laughing and having himself a high time. It worked in reverse, too, but the others had long ago come to accept those things.

Early laughed. "Same thing happens come summer, though," he said. "Waugh! Them *señoritas* is fine, for certain. But, goddammit, after a couple of months dealin' with their fathers and brothers and other such goddamn critters as want to stand in your way, ye just want the freedom of your own woman and your own lodge." He paused, thinking. He did not often give voice to such things. None of the mountain men did, and so he had to think over every word.

"There's more'n that though, goddammit," he continued after a little. "Ye get tired of *cigarrillos* and food filled with beans that make ye fart as often as Lucien wants to hump some unfortunate woman. Ye get tired of Mexican officials and their connivin' and all such doin's. Makes ye just want to get up in some high mountain valley with your squaw and your possibles in your lodge and breathe free again."

Adams nodded. There was more to these men than he had thought. He knew they didn't very often speak about their feelings or desires and such, and it was an eye-opener for him. They tried to come off as simple men, but they were, Adams now realized, more complex than they would admit. He also felt good that they had opened up to him today. It made him feel more a part of the small group.

32

A WEEK AFTER THEY returned from Taos, Rawlins and Chardonnais made another trip there to pick up supplies. This time when they came back, though, neither was in good humor.

Adams wondered about it but said nothing, since Early did not. Adams might feel more a part of this select group, but he still wasn't really one of them. So he did not think it his place to question Rawlins or Chardonnais. Early simply acknowledged that his two longtime friends were in no mood for chatting, then turned and left with Adams in tow.

That night they sat around the fire, filling their bellies on deer meat, beans, and coffee. After eating they sat back, smoking. Rawlins, who had regained most of his humor during the afternoon, stood and walked to the supplies. He returned to the fire with two jugs of whiskey.

"Here, ye sour-faced ol' fart," he said with something approaching glee as he set one of the jugs in front of Chardonnais. The French Canadian said nothing, though he scowled and jerked the cork out of the jug. He hefted the vessel and drank deeply.

Rawlins shook his head and eased himself down. He started the other jug. After a healthy swallow, he passed it to Early, who drank and handed it to Adams. He took only a small sip before giving the jug back to Rawlins.

Chardonnais continued to sip more frequently and deeply than the others, greedily slurping the fiery brew.

"Hell, Lucien, ye aim to drink it all by your goddamn self?" Early asked after a while.

"An' suppose I am, eh?" Chardonnais said belligerently. "What of it? I am 'alf froze to 'ave a good drunk." He glared at the others.

"If that's where your stick floats, ol' hoss, this chil' ain't gonna stand in your way," Early said evenly. "But what'n hell's got your balls all in an uproar?" He had his suspicions.

Chardonnais only scowled again and took another drink.

A grin lit Rawlins's face. He scratched his greasy head after pulling off his hat and tossing it aside. "Seems ol' Frenchie there nary got his lance wet this trip." He stifled some chuckles. "Weren't enough time, I reckon, since we needed to get back here."

"It don't take that long," Early said, smiling, his suspicions confirmed.

"It takes some goddamn time for a chil' to find his-self a woman when his reputation proceeds him. Seems like all them *señoritas* he's humped don't want nothin' to do with him again." He could no longer contain the laughter. It came up and out, softly and steadily. "And, would ye believe it, all the trollops in Taos was *ocupado*." He was laughing full out now.

Early was, too, and could find nothing more to say.

Even Adams was amused. He decided to test his place here a little. "You see, Lucien," he said quietly. "If you had brought your Ute woman with you, this never would have—"

Chardonnais's burst of agitated French stopped Adams cold. The easterner looked scared but kept himself under control. When Chardonnais paused for a drink, Adams said stiffly, "If you want to insult me, *Mister* Chardonnais, please do so in my language so I know what you're saying."

"I will tell you what I said," Chardonnais growled. His dark face was contorted with anger. "I said you are a no-good *fils de garce,* a son of a bitch, eh? I said you 'ave no balls, and dat you couldn't fin' a woman to 'ump you if you 'ad a sack of gold as big as a 'ouse. *Vous êtes nullissime.* You are useless, and you 'ave no *kiquette,* no pecker, as *mes amis* might say. An' I said you—"

"That's enough!" Adams growled. His face was red with anger and embarrassment. When Chardonnais had clamped his mouth closed in angry surprise, Adams said, "I was joshing you, as Mister Early and Mister Rawlins often do," he snapped. The words were strangled by his rage. "I thought I was considered your friend as well. Apparently I was wrong in my thinking."

"*Mais oui!*" Chardonnais muttered.

Early and Rawlins looked on silently. This was not their affair; it was between Adams and Chardonnais. Adams would have to deal with it as best he could. If he got rattled now, he'd never be able to take Parfrey.

Adams nodded. "Then you have my apologies for assuming more than I should have."

Chardonnais grunted an acknowledgment and took another drink.

"But," Adams added firmly when he realized that was going to be Chardonnais's only response, "I expect an apology from you, too."

"From *moi?*" Chardonnais asked in surprise, almost choking on his whiskey. "What in 'ell for?"

"For all those names you called me," Adams said calmly. "I might've misjudged when I assumed we were friends, but that's no call for you to say those things to me. No, sir, no call at all."

"*Merde,*" Chardonnais snapped. "I ain' going to apologize to you, nor nobody, *monsieur. Mais non!* Nevair."

"You, sir," Adams said flatly, hoping his fear was not evident, "are a clap-ridden whoreson. A festering, disease-carrying cockalorum."

Chardonnais was off the ground like a bolt of lightning, storming across the fire. He crashed into Adams's chest, knocking him onto his back. Chardonnais's dagger gleamed in the firelight.

Early and Rawlins moved, fast. Both knew Adams was no match for a knife-wielding Chardonnais. But they were not fast enough. Adams grunted in surprise and with the impact. But he fought back the fear that threatened to overwhelm him, letting his body react.

He bucked twice, gaining enough momentum to flip Chardonnais off him. He scrambled up, drawing his own knife. He was breathing heavily.

Early and Rawlins quickly stepped between the two. Early placed the flat of his bandaged palm against Adams's chest, but he addressed both when he spoke. "Ye boys put them blades away," he snapped.

When both combatants hesitated, Early said, "Ye critters best listen, goddammit. Now I know ye two goddamn fools don't want to go killin' each other. Ye want to kick the shit out of each other, that's one thing, but I ain't aimin' to let ye carve each other into wolf bait. Ye drop them knives and ye can fight all ye want."

"Don' get in my way, *mon ami*," Chardonnais said flatly. "This is not your fight. I am sick of dis *fils de garce* and all 'is big talk and 'is fancy words. Now, move out of de way before I 'ave to cut you, too, before I make de wolf bait out of dat *grande gueule*— loudmouth."

Early's eyes narrowed, and he whirled, his Green River knife in his right hand. "Ye aim to move me, ye shit-eatin' little fart?" He had seen Chardonnais in some very sour moods, but never this bad. He was prepared to excuse a lot of rancorous behavior in his friend, but this baffled him.

Rawlins still had a tight grip on the short, rugged Frenchman, but Chardonnais made no effort to go against Early. He was filled with rage and was a little drunk. But he was not crazy, and he knew better than to try facing Early with a knife. Chardonnais spit and flipped his knife. It stuck into the ground. "Dere. Are you 'appy, eh?"

Early turned back to face Adams again, sliding the knife back into the sheath as he did. "What's it gonna be, boy?" he asked.

Adams dropped the weapon. "I don't need the knife, Ezra."

Early stepped out of the way. "Let him go, Abe."

Rawlins released Chardonnais, and the Frenchman immediately charged. He slammed into Adams, shoulder into abdomen. His momentum carried both a few feet before they tumbled to the ground.

Adams struggled and wriggled, trying to free himself. He also fought his own fear. Letting the fear get the upper hand, he knew, would be his undoing. He would have his hands full in battling Chardonnais without that, too. He finally managed to kick himself loose and he shoved Chardonnais away. The two stood, a little more slowly than the last time. They were gasping for air and watching each other warily. Chardonnais seemed cocky, though, and charged again, arms widespread. He resembled an angry buffalo bull.

Adams was more prepared this time than Chardonnais had figured on. Indeed, Chardonnais had maintained a mighty low opinion of Adams's abilities. Adams, though, stepped lightly to the side and clubbed Chardonnais on the back of his thick neck with interlocked fists.

The mountain man stumbled ahead a few steps and stopped, spinning. The punch had had no effect, it seemed. He grinned viciously. "You will not do such a t'ing again, *monsieur*," he hissed. He was almost as angry at himself for having gotten hit as he was at Adams for hitting him.

Adams surprised everyone by charging, hoping to catch Chardonnais off guard. He almost did, but Chardonnais recovered swiftly and was ready when Adams actually ran into him.

It was Adams's turn to be surprised when he hit Chardonnais. The Frenchman did not budge. Adams bounced off the mountain man and then fell as he caught Chardonnais's powerful fist on the side of the head. He gave silent thanks when Chardonnais's kick missed his groin.

Chardonnais moved forward, very lightly for such a stocky, bearlike man. But the fight had not gone out of Adams yet. The young easterner kicked out with both feet, knocking Chardonnais's legs out from under him. Chardonnais fell, grunting when he hit the dirt. Adams crawled and scrabbled onto Chardonnais's chest, lashing out with his fists. He heard yelling, and realized after a moment that he was the one making the eerie sounds. He decided he didn't care.

Chardonnais fought back hard, raining heavy blows on Adams wherever and whenever he could. He had the strength of a grizzly and was a veteran of many a brawl. Worse for Adams, Chardonnais did not like losing at anything, least of all a fight.

Adams had learned well from his mentors, however, including the one he was savagely trying to gouge, bite, and strangle. Finding an opportunity, he clamped his teeth onto Chardonnais's left ear and bit down hard.

The mountain man howled in rage and let loose a string of torrid, unintelligible French. He also jammed a thumb into one of Adams's eyes.

Adams yelped and jerked his head back a little, out of range of Chardonnais's searching thumb. Then he returned the favor. As Chardonnais grunted with it, Adams bit Chardonnais's ear again. He pulled his own shoulders up to protect himself and gnawed with determination while Chardonnais pounded his sides and back with punishing blows.

Realizing his fists were not doing much good, Chardonnais suddenly grabbed the back of Adams's hair and yanked with all his strength. Adams's head moved back slowly, but when it did, there was a small piece of Chardonnais's ear in his teeth. Blood dripped down his chin, and covered Chardonnais's ear. Adams tried to gouge Chardonnais's eye again, but he missed, and his finger hit Chardonnais's forehead and slid off. It did serve to make Chardonnais release his hair. Adams pushed himself to his feet, where he stood unsteadily.

Chardonnais also got up, feeling his bleeding ear. "*Le lèche-cul,*" he hissed. "Ass licker. You took part of my ear. I'll make you pay for dat."

Adams spit the tiny piece of flesh out. He looked queasy, but he stood defiantly. He wiped away the blood on his chin, and then cleaned his hand on the buckskin pants Chardonnais and Rawlins had brought back for him after their first trip to Taos. "Do your worst," he said calmly.

With a roar, Chardonnais charged. He rammed into Adams, enveloping him in his arms. They fell, but as they went down, Adams shifted. They landed hard and rolled over and over. The struggling men rolled through the fire, not noticing. Each fought for an opening.

Punches flew and legs flailed but with little effect now. Finally they fell apart, too tired to keep up such exertions. Both struggled to rise, their chests heaving as they fought to breathe.

Chardonnais made it first. Balling his fist, he staggered toward Adams. He swung at Adams's head, but the easterner, who had managed to rise only as far as his hands and knees, had fallen back down, so Chardonnais's punch hit only air.

Before Chardonnais could gather up his strength for another shot, Adams had managed to get up. He was unsteady but ready.

Early and Rawlins, who had stood by quietly through it all, suddenly burst into laughter.

"Ye ought to see yourselves, boys," Early said. "Ye are two of the sorriest-lookin' critters this chil's ary seen."

Chardonnais and Adams looked at each other, seeing in the other man an image of himself. Both were caked with sweat, dust, and blood. Suddenly Chardonnais grinned. Once again, his rage and melancholy had fled in the blink of an eye. "You are a sorry-looking child, *monsieur*," he said quietly, still puffing.

"Hell, you don't look too good yourself," Adams gasped stiffly. He thought perhaps he had missed something here. A moment ago, he was fighting for his life. Now Chardonnais was standing here grinning at him. It mystified him.

"Why'n't ye hosses quit this here foolishness," Early said.

"I'm willing if he is," Adams said with as much eagerness as he could muster.

Chardonnais nodded and grinned. "You did well, *mon ami*. You made dem come now. *Mais oui*." He took a step forward, holding out his hand.

Adams warily took the proffered hand, half expecting some trick. But Chardonnais merely gave one strong squeeze and released the hand. Then he threw one strong arm around Adams's shoulders, and the four men returned to the fire.

As they all sat, Chardonnais said, "Pass me dat jug, Ezra. I 'ave worked up a big thirst. *Oui. La grande soif.*"

Early looked at him with a question in his eyes. "Ye sure, boy?"

"*Oui.*"

Early shrugged and passed him the jug.

33

ADAMS AND CHARDONNAIS REFUSED doctoring. Not that Early and Rawlins could have done too much anyway. Their medical supplies consisted of a small bottle of laudanum, some roots and herbs of unknown vintage, and a needle and some sinew for stitching wounds closed.

Adams had wanted some medical attention, but he was not about to appear weak before these other men. Not after what he had been through. Besides, he had no real wounds, and there was no medicine he knew of for bruises and small cuts. He could, he supposed, take some laudanum for the pains, but that would knock him out. He figured the harsh whiskey they were sipping would be enough of a painkiller for him.

More meat was put on the fire, to be ready whenever the men felt like partaking. As the two jugs made the rounds, Rawlins offered Adams a cigar. "Picked me up a new supply whilst me'n Lucien was in Taos," he announced. "I reckon ye deserve one." He was much impressed with Adams, something he hadn't been until a few minutes ago. He had always thought Adams would be a weakling, but the easterner had shown him something about courage and determination.

"Thanks," Adams said. He lit it and leaned back against his saddle. The pain was really starting to get to him now. He felt like he had been kicked by a herd of mules. He knew his face, as well as most of the rest of his body, would be discolored. He wanted to look, to check himself out, but that would not do. He must pretend to be unconcerned. He drank deeply of the whiskey jug when it came to him, hoping to ease the pain.

With his pipe going, Early asked, "What'n hell come over ye, Lucien? Ye've been overcome with the melancholy afore, but ye ain't ary been that bad I can recall. It had to be somethin' more'n you just not gettin' a chance to stick your pizzle in some poor *señorita*."

"Aw, hell," Chardonnais said, looking more than a little ashamed. He took a drink, then puffed on his pipe. "What you say is true, *mon ami*. Dere is more, though," he sighed heavily, remembering lost opportunity, "dem *mademoiselles* dere in Taos was cold toward me. I can't understand dat."

"Shit," Rawlins drawled. "Ye keep your pecker in your pants more often and think about somethin' else, them women might be more likely to spread for ye."

Chardonnais ignored the jibe.

"Ye said there was more?" Early asked.

"Oui." He grinned with regret. "I lost nearly all I 'ad on some damn 'orse race. Left me mostly a *vide-poche,* an empty pocket."

"Ye should've known better'n to do such a damn-fool thing, boy."

"Oui." He didn't sound like he regretted it much. "But dis young Mexican buck 'ad a fast 'orse. Or so everybody said, eh." He shrugged.

"Heard wrong, did ye?" Early asked with a low chuckle.

"Mais oui!" Chardonnais said with a touch of rue. "Damn race wasn't even close. Damn."

"And where'n hell was ye durin' all these doin's?" Early asked Rawlins.

The rangy Kentuckian shrugged. "Off doin' what I was in Taos to do—gettin' us some supplies. Lucien there tol' me he was headin' off to see if'n he could find someplace to dip his wick. Next thing I know, ol' froggie there is rantin' and ravin' and puttin' up all kinds of a fuss."

"Oui," Chardonnais admitted. "Between dat damn 'orse race and remembering I 'ad not 'umped any of de *femmes,* I work myself into *le grand* fit. I got madder an' madder de closer we got to 'ere. I was more dan 'alf froze for a fight, and *mon ami* over dere"—he pointed to Adams—"was good enough to accommo-date me by opening his mout'." Chardonnais grinned at Adams. "But you showed this child a t'ing or two. *Mais oui!*"

Adams felt a flush of pride, but he remained silent. He had learned well, and he was proud of that. Still, he was racked with pain and rather baffled about Chardonnais's mood swings. *How's a man supposed to know what to say and when to say it if he doesn't know how someone's going to react?* he wondered.

Still, even as his euphoria wore off, he knew that he had done well this night.

Early let Adams lie around the next day so he could recover. But the following morning, training continued. Still, there was little more Early, Rawlins, and Chardonnais could teach Adams. Whatever was done now was more a matter of practice and repetition.

After the four men had finished their evening meal two days later, Rawlins said through the fog of cigar and wood smoke, "I reckon it's time for us to be movin' on, Ez. He ain't gonna get no better'n he is now, I don't reckon. Not 'less'n ye reckon to spend the winter here helpin' him."

"Wasn't plannin' on it," Early said easily.

"Didn't reckon ye had." Rawlins paused a moment. "Bart's done purty well for hisself, but we can't go on babyin' him. I reckon he's about as ready as he's ary gonna be to go agin that Parfrey feller."

"What's your thinkin', Lucien?" Early asked, reserving comment.

"It don' matter what I t'ink, *mon ami.* It only matters what Monsieur Adams t'inks about all dis." He shrugged. "But since you ask me, I will tell you what I t'ink, eh. I t'ink we need to get our asses up into Ute country and goddamn soon. We ain' going to make no bevair come if we don' get up dere and set our traps. Everybody we know was nearabout ready to leave Taos when me and Abe rode in dere de udder day. We won't even find de bevair if we don' hit de trail soon."

"It don't matter one goddamn bit when we leave out, *amigo,*" Early said fiercely. "This chil' can make beaver come anytime, anywhere." He puffed. "But ye're right," he added. He looked at Adams. "Well, boy?"

Adams knew all the eyes were on him, and that made him more than a little uncomfortable. He thought about it. There was so much he didn't know, yet he had learned quite a bit in a short time. He knew Rawlins was right, that there was little more that these men could teach him. At least here and now. If he traveled with them, lived with them for months, yes, they could teach him so much more. But he didn't have that luxury.

"I've kept you men here far too long already," Adams said slowly. "I'm grateful for all you've done. But like Lucien said, if you don't get on the trail soon, your trapping will be ruined. I can't have that on my head."

"Don't ye worry none about that, boy," Early said. "Just 'cause ol' Lucien's a goddamn worry wart don't mean we can't make beaver come. I just don't want to see ye get rubbed out by the likes of Parfrey."

"That's touching," Rawlins said with a healthy dose of sarcasm. "Ye aimin' to marry him soon?"

"Shit. It ain't so much that I'm overly fond of him, but I'd hate like hell to know we wasted all this time and effort."

"That makes sense," Rawlins agreed.

" 'E will rip dat Parfrey's 'ead off," Chardonnais said firmly. Since his fight with Adams, he had become far more friendly toward the New Yorker. And much more of a booster.

"Maybe *ye* ought to marry him, Lucien," Rawlins said.

"Bah," Chardonnais spit. "I just know what 'e can do. I was de one fought 'im, not you. If you 'ad fought him, you wouldn't be sitting 'ere now. You would be gone under."

"Bart?" Early asked. "It's your goddamn choice, boy."

"Well, much as I'd like to believe in Lucien's faith in me, I don't think I'm as good as being able to take Abe easily," Adams said diplomatically. "But I do think all of you are right in saying there's not much can be done with me here." He took a deep breath and let it out slowly. "I say we go back to Santa Fe and get it over with." He was filled with a mixture of eager anticipation and fear.

Early nodded. "If'n that's where your goddamn stick floats, boy, I ain't gonna be the hoss to stand in your way." He knocked the ashes out of his pipe into the fire. As he put the pipe into the piece of buckskin around his neck, he added thoughtfully, "But I expect we ought to wait another couple days."

"Why?" Rawlins asked, surprised. He thought the decision had been made.

"Bart's still some stove up from his fight with Lucien the other day."

"So's Lucien," Rawlins said.

"Ain't Lucien gonna have to go agin a hard ass like Parfrey," Early said simply. "He's gonna have his hands full as it is. We don't need to cut the odds no more by havin' him gimpin' around when he sets on Parfrey."

Rawlins nodded. "When do we leave?"

"Day after tomorrow, I expect," Early said thoughtfully. "We take our time heading back to Santa Fe, that'll be another day or two. He ought to be recovered full by then."

"I'm fine, Ezra," Adams interjected. "We can leave in the morning."

"Couple more days ain't gonna hurt us none." He looked from Rawlins to Chardonnais. "If you boys're in a hurry, ye can head on to Taos come mornin'. Me'n Bart'll follow ye when we can and meet ye there."

"What do ye say, Lucien?" Rawlins asked. It was not so much that he wanted to get back to trapping grounds. Another couple of days here wouldn't make any difference. It was just that he was bored stiff. Watching Hobart Adams toss a tomahawk at a tree stump hour after hour was not his idea of something to do.

"I am 'appy 'ere to wait, I t'ink. But you are not?"

Rawlins shrugged. "Just half froze to be on the move is all. We can wait around."

"We will go 'unting tomorrow. Dat will give you somet'ing to do, eh?"

"I reckon."

"You gonna be all right, Lucien?" Early asked. "Ye was some busted up in that fracas, too."

"I will be fine, *mon ami.* Maybe a little slower dan is usual, but dat is all." He grinned, brightening his bruise-colorful face. "Is not so bad as dat time we 'ad dat little *fandango* with de Crows t'ree wintairs ago, eh?"

"We made them goddamn red devils come that time," Early said.

"What happened?" Adams asked, then hastily added, "If you don't mind talkin' about it."

"Ain't much to tell," Early said. "We was trappin' up

along the Wind River. Couple Crows run off some of our horses and such. Them fractious bastards're the best goddamn horse thieves this chil' ary saw. Anyway, me'n Lucien hauled ass out after them Crows."

"Yeah, leavin' me behind to watch over the women and goddamn young 'uns," Rawlins groused.

"Well, we needed to 'ave de best fighters to catch dem Absarokas," Chardonnais said with a chuckle.

"Shit, ye think Bart whomped your ass good, ye wait'll ye recover. Then I'll show ye a real whompin'. Son of a bitch." He sounded a lot more angry than he looked, or was.

"Christ, will ye two knock this shit off," Early said with a shake of his head. "Goddamn, ye're like two bickerin' old women." He faced Adams. "Lucien caught up to 'em first, and he leaps on the back of one of them red devils. The two of 'em fall off the horse and go bouncin' around in the dirt. I figure he's got things under control, so's I drop the other Crow and then round up them horses them Injins stole from us."

He laughed a little. "Shit, this is the good part." He stopped, trying to control the guffaws with no success. "When I get back, I find this big-ass ol' Crow—I mean this hoss made up nearabout two of Lucien—poundin' the shit out of Frenchie, with Lucien hollerin' like a stuck hog."

"An' dis big oaf," Chardonnais said, laughing and pointing to Early, "stands dere laughing while dat Crow is trying to mash me to pulp."

"Well, I couldn't help it, dammit. It was some funny."

"So what happened?" Adams asked.

"I finally managed to stop laughin' long enough to

brain that goddamn Crow. Then I had to practically carry that fat Frenchman back to our camp, while herdin' the goddamn horses. Ye've always been a pain in the ass, Lucien."

The men dissolved into laughter.

The next morning, Early and Adams lazed about the camp, while Rawlins and Chardonnais rode off. Chardonnais returned a few hours later with two turkeys.

"Where's Abe?" Early asked.

" 'E is stayin' out dere with an elk we kill. I came to get de mule."

34

CHARDONNAIS HAD A LEISURELY cup of coffee and a couple of sips of whiskey. Then he ambled over to put the pack saddle on the mule.

Just as Chardonnais finished, he looked up in surprise to see Rawlins riding hell for leather toward the camp. He hurried toward where Early and Adams stood at the fire, watching.

Rawlins pulled his horse to a foamy, jolting halt near the fire. Before the horse had fully stopped, Early had noted the arrow sticking out of Rawlins's left thigh, and the two others stuck in the saddle.

Early and Chardonnais did not need to ask what had happened. The sign was all too plain. The arrows even told them that those who had attacked Rawlins were Jicarilla Apaches. All Early asked was, "How far?"

"See for your own goddamn self," Rawlins growled. He pointed over his shoulder. Six Apaches were racing toward them through the scattered trees about three-quarters of a mile to the south.

Early spun and saw Adams frozen, dumbly watching the rushing Indians. Adams's face was white with fright. "Bart!" Early yelled as he grabbed his rifle and headed east for a large cottonwood log. "Move!"

Chardonnais was right behind Early. He jumped over the log, caught his foot on a dead branch. He fell and rolled several times. When he stopped, he crawled swiftly to the fallen cottonwood. Rawlins rode east past them, herding the mule and the three other horses ahead of him. As the trees thickened, he stopped and slid off his horse.

Adams finally moved, running hard after the others. As he did, he hunched his shoulders, pulling his neck down, waiting fearfully for an arrow or rifle ball to find him.

None did, and he soon found safety behind a jumbled clump of logs, brush, and weeds a few yards east and just behind Early's cottonwood log. He scrunched up behind his feeble barrier and tried to calm his breathing and his pounding heart.

"Abe," Early called, once he had seen that Adams was protected, "stay where ye are and watch the animals." Both figured the Apaches would head for the animals first, trying to steal the horses and mule.

"Them fractious ass wipes ain't gettin' these goddamn animals," Rawlins responded.

There was no fear in his voice, Adams noted. Nor had there been in Early's. He wondered how they could be so calm.

"Lucien," Early said quietly to the man next to him, "get your ass back over there by Bart and keep him company."

As Chardonnais started slithering at an angle toward Adams's small fortress, Early called, "Bart, ye all right, boy?"

"Yes." To him, it sounded like he was using someone else's voice.

"Ye got your rifle, pistol, and fixin's?"

"Yes."

"Ye listen to Lucien, boy. Do what he says."

Adams nodded, not even thinking that Early could not see him. He finally gained some courage and peered out at the Indians. Though they were still some distance away, he thought they looked much like the warriors who had accosted him and Early back on the Santa Fe Trail, the ones from whom Adams had gotten his horse.

"Are they Jicarillas, Lucien?" he asked.

"*Oui.*" He let fly some French that offered his opinion of these Indians, their parentage, and their sexual habits.

"Can't we deal with them?" he asked. "Ezra and I encountered some of them one time and managed to trade with them for my horse."

"Dese boys don' seem to be in a mood to parley, eh? Even if dey was, I ain' so sure we are. Not after dey tried to rub out ol' Abe."

Adams decided to shut up.

Early looked over the log. The Apaches had stopped some distance away, and four had dismounted.

"Ye need help tyin' them horses down, Abe?"

"No, I don't need no goddamn help from the goddamn likes of ye to help me hobble some goddamn horses to keep them out of the goddamn clutches of some goddamn mule-eatin' goddamn Apaches."

"I t'ink Abe is all right, Ezra," Chardonnais called out with a chuckle.

"I expect," Early answered, watching the Jicarillas. "I thought mayhap that arrow'd slow him down a mite."

"Maybe it will," Chardonnais said, chuckling. "But it don' slow down his blabbering."

"Ye boys just worry over your own hair, goddamn ye both," Rawlins snapped. He had worked the four horses and one mule as deep into a tight copse of trees as he could and was busy hobbling the animals. Then he tied them to trees, so the Apaches could not run them off.

"They're not coming anymore," Adams said with relief.

"Dey will be back, *mon ami*," Chardonnais said next to him. He wiped the sweat off his forehead. "And while we wait for dem, you should make sure you 'ave your rifle loaded and primed, eh?"

Adams nodded and checked. He needed priming powder in the pan, and corrected the oversight.

Chardonnais had rolled over onto his back and was half-sitting up, looking around. Then he rolled back onto his stomach and looked over the glade. "Is dere anyt'ing different about dem Apaches, *monsieur?*" he asked.

"No, sir," Adams said firmly. "They're still sitting or standing there."

"And 'ow many of dem do you see?"

"I count four."

"And 'ow many 'orses?"

"Six."

"Doesn't dat tell you something, eh?"

Adams nodded in slow recognition. "A couple of them are sneaking up on us, aren't they?"

"*Oui.*" He paused and looked about. All around them were trees, in some places thick, in others, like here, widely spaced. There were only a few places the Apaches could use to sneak up on them. But all led straight to the copse that sheltered the horses. "I want you to crawl up dere by Ezra."

"Where're you going to be?"

"I am going over dere by Abe, to 'elp 'im watch over de 'orses."

"Why?"

"Never you mind. Just do what I tell you, eh." He glanced over the thin barricade. "Our frain is comin' to you, Ezra," Chardonnais called. He waited a moment, until he saw Early nod. "Go, *mon ami.*"

The two moved off in opposite directions. Within moments, Adams was lying behind the big cottonwood log two feet or so to Early's right.

Without taking his eyes off the Jicarillas, Early asked, "Where's Lucien gotten off to?"

Adams explained. When Early did not comment, other than to nod in acknowledgment, Adams asked, "What're we going to do?"

"Wait. Them ones sneakin' through the woods'll have to show themselves sometime." He reached into his possible sack and brought out some tobacco. As he chawed it into a comfortable consistency, he said, "Those bastards out there'll most likely start movin' toward us afore long. They'll be hopin' to keep us fixated on them whilst the others sneak up on us and try'n get our horses."

Adams was pasty with fear. "Why didn't they just attack us when we were out in the open? That's what they seemed to be ready to do," he asked with dry mouth.

"They was of a mind to, I expect. But they couldn't get to us afore we got behind these here logs. So they stopped and pulled back to where they are and devised another goddamn plan."

"But . . ."

"Look, Apaches ain't no goddamn fools, boy. They know a bunch of mountaineers could sit back here and drop nearabout all of 'em afore they even got close to us. Besides, Apaches're sneaky bastards. These are mountain Injins and desert Injins. They ain't like the Comanches and Cheyennes and other such devils. They don't set a horse for war like them Plains Injins. But make no mistake, boy, these here warriors is ary bit as fierce as any Comanche. Mayhap more so. It's just that they go about things in diff'rent ways." He almost smiled. "Kind of like Abe and Lucien."

Adams nodded and shut up. He was fidgety, though, squirming around and nervously fingering his rifle.

"Settle your ass down, boy," Early said harshly. "I can't hear shit with ye bein' so itchy."

"I'll try." Adams fought hard to keep the terror from overcoming him. He was mostly successful, though he still felt rather numb. Nor did the waiting get any easier. Despite the shade and their altitude, the heat was fierce. With nothing to break the rays of the sun, it beat down forcefully. Sweat formed on his head and dripped down into his eyes. He wiped it away as surreptitiously as he could. He could still feel trickles of sweat running from his back down his sides.

Early lay perfectly still, watching, eyes and ears alert. He was tempted more than once to try a shot at one of the four Apaches still standing out there with their horses. But they were well out of range, and he knew it, so he resisted the temptation.

He and the others were in a pretty defensible position. The stream was almost directly behind them, to the north. It wasn't that big a stream, but along this stretch, the bank on the other side was a slick, medium-tall cliff. The fire they had used, and their supplies, were twenty or thirty yards due west of Early's position. The fire was only a few yards from the stream bank, which at that point was flat and easily accessible. It was the only point nearby where the Apaches could easily cross the stream, if they were so inclined. Early gave no thought to their supplies being out there. Not when they were this close to Taos or Santa Fe.

Due east, about thirty yards or so, was the copse where Rawlins and Chardonnais were watching over the horses. The copse ran to the water's edge on the north and up to a tall, sharply defined cliff on the east. South of the copse, the trees were still rather thick, gradually thinning the farther south of the copse one went. The band of trees curved around toward the east, thinning until the pines and aspens were quite scattered.

Almost directly south of Early's position, where the band of trees thinned almost to nothing, about half a mile away, sat the four Apaches. Early knew that the other two Jicarillas had to be sneaking through the thick trees south and east of his position, since to the south and west the scattered spruces and junipers offered little protection.

There was a jumble of gigantic boulders piled haphazardly atop one another in a towering monolith of stone. It offered a fine place for a warrior or two to rest for a few moments before making the short dash across the small open space to the copse.

Early caught a small movement in that massive pile of rock. He stared hard, waiting for it again. "Keep your eyes on them other goddamn Jicarillas out there, boy," Early ordered. "Let me know if'n they move any."

He continued to watch the rock formation, ignoring the perspiration that rolled down his nose and then dropped off the flat end. A rock skittering down the face of the monolith got his attention. He rested the Dickert across the log and pulled back the hammer to full cock.

"You see something, Ezra?" Adams asked worriedly.

"Shut your trap, boy, and watch them goddamn Injins."

Early thought he saw another movement up among the rocks, but he wasn't sure. Still, he kept his eyes fixated. There was no more movement for what seemed like a long time, but still Early lay there, rifle ready.

Sometime later—Early didn't know how long it was—Adams said quietly, "All those Apaches out there have mounted again, Ezra." He sounded more worried.

Early grunted, but said nothing. Then Early heard the thunder of the Jicarillas' drumming hooves.

"They're coming," Adams croaked. He felt like his

heart had inched its way up into his throat and was trying to fight its way past his Adam's apple. He wiped his perspiring palms on his pants, but it seemed to do little good, since they immediately sweated up again.

"Just hold yourself steady, boy," Early said. "And remember what we taught ye."

35

EARLY PULLED THE TRIGGER, and the Dickert roared. A splotch of deeper brown danced against the reddish-tan rocks and then bounced down the pile of boulders. Early jerked his head around as he hurriedly reloaded, but the charging Apaches were gone. They had cut east and into the dense trees just south of the pile of rock. He hesitated only a moment, trying to fix where the warriors were.

"C'mon, boy," he ordered as he jumped up.

A startled Adams followed Early into the brush to their east, a little north of the monolith. Adams's heart pounded as he followed Early's buckskin-clad back. Then he lost Early in the trees. He stopped, very frightened. There was only the sound of the rushing stream, the wind rustling through leaves and pine needles, and the thumping of his heart. He heard a yell, followed by a curse in French.

"Oh my God, the horses," Adams muttered, then he ran hard for the copse where Rawlins and Chardonnais were watching the horses. The fear seemed to have disappeared in the heat of the moment as he crashed through brush and around trees.

He pounded into the copse and saw Chardonnais grappling with two Apaches. The short, bulky mountain man fought like a cornered wildcat, knife in one hand. The Apaches, however, were his equal in ferocity.

Without pausing for thought, Adams dropped his rifle and charged, slamming as hard as he could into the mass of struggling men. The four went sprawling. As he scrambled up alongside Chardonnais, Adams heard a shot to the south. Then two more, the last from deeper in the copse, toward the stream. He assumed it came from Rawlins. But the two grim, painted Apaches, their two dark faces fierce, were of immediate concern. Chardonnais, who had lost his knife when Adams slammed into him and the Apaches, pulled out his tomahawk. Adams nervously did likewise.

The warriors were almost carbon copies of each other. They were short, dark, and bandy-legged. They had big chests and looked like they could run or walk—or fight—for days without tiring. Their eyes were almost black, and set deeply in the skull, under a thick forehead. Each wore soft moccasins up over the knee, long buckskin breechcloths and shirts, and cloth headbands tied around straight, dull black hair. One held a knife in one hand and a tomahawk in the other. The second, the one closer to Chardonnais, carried a stone war club with a scalp hanging from the end.

Adams's assessment of the warriors took perhaps three heartbeats. Then Chardonnais leapt at the Jicarillas. Adams gulped and did the same. He swung his tomahawk crazily, afraid not to, or even to slow down. He lost sight of Chardonnais, as he moved toward the Apache who held weapons in both hands. The warrior moved slowly backward, biding his time.

Adams could not keep up the onslaught for long. His arm grew tired and his swings began to grow slower and fewer as seconds, or maybe it was minutes, passed. As the arm motion continued to wind down even more, the Apache suddenly swept in, underneath the tomahawk.

Adams jerked himself sideways, not quite knowing how he had managed it. The knife blade bit into his side, chunked off a rib, gouging out a hunk of flesh. Adams could feel the blood seeping out, but there was no pain, which surprised him. That would come later, he would learn.

He retaliated instinctively, swinging both hands on the tomahawk at the Apache. The haft of the weapon caught the Jicarilla in the back of the neck. The Indian grunted, more in surprise than in pain.

Adams thumped him again, and the warrior fell to the side. As the Jicarilla went down, Adams pounded him unmercifully with his left fist. He was not himself any longer. He was a wild man, intent on only one thing—killing. It was not a conscious thought, just the action forced upon him by his rage and fear.

Then Adams viciously brought the tomahawk into play. It came down twice with all his fury and fright, splitting the Apache's face and head. Still without thinking of what he was doing, Adams raised the weapon to strike once again. But a brawny hand grabbed his arm and stopped it.

He looked up, eyes clouded with fear and wildness. The voice began to filter through to him, though: "Let that Injin be now, boy. Ye done him enough damage."

Slowly Adams's mind and eyes cleared, and he saw Early, still holding firmly onto his arm. He blinked and looked down at the bloody mess that moments ago had been an Apache warrior's face and head.

Adams jerked his head to the side and threw up, his vomit splattering the bloody ground. Early let his arm go, and the tomahawk fell.

"What's ailing our frain?" Chardonnais asked, walking up and stopping next to Early. He looked down at Adams, who had fallen to hands and knees and was still retching.

"Got himself a good look at his handiwork." He laughed lightly and waved vaguely at the remains of the Apache. "It ain't a purty sight, I'd be sayin'. Hell, he plumb butchered that critter."

Chardonnais shrugged. " 'E sure does puke a lot, don' 'e? I am amaze."

Early chuckled. "He can puke all he wants as long as he makes them goddamn Apaches come like he done today." He paused, looking around. "Ye seen Abe?"

"Not since de attack come on us. 'E took de animals down toward de water at de north end of de copse. I t'ought I 'eard a shot from over dere a while back." He shifted his rifle onto his shoulder. "I go look for dat rascal."

"No need for such doin's," Rawlins said, hobbling up. "I were comin' up to help ye boys, but it don't much look like ye need it." He glanced at Adams, then ignored him. **"Thar any** more of them bastards lurkin' about?"

"Don't expect so," Early said. "I got me one on them rocks over yonder to set things agoin'. Got me another back over there 'tween the rocks and the cliff. Missed me one other when that son of a bitch ducked behind a rock." He sighed. "Seemed like that bastard could see the ball comin'. Ah, well, I expect someone else finally rubbed him out. Lucien got one right here, and Adams took care of this hoss. That leaves two."

"I only got me one of them devils tryin' to make off with the horses," Rawlins said.

They all tensed. There was one Apache unaccounted for. Then they heard a horse riding hard. Through a brief break in the trees, they saw a lone Indian racing off, leading three empty horses behind him.

"Dat's all of dem," Chardonnais said with a grin. "We made dem come now." He stopped and watched with some surprise as Rawlins spun and ran as best as his wounded leg would allow.

"What de 'ell . . . ?" Chardonnais wondered aloud.

"I expect he aims to get that last goddamn Apache," Early said. He bent to help Adams up.

"I can do it," Adams snapped. Early shrugged and watched as Adams struggled up. He was a little unsteady, and his face was ghostly pale, but he was on his feet. "Why's he going after that Apache?" he asked, voice cracking.

Early shrugged. "I expect he figures he owes 'em somethin' for putting that arrow in his leg." He sighed. "It's probably best. We don't need that son of a bitch comin' back here with a passel of his goddamn friends."

Chardonnais nodded, as if he had just made a momentous decision. "I am going after him," he announced.

They heard Rawlins's horse galloping off. Chardonnais spun and ran. Early and Adams watched silently until they heard Chardonnais's mount racing after Rawlins. Early turned and looked at his companion.

"Ye feelin' all right, boy?" he asked.

"Yes," Adams said in irritation.

"Good. Ye want that there buck's scalp?"

Adams grew even more pale. He belched, trying to keep down what little remained in his stomach. "No!" he said sharply.

"Suit yourself, boy," Early said with something approaching glee. "I took one of mine, and I'm still fixin' to get the other."

For the first time, Adams noticed the bloody shank of hair dangling from Early's belt. He wanted to be sick again. "You're as bad as they are," he said. "A bloody savage."

Early's eyes narrowed, but his voice was calm. "I ain't the first white ary took a scalp. Wasn't so long ago the goddamn British were payin' good money for Injin scalps back where ye come from, boy. The goddamn Mexicans still do it."

"Doesn't make any of it right."

Early shrugged. "It's somethin' the goddamn Injins, near all of 'em, understand. Most of 'em believe that if'n ye raise hair, their spirit'll nary be free to go to the spirit world. Means ye won't have to face him again when ye get to the Land Beyond. I ain't sure the Apaches feel the same, since ain't nobody this chil' knows of ary got near enough to 'em to find out, but even if they don't believe in such, they understand it."

Adams looked at him in disbelief. "That's one of the dumbest things I ever heard of," he commented.

"Mayhap. But to them it makes sense. To most of us mountaineers, too. Look at it this way. It's the Injins' hell. Ye got your fires and such, they got their wanderin' spirits. I expect it's all the same in the end."

"Never thought of it that way," Adams said grudgingly.

"Hell, boy, your ways ain't always the right ones."

Adams nodded distractedly and held his side. The pain was beginning for real. He pulled his hand away. It and his shirt were covered with blood.

Early grinned. "Ye been blooded in war now, boy," he said joyfully.

Adams smiled wanly.

There was a shot from far off. The sound drifted slowly over them, hit the cliff back beyond the copse and washed lightly over them again. "*Bueno*," Early whispered. "It's over."

He looked over at Adams and smiled easily. "C'mon, boy, let's go'n get them horses and then see about fixin' ye up."

They walked slowly into the copse. Early untied his Appaloosa, Adams's bay, and the mule. Holding ropes looped around the animals' necks, he led the way back toward the fire, which had burned down. "Set your ass, boy, and take your leisure for a spell," Early said.

Early quickly hobbled the horses nearby and then built up the fire. Just about that time he had the flames glowing bright and hot, Rawlins and Chardonnais came thundering back toward camp, whooping it up.

Early stood and watched, real pleasure on his face.

Suddenly a thought occurred to him. "Ye see the way they're ridin', boy?" he asked.

"Sure," Adams nodded. Fear began to envelope him again. "Like those Apaches are after them again."

"They're haulin' ass, all right. But there ain't no danger."

"How can you tell?" Adams was interested.

"Ye remember when Abe rode in with them Apaches after him?"

"Yes," Adams said with a baffled shrug. "I don't see anything different."

"He was ridin' straight for us. How're they ridin' now?"

Adams stared at the two riders a moment. "They're zigging and zagging, back and forth."

Early beamed. "Ye catch the difference now, boy?"

"Zigzag riding means no danger. Riding like hell straight on means there's danger?"

"Waugh! Ye can make 'em come with the best of 'em now, boy," Early said with a chuckle. "Ye know why that is?"

Adams thought for a few moments. "Coming straight on is more direct, of course," he said with a nod. "Riding the way they are now would take too much time, and might endanger everyone in camp."

Chardonnais hit the camp first and jerked his horse to a stop. A few eye blinks later, Rawlins arrived in a cloud of dust and foam. Both horses reared, and the men gave a final whoop.

36

"ALL RIGHT, BOY, PULL off your shirt and stretch yourself out there so's I can see what the damage is," Early said. Rawlins and Chardonnais were tending to their hard-used horses.

Adams gingerly removed his shirt and then lay on his blanket. Early knelt next to him and none too gently probed the skin. "Shit," he growled, "'tain't nothin'." He looked up. "Hey, Lucien, fetch one of them whiskey jugs over here."

Chardonnais grabbed a jug and walked toward Early and Adams, muttering, "Goddamn, why is me all de time 'aving to do dese t'ings. *Merde.* I always 'ave to do de shit work around de whole damn camp. All de women's work. I am beside myself with anger at dese insults."

"Christ, Lucien, ye gonna piss and moan the rest of

your life?" Early snorted. "Just get your ass over here and help out."

"What you want, *mon ami?*"

"Just stay here in case I need ye to hold ol' hoss here down. And ye, boy," he said to Adams this time, "best bite down on a twig or something. This's liable to burn a mite."

Adams started to argue, but Chardonnais jammed a stick in his mouth, shutting him up. *"Procéder, mon ami,"* Chardonnais said smugly.

Early grinned and poured raw liquor on the open wound. Adams gasped around the twig. He wriggled, splashing whiskey over his blanket. Chardonnais clamped two strong hands on him and pressed him down.

"T'ink we should put fire to it?" Chardonnais asked when Early had stopped pouring whiskey on Adams's wound.

"Naw. But I expect we ought to sew it up and then poultice it."

Adams spit the stick out of his mouth. "What?" he asked, worried.

"Ye heard me, boy. Now shut up, I got work to do."

"You aren't going to do any sewing on me, Ezra Early," Adams said with determination.

"Who's gonna stop me, boy?" he asked flatly. "Ye?"

"If I have to."

"We don't stitch that goddamn wound up, boy," Early said harshly, "it'll fester on ye."

"But . . ." Adams started to protest. He did not finish, since he knew Early was right. He licked his lips. "You ever done this before?"

"Mais oui!" Chardonnais laughed, rocking back

with his buttocks on his heels. "Look at dis." He yanked up his shirt, showing a long, jagged scar running from just under the left nipple down the left side and curving in toward the belly button. "*Mon ami* did dis. Four years ago. I t'ought I was gone under for sure, but Ezra, 'e fix me up good as new."

Adams found it hard to pull his eyes away from the ugly scar on Chardonnais's torso. He did when Chardonnais finally dropped his shirt again. Adams turned his eyes on Early with new respect. He was still worried, though. "You going to be able to do this with your hand all bandaged up like that?" he asked nervously.

"Hell, this little thing?" Early snorted, holding up the hand that was covered by a now-filthy bandage. "That's my left hand, boy. I'll do the sewin' with my right." He chuckled.

The laugh did not fill Adams with confidence. Gulping, he said, "Do what you have to, Ezra."

"I will get de doctoring kit," Chardonnais said, pushing himself up. He wandered off to the supplies.

Early looked around. Rawlins was done currying his own horse and was working on Chardonnais's. Early knew he would have to go through all this again as soon as Rawlins was done with his chores.

Chardonnais returned with the small bundle of medical supplies and set it down. He opened the bag and pulled out some roots and an old tin cup. "I will make de poultice, eh?"

Early nodded. "Best make enough for two."

Chardonnais's eyes followed Early's glance to Rawlins. He, too, nodded. "*Oui.*"

"Ye want some laudanum to knock ye out, boy?" Early asked.

Adams shook his head. "Just do it."

Early pulled out a needle and some sinew. Turning to the side, he poured a little whiskey over all the items. Then he painstakingly threaded a string of sinew onto the curved needle. "Ye ready, boy?" he asked.

Adams looked up and saw the twinkle in Early's usually hard eyes. "You're enjoying all this, aren't you?" he accused in friendly tones.

"I am," Early said with a grin.

Adams sighed. Somehow, his fear seemed to have dissipated in the friendly banter. "All right, then, do your worst." He paused, then laughed. "On second thought, my friend, do your best."

Early stuck the twig back in Adams's mouth. He bent and stabbed the sharp point of the needle through the skin on the underside of Adams's wound. He pulled it through, the sinew making the skin do a little jig.

Adams gasped and bit down on the green twig. His legs tensed and his fists clenched. But he did not cry out.

Early pulled the sides of the wound together and made a knot with the sinew, then cut it. He repeated the process four more times, then leaned back and surveyed his work. "Waugh! This chil' shines when it comes to doctorin'," he boasted. "Plumb shines. Ye'll nary be able to tell ye was hurt."

Adams took the twig out of his mouth and tossed it away. "Whiskey," he whispered. The pain was sharp and unceasing, but he could handle it. Still a couple of jolts of Taos Lightning would do a heap of good, he figured.

Early helped him into a sitting position and then got him braced against his saddle. He handed the easterner the jug and watched with amusement as Adams poured a goodly portion down his gullet.

Chardonnais strolled up with a blackened tin mug full of goop.

"What's that?" Adams asked.

"Yarrow root for a poultice," Early said. "It'll keep the poison out of that wound."

Chardonnais knelt and slathered some of the yarrow root mush on the wound. Adams watched dispassionately. It didn't hurt nearly as bad as he had thought it would. Finally, with Early helping to hold Adams up, Chardonnais wrapped some old cloth around the patient's torso, covering the wound.

Early set Adams back down. "Ye set there and rest a spell, boy. Ye get to movin' around too much, and ye'll set yourself to bleedin' again." He stood and looked at Rawlins, who had sat on a log nearby and was looking down at the stump of arrow in his leg. "Your turn, *amigo,*" he said.

"Ye ain't comin' near me with your goddamn medicine, Ezra Early. Ye plumb sure as shit ain't."

"Jesus, Abe, I nary figured ye for a weaklin'. Now ol' Bart there, he just sat and took his doctorin' like a man. But ye, ye set there squawkin', lettin' everybody see ye're scared shitless."

"Ye ain't gonna sweet-talk me into lettin' ye butcher me up, ye son of a bitch," Rawlins said.

Early sighed. "Ye gonna let me look at your leg, or am I gonna have Chardonnais sit on ye, too?"

"I can do dat. *Mais oui!*"

"Aw, shit, ye ain't gonna be happy less'n ye're pokin' around tryin' to patch up this ol' hide. Christ, ye're worse'n my ol' mam was, damn ye." He stretched out his legs. "Do it."

Early slit through the tough, greasy buckskin pants

until he had some working room. "Hell, don't look so bad. No worse'n what Bart got."

"I know that, goddammit. Just get it done."

"Ye want a stick to chaw on?"

"No, I don't want no goddamn stick to goddamn chew on," he snapped. Then he grinned. "But I could do with a swaller of Lightnin'."

Early grinned back at him, as Chardonnais handed Rawlins the jug. Rawlins drank long and deeply. He kept the jug near his hand. "Have at it, ye goddamn butcher."

Early tugged gently at the broken arrow shaft, twisting it a little to see how deeply and securely it was imbedded.

"Why don't you just yank it out?" Adams asked quietly.

"Most arrows Injins use for war are barbed on the end," Early answered. "They can cause a heap more damage when they're yanked out than they do going in." He paused. "It's set in there pretty goddamn good, Abe," Early said quietly.

"Shit," Rawlins commented before taking another drink. "Ye just want to go diggin' around in there with your goddamn knife."

"I ain't gonna feel nothin'," Early responded honestly. He pulled his patch knife and splashed whiskey over it. Without preliminary, he cut into Rawlins's leg, carefully working the short blade around the arrowhead. He tugged on the arrow shaft every few seconds, constantly testing how tightly it was seated. Finally he pulled the knife out and slid it into the sheath sewn onto the front strap of his shooting bag.

"Ain't ye done yet, goddammit?" Rawlins asked. His

voice was level and he seemed unaffected by the pain.

Adams watched, amazed at Rawlins's calmness and wished he was as brave.

Early suddenly yanked the arrow shaft, and the arrowhead was out before Rawlins knew what he was doing. The blood flowed freely though not copiously from the wound. Early let it run a few moments, allowing it to clean out the wound.

Looking down at it, Rawlins said quietly, "I wonder how much blood a man's got in him." He took another drink. "Reckon it don't matter none. With all I've lost in my life, if a body didn't replace it, I'd of been gone under a heap of years ago."

It was a strange comment from Rawlins, who was not known for such musings. Early just shrugged it off, figuring the statement was the result of the excitement, the pain Rawlins was masking, and the whiskey.

Early threaded the big curved needle with sinew. It took only three of his crude stitches to close up the arrow wound. Chardonnais poulticed it, and Early wrapped it with the last of the cloth.

"Dere," Chardonnais said, as he pushed to his feet. "Dat will 'old you."

Early put away his primitive doctoring equipment, then grabbed the jug. He took a healthy dosage. "Waugh! That's prime. Plumb prime." He stood. "Ye boys'll be just fine in a few days. Just don't go gettin' too feisty or ye'll set yourselves to bleedin' agin." He grinned maliciously. "Then I'd have to go back and stitch them wounds again."

"Ye come at me with that goddamn needle again, Ez, and . . ." Rawlins said.

"And what?" Early asked with a grin.

"Ye'll find out, ye son of a bitch." Rawlins hoisted the jug and winked at his old friend.

Early put the medicine kit away and washed in the stream. When he returned to the fire, Chardonnais had tea and meat cooking. Early sat.

"Ye think ye can refrain from causin' us any more trouble, there, Abe?" Early asked with a grin.

"I ain't seen no trouble," Rawlins said blandly. "Ye seen any trouble there, Frenchie?"

"*Mais non!*" Chardonnais laughed. "But, den, I ain't de one sitting dere with an arrow wound in de leg."

Rawlins laughed. It was a deep, rich sound that carried up to the treetops. "Well, hell, we sure made them devils come. Goddamn, even ol' Bart there."

"Ye hear that, boy?" Early said after taking a pull from one of the jugs. "Ol' Abe give ye a compliment. Waugh! I ain't heard the likes of it since—" he paused and sipped again. "Shit, I ain't ary heard the likes of it."

"Hell, ye noticed I didn't offer ye no goddamn compliments, ye ol' fart. Christ, ye're worse'n goddamn ol' squaw. Ain't that right, Frenchie?"

"Don' get me in de middle of your arguing, *mon ami.*" He grinned and looked through the fire smoke at Adams. "But I would like to tell ol' Bart dere *merci.*"

"For what?" Adams asked, surprised.

"For coming to my rescue, of course." As always his hands flew all which ways as he spoke, adding emphasis. "Now, I ain't saying dat I couldn't 'ave 'andled dose two bucks by myself, but you was some 'elp to me, and for dat, I say, '*Merci, monsieur.*'"

Adams nodded, flushing with pride.

"Don't talk him up too much," Early said with a

chuckle. "He'll get to thinkin' he's too goddamn big for his britches. 'Sides, ol' hoss there was too squeamish to raise the hair on that buck he put under."

Adams wanted to protest, but he wisely decided to wait a bit, to see what transpired. Early didn't seem angry about it. Indeed, it seemed to Adams that he was being joshed, making him a true part of this small group.

"From what I saw," Chardonnais said in Adams's defense, "dere wasn't enough of dat Apache's 'air to be raise."

"I expect that might explain it," Early said. He reached for a piece of meat.

Adams, sitting there, felt fine.

37

THE FOUR RODE INTO Santa Fe quietly, not wanting to raise much of a fuss. It had been only three weeks or so since Early and Adams had been broken out of jail, and Governor Castillo might still be holding a grudge.

Besides, none of the four had any real fancy outfits to wear to make a grand entrance. Their buckskins were covered with grease, blood, dirt, and were dotted with holes.

They had spent three more days in the mountains south of Taos, letting Adams and Rawlins recover. There was no reason for them to stay longer. Adams had proven himself, and there was little more that Early, Rawlins, and Chardonnais could do for him.

Nor were the wounds enough to slow Rawlins and Adams very much.

Adams had been surprised at how fast he recovered. He had never been wounded before, had never even suffered more than minor illnesses, so he had not known what to expect. There had been a considerable amount of burning pain the first day and certain positions gave him a short, sharp reminder of the wound, but otherwise he was fine. By the second day he hardly noticed it. Either the pain had gone away, or he was simply unaware of it.

They were in no hurry on the trail toward Santa Fe, taking two days to make the trip, riding into town early in the morning. After seeing that their horses were safe in the livery stable, they headed for Mendoza's, a low dive of a tavern frequented by some of the rougher wagoneers. It was a likely place to find a man like Ebenezer Parfrey.

He was not there. As they took seats at a rickety table, Early tried to calm the tense Adams. "Don't get your feathers all ruffled, boy. Just set your ass down there and have a cup or two. Ye've earned it."

Adams scowled, but he sat. A surly, foul-smelling, one-eared, cadaverous Mexican slapped a jug and four filthy crockery glasses on the table. Early tossed a coin at the man, who clomped off.

Early looked with distaste at the cups. Then he shrugged. The whiskey was probably horrid, and Early didn't figure anything could live in it. He reached for the jug and poured them each a brimming mug full.

Adams almost choked on the nasty liquid, but the three mountain men seemed to down the whiskey without gagging. Adams admired them for it.

Early refilled his cup and took another drink. "Damn! This chil's drank mule piss better'n this." He grinned. "Then again, I've drunk worse, too." He poured some more into his mouth. "Ye know, boy," he said quietly, "we might not be able to find Parfrey. Most of them boys who haul goods 'tween Missouri and here has left already. Parfrey might be among 'em."

A burst of anger blossomed in Adams. "Then goddammit, why'd you go through all that nonsense in the mountains, and then come back here? You knew it all along. Hell, before we left the last time, we made sure Eakins had my package to take back."

Early shrugged nonchalantly. "I expect we could've let ye go try'n take Parfrey then, and gotten yourself put under. Or gotten tossed back in jail by the governor's troops. That would've been shinin' doin's, for goddamn sure."

"But—"

"I ain't finished yet, boy," Early barked. He turned a baleful glare on Adams. "Mainly, though, I was thinkin' that ye'd be tougher and learn how to handle yourself in a week. Not three or so. 'Sides, not all them boys leave at the same time. Parfrey struck me as a man who'd like to linger here where things're comfortable, where he can have his fill of willin' *señoritas*. Hell, back in Independence or St. Louis, no self-respectin' woman'd have anything to do with him. But sometimes these *señoritas* down here ain't so choosy, 'specially when it comes to Americans. These women down here think all Americans're richer'n God, and are free about passin' it around."

They all drank quietly for a while. Adams was still angry, but it was anger born of nervousness. "So, what do we do now?" Adams asked tensely.

"Ye know, Ezra," Rawlins said quietly, "it might be this Parfrey feller ain't gone yet." He rolled the dirty pottery glass in his big hands, seeming to stare at it dreamily.

"How's that?"

"Well now, I don't know this goddamn Parfrey all that well, ye understand. Hell, not at all really. But from all I've heard spoke about him, he's one fractious ass-wipe."

"He's that all right," Adams said fervently. "What does that matter?"

"Means he might not've been able to hook on with a large train headin' back East. Means if he's got his own small wagon or two that he'll be afeared of travelin' alone, with just his few companions, especially since on the way back there he'll be cartin' gold and maybe pushin' a herd of Mexican horses."

"You think so?" Adams asked, nervous excitement building in him again, as it had on the two-day ride down from the mountain camp.

Rawlins shrugged, and set the glass down. "Could be it is, boy," he said as he poured himself another glass of whiskey. He grinned. " 'Course, could be I'm full of shit, too."

"What do you think, Ezra?" Adams asked.

"Makes some sense," Early allowed. "Guess we could try'n find out." He looked at the bartender. "Ye Mendoza?" he called out.

The man simply stared, no expression on his scarred face.

Early scowled. Loud enough to be heard by the man, he said to his companions, "Jesus, it just don't shine with some critters to be friendly to him." He shook his head. "All ye do is ask a man's name so's ye can talk to him nice, and ye get some nasty ass stare."

"His loss," Rawlins offered. "Could've picked himself up a bit more goddamn gold than just dolin' out drinks."

Early glanced out of the corner of his eye and saw that Rawlins's statement had caused at least a bare minimum of interest to show in the Mexican's face.

"Well," Early added, "I expect we can take us a *paseo* over to Manuelito's and see if them boys is some friendlier."

"I am Mendoza," the man said.

"I think ye're a lyin' son of a bitch," Early said. "Ye go'n tell us you're Mendoza just to squeeze some specie out of us." He looked around. Several tables in the small *cantina* were occupied. Early picked up his glass and threw it at one table of three Mexicans who appeared to be making a studied effort at ignoring Early and his companions.

The crockery smashed against the adobe wall near one man's head. The three men at the table looked, half-fearfully, half-defiantly at Early. "Is that Mendoza?" he asked, pointing at the bar man.

"*Sí,*" one said.

"*Gracias,*" Early said sarcastically. He looked at Mendoza. "Ye know a man named Parfrey?" he asked.

Mendoza moved up toward the table. His arms were at his sides, but his right hand formed a right angle with the arm.

"Christ, the son of a bitch's got his hand out already," Rawlins said in annoyance.

"Ye'll get your goddamn money, boy," Early growled. "Soon's ye tell me somethin' I figure is worth payin' for. Now, do ye know Parfrey?"

The squashed-thin face bobbed down once and then returned to its normal position.

"He leave with one of the wagon trains heading toward the States?"

The skull-like head moved from one side to the other.

Adams bit back a cry of joy. "Then he's still in Santa Fe?" he asked, managing to keep relatively calm.

Again the shake of the head.

"Then where in hell is he?" Adams asked, anger rising. He had gone from despair to euphoria and back again, in seconds.

The long, thin hand and the end of the long, thin arm waggled.

Early, sitting nearest to Mendoza, considered for a moment spitting into the hand. That would go pretty far toward teaching Mendoza to be less greedy. But he decided that doing so would accomplish nothing other than to make him feel better. He reached into his possible sack and pulled out a small pouch. From it he extracted a copper coin and dropped it in the hand.

The fingers wiggled again.

"The only thing else ye're gonna get from me, boy," Early said flatly, "is a lead pill. Now answer my *amigo*'s question afore I gut ye."

Mendoza's eyes narrowed in anger. He hated these damn swaggering *Americanos*. Especially the free trappers. They were arrogant, strutting peacocks, who thought they were the cocks of the walk. They tossed their money around with abandon, got drunk and brawled. They sported with the *señoritas*, turning the young ladies against the true residents of Santa Fe.

The Santa Fe Trail traders were almost as bad, in his

thinking, since they brought in huge wagons of goods that co-opted the Mexican merchants. In return, the traders took out gold and fine Mexican horses, leaving only shoddy cotton goods and other cheap manufactured items.

Those bandits would come into his *cantina* and raise havoc, leaving the place a shambles more often than not. And they often complained that his whiskey was too watered down, or poorly made. As if they had any taste in such matters, Mendoza had thought angrily on more than one occasion.

He looked with fresh hatred into the unforgiving eyes of this rangy, buckskin-clad man, and wanted to kill him. But he knew it was impossible, especially with four of them. Not that Mendoza thought he could take even one of them by himself. Not in a fair fight. Though with a pistol . . .

Such thoughts were useless, he decided. He opened his mouth to speak, to lie to these hated *Americanos,* to tell them what he thought they wanted to hear. But he closed his lips without saying anything a moment later. An idea had sprung up and he gave it a moment to develop. It was not a great idea, just a workable one, and one filled with enough poetic justice to agree with Mendoza's poetic soul.

He need not lie, he decided. That would only make these men angry, and they were men who would come back and kill him for having lied to them. No, he would tell them the truth. It was evident that these men were after Parfrey for violence, not for friendship. So, Mendoza reasoned, why not let these damned *Americanos* kill each other. For every one who died at the hands of a countryman, another might swing at the end of a rope. It might not rid Mendoza's land of them, but it could eliminate a few. And that was far better than nothing.

"I heard, *señor*," Mendoza said in heavily accented English, "that Señor Parfrey has gone to Taos."

"Taos?" Adams burst out. "You sure?"

"No, *señor*," Mendoza said, hoping he showed the proper amount of sadness. "I only heard that. I did see him riding north several days ago. And word has it that he's picking up some things to take East."

"*Gracias,* Señor Mendoza," Early said. He dropped a gold coin in Mendoza's hand and stood. "I don't expect ye boys'll have any objections to makin' a *paseo* up to Taos?"

Adams got up so fast that he knocked his chair over. They hurried out, while a confused Mendoza switched his glance from the departing Americans to the gleaming gold coin in his hand.

The four wasted no time in getting their horses and riding out of town. They stopped just before dark and made camp. Adams fidgeted and had trouble sleeping, so eager was he to get to Taos.

They were up before dawn and on the trail again just after first light. They arrived in Taos before dark. As they were turning their horses in at a livery, they heard that there would be a ball that night.

"Best get us some fancy outfits, boys," Early said.

"I'm not going to a ball until after I find Parfrey," Adams said in determination.

Early clapped a hand on his shoulder. "Where better than a *fandango* to look for that son of a bitch?"

A slow smile began growing on Adams's face, as he nodded. "Yes," he whispered. "Yes."

"And, I expect," Early said with a chuckle, "that a certain *señorita* also will be there."

Adams's smile grew to immense proportions. *Dolores.* The word rolled around in his mind comfortably. He had hardly thought of her while they were south of Taos, but now her name filled him with warmth and expectation.

38

ADAMS WAS TENSE AS he, Early, Rawlins, and Chardonnais joined the throngs heading toward the torchlit plaza. The musicians were playing, and the tables were piled high with succulent foods, the aromas mingling with the acrid odor of burning torches.

The four men were dressed similarly in the best finery they could find at the Bent and Saint Vrain store. All had creamy buckskin pants, heavily fringed down the outer seams, the bottoms flaring slightly. Each wore dyed leather *botas* that matched the color of his shirt. Early wore a green calico shirt; Chardonnais, one of bright red; Rawlins's was blue; and Adams's a plain off-white. Short, Taos-style buckskin jackets, beaded on front and back, covered the shirts. Knives, tomahawks, and pistols were stuck into or hung from wide leather belts or colorful sashes. Adams wore a dark blue *sombrero,* Rawlins and Early each sported a beaver-felt top hat, and Chardonnais wore a plain, flat-crowned, wide-brim hat.

They took up posts on the perimeter of the plaza and watched the swirling, gaily dressed dancers. As they did, Adams scanned the crowd intently, trying to spot Parfrey. He did so with a mixture of worry and anticipation. He did not see the lanky ruffian, though.

Then, without a word, he moved hurriedly away from the others. Early, Rawlins, and Chardonnais stared after him for a moment, before searching the crowd. "I don't see no sign of Parfrey," Rawlins said.

"Me neither," Early responded. "But ol' Bart must've seen him, the way he took off like he did."

They remained alert, watching Adams's retreating back, ready to act in an instant, if it became necessary.

It had not been Parfrey, though, whom Adams had seen. Instead, he moved with a newfound grace through the crowd toward a brightly dressed woman. As he reached her, from behind, he said, "Dolores, *por favor.*"

The young woman spun away from the female companion she had been speaking with and stopped, staring haughtily at Adams. "Do I know you, *señor?*" she asked icily before beginning to turn away.

"Wait," Adams said urgently, letting his hand fall gently on her shoulder. He tugged her lightly around to face him again. "Please, Dolores, let me explain," he said softly.

Dolores stood staring coldly at him. One hand at her bosom gripped the lace *mantilla* that cascaded down from her glossy black mane and over bare shoulders rising duskily from her low-cut dress of dark blue wool. The other hand held a closed fan. She did not seem the least bit receptive.

Hastily, trying to keep any tone of pleading out of his voice, Adams succinctly explained his prolonged absence, all that he had been through—the brief encounter with Parfrey, the week in jail, the time in the mountain camp, the battle with the Apaches.

Dolores's frosty exterior began to melt as the soft, quiet explanation wound on, and she looked at him with considerably more warmth. Still, by the time he finished, he was not certain that she had accepted what he said. He ended, his voice fading out, and looked hopefully at her.

For what seemed an eternity, Dolores Ortega y Delgado stared at Hobart Adams. In the short time they had been together before he left, she had come to love him. Because of that, she was very hurt when he did not return after a few days, as he said he would. She figured that she had been used and then discarded. For a woman of her station and breeding, the insult was almost too much to bear.

Now, though, her love for him returned in full bloom. She saw the way he held himself, as if he had been wounded. And, she had heard that a couple of *Americanos* had been arrested and imprisoned down in Santa Fe, right about the time he said he had been in Governor Castillo's *calabozo*. In addition, she had caught a glimpse of two of his companions—the hard-eyed American and the short, swaggering Frenchman—riding hard into Taos, and then back out soon after at the head of a force of American ruffians led by Ceran Saint Vrain. She decided, suddenly, that she would believe him. She had no other choice. She loved him too much not to. She only hoped, in her deepest soul, that he felt the same way about her.

"I forgive you," she finally said in soft, velvety tones. She betrayed none of the worry she felt in her heart.

He grinned widely, happiness flooding over him. He hadn't realized until now just how tense he had been waiting for her answer. He bowed deeply at the waist, sweeping his *sombrero* before him so that it almost brushed the ground. "May I have the honor of this dance, *señorita*?" he asked when he had straightened.

"With pleasure, *señor*." Dolores curtsied. She, too, was greatly relieved. There could be no mistaking the real pleasure on his face when she had forgiven him. He loved her, she was sure of that now.

Adams took Dolores's hand, and they glided into the flow of dancers. He was still not a very accomplished dancer, and he sweated as he strained to keep his leather boots off her dainty, slipper-clad feet. He worried enough about whether she really loved him, and did not want to turn her against him by being some boorish bear of a dancer.

Dolores, though, was delighted to be with him. She was happy to stay with him, too, and she spurned all other offers but Adams's to dance.

Across the plaza, Early, Rawlins, and Chardonnais watched the couple.

"Looks like ye ain't gonna see that chil' this night, *amigo*," Rawlins said with a chuckle.

"Can't say as I figured on gettin' home too early— if at all—myself," Early said. "This chil's got his eyes set on that little *señorita* yonder." He pointed to a young woman in a solid black dress. She had taken the *mantilla* off her hair and let it rest on her shoulders, around her long, graceful neck.

"Shit," Rawlins drawled. "This chil's got a brand-new Green River I'll wager that says ye cain't get that purty thing away from the band of young bucks hangin' on her every word."

"I expect I could use me a new knife," Early allowed. "Ye're on, *amigo*. I'll put my knife sheath—this here one I'm wearin'—against it."

"Suits this chil'."

With a grin, Early swaggered off in the direction of the young lady.

As he did, Chardonnais said with a grin, "Well, dis chil' ain't goin' to sit 'ere all de night just watching all dese lovely *mademoiselles*. I fix to 'ave me one of dem. Maybe two or even t'ree, eh." He laughed and wandered off, jauntily singing some obscure French tune. His companions had always figured the song was one of his own making, since they had never heard any other man, French or otherwise, singing it.

"Well, shit," Rawlins mumbled, suddenly finding himself alone. "This chil's fixin' to see some action, too." An hour later, while dancing some young *señorita* around the plaza, he smiled as he spotted Early slipping down an alley. Early was alone, but Rawlins's alert eyes noted that the *señorita* with the black dress was also missing. He grinned again, dazzling the woman in his arms. He was about to try talking her into slipping away with him.

In the morning, Rawlins handed his Green River knife to Early across the table. He scowled, but he really didn't mind losing the bet. He had had himself a fine time, too, which is what mattered. Early gleefully picked up the knife and ran a thumb along the blade, testing its keenness. There was no real reason for doing it, though, since he knew as well as anyone that Rawlins, despite his wild and fractious ways, took excellent care of his equipment.

"I told ye so, goddammit," Early crowed. "Plumb told ye."

"Shit on ye," Rawlins growled. But he grinned. "How was she?"

"She shined, she did. Damn, I ain't had me one that willin' in a spell." He laughed. "Hell, I thought for a while there she was gonna hump this poor ol' hoss plumb to death. Like to wear my ass out, she did."

"Sign of age, *amigo*," Rawlins said with a chuckle. "Ye're slowin' down, ye ol' fart."

"Hell. How about ye? Ye find yourself some *señorita* to do more than *fandango* with?"

"Hell, I'm insulted ye even asked me such." He laughed. "Tellin' true, though, me'n her wasn't the best of fits. She was out for some foofaraw was all, I reckon. Too damn skinny, too, I'm thinkin', once her duds was off."

"I hear she's spoke highly of ye, too," Early said with a belly laugh.

Rawlins shrugged. "I ain't ary said I was God's gift to womankind. I ain't exactly as suave as most of these young Mexican bucks, that's for goddamn certain. Any woman can't see that straight off and is expecting something more is in for a real disappointin' time." He winked. "Of course, if all they're lookin' for is a hoss with a heap of willin'ness and a big, hard pizzle, they can't go wrong with this chil'."

"Nor if they're lookin' for one who's so full of shit his eyes is brown," Early added, joining his friend's laughter.

Rawlins pointed to the door. "Well, lookee who's here."

Early turned in his seat to see a bouncy, grinning Adams arrive at the table. He sat and grabbed Early's coffee cup. He drank some before setting the cup back in front of Early. "Mornin', boys," he said cheerily. "Hope you all spent a pleasant evening."

Early looked at him in surprise. He had never seen Adams so happy or so cocky, though not in a bad way. "We was just discussin' such doin's," Early said. "We had us shinin' times last night. How about ye, boy?"

"Pleasant, most pleasant." Adams grinned widely and ordered breakfast. It had been more than pleasant. More like downright outstanding. After dancing with Dolores for an hour or more, Adams had hinted that he would like to see her again in private. He licked his dry lips, worried that she would refuse. He was not sure it was right to suggest such a thing, and after he had disappeared on her for some weeks, she might want to punish him. But he ached with a need for her, and so he hinted at his desire since he felt too discomfited to come straight out and ask.

Dolores smiled at him and then whispered breathlessly in his ear, "At my friend's house. In quarter of an hour."

He remembered the way easily as he strolled down the dark streets. Then once more he was in the small, dimly lit bedroom. Dolores was pressed against him, her lips hungry for him. In what was far too brief a time, they were reclining, naked, entwined in each other's arms, trying to recover their breath.

"I missed you, *señor*," Dolores said softly. Her wide, deep brown eyes stared into his, hoping to see her love returned there.

"Not half as much as I missed you," he replied, smiling gently.

Her relief was palpable, though she did not let on other than to scrape her fingernails lightly across the tangle of hairs on his chest. The chest hair still seemed strange to her, and she wasn't sure whether she liked it or simply tolerated it because she loved Adams so much.

"But why do you keep calling me *señor*?" he asked, a little worried. The use of the term seemed to him to indicate some standoffishness on her part.

"It is the right thing to do, no?"

"No. Not for people who lo—who . . ."

"Do you?" she asked, hope glowing in her heart.

"Do I what?" Adams responded. He knew what she was asking, and he didn't mind admitting it. He just wanted to be sure she felt likewise first.

"Love me?" Dolores asked flatly.

He looked at her soft, brown face, with the high, smooth forehead, the prominent cheekbones, the fine skin, slightly parted full lips. He decided he could not hold off any longer. "Yes," he said without fear.

"*Gracias a Dios!*" Dolores breathed fervently. "Thank God."

"And do you love me?" Adams asked, fighting back the fear.

"*Sí.* Oh, yes!" she said, eyes wide and intent. "*Mucho. Muy muchísimo.* Much. Very much."

Adams wasn't sure he would be able to speak. Not with his heart swollen up in joy like it was, growing so big as to be pushing out of his chest, crowding his vocal chords. So he leaned over and kissed her, long and deeply. Elizabeth Luyuendyke was but a distant and fast fading memory. Had he bothered to think about her at this moment, he would have wondered how he could ever have thought he loved her.

An hour and a half later, Adams and Dolores reluctantly dressed and went back to the ball separately. Shortly thereafter, Dolores brought Adams to meet her father.

Don Francisco was an old but still imposing man, with a fierce look aided by the wild mane of white hair. Still, he seemed to accept Adams, at least on the surface. He would have, of course, preferred that his daughter become smitten with a young Mexican of a good family. But Don Francisco reasoned that having a rich *Americano* as a son-in-law, if indeed that was where this was heading, might not be all that bad.

39

"WHAT DO YOU BOYS have planned for today?" Adams asked as he finished off his spiced sausage and eggs.

"Well now," Early said around the wad of tobacco in his cheek, "the way I heard it, there's gonna be a heap big fiesta of some kind. These here folks're always celebratin' one damn thing or another." He did not think that such a bad way to live.

"Sounds like a good time," Adams said, leaning back and lighting a cigar from the candle on the table. He had almost forgotten about Ebenezer Parfrey and his vow to get the wagoneer. He was feeling too good about life. While he and Dolores had not exactly pledged their troth, they had made a commitment to each other. There had been no reason for words. Both knew it, and accepted it.

"Ought to be," Rawlins said. "There'll be horse racin' and a heap of other doin's. I aim to win me some specie this day, for goddamn sure."

The noise in the street was already growing, and they did not want to miss it. Within minutes they strolled out into the bright, warm sun. People in festive costume hurried about, seeking friends, food, drink, and excitement. The three men walked toward the plaza, where most of the activity would take place.

"Looks like they're fixin' to start a horse race," Rawlins said.

"Expect so." Early grinned. "I misdoubt it'll be the only one this day. I expect I'll wait afore bringin' the Appaloosa out. Give me a chance to see just what she's facin'."

"Well don't wait all goddamn day," Rawlins growled. "I aim to wager a heap on that ol' hoss."

"His Appaloosa fast?" Adams asked.

"Ain't a goddamn horse in Taos can beat it, boy," Rawlins said. "Ye wager all ye can on her and ye'll be a rich man afore the day's done."

Adams nodded and watched as a shot rang out and seven horses thundered out of the plaza and onto a street heading north. Early also watched closely. Many Taoseños had seen the Appaloosa run, but he had not raced the animal here in a few years. There should be few eyebrows raised when he brought the horse out and wagered heavily on her.

From what he could see, none of the horses in this race would give the Appaloosa any competition. He figured he would be in some big winnings today.

Another race started almost immediately after the first finished. Chardonnais wandered up, his usual jaunty self, and watched along with his companions. Afterward the four strolled around the plaza, betting occasionally on a game of monte or a wrestling match or whatever they happened to be close to at the time.

"Well," Early said, "I best get the Appaloosa afore they finish up all the horse racin'." He strolled off. Ten minutes later he was in a line with five other riders.

Someone fired a gun and the horses bolted.

Chardonnais and Rawlins did not even watch. They were too busy wagering all they had or could beg, borrow, or steal on Early's horse. With a pounding heart, Adams bet all the money he had. It wasn't much, but it would hurt if he lost.

The wagering ended as they could hear the crowd announcing with a burst of cheering that the race was in its final stretch. Early's Appaloosa trotted home a hundred yards ahead of the second-place horse. Crowing cockily, Rawlins, Chardonnais, and Adams collected their winnings. They were counting it when Early walked up, towing his horse. "How ye boys do?" he asked.

"How you t'ink, eh?" Chardonnais said with a grin.

"I just hope we ain't cleaned out all these here boys," Rawlins grumbled. "There's bound to be a heap more doin's to be wagerin' on."

"Christ, Abe," Early said with a laugh. "Ye ain't ary happy, are ye?"

Suddenly there was a shout and a roar. The four spun and grinned. "Watch this, boy," Early said to Adams.

People lined a street leading away from the plaza. In the center of the street, barely visible, the head of a chicken stuck out of the ground.

A mounted *vaquero* sat in the plaza waiting. Then he punched his big spurs against his horse's side. The animal bolted, flying across the plaza. As the rider neared the chicken head, he swung low over the horse's side. As he swept past the buried, live chicken, he reached out a hand and squeezed. The chicken squawked loudly to the jeers of the crowd. The humbled rider pulled to a stop farther down the street and rode sedately back to the plaza. He hung his head, muttering.

Another rider swept down the street, and he, too, failed. Then another and another.

"What're they trying to do, Ezra?" Adams asked.

"What'n hell's it look like they're tryin' to do, boy?"

"Pull the chicken out of the ground."

"Ain't so easy as ye might think, is it?" Early laughed.

"No." He watched as another rider failed.

"Hey, Frenchie," Rawlins said with a grin, "why'n't ye try it."

Chardonnais scowled and blasted his friend with an earful of profane French.

"What's wrong, Lucien?" Adams asked.

Chardonnais turned burning eyes on Adams. Then he relented a little. "My arms are too short for such t'ings," he said stiffly. "And dese bastards, dem wit' their long arms, damn well know it. Dey jus' try to make fun of me, 'cause dey are afraid to try it. Dey will look de fool."

"Shit," Early and Rawlins muttered in unison.

"Well, why don't one of you try it?" Adams asked.

"Well, damn, boy, I just might," Rawlins said. "But maybe I won't neither. I don't need me no goddamn chicken."

"You are jus' scared of fallin' off your 'orse," Chardonnais needled. "You don't 'ave de 'eart for such t'ings. Or *les couilles*—de balls."

"Ye got anything worth more'n a Digger's ass ye'd like to wager on whether I can do it, ye short-legged little shit?"

"My sleepin' robe. De one of wolf fur."

"That shines with this chil'. And just to show ye I can do it, I'll put up my goddamn saddle."

"I accept," Chardonnais said, his round head bobbing.

Rawlins ambled off toward the stables, stopping by to tell the officials that he would be making a run at things. The officials nodded but urged him to hurry a little. There were still several more men waiting to make the run, but they could not wait all day for one man.

"You sure you want to do that, Lucien?" Adams asked. "If you win, Abe won't have a saddle."

Chardonnais grinned. " 'E will not lose. And I can get a new sleeping robe as soon as I get to de village."

"Then why?" Adams asked, curiosity aroused. "Just for the gambling?"

"That's part of it," Early answered. "But this here's a good chance to collect some big winnin's. Ain't that right, Frenchie?"

"*Oui*. Watch dis." He grinned and then yelled, "*Allons, mes amis.* I 'ave *beaucoup* specie to bet. My frain is going to get dat chicken out of de groun'. I 'ave many gold pieces to say 'e can do it."

An excited buzz ran through the crowd nearby, and then spread as word was passed. Soon men and women gathered around, nearly all betting heavily against

Rawlins. After all, if their best *vaqueros* hadn't been able to do it, no *Americano* was going to be able to.

Early and Chardonnais covered every bet that came along, whether in coins or goods. Catching the excitement, Adams got into the action by taking some modest wagers.

A yell went up as Rawlins entered the plaza. He doffed his top hat and tossed it to a young peasant woman. With a roar and a shout, he was off. He didn't look good riding a horse, seeming to be all flapping arms and legs, his ass bouncing in the saddle. He thundered past his three companions, then swooped low over the side of his horse. The long, strong fingers of his right hand reached down. There was a horrendous cackling. Rawlins, still riding hard, straightened up, holding the chicken high above his head as he slowed the horse. A wide grin splayed across his face.

He rode back to the plaza. Still on horseback, he handed the chicken to the *señorita* to whom he had tossed his hat earlier. She was a pleasantly plain-looking woman dressed simply in a cotton dress that reached midcalf. She was too poor to have fancy dresses and *mantillas* and such. She was also quite happy to have the chicken. It would serve her poor family well.

Rawlins grinned as he rode away. He knew he would also be served well. He trotted to where Early, Adams, and Chardonnais were gleefully collecting their winnings, gloating. "Well," he said laconically, "looks like ye boys did all right."

"Judgin' by what ye done with the chicken, I expect ye didn't do so bad your own self," Early said with a laugh.

They were distracted by a roar from the crowd. They

turned to see four oxen hauling a wheeled, wooden cage into the plaza. The cage contained a snarling grizzly bear.

"Now here's somethin' I can take a shine to," Early said. He grinned, mounted the Appaloosa, and walked off.

"What's this all about?" Adams asked.

"They're gonna let that goddamn griz loose, so's some of these boys can try'n rope it," Rawlins answered, dismounting. He held the reins to his horse loosely in hand.

"What the hell for?"

Rawlins shrugged. "Prize money's part of it," Rawlins said nonchalantly. He didn't really expect Adams to understand. "These boys don't make a whole hell of a lot of specie workin' the ranches. It's also a good chance for them to show off their skill . . . and their bravery." He grinned. "Impresses hell out of the *señoritas.*"

"Seems absolutely foolish."

Rawlins shrugged.

"Can Ezra really do it?"

"He's done it onct before. A few years back. He ain't real good with a rope. Not like the *vaqueros.* Them boys live by the rope and can usually rope the b'ar purty easy. Trouble is, holdin' on afterward."

They watched as gaudily dressed *vaqueros* grouped in the plaza. A peasant yanked open the door of the wheeled cage and ran. The bear, sniffing freedom, shuffled out, its big, cinnamon-brown head moving slowly from side to side. The bruin reared, testing the air. He fell back on front paws. Someone fired a gun, and the bear suddenly began moving quickly across the plaza.

One of the *vaqueros* shouted, and then everyone was off in pursuit. The bear, sensing danger, stopped and looked back. He seemed somewhat bewildered, as he sniffed the air, trying to find the danger. Then he lumbered off again.

Yelling *vaqueros* swarmed around the beast, twirling their *reatas*. One after another they threw their rope loops. Some missed, but a few neatly circled the bear's massive head and settled down over the brawny neck. They tightened as the bear backed off.

The bear reared, bellowing in rage and frantically waving its huge clawed paws in the air. He plopped down and rumbled off, dragging one *vaquero* off his horse. Whirling, the bear was on the man in a flash, raking him with his claws, snuffling and snorting, venting his rage. He bit the man's leg and pulled him about for a moment, then went back to clawing him.

Two other rope loops encircled the bear. The riders hastily dallied the rope around saddlehorns. Working in concert, they moved their horses backward. Slowly the power of four horses pulled the bear a little off the man, but the grizzly was still close enough to keep his claws on the man.

Another *vaquero* swept by and with his *sombrero* he swatted the bear on the snout. The angry bruin let go of the man on the ground and reared, displaying his displeasure.

Early slid off his horse and slipped in under the bear's deadly claws and fangs. The other *vaqueros*, seeing what he was doing, jerked the horses backward, pulling the bear over onto his back.

Early grabbed the downed *vaquero* and pulled him away by a few feet. He scooped the man up with an easy effort and ran off to safety.

The bear had regained its paws, and with a frightening bellow hunched his neck, pulling furiously at the ropes. Its strength was awesome, and it slowly gained way. One rope snapped. With one fewer horse dragging on him, the bear made more headway. Suddenly it whirled and charged, slashing one of the horses with its claws.

The mount screamed and reared, dumping its rider. Stunned by the hard landing, the man scuttled through the dust, away from the frightful fangs and claws. The bear chomped on the horse's shoulder and clamped down, holding the squealing mount firmly. Curses in Spanish, English, and French filled the street as people nearby fled, afraid the bear would be after them next. Then there was the roar of a heavy rifle. Then another.

The grizzly let the horse go, bellowing again. He whirled, seeking somewhere, something into which to sink its fangs.

At the sounds of the first rifle, Early had glanced around and seen that Rawlins had fired, followed by Chardonnais. As the bear let go of the horse, Early yanked out his own rifle. He dropped to one knee and fired, hitting the bear in the chest.

The grizzly charged him, but Early merely grinned humorlessly, rose and slipped into the saddle. The big Appaloosa carried him easily out of the way of the rushing bruin. The bear stopped near the center of the plaza, blood streaming from mouth and nose and covering the dark chest fur.

Once again Rawlins fired, and Chardonnais again. The bear reared one last time before crumpling to the ground in a cloud of dust. Still, it struggled to rise until Early moved in close and fired a pistol ball into the beast's brain from a couple of yards away.

People who had fled began creeping carefully out of

buildings again. Early dismounted, as Rawlins, Chardonnais, and Adams walked up. They looked down at the carcass.

" 'Less'n ye hosses got a complaint, this chil's got a hankerin' for them claws," Rawlins said, leaning on his rifle.

"Suits me," Early said. "I'll take the teeth. I expect they'll shine for fancyin' me up."

"Dat leaves me wit' de hide," Chardonnais said. "Dat's fine wit' me, seeing as 'ow dis shit"—he jabbed Rawlins with a not-all-that-gentle elbow—"won my sleeping robe. I can use dis 'til Looks Again can make me a new one."

While the three went about their job with bloody, swift efficiency, trying not to get any of the gore on their fancy clothes, a small crowd gathered. When they were finished, several peasants swooped in, carving the meat off the quivering carcass.

"Excuse me, *señors*," a *vaquero* said as the four walked off. When they stopped and looked up at the mounted Mexican, he said, "My *amigos* and I are grateful for your help."

"Weren't nothin'," Rawlins said.

"But yes it was." The *vaquero*'s speech was accented, but not too heavily. "If it wasn't for you, Manuel would've died. He might anyway, but, well, you tried to save him. We are thankful, and we would like to buy you a drink in the *cantina* there." He nodded with his head.

Early grinned. "That, ol' hoss, is the kind of thanks this chil' likes."

40

THE FOUR PARTOOK OF more than one round of Taos Lightning and mescal with the *vaqueros,* enjoying the hospitality of those Mexican horsemen, as well as some of the *señoritas* and the owner of the *cantina.*

Adams had only a few drinks and quickly tired of trying to fend off two particularly aggressive young women. "I'm heading off, boys," he finally said, thoughts of Dolores omnipresent.

Not long afterward, Rawlins decided to leave, too.

"Can't keep up with us real *hombres,* eh?" Early said sarcastically.

"I got me better things to do." He grinned.

Early looked at him in surprise, then he, too, grinned. "That little peasant girl, eh?"

"Ain't none of your concern," Rawlins said in a friendly growl. Then he was gone.

After a while, though, the *vaqueros* began drifting off to take part in other contests, or to rendezvous with some young ladies. Early and Chardonnais, who had taken two of the *señoritas* into the back room in the three hours they had been in the *cantina,* bought two bottles each of Taos Lightning and mescal. They found a spot in the shade of a tree from which they could watch the fiesta swirling around them.

They were still there the next morning, blissfully snoring away. The passersby generally ignored them. Some simply looked in disgust at the two slovenly, drunken mountain men. Others laughed.

Until Rawlins came along. He was on his way back to his room when he spotted the two sleeping figures. A sly grin spread across his face, and he looked downright malevolent when he got a bucket of water from the town well. He walked to where Early and Chardonnais were and doused the two of them with the water.

They sputtered awake, groaning, sick with fresh hangovers. "Jesus goddamn Christ all goddamn mighty, Abe," Early swore. He was still lying on his side, but now holding his throbbing head in his hands. "Weren't no goddamn call for such doin's."

Rawlins grinned. "Ye two ass-wipes ought to see yourselves. Ye sure are some goddamn sight, the both of ye."

"Piss off," Chardonnais groaned.

"If'n I do, boy, it won't be all over myself, like some other hosses I know," Rawlins said with a malicious grin. He was enjoying himself.

"I been worse off," Early managed. He wanted to vomit more than anything, but he would not allow himself to. Not while Rawlins was standing there so smugly.

"I reckon ye have." Rawlins laughed.

"So've ye, ye goddamn peckerless bastard."

"Nary," Rawlins said with rare joy. "Nary have I been so bad as ye two are now." It was a bald-faced lie, but he didn't care a whit. Generally, he was one of the worst, and more than once the others had gloated over his suffering from a hangover. This was a rare chance to return the favor.

"Go away, damn you." Chardonnais gasped. He had not been able to fight off the nausea that overpowered him, and he had been retching for the past few seconds.

"Ye boys aim to break your fast?" Rawlins asked. He laughed all the more at the black looks Early and Chardonnais shot at him. He shook his head. "Well, boys, I sure as hell aim to. Yep. Just the thought of some greasy *chorizos* and maybe a couple of nice runny eggs from Rosalita's hens. Have me some big, thick biscuits covered over with honey, a couple pieces of cheese, maybe some goat's milk."

Early could no longer hold back the raging flood of nausea. He did, however, manage to roll over and get to hands and knees before his stomach erupted.

Still laughing, Rawlins strolled away.

Early rolled over onto his buttocks and leaned back against the adobe wall of the building. Chardonnais slowly followed suit. They looked at each other forlornly.

"You t'ink we're getting too old for dis shit, *mon ami?*" Chardonnais asked in between gasps.

"Mayhap ye are, but I sure as hell ain't." He pushed

with his feet, sliding his back up the wall. He figured that would be the easiest way to get upright. It worked, though it was an effort. He stood there, legs shaky, using the wall for support. His stomach felt like someone was twisting it violently. His head pounded, and the people walking by wavered in his vision. His mouth was sour and felt like the bottom of a chicken coop.

He looked at Chardonnais. "Christ, I hope I don't look as bad as ye."

"I t'ink you look worse dan me," Chardonnais said unconvincingly. He sat there a moment longer, wishing somehow that he could magically rise. But he couldn't, and he knew he would have to make a conscious effort to do it. Early certainly wasn't going to be of any help to him. He did, though, follow Early's example and use the building to help him. Soon he was on his feet, more or less.

"I expect I could do with some more robe time," Early allowed.

"*Moi aussi.*" He rubbed the snot away from his running nose. "But I ain' so sure I can make it."

"Well, I sure as hell can't help ye none." Early pushed away from the wall, a little surprised when he did not fall down. He experimented with a cautious step, followed by another. It took a little while, but he finally reached his room. He had no idea whether Chardonnais had followed him or not. He could not worry about his friend now. He climbed into bed and was instantly asleep.

Early felt considerably better when he awoke several hours later. His stomach still lurched, but his head was mostly clear and he was hungry. He rose and splashed water into a basin. He washed his face, the cool liquid refreshing him. A few minutes later, Adams strolled in, carrying a sketch pad and writing paper. "Ye ate lately, boy?" Early asked.

"Not for some time." He held up his papers. "I've been busy."

Early grinned. "At more'n sketchin' and such, I'd wager. That so?"

Adams considered for a moment getting angry at the insinuation. Then he realized that for one thing, Early was just being friendly in a crude way that passed for manly camaraderie. For another, if he objected, he wasn't sure it would get him anywhere other than dead. Suddenly he grinned. It was probably no secret what he had been up to, and whom he had been up to it with. Early understood these things. "Yes. Or should I say *sí?*"

"What say we go fill our meatbags, boy?"

"Suits me, *amigo.*" Adams smiled, rather pleased that he was beginning to use his smattering of Spanish, as well as the strange argot of the mountain men.

They walked silently toward a restaurant. When they were seated and had ordered, Adams suddenly blurted out, "Have you seen Parfrey, Ezra?" He had successfully, if only for a little while, put Parfrey out of his mind. His joy at seeing Dolores again, and the time he was with her, had kept the distasteful thought of Parfrey away. Even today, when he had spent several hours sitting in the plaza, when he was not talking with Dolores, sketching had kept the anger and desire for vengeance at bay. For some reason, though, Parfrey had entered his thoughts on the walk to the restaurant. Suddenly, it seemed almost urgent that he renew his quest.

"Nope." Parfrey was Adams's problem, as far as he was concerned. He was not about to worry over it. Still, he knew how much it mattered to Adams. "Don't ye worry none, boy. We'll find that son of a bitch."

Adams nodded, but he sat, staring moodily at the walls. Even the food, when it came, cheered him only a little.

To try to get Adams's mind off Parfrey, Early asked, "Ye sell any more of them drawin's of yours?"

Adams nodded. "Six of them today."

"Hell, boy, your pockets ought to be full."

"And if they are?" Adams asked suspiciously.

"Well, now, I was thinkin' ye might like to try losin' some of it over at Doña Montoya's gamblin' place. Mayhap play a game or two of monte."

Adams brightened fractionally. "It might be nice to partake. But I don't intend to lose."

"Me, neither. Let's go."

Doña Montoya's was crowded as usual. Smoke was thick in the air, and the noise loud enough to hurt. Early and Adams bulled their way to a table and sat, placing their gold coins on the table in front of them.

The cards rose and fell, and neither man gained or lost much. Then Adams got just the right hand, and he bet heavily. He won. With a whoop, he leaned over to rake in his winnings. As he did, Parfrey took a seat directly across the table from him.

"Looks like ya been doin' all goddamn right for yourself, boy," Parfrey said with a sneer. "Your goddamn luck changed, I take it?"

Adams stiffened, still leaning across the table.

"Pick up your winnin's, boy," Early said quietly, gazing evenly at Parfrey.

Adams did so, and then reached for his knife. Only Early and Parfrey saw it. Early gripped Adams's arm. "Not here."

"But, Ezra," Adams hissed. He seethed.

"Just do what I tell ye, boy," Early said sharply, though quietly. "Get your hand off that knife and put both your hands on the table. They're dealin' the cards again. Just keep on playin'."

Adams did as he was told, and looked at the cards before him. He played absentmindedly for more than an hour. Then Parfrey rose and left. Adams rose to follow, but Early stopped him again. "Set your ass back down, boy, and listen to what I got to say," Early said harshly.

Adams sat angrily, and he and Early played the cards that were dealt them. As the game progressed, Early said quietly, "I know ye want to go agin that son of a bitch, but this ain't the place for it."

Early fired up his pipe and gave up on the hand he had. "I stopped ye afore for two reasons. Fust, there's enough soldiers here that ye would've been made wolf bait by 'em nearabout as soon as ye pulled that blade. And second, one of Parfrey's ass-lickers was settin' there with his pistol. If the soldiers hadn't of rubbed ye out, he would've. Ye'd of never made it across the table."

Adams looked at him in surprise, and Early nodded. "I told ye his kind ain't to be trusted. Ye got to get him out in the open, where he can't pull none of his trickery."

"But he's likely to run now, isn't he?"

"Shit," Early snorted. "Run from what? Ye? Hell, he ain't scared of the likes of ye, boy, and that's a damn

fact. He don't know ye wrassled Lucien to a draw and
stood with me and the others agin the Apaches. All he
knows is ye're the chil' he and his men whipped the
shit out of and left out in the Cimarron. And the chil'
they scared shit out of down in Santa Fe."

"That's to my advantage, isn't it?"

"Yep." He paused. "Collect your winnin's." When
Adams had done so, Early said, "I figure he don't even
suspect ye're lookin' for him."

"He'll be surprised then, won't he?"

"Mayhap. On the other hand, if he does think ye
might try'n go agin him, he'll try gettin' ye fust, when
ye ain't expectin' it."

"I'm not afraid of him."

"I know that. But there's no tellin' what a snake-
humpin' son of a bitch like him'll do. Keep your eyes
peeled, since I figure he'll always be with some of his
compañeros." He paused to make a play with the
cards.

Adams's shoulders slumped and he nodded. Then he
straightened. "You've treated me well, Ezra. Done
more for me than anyone's got a right to expect.
Because of that, I'll try to do what you've suggested.
But I don't intend to let Parfrey's infractions pass." He
stared hard at Early.

"I wouldn't call ye *amigo* if ye did, boy," Early said
evenly. "Now, set your mind on them cards afore ye
lose everything."

41

EARLY AND ADAMS STROLLED the dark silent streets, talking softly. They had done well at Doña Montoya's monte tables and were heading back to their room. Suddenly Early slammed his shoulder into Adams, sending him sprawling in the street. As Early dived for the cover of the corner of a building, a rifle boomed. The ball hit the adobe wall to Early's left.

"Get your ass over here, boy," Early said calmly after a few moments, "afore he reloads."

Adams was up and sprinting as Early pinpointed the spot where the shot had come from. The rifle appeared again at the dimly lit window, and Early fired one of his pistols. He didn't expect to hit anything; he just wanted to give Adams time to get to safety.

The rifle disappeared, though Adams didn't know it.

He stopped, kneeling next to Early, breathing heavily. "You get him?" he asked. "Whoever it was?"

"Nope. Wasn't tryin' to. But I expect we won't be bothered no more tonight." He grinned into the darkness. " 'Specially if'n we go on down this here alley and around." He reloaded his pistol, doing it by touch.

Adams grunted an acknowledgment. He was seething inside, enraged that someone would do this. He was frightened, too, and that made him all the more angry. He did not need to ask who had done it.

"How'd you know?" he asked, trying to calm himself.

Early shrugged, knowing that in the darkness of the alley at the corner of the building Adams couldn't see it. How could he explain that, like when he was in the forest, he was ever alert? Things struck him and he processed the information instantly, without conscious thought. Now that he did think about it, there were some clues. A sound of a rifle being cocked, a glint of something in a torch or lantern, a move caught only in his peripheral vision.

"Couple little things," he finally said lamely.

"I see. Well, let's go get him."

"I expect he's long gone now. 'Sides, ye've had more than a little awerdenty. Ye'll not be at your best." He stood. "Let's go."

They strolled down the Stygian alley, walking slowly so as not to turn an ankle on the rubble and garbage. When they got to the room, Early held a finger against his lips, indicating that Adams should be quiet. He positioned Adams on one side of the door. He took the other. Suddenly he flung the door open. Nothing happened.

Early peeked cautiously around the adobe into the room. Moonlight filtered into the room through the shutters over the two windows. It was enough to show no one was in there. Early walked in, followed by Adams.

"Best get some robe time, boy," Early said. "Ye'll need it come mornin'."

"You think something's going to happen tomorrow?"

"It's time an end was put to this devilment, boy," Early said harshly.

Adams felt odd as he pulled off his clothes. When he crawled into bed, he realized that it was because he had no fear, only anticipation. It was, he thought, strange, and he wondered about it for a while. It kept him from falling asleep for a good long time, but finally the whiskey and general tiredness overtook the excitement of the impending action, and sleep came.

Adams awoke groggily with the dawn. He had not slept well, and he had a touch of a hangover. More annoying was the fact that his anticipation at taking on Parfrey had at least partially evaporated, replaced with a gnawing nervousness. It was one thing to be suddenly thrust into danger, like with the Apaches. It was entirely another to go out seeking to do serious harm to another human being.

Early was gone, and that bothered Adams. It wasn't so much that he needed Early around, it was more that he didn't know what to do with himself. He planned, of course, to seek out Parfrey. The problem was, he wasn't sure how to go about it, and for that he wanted Early's help.

With a sigh, he made water in the chamber pot and

tossed the contents out the window into the alley. Five minutes later, he went through it again, scowling at the anxiety that was affecting his bladder.

He was more or less grateful when Early walked in. " 'Bout time ye got your lazy ass up, boy," Early said without preliminary.

"Where were you?" Adams asked, trying to hide his nervousness.

Early ignored the question. Instead, he asked, "Your weapons ready?"

Adams nodded, suddenly needing to relieve himself again. But he grabbed his pistols, stuck them in the sash that served him as a belt, and picked up his rifle. He draped the shooting bag and powder horn over his shoulder and then pulled on a serape. "Ready," he said, wondering whether his voice had quavered.

Rawlins and Chardonnais were waiting just outside the building. They, like Early, wore blanket *capotes.* "Mornin', boy," Rawlins said flatly. He had come to like Adams and would hate to see him go under. But it was a job the young man needed to handle.

"*Bonjour,*" Chardonnais added. "*Allons.*"

They headed down the street and pulled into a small eatery. "I doubt I can get anything in my stomach now," Adams protested.

"I can," Chardonnais said with customary cheer.

"Ye'll need your strength, boy," Early said.

They ate quickly and hugely. Adams picked at his food at first, but then realized that he was hungry, and he put more effort into it. As the food hit his system, the slight hangover and the tiredness sloughed away. In its place grew confidence and a feeling of aggression. Not only did he know he had to get this over with, he now *wanted* to get this over with, and soon. After a last cup of coffee, they lit cigars and pipes as they headed outside. Rawlins and Chardonnais went one way, Early and Adams the other.

They checked shops, boarding houses, and saloons. They scouted the plaza and side alleys and streets. They couldn't find Parfrey, though at a few places they heard he had been there not long before, or that they had just missed him. Early began to suspect that Parfrey had friends here, mostly in the low saloons, who were trying to throw him and Adams off the track.

Soon after they started their search, the sun disappeared behind thick banks of heavy, dark clouds that had blown in from the west. The wind also brought a chill to the air, here at the seven-thousand-foot altitude at which Taos sat. Thunder began rolling ominously off the Conejos Mountains. It dampened Adams's enthusiasm and weighed heavily on him.

The morning slipped away, but still they had not found Parfrey, and the four men finally regrouped in the plaza. The rain had started, though it wasn't heavy yet. Still, they met under the portico of a saloon, protected by the slightly sloped porch roof.

"Don't look like that critter's around," Rawlins growled in annoyance. He hated rain and clouds, and his tolerance for frustration was always low.

"Mayhap so," Early said. "But we ain't givin' up now."

"What you suggest, *mon ami?*" Chardonnais asked. He leaned back against the wall of a saloon and watched the *señoritas* walk by. He smiled, enjoying the sight of the wind whipping their skirts up and about. He was ready for a break from all this searching, perhaps a quick, hot rendezvous with one of these lovelies to take the chill out of the day and the lust out of his system, if only for a little while.

"I expect we ought to check every place again. He's got to be in one of them." He shrugged, his own annoyance growing, despite his deep reservoir of patience. "We don't find him after another *paseo* around town, we'll give it up for this day."

"If'n that's where your stick floats," Rawlins growled, "then I reckon mine does, too." For some unknown reason, he suddenly lost his frustration at the so-far fruitless search.

Early nodded. "How about ye, Frenchie? This really ain't your concern, and ye can go about your own business, if'n ye're of a mind to."

Chardonnais watched for a last, lingering moment as another lovely young woman drifted by, hurrying against the rain and the wind. He sighed. *Yes,* he thought, *some time with one of them would be nice.* But Adams was his friend, and he could not desert his friend. "I t'ink I will 'elp some more, eh." He grinned, the gloom that had arisen sloughing off him.

Early nodded. "That suits this chil'. Ye boys head that way." He pointed to the direction he and Adams had come from. "We'll go the other. Maybe that'll change our goddamn medicine."

They moved off, seeking cover from the increasingly heavy rains where they could. They were happy to duck into stores and saloons, where they were out of the inclement weather and where they could warm themselves at cheery, aromatic fires that burned in the indigenous, rounded-front fireplaces.

The rain drove harder, pouring down in thick

sheets. Thunder exploded in cacophonous blasts, and lightning snapped and spit with dazzling frequency. There were few people outside as Early and Adams hurried from one building to the next as quickly as they could.

At a small restaurant, as they stood letting the flames singe the chill off them, Adams asked, "You said something about changing our medicine to Lucien and Abe. What's that mean?"

Early thought about that for a moment. He had never been called on to explain it before, and was not sure he could. It simply was, and he accepted it. "The Injins, all of 'em I know of, believe in medicine. Before they go on the hunt, before they go off to war, they make medicine. Kind of communin' with the spirits. It guides their lives in most ways." He smiled. "Most mountaineers believe in it, some more'n others."

Adams was not sure he understood, but he nodded anyway. It was, he gathered, a matter of faith. One simply believed in such things, or one didn't. It defied explanation. He didn't believe, since he knew nothing of it, but he did not disbelieve in it either.

They moved on and entered a warm, glowing saloon. They stopped just inside the door of the small *cantina* and shook the rain from their hats. Suddenly Adams stiffened. Through the light crowd, he spotted Parfrey standing at the makeshift bar.

Without a word, he slapped the big *sombrero* back on his head and stalked forward.

Early slipped just to the side of the door and untied the belt of his *capote*, which he had worn against the wind and chill, and opened the blanket coat so his pistols were within reach. He also slid the Dickert rifle out of the blanket rifle case. Though it would be nearly useless in the confines of the small saloon, it might nonetheless come in handy. He waited, watching the crowd warily.

Adams strode quietly toward Parfrey from behind, ignoring two of Parfrey's henchmen who were flanking him.

Parfrey seemed unaware of the two men, having not even bothered to look when the door had opened and closed. His first indication that trouble was brewing was when Adams suddenly grabbed him by the back of the shirt and yanked hard. As he did that, Adams also stuck out his right foot.

Parfrey stumbled and then fell. He hit one of the sturdy wood tables and then rolled off onto the dirt floor.

Still on the floor, Parfrey began scrabbling for one of the big pistols in his belt. His face curled up into a hideous scowl.

Adams forgot about his own pistol. In his determination to deal with Parfrey, he wanted only to use his hands; to treat Parfrey like Parfrey had treated him back there in the Cimarron desert. Moving more quickly than he thought he could, relishing in the icy calmness that had come over him, he stepped forward and kicked the pistol out of Parfrey's hand as the wagoneer tried to bring it to bear. It clattered away.

There was a roar from behind, and Adams instinctively ducked, then turned his head.

Early was standing there, just leaning his smoking Dickert against the wall. His eyes were on Parfrey's two companions. "These here doin's is 'tween ol' Bart and the shit pile on the floor," Early said harshly. "Ye boys stay clear of it."

George Court and Alf McHugh glared at Early. "I got me a score to settle with that donkey-screwin' little puke," Court said nastily. "For kickin' me in the balls that night down there in Santa Fe."

"Ye ain't got no balls to be kicked, ass-wipe," Early said. "Now ye keep your nose out of these doin's. Ye still got the stomach for going agin Bart—or me—when he's done raisin' hair on mule shit there, ye can have at him. 'Less'n, of course," Early added with a sneer, "I get tired of lookin' at your ugly face and shoot ye first."

Adams had turned back to face Parfrey as soon as he knew who had fired the shot. He had implicit faith in Early and knew he would handle McHugh and Court.

Parfrey pushed himself up, a look of malevolence curling his dark face. "I'm gonna kill ya for that, goddammit," he said with a snarl. He went for his big knife. "More'n that, goddamn ya, ya dumb sonna bitch, I'm gonna carve ya like"—a smirk grew on his face—"like I done to that goddamn Comanche bitch." He laughed, a sound that revolted Adams.

Parfrey tapped the small buckskin bag hanging at his waist. "Bitch didn't have much tits, but 'tween the two of 'em, I found me enough hide to make me this here little pouch."

42

PEOPLE BEGAN LOOKING FOR safety. Most made it to the door and outside until only Early, Adams, Parfrey, Court, McHugh, and the bartender remained.

Adams took off his *sombrero* and tossed it aside. Then he pulled his pistol. He smiled just a bit at the sudden look of fear in Parfrey's eyes. But he gently set the pistol on a nearby table. Adams's face hardened. "I'm going to give you more of a chance than you ever gave that girl," he snarled. "And more of a chance than you ever gave me."

"Shit," Parfrey drawled, arrogant once again. "You're a goddamn fool, boy." He grinned evilly and advanced slowly.

"We'll just see about that," Adams said, unafraid. He pulled his own blade and crouched, holding the knife easily in hand, the way he had been taught. He waited.

Early kept his position by the door, certain that Court, McHugh, or both would try something. As Parfrey moved forward, riveting Adams's attention, one of them did. Moving with deceptive slowness, Court eased his pistol out and quietly pulled back the hammer.

Early pulled out a pistol and held it in Court's general direction. "I wouldn't do that was I ye," he said quietly.

Court froze, a cold look on his face. With careful movements, he started to place the pistol on the bar. But just as the weapon touched the old wood door that served as a bar, Court whipped it out and swung toward Early, hoping to catch the mountain man by surprise.

Early fired the pistol. The .54-caliber ball punched through Court's stomach and out the back, sinking at last in the adobe wall behind the bar. Court was slammed up against the bar, his eyes widening in shock and surprise. He stood only a moment, body swaying with the remnants of impact, before he crumpled.

Eyes never leaving McHugh, Early spit a gob of tobacco juice and began reloading the pistol.

Adams and Parfrey had frozen at Early's words and stayed that way through Court's death. As Court fell, Parfrey recovered first. He jumped at Adams, knife thrusting out.

Adams was far faster than Parfrey had figured on. He whirled, sidestepping the charging freighter. He added impetus to Parfrey's movement with a hard punch on the man's back.

Parfrey hit the bar and his breath burst out as the

wood slammed his stomach. He fell, gasping for air. But he was up quickly, using the bar for support. Sweeping his hand along the bar, he came up with a crockery glass and whirled. He threw it at Adams, who ducked.

Parfrey charged again. Adams fell out of the way as Parfrey's knife sliced through his *serape* and nicked the skin. Parfrey whirled and came after Adams again. Adams had fallen, landing hard in the dirt. He grabbed a chair and shoved it in front of him. Parfrey's knife stuck in the wood, and Adams flung the chair to the side. Parfrey kicked him in the side. Adams gasped. Not stalling even a heartbeat, Parfrey kicked the knife out of Adams's hand. Parfrey aimed another kick at Adams, but the easterner grabbed the wagoneer's foot and turned. Parfrey fell, rolling to cushion the landing.

They scrambled up, watching each other with feral faces. Adams charged, head low, arms outstretched. His right shoulder crashed into Parfrey's midsection, who lost his air with an explosive burst. Adams swept his arms around Parfrey. He kept driving Parfrey toward the door.

Raining punches on Adams's head, shoulders and back, Parfrey fought to stop his backward movement. Adams had a full head of steam, though, and kept shoving. He was aware that Parfrey was pounding on him, but he did not feel the blows.

Still locked, the two burst through the door of the saloon and out into the smashing rain. They fell into the mud with a loud splat, Adams on top. Without mercy, he smashed his fists into Parfrey's face again and again. The blows squashed Parfrey's nose and split his lips as well as the skin on both cheeks.

Parfrey was not finished yet, however. He bucked and kicked and swung fists and elbows and knees. He finally managed to jam a thumb into one of Adams's eyes.

With a yelp, Adams clutched at the injured eye, allowing Parfrey to pummel himself free. Parfrey knocked Adams off his chest and into the mud.

Once more they got to their feet, though both of them were a little slower at it this time. Both were breathing hard from the exertions. Parfrey's face was covered with blood, mud, and sweat, despite the cool temperatures.

A crowd gathered, cheering in the rain. Adams and Parfrey charged at each other. They collided and grappled, straining as their feet tried for a purchase in the slick mud.

Chardonnais and Rawlins found Early leaning against the adobe wall of the saloon next to the door. "Don't look like our *amigo* needs our help, does it?" Rawlins commented.

"Expect not," Early said. "But that goddamn Parfrey's got some friends around likely to start some goddamn devilment. I already made wolf bait of one of 'em inside there. I expect ye boys best keep your eyes peeled, 'specially with all these folks about."

Rawlins nodded. "Any of 'em in partic'lar ye think might be thinkin' to cause some trouble?" he asked.

"Well, there's still one inside that I know's gonna be fractious if he gets the chance." He pointed at two disheveled, mean-looking men standing a little apart from the crowd. "And I been watchin' them two critters over there since I stepped outside here. I figure they'll do somethin' foolish soon's it looks like Parfrey's been took care of."

Chardonnais grinned. "Dey won' do not'ing," he said. "We will see to dat. Come on, Abe. We will take us a *promenade* over dere, eh? Just to keep dem company."

He and Rawlins strolled off through the pelting rain, heading toward Tom Hartstone and Dickie Thayer. Early turned back to watch the fight but was always alert to any movement from inside the saloon. McHugh didn't seem to be the type who learned quickly, and Early fully expected him to try something sooner or later.

Adams and Parfrey were still locked together, struggling for advantage. Parfrey tried to head-butt Adams, but Adams jerked his head to the side. Adams tried to bite Parfrey's nose but missed. Adams's foot slipped in the mud, and Parfrey's strength brought him down, flat on his back, left leg curled up under him. Parfrey scrambled onto Adams's chest and returned the onslaught of punches that had earlier been his to receive.

Adams squirmed, trying to get Parfrey off him, trying to get his own leg out from under him. He also tried hitting back, slamming short-leveraged punches at the side of Parfrey's face. He pulled his chin down, trying to block his head from the tirade of blows that had joined the rain in pelting his face.

With a desperate lunge, Adams grabbed at Parfrey's throat. The mud and rain had made the man's flesh slick, but Adams clung on and squeezed as hard as he could. With all his strength, he pulled Parfrey's head slowly toward his own. Ignoring the pain from the many punches he had taken, Adams jerked his head up and latched his teeth onto Parfrey's shattered nose. He bit hard.

Parfrey howled in pain, suddenly grabbing Adams's hair. He tugged, trying to get his nose free. Adams squeezed Parfrey's throat all the harder and suddenly bucked his body. Parfrey came off his chest and splashed in the mud next to him. The two lay, drenched and covered with mud. Their chests were heaving, and the pain in both men was growing.

A knife-wielding figure bolted from the crowd heading for Adams. Early moved to go after him, but then saw Chardonnais racing for the man.

Chardonnais dove and hit the man just as he was kneeling and about to plunge the knife in Adams's chest. Chardonnais heard two of the man's ribs crack as he bowled Dickie Thayer over. Thayer sucked in a breath and sudden pain lanced into the side of his chest. They rolled twice in the slick mud, but Chardonnais ended up with his feet under him. He surged up, all five feet six of him, dragging Thayer up by the shirt.

Chardonnais pounded Thayer in the face three times with a hard right fist. Thayer clawed frantically at Chardonnais's shirt, screeching, "Let me go, goddammit. Let me go!"

Chardonnais released him, and the man fell, splattering mud. "Dis is none of your concern 'ere, *monsieur*," Chardonnais said harshly. "You—"

Two gunshots, coming close together, caught his attention, and he looked up. The crowd had parted and everyone was staring toward the door of the saloon.

When Early had seen Chardonnais darting after Thayer, he figured he would stay put in case McHugh tried something from inside. He simply rested his rifle against the wall and waited, watching the door. He figured Rawlins **would handle** anyone else who tried to interfere.

The door cracked open, then slowly widened a little at a time. He had been right. Early grinned and flattened himself against the wall. It seemed to take a while, but then the door was opened wide. A rifle barrel emerged.

Early suddenly whipped out a hand and clamped it on the barrel. He shoved the muzzle upward and jerked forward. McHugh stumbled out of the saloon. With another jerk on the rifle, Early swung McHugh around in front of him, smashing him in the face.

McHugh's finger jerked instinctively on the trigger, and the rifle fired. The ball lodged in a log beam of the portico. A moment later, he dropped the rifle and reached for a knife.

Still holding the rifle barrel up in his left hand, Early jerked out one of his pistols. At arm's length, he fired. From less than a foot away, the ball slammed McHugh back several steps. The muzzle blast set McHugh's shirt on fire for a moment. The fire went out as McHugh stumbled out from under the portico and fell in the rain. He was dead.

Early slid the metal clip of the pistol on his belt and picked up his rifle. He strolled out into the rain, heading toward Chardonnais. As he did, he saw that Rawlins had a knife to the throat of the other man of the pair Early had first spotted, Tom Hartstone. Early stopped near Chardonnais and looked down at the man still lying there. He grabbed Thayer and hauled him up by the shirt.

"Best get your ass back with your *amigo* there, boy, and mind your own goddamn business."

Wide-eyed with fear, Thayer hurried over to stand quietly next to Hartstone. Chardonnais grinned at Early and followed Thayer, planning to keep an eye on him.

Early turned and walked toward the saloon again. Adams and Parfrey were still lying there trying to catch their breath, since less than a minute had passed since Thayer had bolted from the crowd. As Early strolled between the two, he looked down at Adams and grinned. "Ye'll get rheumatiz for sure ye keep on restin' there in the mud and rain."

Adams managed a wan smile and rolled over. He pushed up on hands and knees. His efforts activated Parfrey, and soon both were standing.

Parfrey's lips curled into a sneer. "You got in a few goddamn lucky shots at me, boy," he said with a smirk, the words a little garbled by the pain and bruises on his face. "But you'll never take me. Never. Ya should've finished me off when ya had the chance, ya idjit sonna bitch." He spit blood into the mud. "Ya ought to go back where ya come from whilst ya still got the goddamn chance."

Adams wiped water off his face. "Losing your nerve, you toad-humping bastard?"

Parfrey's face turned vengeful with fury, but Adams showed no fear. Adams pulled off his thick wool *serape* and tossed it aside. Parfrey's eyes glittered with desire and deviousness when he saw the tomahawk in Adams's belt. Parfrey had no other weapons than his feet and fists right now, and he wanted to get his hands on that tomahawk. He figured that if he could do that, this fight would be over in a real hurry.

43

PARFREY CROUCHED AND MOVED slowly in on Adams. Suddenly he bent, scooped up a handful of mud, and threw it at Adams's face. Then he charged as Adams clawed at his eyes, trying to clear away the clinging mud.

Instead of ramming Adams, though, Parfrey instead went for Adams's belt, scrabbling for the tomahawk. He got it free, but it slid through his mud-slick fingers and splashed in the soppy muck. He dived for it, fingers once more closing around the haft. He glanced up, noting with satisfaction that Adams was still trying to clear his vision.

Fumbling in his haste, Parfrey slipped the rawhide thong on the end of the tomahawk around his right wrist. He wished he had somewhere to dry his hand, but he didn't, so he just grabbed the handle and moved toward Adams, confident now.

Adams had gotten his eyes mostly clear, and he could see. He was frightened, but he was not about to give up. He backed away, trying to think of something to use for a weapon. Then Parfrey stopped, glaring at someone or something behind Adams. Then Adams heard, "Here, boy, take this."

He looked behind. Early was standing under the edge of the portico, with his tomahawk in his left hand. He tossed the weapon easily toward Adams. In his right hand, Early had a pistol trained on Parfrey, preventing him from doing anything while Adams's back was turned.

Adams easily caught the tomahawk and quickly slid his hand through the loop on the end of the haft. He nodded his thanks and once again turned to face Parfrey.

"Shit, you think that's gonna he'p ya," Parfrey said with a sneer he hoped would cover up his reborn worry.

"I've learned from the best, you pitiful whoreson. And I learned well."

"Now ya got me all a-tremble, boy." Parfrey closed off one nostril with a finger and blew snot out the other. He repeated the process with the other nostril. Then he suddenly charged, coming in on Adams hard and fast. He slashed wickedly with the tomahawk, hoping through sheer force and volume of swings to overcome Adams.

Adams mostly stood his ground, giving way reluctantly, fending off the whipping tomahawk as best he could while waiting for an opening.

Suddenly he had that opportunity. Parfrey had tired quickly, and the swipes he made with the tomahawk grew steadily less frequent and forceful. Adams's left hand darted out and grabbed Parfrey's right wrist, stopping the tomahawk in mid arc. He swung his own weapon in low and hard.

Parfrey was too slow to stop it, and the tomahawk sliced deeply across his abdomen, opening a long, gaping wound. A small section of intestines spilled out. Parfrey grunted with the shock of the wound, and his body quivered. His fingers relaxed and the tomahawk fell, dangling loosely from the thong around his wrist.

Parfrey sank to his knees in the mud, with Adams still holding on to his wrist. The easterner released Parfrey's arm, and let his foe fall face downward into the mud with a soggy plop.

Adams stepped back a pace or two. Then he moved up and knelt by Parfrey's side. Grabbing the freighter, he pulled him over onto his back. "Where're my papers and other things?" he asked harshly.

Parfrey's eyes had glazed already, though he still breathed weakly. Adams shook him. "Where're my things, damn you?" he asked angrily.

Parfrey's chest gave up its feeble attempts to bring air into his body.

"Damn," Adams muttered. He shook his head sadly and pulled his tomahawk from Parfrey's wrist. He stood and slid his tomahawk away. With slumped shoulders, he walked toward Early, who had been joined by Rawlins and Chardonnais. They had Thayer and Hartstone against the saloon wall. Silently he pulled Early's tomahawk off his wrist and gave it to his friend.

Early nodded and slid the weapon away under the *capote*. "Ye sure made 'em come, boy, for goddamn sure," he said quietly but with pride.

Adams hung his head. He did so partly from pain, partly from weariness. Partly from shame, too. He found it hard to realize that he had killed a man—a white man—in hand-to-hand battle, cutting the man's stomach open like gutting a deer. It did not set well with him.

"Shit, don't be so goddamn glum, boy," Early said soothingly. "Ye only did what ye had to do. He tried to kill ye more'n one time, and that's somethin' a man can't live with 'less'n he does somethin' about it. And ye remember what he done to that Comanche girl, don't ye? Hell, if them Comanches'd known who done that, they would've come lookin' for Parfrey themselves so's they could raise his hair and set that gal's spirit free. Ye just went and done it for 'em."

Adams's head came up slowly and he squared his shoulders. He was still in agony, but it no longer mattered. He smiled a little. "You're right, Ezra," he said calmly, his smile growing. "Parfrey got better than he deserved."

"That he did, boy." Early returned the smile.

Adams looked at Thayer and Hartstone. "Parfrey died before I could talk to him about my things," he said, voice growing hard. "So I'll ask you two. You were with us on the way out here, and know him well." He paused, letting that sink in. "Where're my things?"

"I don't reckon I'll tell the likes of you," Hartstone said with a show of bravado. "Hell, you kilt our friend, and that ain't somethin' we're likely to forget anytime soon."

"I'd tell the chil' what he wants to know, boy," Early

said easily. He shrugged. "Or I could set him onto ye with his 'hawk."

The man looked at his companion. "Tell him, dammit," Thayer said. His side and chest were on fire from the cracked ribs, and he knew he and Hartstone could do nothing against these men. "There ain't no use in our gettin' kilt dead because of that troublemakin' son of a bitch." He painfully pointed to Parfrey's body.

Hartstone shrugged. Thinking about it, he had no great love for Parfrey. "Your trunk's in Parfrey's room at the boardin' house we was usin'."

Adams nodded. "Where?"

"Don't think I could tell ya."

"You will show me, though, won't you, boy?" The hardness of Adams's voice surprised everyone.

Hartstone nodded vigorously.

"Just one more thing," Adams said. "Where are Jenkins and Maines? I don't want to have to worry about one of 'em back-shooting me."

"Bob 'as killed by some greaser down in Santa Fe," Thayer said. "Ivor went back with Eakins's caravan. Chickenshit that he was."

A week later, Early, Rawlins, and Chardonnais rode out of Taos with a flourish, a roar of guns, and a burst of speed. Their horses were painted and festooned with bits of color. A half-dozen braying mules trotted in ungainly splendor behind them.

In the plaza, Adams stood with his arm draped lightly around Dolores's shoulders, watching his new friends leave. He was grinning so wide he thought his face might crack.

Adams considered himself the luckiest man alive. He showed few effects now of the fight with Parfrey, except for some lingering bruises. He had good friends in the three mountain men. He and Dolores had pledged their troth, planning to marry the next summer, when Early, Rawlins, and Chardonnais returned from the mountains. He had retrieved his trunk, mostly intact, and found almost all the stories and sketches he had made, though his money was gone. He had made arrangements with Ceran Saint Vrain, who also had become a friend, to have a package of sketches and articles taken with a late train heading east.

Saint Vrain had offered Adams the chance to go along, too. Adams had thought about it and even discussed it with Early.

Early was preoccupied with preparing to leave, and was short with him. "I can't tell ye what the hell to do, boy," he finally said in exasperation at Adams's interruptions. "Ye got to make up your own mind." He paused, then asked, "Ye got anything there makes ye want to go back to New York?"

Adams didn't have to think about that long. "Just the job."

"Ye can do that from here. It's why they sent ye in the first place. Do ye have anything to keep ye here?" A twinkle grew in Early's eyes.

Adams didn't have to think about that long either. "Yes," he said. He had told Early about Dolores, and the mountain man knew how he felt about the woman.

"Then stay here," Early said finally. "Ye can make your way with your sketches and such. Send your booshway a letter with the dispatches you're sendin'

back through Ceran, tellin' him you're stayin' here for
the winter. After me'n the boys get back next year, ye
can decide what ye want to do."

Adams smiled. It was what he hoped Early would
say. Somehow he didn't think such a decision was
valid without the mountain man's approval. "I'll do
that." He paused, hesitating. Then he decided to
plunge on. "I'd like you to stand up with me when . . .
when . . ."

"When ye marry that pretty little *señorita*," Early
said with a laugh. "I know. Such doin's'll shine with
this chil'. Plumb shine."

It was with mixed feelings that he watched his three
friends leave Taos. He would be alone, he thought.
Then he smiled at his foolishness. He would not be
alone. He had Dolores, and her family seemed to be
warming to him. And he had other friends in Taos
now. He would do well.

Early and his two companions were out of sight
now. Adams turned and smiled at Dolores. Offering
her his arm, they strolled off.